FUENTE OVEJUNA

Frontispiece – Final scene in the Dublin production. The roles of Ferdinand and Frondoso, and of Isabella and Laurencia, were deliberately doubled.

ARIS & PHILLIPS HISPANIC CLASSICS
Golden Age Drama

LOPE DE VEGA

FUENTE OVEJUNA

Text, Translation, Introduction and Notes by

Victor Dixon

Aris & Phillips is an imprint of
Oxbow Books, Park End Place, Oxford OX1 1HN

ISBN 0-85668-328-0

First published 1989, reprinted 1991, 2005

A CIP record for this book is available from the British Library.

The publishers gratefully acknowledge the financial assistance of the
Dirección General del Libro y Bibliotecas of the Ministerio de Cultura
de España with this translation.

CONTENTS

ILLUSTRATIONS

For 'Taffy' (Keith Davies)
who first taught me Spanish
and a love of translation.

I know that when reading my plays you will remember the acting of those who gave this body a soul, so that you may derive more pleasure from its characters, who look only to your grace to lend them movement.

LOPE DE VEGA, to the readers of *Fuente Ovejuna*

Please God I may not be brought by necessity to such misfortune as to translate books from Italian into Spanish, which to my mind is a worse crime than smuggling horses into France.

LOPE DE VEGA

Well, here it is;
and if some critic claims it doesn't scan,
I say let him do better if he can!

Fuente Ovejuna, 2032-4

I should like to thank all who were involved in the first production of this translation, by the Samuel Beckett Centre for Drama and Theatre Studies, in the Atrium, Trinity College, Dublin, March 1989.

A modern portrait of Lope de Vega by Anthony Stones

INTRODUCTION

Lope de Vega's productivity as a playwright is literally legendary, and was so in his own time.[1] His disciple Juan Pérez de Montalbán asserted that he wrote 1800 *comedias*, and he himself referred repeatedly to *mil y quinientas* (meaning, probably, 'an enormous number'). But the best guess is that he turned out, over nearly half a century, about half that amount, less than 800.[2] In his most productive years, this must have meant an average of a play a fortnight; in view of his undoubted facility, and his not wholly unsupported claim that he had on occasion completed one (some 3,000 lines of verse) in twenty-four hours,[3] such an output in his principal field of activity need not provoke incredulity – let alone suggest, in the face of over forty autographs, that he did not himself write every line[4] – even when we take into account the time and energy he devoted to all the other genres of his day, and his many other preoccupations, especially religion and sex.

Such sustained creativity nevertheless demanded a readiness to look anywhere and everywhere for inspiration, and the three-hundred-odd undoubtedly authentic plays which have survived are of almost every conceivable kind.[5] A large proportion are romantic comedies of contemporary life, set especially in his native Madrid, though also in the countryside and other Spanish cities (Seville, Valencia, Toledo...), often against the background of popular festivities and folk-customs. Very frequently, however, he sought source-material in literature of every sort; in Classical writings (especially the *Metamorphoses*) the Bible and hagiography, Italian romances and *novelle*, the *Celestina*, and chivalresque and pastoral prose and poetry. But often and inevitably he turned his hand also to historical subjects, whatever their period or geographical location (Ancient Greece and Rome, modern Europe, the Indies); above all, he returned repeatedly to the legends and history of Spain, from the Dark Ages to his own day, as recorded in ballads and chronicles of every kind, and even (in his 'journalistic' dramatizations of recent events) in news-letters hot from the press. Collectively, therefore, his disordered sequence of Spanish historical plays afforded his spectators a panoramic view, midway between myth and documentary, and of course from the perspective of their own day, of the whole of their country's past – a series of history-lessons, so to speak, in the 'open university' of the *corral* theatre.

In *Fuente Ovejuna*, written in the very middle of his career, probably between 1612 and 1614,[6] he turned, as he had at least six times before, to the most critical period of that history, the reign of the Catholic Monarchs, Ferdinand of Aragon and Isabella of Castile and Leon.[7] By the union of their kingdoms, the completion of the Reconquest, and the discovery and first settlement of the New World, they could be seen to have created the Spain their descendants ruled, by Lope's time the greatest power on earth. As R.I. Rosaldo has written, 'when the Spaniard of Lope's age looked back on his own history, he divided it, as though it were a three Act play, into three periods: (1) the medieval period when giants of men maintained the basic Spanish values of loyalty, honour and faith, (2) a middle period (the fourteenth and fifteenth centuries) when arrogant nobles threw Spain into a turbulent state of anarchy, and (3) the age of Lope, which began with the accession of the Catholic Monarchs and the reaffirmation, with renewed zeal, of the basic Spanish values.'[8] *Fuente Ovejuna* belongs, in such a programme, to the beginning of the final great act. It is set, essentially, in 1476, the very year in which (in March) the battle of Toro confirmed Isabella's claim (against that of Juana 'la Beltraneja' and her husband Alfonso of Portugal) to the Castilian crown, and in which she began the process of bringing under royal control the over-powerful Military Orders of Santiago, Calatrava and Alcántara.[9] It is based on two events of the time, which were not directly connected, but in both of which the second of those Orders was centrally concerned. One of those events was the seizure by its young Grand Master, Rodrigo Téllez Girón, in support of the Portuguese claimants, of the strategically situated Ciudad Real, only for it to be recaptured for Ferdinand and Isabella by a force led by the Master of Santiago and the Count of Cabra, and for Rodrigo Téllez, after submitting to the Monarchs, to die heroically in their service at Loja in 1482, on an expedition against the Moorish kingdom of Granada, ten years before its fall. The other was the rebellion against its Grand Commander, Fernán Pérez de Guzmán, by his feudal vassals in the town of Fuente Ovejuna in the province of Cordoba. Incensed, apparently, by a series of tyrannical acts, in April 1476 they attacked his house, put him to death and mutilated his body; but when an emissary of the Monarchs arrived to investigate the murder, those he interrogated would only say, under torture, that 'Fuente Ovejuna' had done the deed. Thus no individual culprit could be identified, and their crime was left unpunished.

How and why Lope decided to dramatise those events is a matter of conjecture. C.E. Anibal plausibly proposed in 1934 that a lost play, written by Lope before 1604 and entitled *La muerte del Maestre*, had told the tale of the death of the young Girón, the most famous forbear of one of his principal patrons, the third Duke of Osuna, and that in the hope of pleasing the latter he went back in search of material to Francisco de Rades y Andrada's *Chronicle of the three Military Orders* of 1574.[10] There, the theory goes, in the account of the seizure of Ciudad Real and its aftermath, and especially in the story of Fuente Ovejuna, he found an irresistible subject; and there can indeed be no doubt that five pages of that *Chronica* (see Appendix) were the principal source of our play.[11] Duncan Moir, by contrast, in 1971, no less plausibly suggested that his recourse to the *Chronica* may have been prompted by No. 297 of Sebastián de Covarrubias Horozco's *Emblemas morales* of 1610, a work with which he was certainly familiar at the time.[12] On the other hand, as attested by the same author in his more famous *Tesoro de la lengua castellana* of 1611, as well as by other contemporary allusions, the gist of the Fuente Ovejuna story was generally known, and had given rise to a familiar proverb: 'Fuente Ovejuna lo hizo'

('Fuente Ovejuna did it'). What else Lope may have known of that story we cannot ourselves be sure. It had been recounted (rather differently) by the fifteenth-century Alonso de Palencia,[13] and in 1601 (probably after Rades) by Juan de Mariana;[14] but it cannot be proved that our author was aware of their accounts, or indeed of others, written or merely oral.[15]

Studies published this century have of course clarified and reassessed the nature and significance of the historical events in question;[16] but many critics, in studying the play, have properly concentrated instead on the one account that Lope undoubtedly knew, and have described – not always accurately, and never, perhaps, in full – the ways in which in his dramatization he chose to reinterpret it.[17] They have noted Lope's eagerness to exculpate Osuna's ancestor for having acted against Isabella and her consort, which by Lope's time could have been seen only as high treason. Lope portrays him consistently as a young man easily misled and duly humbled by experience (though his repentance seems much more rapid than in the Chronicle, according to which it took place only 'after some years had passed'), and no less consistently underlines his noble qualities, recalling repeatedly his later loyalty and prowess. They have stressed even more the inculpation of Fernán Gómez in the matter of Ciudad Real, for it is on him (rather than, as in the Chronicle, on the Master's cousin the Marquess of Villena and his brother the Count of Urueña) that blame for the young man's error is made to lie (679–82, 2318–20). We should note, however, that as pointed out by Anibal, 'Rades does declare that the Commander supported the Portuguese faction in the war of the succession and does indicate that his relations with the Grand Master were those of an ally.' Although Rades does not connect Fernán Gómez with the expedition against Ciudad Real, 'Lope has simply *assumed* that the Comendador *must have* been on friendly terms with his superior and that, being evidently a villainous character, he would naturally have joined the latter in such an attractively unscrupulous venture'.[18] Indeed Lope goes further, and makes Fernán Gómez the young Master's 'evil genius'; the tyrannical villain of the story of Fuente Ovejuna thus becomes also the traitorous instigator of the seizure of Ciudad Real, and so the central figure of the play as a whole, to which his character and his conduct and what they represent give, as we shall see, both an organic and a thematic unity. Lope in fact depicts Fernán Gómez in far blacker colours than the Chronicle, presenting him as an utterly selfish and unnatural monster. Rades had referred once to his 'tyranias'; Lope uses this word and its cognate tirano(s) no less than 17 times in Act III. The Chronicle had said that he 'had inflicted great wrongs and dishonour on the inhabitants of the town, taking their wives and daughters by force, and robbing them of their property, to maintain the soldiers he kept'; Lope refers to other offences (1710, 2399), but chooses to stress throughout – in part, no doubt, to play the more strongly on the spectators' emotions – his physical cruelties and especially his sexual depravity.

The peasants of Fuente Ovejuna, none of whom the Chronicle had identified, are represented in the play by eleven named (and a few unnamed) individuals. They offer their feudal lord loyal service, even love, and are turned against him only gradually by his utter failure to reciprocate their respect and by a long series of specific affronts.   At last they rebel; but whereas Rades had stated merely that 'they all decided with one consent and will to rise up against him and kill him', Lope stages a protracted debate among their representatives, at which restraint is urged and other alternatives are discussed.   It requires an impassioned tirade by one of his female victims finally to spur them to action, and they are moved, as much as by vengeance, by the urgent need to defend her, her lover and their collective sense of honour.   The murder itself, and the mutilation of the corpse recorded by the Chronicle, are not shown, though such horrors were not usually staged, and they are described later.   By contrast their unanimity under torture is repeatedly emphasised: in a comic rehearsal, an off-stage scene and the investigator's report.   Their loyalty to higher authority is similarly stressed.   Rades had recorded that they cried not only 'Fuente Ovejuna, Fuente Ovejuna' but also 'Long live the King and Queen, Ferdinand and Isabella, and let traitors and bad Christians die'; Lope has them proclaim the supremacy of the Crown before the rebellion and to the end.[19]   Their rejoicing after the murder is less a vindictive triumph than a celebration of the royal couple, and their victim's head is paraded only for them to display in its stead the arms of the Catholic Monarchs – an act not recorded in the Chronicle, but referred to twice more in the play (2071–80; 1992–5, 2436–7).   Rades had suggested a degree of self-determination (and hinted perhaps at the historical fact that the city of Cordoba had fomented the rebellion) by stating: 'The people of Fuente Ovejuna, after having killed the Grand Commander, took away their rods and offices from those appointed by this Order, to whom jurisdiction belonged, and gave them to whoever they wished.   Then they had recourse and entrusted themselves to the city of Cordoba, saying that they wanted to be subject to its jurisdiction, as they had been...'   Lope's peasants, by contrast, in an unhistorical (but dramatically and symbolically necessary) confrontation with the Monarchs, seek only direct dependence on the Crown (2434–7; cf. 2138), which Ferdinand accepts, although he circumspectly suggests that control may be deputed to a more worthy Commander (2446–9).   Similarly, they ask not only for clemency but for exoneration (2438–41); the Crown, which according to the Chronicle had called off the investigation after the Commander's guilt had been established, insists that the lynching was nevertheless a serious crime, but accepts that their solidarity has won them immunity from reprisal (2442–5).

These prudent decisions are in line with the prominent and idealised presentation of the royal couple throughout the play, both in their three appearances and by frequent allusions.   But the Catholic Monarchs – the adjective is used repeatedly[20] – are conceived of as ruling only by the authority of God and with His blessing.[21]   The secular-minded Chronicle had made no reference to God; but His favour and intervention are sought and acknowledged by the peasants throughout.[22]

Fernán Gómez, by contrast, as Duncan Moir pointed out, 'is a devil-figure, surrounded by devil-imagery, in the play.   In what is basically a religious drama, we delight in his destruction and we experience a type of Christian triumph.'[23]   Enjoying that triumph, Lope's spectators would have seen behind the royal pardon the will of God Himself, 'judging that the Commander's death was a

punishment from Heaven', as Andrés Morales was to write in 1620 of the story of
Fuente Ovejuna.[24] In this their English contemporaries, witnessing similar plays,
would certainly have concurred. To quote Robert Pring-Mill: 'Fuente Ovejuna,
like the Elizabethan plays of order and disorder, reflects a pattern of society
dominated by the idea of absolute monarchy, with the sovereign seen as God's
minister on earth and as the instrument of justice.'[25] Lily Campbell asserted,
over fifty years ago, with reference to English revenge drama, that 'God's
revenge is the typical theme dominating all the tragedy of the period',[26] and Roy
W. Battenhouse has similarly said, of Tamburlaine: 'It is now an established
point that Englishmen of Marlowe's day thought of history as the record of God's
Providence, and of the world as the theatre of His judgements.'[27]

In 1950 Courtney Bruerton argued that Lope's own play La quinta de
Florencia (ca. 1600) had been the first of a series of so-called comedias de
comendadores by Lope and others, and was the source of the non-historical parts
of Fuente Ovejuna, his later El mejor alcalde, el Rey (1620–3), and especially
his earlier Peribáñez (probably 1605–8).[28] The verbal parallels Bruerton
adduced, and his arguments about the genesis of Peribáñez, are unconvincing;[29]
but his suggestions about our play (and about El mejor alcalde) do have a limited
validity. La quinta de Florencia was based on one of the Novelle of Bandello
(II, 15), which tells of a nobleman (Pietro) who abducts a peasant-girl and is
later forced by the Duke of Florence to marry her. In expanding this brief tale,
Lope names his villain César and his heroine Laura; in Act I she is beset by
three peasant lovers, Roselo, Doristo and Belardo, but fobs them off with a task
apiece. As she tells herself, beside a spring, she prefers her own company.
Teodoro and Dantea attempt with gifts to seduce her for their master César, but
to no avail. In Act II, still immune to love, she is found and courted, also
beside a spring, by César himself, but she tricks and escapes him, to his despair.
At the end of this act, he and his followers, armed with guns as if hunting,
abduct her – like a dove seized by an eagle, or a doe by a wild boar, says the
imagery – from the home of her wise old father Lucindo. The peasants hope for
justice from Heaven and from the Duke, to whom in Act III they appeal, with
ultimate success.

At about the same time, Lope similarly dramatised, as El ejemplo de
casadas (1599–1603?), one of Boccaccio's novelle (Decameron, X.10), his tale of
'patient Griselda', a shepherdess who is subjected to a series of cruel trials of
constancy by her noble husband Gualteri. Renaming her Laurencia, he imagines
in Act I her life before their marriage. She is congratulated by her friend
Fenisa, beside a stream, on her immunity to love. They are joined there by
three shepherds, Danteo, Lucindo and Belardo, who ask Laurencia to settle a
debate about love on which they have been betting. Interrupted by the
appearance of a huntsman, Count Enrico, who is impressed by her wisdom, they
return to the debate; but she proposes instead a riddle. Enrico asks her
philosopher father Lauro for her hand, and Belardo sees in this marriage an
answer to the riddle. In the last act, however, he finds another answer – the
correct one – which appears to settle the original debate.

In La quinta de Florencia, and even more clearly in El ejemplo de casadas, we can note the appearance of names, characters, scenes, devices and images which will reappear in *Fuente Ovejuna* (as well as for example in *El mejor alcalde* and *El villano en su rincón*). We cannot speak confidently of either as a direct source of our play, for such motifs became the dramatist's stock-in-trade, though it may well be that Lope remembered them as he wrote. What should interest us more is that when faced with the need to add flesh and blood – peasant characters and scenes – to the bare bones of an historical narrative, he worked on very similar lines to those he had followed a decade before in expanding two short *novelle*.

As comparison with its main source shows, *Fuente Ovejuna* is a remarkably faithful dramatization, albeit with significant modifications and additions, of one chapter of a Chronicle, and one trend of scholarly criticism, represented recently by Javier Herrero and David H. Darst, has been to see it primarily as the kind of history-lesson I have suggested. Herrero, not disregarding and indeed incorporating other interpretations, has written that 'Lope de Vega's poetical purpose in *Fuente Ovejuna* consists in a glorification of the triumph of *absolute monarchy* over the forces of feudalism, of *anarchic aristocracy*. By choosing the notorious Order of Calatrava and confronting it with the Catholic Kings, Lope is making of their struggle and the consequent defeat of the order, the image of the end of *feudalism* and the emergence of a new order, which, for him, is embodied in the Spanish universal monarchy...'[30] Darst, similarly, has described the likely impact of the play on its first spectators: 'The audience, who views these events from a historical perspective of one hundred and fifty years, would immediately perceive that the events on stage portray the "coming to be" of the unified Spanish State, a process hampered on the national and political levels by the razing of Ciudad Real... and on the local and personal levels by the tyranny of Fernán Gómez in Fuente Ovejuna.'[31] Over the last half-century, however, the predominant trend among serious scholars has been to regard the play rather as a lesson in morality, and even in metaphysics.[32] They have seen it, that is, as one of those historical fictions, characteristic of its epoch, which (as Northrop Frye put it) 'are not designed to give insight into a period of history but are exemplary'. 'Shakespeare and Jonson' (he added) 'were keenly interested in history, yet their plays seem timeless';[33] we can say the same of Lope and *Fuente Ovejuna*.

I personally have sympathy with both interpretations – though more, as will become evident, with the second – and indeed consider them compatible and complementary. I have little or none, on the other hand, with the even commoner tendency, of even longer standing, on the part of some critics and especially of many performers, to present it as a political tract, either reactionary or (more often) revolutionary, for Lope's time or their own; to do so, they have invariably been obliged to disregard or even excise whole portions of Lope's text.[34]

Such misunderstanding or mutilation has often involved the so-called sub-plot or secondary action concerning Ciudad Real. This was once indeed regarded even by respectable scholars as irrelevant to the 'main plot' concerning Fuente Ovejuna;[35] but increasingly they have been seen as perfectly integrated.

H.B. Hall has gone furthest, pointing out that 'Lope, while linking his plots thematically, further unifies his material by drawing important formal or structural parallels between them'.[36] Perhaps one should go even further; as I shall hope to show, the play has essentially a single action.   In addition, adaptation has often meant a modification of the role of the Catholic Monarchs, or their complete elimination.   Commenting on a whole series of twentieth-century productions in which at 'moments of fundamental political crisis' such changes were made, Juan Manuel Rozas, a sadly-missed Spanish scholar, pointed out that *Fuente Ovejuna*, 'with the secondary action, is one work, without it, another.   I believe there is no better proof than this of the radical importance of its secondary action.   And I do not believe that there is a more tangible proof of *Fuente Ovejuna's* universality and worth as a classic than to observe that its adaptation to future vicissitudes was already assured by its very structure.   Lope writes a play on the Middle Ages; he gives it a baroque structure; and he leaves it ready for posterity, by virtue of the inclusion or exclusion of the secondary action.   As a definition of what a classic text should be.'[37]   In so saying Rozas, although he surely underestimated the difficulty of disentangling the two 'actions', would seem to have seen the play's capacity to withstand mutilation as a proof of its vitality, as the hallmark of a classic. Perhaps it is; and in some historical contexts, such adaptation may serve a political purpose, though the result should not in honesty be billed as Lope de Vega's work, and the adaptor would in my view do better to retell the Fuente Ovejuna story in a completely new play.   To adapt can only immeasurably impoverish the work Lope wrote and destroy its intricate structure.   In his *New Art of Writing Plays* of 1609, as Rozas recalled, he himself advised – almost literally versifying Aristotle – that it should not be possible to remove any part of a dramatic work without demolishing the whole.[38]   And in more 'normal' contexts, it is surely unnecessary, and even inapposite.   In writing *Fuente Ovejuna* Lope was not concerned to strengthen, and certainly not to subvert, the essentially stable political structures of his day, which he and his spectators simply took for granted.   While I agree, as suggested above, that he was probably interested in understanding how they had evolved, he regarded the perfectability of their operation as dependent on the behaviour and treatment of the individual, on the exercise by all, within those structures, of high moral and social principles.   If the play as written seems therefore to have too little to say to those who seek urgently to strengthen or subvert their own, to members of comparatively stable societies like his – I think, in our own day, of Western Europe, including post-Franco Spain, of the U.S.A. or of the U.S.S.R. – it will always have a powerful relevance and an inspiring (though some might say over-optimistic) message.

The besetting sign of weak students, as any teacher of literature knows, is to 'tell the story' of the work they are discussing.   That sin I shall now commit; but in summarising the plot of *Fuente Ovejuna* I shall hope to show schematically how the two events it dramatises are inextricably intertwined in a single organic action, informed by a single theme.   That theme, though expressed in the play with great complexity, may be simply stated.   As John Donne wrote a decade later: 'No man is an island'.[39]   Selfishness, variously displayed throughout by Fernán Gómez and his henchmen (and initially, at his direction, by Rodrigo Téllez), is an intolerable assault on human relationships, on the framework of society, on the God-given harmony of the universe, and results if not transcended in the elimination of its exemplar.   It must be replaced, as all the other characters know or learn, by selflessness, manifested in interpersonal love, in respect and consideration for the human rights and dignity of others, in altruistic concern for the well-being of one's fellows (of whatever social rank), in loyal solidarity with one's community, small or large, which will inspire, at one moment of crisis, a reluctant recourse to violence, and at another, a willing submission to suffering.   To coin a phrase or two, 'love is all you need'; but in *Fuente Ovejuna* 'love is a many-splendoured thing'.[40]

The first forty lines of the play reveal to the spectators, directly and economically, the name, rank and arrogant nature of its central character; but they also announce explicitly (though obliquely and ironically) the theme which his story will illustrate.   As he and his servants sententiously state, whereas courtesy, respect for others, wins love, its opposite wins only hatred.   Disrespect for one's equals is folly; disrespect for one's superiors or inferiors is treason or tyranny, an intolerable assault on society.   The remainder of the scene establishes the political state of the nation, and shows the Commander as himself a devious traitor, well able to seduce the young Master of his Order into joining him in an act of violent self-assertion against his superiors and the commonwealth at large.

A conversation in Fuente Ovejuna between two peasant-girls, Laurencia and Pascuala, shows by contrast what hostility his seduction of women is already arousing amongst his inferiors, although at this point they see his self-centred lust as only typical of males in general.   When three male peasants appear, Frondoso's list of euphemisms, and Laurencia's reply, refine the concept of courtesy; what passes for respect may be lying flattery, and disrespect may turn to slander.   There follows a Platonic debate, which might seem implausible and digressive; in fact it restates the socio-political issues in a philosophical way.[41]   If love, as Mengo concedes, is the harmonious, cohesive principle of the macrocosm, the visible and invisible universe, and the self-preserving instinct of the microcosm, the human individual, is it also true, as he appears to prove, that what passes for love *between* humans is always self-interest, that altruistic concern for others cannot exist?   Flores' florid account at this point of the seizure of Ciudad Real, against the will and despite the loyal resistance of its inhabitants, describes an apparent victory for the kind of self-interest which is treason, and the Commander reappears in temporary triumph.   He is welcomed, innocently enough, by the whole of the peasant community; they offer well-meant proofs and protestations of love, which he accepts with little respect as no more than his due.   Indeed what he demands of their women is far more: complete subservience to his selfish desires.

The third scene shows the Catholic Monarchs, at the apex of the social structure, zealous to protect the peace and wellbeing of the whole realm, and responding promptly to the loyal representatives of Ciudad Real (who refer, as if incidentally, to the Commander's tyranny of his vassals) by sending two loyal noblemen to remedy his excess. Back in Fuente Ovejuna, near the bottom of the social hierarchy, the hitherto loveless Laurencia begins to respond to the love of Frondoso, directed as it is toward a Christian marriage expected by their whole community; but the incipient idyll is disrupted by the predatory Commander, who brags of his adulterous conquests. His attempt to overcome her resistance too by violence, and Frondoso's readiness to risk his life to protect her, reveal the peasant as a champion of unselfishness (who is nevertheless restrained by respect for his superior's rank), and the nobleman as lacking again in love or respect for anyone, or indeed for anything other than his own misconception of the code of chivalry.

The second act opens peacefully with two leaders of the rustic '*república*' responsibly discussing its welfare (and one of its more educated members debating 'progress' with a probably shrewder companion); but tension returns with the appearance of the Commander, just as an unnamed peasant is railing against his excess. He quickly displays his utter insensitivity to his inferiors' desire for mutual respect, his vindictiveness towards Frondoso and his lecherous designs on their womenfolk, until news of the impending failure of his treason against his superiors impels him to seek to sustain that other manifestation of his arrogant self-assertion. On his way to do so, he commits more tyranny. Three of his already terrorised peasants encounter another, Jacinta, who is fleeing from two of his soldiers. Mengo, displaying (like Frondoso) the kind of altruism which he had refused to believe could exist, attempts heroically to defend her, and appeals, when the Commander appears, to his supposed nobility. Fernán Gómez merely has him cruelly flogged, and no less cruelly misuses the defiant Jacinta.

The charming scene which follows has received scant comment from critics, but provides a crucial counterweight to the Commander's incapacity for love and 'courtesy'. Laurencia, now as much in love as Frondoso, at last agrees with him, and their community, that they should be married, but urges him to seek the consent of her father, the magistrate Esteban. The latter appears, discussing the Commander's most recent tyranny (and his treason), and readily accedes, once he can confirm that his daughter and Frondoso's father are also willing.

The lovers' exultation at the prospect of their union is counterpointed by defeat and division for the traitor and his dupe, but is soon reinforced (despite new allusions to his tyrannies) by the festivities of their harmonious, heaven-blessed marriage, in which their whole community joins. But the romantic lyric sung at the height of the rejoicing, hinting darkly at the triumph of violent desire over terrorised innocence, presages the dramatic reappearance of the Commander. With hypocritical words and savage force he arrests the bridegroom, responds to the old magistrate's reminders of superior authority by belabouring him with the very symbol of the rule of law, and abducts the bride. The community seems paralysed before the triumph of tyrannical self-love.

Act III begins, however, with that community considering its response: canvassing milder alternatives, including an appeal to the crown, but convinced increasingly that collective resistance, however risky, is the only emergency solution. It is nevertheless Laurencia, the disfigured but defiant victim of the Commander's tyranny, whose scornful rhetoric rouses them to defeat his violence with a violence in which she summons their womenfolk too to join. Fernán Gómez, surprised as he is commanding further cruelty and murder, learns only in death that he has forfeited all respect, which the community, in its triumph over the tyrant and his accomplices, reserves for itself and for higher authority.

That higher authority now receives news of its own triumph over his treason, but also of what appears to have been another violent assault on the commonwealth. Its proper, parallel response is to dispatch another representative to remedy the excess.

Back in Fuente Ovejuna, by contrast, the community demonstrates its essential allegiance to that commonwealth. In celebrations closely similar to those at the wedding of Frondoso and Laurencia, they view their action as another triumph by Ferdinand and Isabella, the married couple at its head. Esteban warns, however, that those new upholders of order and the rule of law will insist on an investigation, involving torture, that the murderers must demonstrate that they were inspired, fundamentally, by love. That love in fact must now face fearlessly its sternest test, for which he prepares them. As a magistrate, he plays himself the role of the royal Judge, until the real Judge is announced.

After an economical scene in which the errant Master is forced to acknowledge that in both matters he too must submit to higher authority, the community duly demonstrates its self-denying solidarity. But the suffering to which those who have espoused violence now submit takes place offstage; framing it, Lope foregrounds instead its gentler counterpart, the love of Frondoso and Laurencia. Each is utterly, selflessly concerned for the wellbeing of the other and that of their kinsfolk; both agonise at the sufferings but enthuse over the heroism of the individuals who are put to the question and give the same collective answer. Significantly, it is the fleshly 'weakling' Mengo (who had believed in self-preservation but not in unselfishness) who scores the ultimate triumph by turning it into a jest, and who in an episode nearer to farce than simple comic relief is properly feted for it. But the final variation on the phrase, setting the seal on a complex and crucial scene, appears in a charmingly sentimental exchange between the pair of rustic lovers.

The royal pair who replace them on stage are similarly loving, albeit in courtly terms, and similarly concerned with the well-being of their community, the whole kingdom of Castile. The ever-loyal Master of Santiago announces, first, the Master of Calatrava (who both repents his former treason and promises future service), and second, his own counterpart the Judge (who describes again, admiringly, the unanimity of the Commander's killers). The 'assassins' themselves appear, bear witness to his tyrannies, and submit like his erstwhile dupe to the highest temporal justice. Covarrubias' 'Christian Judge' accords them (though only provisionally) the direct dependence they desire, and concedes (though he cannot condone their crime) that their solidarity – an earnest, ultimately, of the wider loyalty they proclaim – has obliged him to pardon it. Frondoso, for the peasants, applauds these balanced judgments, and the play ends with order and harmony restored, on an idyllic note of mutual admiration and love. As Spain's leading contemporary dramatist wrote in 1958, '*Fuente Ovejuna* is a splendid example of social and collective tragedy... The act of mutual understanding which allows at its conclusion a reconciliation betweeen the people and the monarchs... recalls, like that of Calderón's *Life's a Dream*, the conciliation traditional in the tragedies of the Greeks'.[42]

THE CHARACTERS

It has long been held that the characters of Golden-Age drama lack individuality and complexity, depth and development; that though often dynamic and vivid, they are rarely more than types, even stereotypes. This generalisation, like most, has much validity, but stands in need of qualification. The public of every social rank which thronged the *corrales*, like the filmgoers and television audiences of today, demanded a constant stream of new works, which would usually run for only a very few performances. It expected comic and poetic (lyrical, narrative and rhetorical) passages, but above all it demanded a good, complete story (or stories), rich in incident.[43] The companies of varying size who served it were of constantly changing composition but conserved a standard structure. Whoever he hired each spring, the actor-manager would invariably play the leading male part, and his wife the leading female. He would have at least one *barba* for older roles, at least one *gracioso* and one *graciosa* to play the comic menials which almost every *comedia* could be expected to include. Such mechanical casting and specialisation, the shortness of runs and the lack of rehearsal time must have meant a great deal of routine performance. The many and mostly prolific writers who attempted to meet, often at speed, the insatiable demand for a fairly standarised product, tended naturally to lapse into facility and a lack of invention, repeating themselves and borrowing from each other. They generally contrived, however, that their plays should not only entertain but edify, that the action should illustrate a leading theme, a universal and important judgement on some aspect of human life. The detailed analysis of its characters was not normally, therefore, their primary concern.[44] On the other hand, those characters' nature and behaviour could hardly be wholly conditioned by the exigences of theme and plot; as Hall has pointed out, the action had to be 'determined by the kind of people the characters are and by the manner in which they choose to behave, since Golden-Age drama takes for granted the notion of free will and moral responsibility. Man, for Lope and his contemporaries, is not the plaything of fate or the victim of some inevitable destiny, despite the acknowledged influence of temperament and environment.'[45] Some leading characters, like the Mayor of Zalamea, in fact themselves embody the theme, and exemplify it by contrast and in interaction with others. Some, like the Trickster of Seville, Alarcón's famous liar and later *figurones*, are surely more interesting than either the theme or the action to their authors, their audiences and to us today. Some, like the Dog-in-the-Manger Diana, or the protagonists of *Life is a Dream*, undoubtedly have conflicts and contradictions, expressed at times in soliloquies and asides, though more often revealed in their actions and relationships. And in any case the most sensitive writers, in their finest plays, are by no means precluded by an overriding concern with the story and its message from the 'imitation of nature' by the creation of convincing human characters.[46]

Fuente Ovejuna is a case in point. It is a chronicle-play, with a unified plot based heavily on history, with (as I have argued) an evident moral and socio-political theme, which its characters function by their interaction to illustrate.   Yet many are sharply-etched individuals, and some, within an overall consistency, reveal progressively a range of different traits, or indeed are moulded before our eyes by their experience.   Critics in general have paid them too little attention, and even Hall, who discusses them ably and at length, seems to me too apologetic.[47]   I shall consider them here, unashamedly, in as much detail as limited space permits.

The roles of the young Catholic Monarchs – in 1476 Ferdinand was 24 and Isabella 25 – are those which have most frequently been misunderstood and misrepresented.   The play was surely not written as propaganda for the monarchical principle and the hierarchical structure of society,[48] which Lope and his audience, as I have said, took unquestioningly (if not uncritically) for granted, but it does suggest approval, like El villano en su rincón (1611–6), or El mejor alcalde, el Rey (1620–3) for direct involvement and concern on the part of Spanish rulers – something increasingly lacking at this time – with their individual subjects.[49]   Ferdinand and Isabella are not, like the kings in those plays, the protagonists of Fuente Ovejuna; their parts are less prominent than those of the noblemen or the peasants, and they are perhaps so idealised as to seem more like abstractions than rounded characters.   But their role is essential to the conception of the play and the view of society it depicts.   They do not descend like gods ex machina at the end, as do monarchs in other comedias, like Calderón's The Mayor of Zalamea, to ratify a fait accompli.   On the contrary, they appear throughout three of the play's sixteen scenes; their representative the Judge is heard offstage in another, and in all but two of the rest their role in the state is referred to, with no hint that as its rulers they are other than exemplary. This is hardly surprising; for in the seventeenth century Ferdinand and Isabella were the object of a 'veritable cult'; their reign was seen as a Golden Age in which together they had created modern Spain.   González de Cellórigo wrote in 1600 that 'our Spain in all things reached its highest degree of perfection in those times'.[50]   Two of the country's greatest writers, Saavedra Fajardo and Gracián, were both in 1640 to publish works in which Ferdinand was idealised as an unsurpassable model for all rulers, past or future.[51]   Lope himself, as shown by Joaquín de Entrambasaguas, brought them on stage in no less than eleven plays, as well as praising them in others.[52]   In some eight they appeared as ideal rulers, in five as a loving couple.   Most interestingly, perhaps, in El mejor mozo de España (1610–1), he gave a romanticized account of their courtship in 1469, without failing of course to see in their union the will of God for Spain.

Their first function in Fuente Ovejuna is therefore to establish its moral and socio-political parameters.   When Fernán Gómez discounts Isabella's right to succeed to the throne of Castile (95–9), a right so divinely ordained, in the mind of Lope's audience, as to be beyond dispute, he is identified immediately as a lying traitor; the enterprise he persuades the young Master to undertake can only be seen as an act of treason, doomed to ignominious defeat.   The Monarchs, from their first appearance, are shown as in agreement on the need for prudent foresight and prompt action to defend that right; throughout the play they are seen and described as striving incessantly to bring peace, order and the rule of law to different parts of a realm which is unquestionably theirs.[53]   When the aldermen of Ciudad Real are announced, they are immediately admitted to the presence (651–4); the Monarchs' readiness to give audience to all is an historical fact, well known no doubt to the spectators, which will be exemplified again repeatedly (1948, 2302–6, 2382–5).[54]   They are praised, as they will be throughout, as a Heaven-sent support and succour to their subjects (655–62, 1948–51, 2341–5); the humblest of those subjects are eager for their direct rule (663–6, 683–6, 2138, 2434–5).   On receiving the report, they agree at once on urgent and opportune action, by nobles whose bravery and competence they recognise now and later (699–722, 1932–47); the success which crowns that action will be reported and seen in four of the subsequent scenes.

They do not appear in Act II, but the peasants in particular voice an increasing awareness of their role (1007–8, 1325–32). At its end Esteban foresees that they will bring order in place of the disorderliness of the Orders (1620–30).[55] In Act III he proclaims that, after Heaven, the Monarch alone is lord; this idea is reiterated throughout the rebellion, and especially at the Commander's final exit.

When Ferdinand is informed, hot on the heels of Manrique's report that one disorder has been set to rights, that another has occurred, he again acts promptly and properly (disregarding the fact that the victim had been his enemy) to re-establish the rule of law, as the peasants will soon predict (2014–25, 2085–8). What may seem severity is notably tempered by his compassionate concern, as he exits, for his informant's wounds (2026–7). The peasants view their action as one which furthers the aims of the Monarchs, whose praises they sing with affection and admiration, whose arms they display and whose rule they welcome as a blessing to themselves and the state.   The Master, by contrast, sees it only as an affront and threat to his Order (cf. 1594–1606), which he is eager – and will continue to be eager, until corrected by the Crown (2351–4) – not to investigate but to avenge with intemperate violence against the villagers (2131–6, 2351–3). But he too must admit the supremacy of the Monarchs, in their case and in his own.   They accept his submission and service with a 'divine' benignity (2338–45), and Ferdinand resolves the 'action of Fuente Ovejuna', though he offers to leave judgement to Isabella (2350), with a statesmanlike prudence for which he is justly praised.[56]

Fernán Gómez, the central character, is 'an impressive study in villainy'.[57] But the varied facets of this villainy are only gradually revealed, confirmed and exemplified (not always predictably) in action and dialogue.   He seizes our attention from the outset by the obsessive, ill-natured arrogance with which he asserts the rights and privileges attendant on his name and rank.   But he reveals himself too as a ruthless and devious politician, exploiting both the strengths and the weaknesses of the young Master to seduce and hector him into a violent act of treason against their sovereigns.   At the end of the scene he betrays a contemptuous disregard for his vassals, which many later comments will underline.[58]   In the next, two of those vassals reveal another aspect of his depravity: irresponsible lust. Flores' fulsome praises, and the villagers' songs and speeches, present him as an impressive and powerful warrior, but the demands he makes of Laurencia and Pascuala are both peremptory and excessive, and the emissary of Ciudad Real confirms him in the character of a tyrant (691–4). The last scene of the act portrays him as an insatiable predator, quick to resort to physical violence and savagely vengeful when thwarted (856–7; cf. 1029–58, 1165–6).

In Act II he so utterly fails to understand how his behaviour outrages his vassals that he is himself outraged by their reactions. He revels in contemplation of his lecheries, and despises those who succumb (1059–1102). In his treatment of Mengo and Jacinta he evinces, by no means for the last time, a sadistic cruelty, and a complete imperviousness to appeals to his presumed nobility.[59] From the following scene, he is not only seen as increasingly disruptive of all law and order but as dishonest and hypocritical, as when he dissociates himself from the enterprise he now calls the Master's, or feigns concern for the Master to cloak his own vengeful intentions.[60] In the scene of his murder, he continues to bluster, but is utterly blind to the physical and psychological realities of his situation. He is essentially irrational, unintelligent and unperceptive; a man without patience, prudence or foresight, who imposes his will for the most part by imperious commands and violent action.

Love, throughout, is beyond his comprehension because foreign to his nature. He uses the word *amor* only three times, essentially in the sense of loyalty (12, 46, 546), and *amores* (1095) only for lust, which is one of his main motivations. Yet even sexuality seems less important to him, as to Don Juan Tenorio, than domination and deceit. As Hall has stressed, he is characterised by perversity.[61] Making love a mere sport, he glories in the subversion of marriage by adultery, and turns a wedding into a wake (1642). He uses Mengo's defensive sling as an aid to assaulting him, a medical treatment as a torture, a symbol of legality as an instrument of injustice. 'Scorning and violating the three vows of poverty, chastity and obedience which, in *his* day, he had to take when he entered his Order',[62] he similarly subverts its crusading mission in making war on the Catholic Monarchs (465–8). The symbols of cross and sword to him mean only violence and bloodshed, and his references to knighthood imply a pagan ideology (121–8, 138–40). He and his followers are rightly labelled barbaric, and so provoke barbarity (937, 1485, 1668, 1701; cf. 2011). They are compared to beasts of prey,[63] whereas the peasants (until 1762) are always associated with weaker, innocent creatures.[64] He is likened to two pagan tyrants, Heliogabalus and Nero (1173–80, 2422), and on two occasions to a devil (810–2, 1143–4). His few references to the Deity are merely formulaic (589, 598, 1597), and his final appeal to God's mercy (unlike, say, those of his counterpart in *Peribáñez*, a true tragic hero) can only be heard as ironic (1895). If, as Varey has shown, *Fuente Ovejuna* amply illustrates the topos of the World Upside-Down, and as Hall says it 'abounds in examples of how sin (defined by Aquinas as a fall from coherence) disturbs the divinely-established order',[65] Fernán Gómez is the first cause and prime example of that disturbance. Only when he is destroyed can harmony be restored.

In Act III, by way of justification of his destruction, he is incessantly labelled both a *tirano*[66] and a *traidor*[67]. In fact he incarnates the utter selfishness which Mengo in Act I mistakenly implies is the mainspring of all human motivation. He is thus a sinister Vice, more menacing monster than man; but as Hall points out, 'although he remains a type, the exploration of his personality offers something of the variety found in a more complex, manysided character. Similarly, the progressive revelation of the depth of his wickedness approximates to the interest which derives from the contemplation of a character who genuinely undergoes development and change.'[68] His dynamic energy, like that of Richard III, ensures that he dominates the greater part of the drama, and makes his role (*experto crede*) an exciting one to play.

Flores and Ortuño are his cowed and cowardly accomplices and pimps; they act as his self-ingratiating echoes. But they remain detached, keep their own counsel, and are no less clearly motivated by self-interest (627–34). They are often conciliatory and cautiously critical, and even allow themselves some irony, which the Commander, characteristically, does not detect (e.g. 17–28). Ortuño, described as sly (202), seems the quieter and more reflective; Flores is the more prominent and more vicious.[69] With a smattering of philosophy reminiscent of Sempronio in the *Celestina* (974-6, 1090-3), and a gift for flattering rhetoric, he is his master's able apologist, offering versions of events which are heavily slanted, though not free from revealing *faux pas* (468, 1968-9, 1993-5). As Hall has put it, 'despite the occasionally coarse comic line (see for example 615–25)', Flores and Ortuño 'are not amusing characters but rather a couple of immoral toughs who will not scruple to do anything to please their master and thus profit themselves',[70] and their punishment, though less explicitly extreme than his, is poetic justice (see esp. 1911–5).

The Master of Calatrava, in many respects, offers a striking contrast to its Commander. Throughout the first scene, and no less than six times later, Lope stresses his youth and inexperience.[71] Not surprisingly, therefore, he is headstrong and naive, too eager for instant glory and too easily led by the older man, whose words he almost parrots (129–37, 153–6). But his bravery, his loyalty (however misconceived) to his ancestors, his kinsfolk and his Order, displayed throughout (672-3, 1453-5, 2141-2), and his readiness to follow what he is persuaded is his duty, can only augur well for his future. Unjustly accused of discourtesy, he is as gracious as his critic is the reverse. Flores' account of his riding forth depicts him as gallant and handsome, and though Lope paraphrases the *Chronica* in describing his vindictiveness after taking Ciudad Real, he surprisingly and significantly adds that the young man is as loved there as he is feared (513–4), and that he was generous to all in his hour of victory (521–4). In defeat he is too ready to seek excuses, too proud that at least the banner of his Order has not been lost, and too quick to interpret his failure fatalistically as a vagary of blind Fortune, rather than as a divinely-willed triumph for the Catholic Monarchs (1450-8). But the couplet with which he exits and ends the scene suggests a recognition that he had erred out of inexperience, and a readiness to learn from his mistake (1470-1).

In his reactions to the news of the Commander's murder, he is once again, initially, both impetuous and reckless (2125–36). Yet he is quick this time to see realistically the need to act with restraint, to submit to his superiors and confess his guilt. His shame will be conquered by his sense of honour, ever his highest concern (2157-60). His humble confession of his past misdeeds, which again inculpates Fernán Gómez (2315-20; cf. 680-2), and his promise of future service, which again recalls his later glory (2326-38; cf. 515-20), are exemplary, and win him royal approbation, though an excess of zeal for the honour of his Order has again to be held in check (2351-4).

Exemplary throughout, by contrast, are Manrique, the Master of Santiago, who merits his Monarchs' trust by his obedience, efficiency and prudence,[72] and his unseen ally the Count of Cabra, a soldier who is praised for his daring and diligence, and as 'a loyal sentinel who seeks to serve his country's need' (711-4, 1940-7). The message is clear; knights who conspire against the state must die or be brought to heel, but those who afford loyal service are admired and honoured. The play contains no hint of hostility, as has often been argued, against the nobility as a class; they must be judged on their merits, as individuals.

The peasants, too, although increasingly they speak and act as a community, are individuals. To the contemptuous Commander – as also to the Master, and initially to the Monarchs and their Judge – they are only *el pueblo, villanos, villanaje*; apart from his conquests, he hardly ever alludes to them by name.[73] Yet those who speak are rarely not identified;[74] and eleven (all of course invented) are lent the individuality of names, which indeed serve, as noted by López Estrada, to set some apart from the others. Most of these are realistically rustic, but *Barrildo* was used by Lope in no other play, and *Mengo* only in one, whereas *Frondoso, Laurencia* and *Leonelo* are names of literary origin. Their speech, as he also showed, is laced intermittently, for effect, with archaisms and rustic words and pronunciations, but less probably with legalistic and philosophical terms.[75] In accord with the reality of Lope's day, they are proud to be Old Christians, free (unlike many noblemen, including some in the Military Orders, despite their rules) of any suspicion of unorthodoxy or racially impure ancestry (989-91). Their exemplary religiosity, their respect for God and the sacrament of marriage is constantly emphasised; more realistically, Fernán Gómez and his followers claim that many of their womenfolk were ready to commit adultery, but none of these appear on stage. The picture of rural life which the peasants' words (and songs) evoke, thus owes much to observed reality, but much also to idealistic convention. Lope's many rural plays were written, after all, primarily to please an urban public, many of whom were first- or second-generation immigrants, refugees from the actual poverty of an increasingly neglected countryside.[76] Yet the degree of stylisation diminishes as the play progresses.

Laurencia, early in Act I, gives a true-to-life but lyrical account (introduced by the topos *más precio*)[77] of the gastronomic pleasures of a typical rural day;[78] by contrast both she and Frondoso satirise the deceitful language of city-folk, implying in traditional vein that their country cousins are more honest and straightforward; and they and others engage in a debate on love of a type familiar in pastoral. In the same scene Esteban and Alonso describe at length, with a modesty which barely conceals the *beatus ille* notion that the simple gifts of nature are at least as precious as those of 'civilization',[79] the abundant tributes (mostly of food) which the village is able to offer to its victorious overlord, in ignorance apparently of the nature of his campaign.   The initial impression is of a prosperous, carefree, loosely-knit community, not unaware of but contentedly isolated from the wider world.[80]

In the first scene of Act II we are shown, more realistically, their concern with economic problems, their commonsensical reactions to ideas from outside. The Commander's ever more intolerable behaviour, which inspires both joint protests and personal acts of defiance, produces a mounting sense of common outrage, accompanied by inklings of a wider perspective of possible relevance to themselves.[81]   The marriage of Frondoso and Laurencia, long anticipated by all, and prepared for with exemplary consideration and courtesy, brings them all together in a joyous and harmonious celebration; but when violence shatters the idyll, they are reduced to uncertainty and disunity.

The meeting which opens Act III expresses their shared distress at the state of their little *patria* (town), though also still greater awareness of the nation beyond (1675–83, 1700–1); but its varied members are unable to agree on corporate action.   Even the crucial irruption of Laurencia, describing her personal sufferings and reviling their collective passivity, provokes initially individual reactions (1794–1800).   These quickly give way to a new sense of common purpose, but equally and simultaneously to a new sense of solidarity with the nation as a whole.   Indeed their first slogan is 'Long live our lords the King and Queen'; only 63 lines later do they raise the cry 'Long live Fuente Ovejuna'.[82]   In their celebrations after the murder, they see their joint action as a victory for the whole realm and its rulers, but also as one which they must show still more unity in defending, since those rulers will properly call them to account.   The giving of that account, in the torture-scene, is framed by expressions of individual emotion by Laurencia and Frondoso, with whom we witness four individual though representative instances of collective solidarity.   As Francisco Ruiz Ramón has said: 'The community which has learnt to unite in its revenge, acquires an awareness of that unity in the torture-scene.   This, not the revenge, marks the high-point of its heroism.'[83]   The unity and unanimity of the villagers depends, though, on the selflessness of each, on his refusal to save his own skin by accusing others.   When all confront the rulers of the larger community, Esteban speaks for Fuente Ovejuna (though Frondoso and Mengo bear witness to individual sufferings), both to defend their collective action and to express their collective desire for direct dependence.   But we should guard against exaggeration in regarding *el pueblo* as a collective hero, let alone as the sole protagonist of the play.[84]   It remains an agglomeration of individuals, who identify progressively with their little *patria*, but *pari passu* with the larger *patria* to which they and it belong and are bound in love.

Esteban 'would offer a good part for the *barba*, the actor who specialised in old men's roles'.[85]   He stands out clearly from the other village elders, his fellow magistrate Alonso and the aldermen Juan Rojo and Cuadrado.   The loving father of Laurencia, he is delighted at the worthy Frondoso's proposal, which he handles with prudence, generosity and a charming sense of humour (1373–1440). Shocked by the shamelessness, by contrast, of the Commander's designs on her, he is pathetically agonised by her abduction and disfigurement (1656–62, 1716–23).   In his public capacity, he takes seriously his obligations to his little *república* (860–7), and acts as the villagers' spokesman, both (like the *regidores* of Ciudad Real) before the Catholic Monarchs, whom he constantly venerates (1007–8, 1620–30, 1700–1, 2072–88) and before the Commander.   In the town's name, he shows Fernán Gómez initially admiration and love (549–78), deference (867), and a courtesy not untinged with irony (941–7, 954–6).   His reproofs, though unanswerably 'eloquent', are restrained (970–80, 1607–14); but the Commander's excesses move him to increasingly outspoken indignation (997–1008, 1317–64, 1619–30), though he submits to a cruel beating with exemplary humility.   He is the first to suggest collective resistance (1664–73), and the first to be stung into action by Laurencia's tirade (1794–8).   Fernán Gómez seems to suppose that he is the rebels' ringleader (1863); he heads those who confront the tyrant (1877–8), and perhaps strikes the first fatal blow (1894).   But in the hour of apparent triumph, he shows an old man's cautious foresight; he proposes the community's unanimous reply to the torturer's question, rehearses and confidently encourages them in making it, and indeed wins praise for showing the way (2081–2124, 2203–9).   He appears throughout as a God-fearing Old Christian,[86] with touches of the rustic philosopher whom Lope so loved to portray, most memorably in Juan Labrador and old Tello de Meneses (e.g. 868–91, 1437–40).[87] He is a man of dignity, integrity and honour who *because* (for all his apparent propriety) he knows his place rebels, under intolerable provocation, in order to maintain it.

The most enigmatic member of the community is Leonelo, the student just back from Salamanca.   He appears in only one scene, and apparently takes no part in the rebellion.   Salomon, observing that in Lope's time some sons of rich peasants were sent to the universities, suggested that his inclusion was intended to add realism to the picture of contemporary rural society; Kirschner, that it was meant to modify the notion of peasant ignorance, and to deny a necessary correlation between book-learning and wisdom.[88]   But how are we to interpret his comments on the invention of printing?   Some critics have found him blasé and pedantic, but others see him as prudent,[89] and certainly his complaints about false attributions sound very like some of Lope's own (918–23).   When the peasants confront the Commander, it is hard to know which he agrees with; his protests could be directed against either (981, 1021);[90] indeed 982–3 suggest that 981 should perhaps be attributed to the Alderman.[91]   On the whole I would play him as a negative character; his ill-tempered objections to the wider diffusion of knowledge are rightly reproved by Barrildo.

Barrildo, in the debate on love, is neither ignorant nor a fool (366–70, 379–82).   Though he seems to be bettered by Mengo, his recollection of a sermon, which 'is meant to underline the basic unity of Christian and Platonic thought',[92] anticipates its resolution by the drama (421–6).   Again, in the deliberations at the beginning of Act III, his interventions are shrewd and cautious (1680–3, 1699).   I believe that he is the author of the song at the wedding, and of its *copla*, both of which are criticised by Mengo, and that he tries to make amends, with limited sucess, with his *copla* in the similar later scene.[93]

Mengo is clearly the part – a complex, challenging one – for the company's principal clown.   But the *graciosos* who, thanks to Lope, became a standard feature of the *comedia*, are very varied, and perform many different functions apart from the provision of coarse humour.   Their antecedents, too, were many. One was the crafty servant of Classical and Humanistic comedy (with whom Flores and Ortuño, though not comic, share some characteristics); but another, in peasant plays, was the foolish rustic, whose original home was the liturgical shepherd-play.[94]   Mengo is undoubtedly descended from this type; but like many of his sixteenth-century predecessors, he is by no means merely a simpleton. Undoubtedly he should present a ridiculous appearance, and be a figure of fun. We are meant to recognise him, as does Laurencia, when the Judge calls offstage for 'that fleshy one, who looks half-naked; that fat one' (2236–7).   At the meeting which opens Act III he speaks for the lowest, most afflicted stratum of the peasant community, the '*simples labradores*' (1703–7).   He carries a shepherd's or swineherd's sling (1169–72); he relies on herbal remedies (2430–3); his most prized possession is his boxwood fiddle (286–8).   His speech contains more rustic expressions than anyone's.[95]   When he tries to compare Fernán Gómez to tyrants of Antiquity, he can manage Nero (2422), but makes hilarious mistakes over Heliogabalus, and has to admit that he knows no history (1173–80). He is critical of other folks' verse, and in the play's most delightful speech makes fun of – in true Lope style – the sort of slapdash poet his creator was accused (and is still accused) of being (1512–33); but when he tries himself, his *copla* (on his obsessive theme) is crudely comic, full of ridiculous rhymes (2061–7).   He cannot philosophize, he says, and only wishes he were not illiterate (371–2).   But he proves to be well versed in the theory of humours, is well able to distinguish three kinds of love, and exploits the Socratic method to prove, apparently, that the third – unselfish love between human individuals – does not exist, that all mankind, like himself, are not made to love (371–434).

At his next appearance, however, Mengo disproves his own proposition by an act of selfless bravery.   When Jacinta appeals for help, her friends Laurencia and Pascuala run away, moved no doubt by the instinct of self-preservation he had described in the debate.   He by contrast finds that his nature requires him to be manly, to act the unselfish hero.   This 'natural man', with no weapons but 'the first God gave us', attempts to defend her, not only with words but with his sling and the stones at his feet; an Adam, he becomes a David (1199–1216).   His bold stand, however, earns him not victory but a cruel martyrdom, which he and others will recall – ruefully, humourously and vengefully – throughout the rest of the play.[96]   For all his resilient jesting, it makes him a constant reminder of the Commander's cruelty and a spokesman for the terror it inspires, both at the disrupted wedding and at the meeting which follows (1644–51, 1687–8, 1703–7).

Yet he is as moved as the rest by Laurencia's tirade; he is the first to propose that their action should be collective (1806), the first to raise the cry of loyalty to the Crown, which he continues to lead (1811–4, 1865).   After exacting and exulting in his revenge, he is the pretend-victim picked on by Esteban for the torture-rehearsal, and quickly learns his part (2101–24).   In the torture-scene itself, Frondoso, Laurencia and the Judge expect him to 'break'; indeed he pretends to, as in the rehearsal, but only to produce a jokey variation of the unanimous reply – a *'pirouette sublime'*, in Mercadier's phrase[97] – which finally defeats the torturer and inspires new confidence in his hearers (2244–57). Despite his fear the most defiant victim, he is deservedly feted (and demonstrates, amid his comic complaints, a characteristically impressive capacity for drink). The humblest, weakest and most fearful of the peasants, he has shown for the second time more selfless courage than anyone, has proved more than anyone the reality of altruistic love, and offers the starkest contrast to the truly loveless nobleman.

Jacinta, whom Mengo attempts to defend, shows (as he does) both terror and defiance. She begs for mercy (as he does) from the 'noble' Fernán Gómez (1223–5, 1247–9, 1274). Similarly denied it and cruelly misused, she appeals instead (as he does) to the judgement of Heaven (1251–2, 1275–6). But in Act III she succeeds herself (as he does) in achieving personal revenge by playing (as he does) a leading part in the collective execution of that judgement (1828–35, 1888–1919).

Pascuala serves rather as a foil to Laurencia. A gentler soul, she underestimates her companion's determination to resist the Commander's intentions, reflecting the more submissive attitude which Lope reveals was adopted by other women of the village.[98] But while she shares Laurencia's suspicions of men in general – witness her comparing them, amusingly, to sparrows (250–72) – she shrewdly anticipates her friend's susceptibility to love, believing, as she insists to Mengo (despite her lack of personal experience), in true affection between male and female (403–7, 442). She repels Fernán Gómez's solicitings as forcefully as Laurencia (599–626), and in Act II is both as fearful and as hostile toward him (1137–98). Characteristically, though, she appeals to him not to disrupt the lovers' wedding, and is more agonised than angered by his savagery (1590–4, 1636–42). She nevertheless takes an active and avenging role in the rebellion (1819–47, 1888–1919), and in the torture-scene is heard – giving twice the common reply – to show perhaps more solidarity than anyone (2221–35).

The role of Laurencia herself is the most demanding. She has more lines than even the Commander, and when not on stage is kept, like him, in the forefront of our minds.[99] Her character shows most complexity and most development, yet remains essentially self-consistent. Initially she seems fierce, hard-hearted and too self-sufficient, even in her affecting praise of the pleasures of country life (179–88, 215–44), for she rejects not only the Commander and his pimps but men in general, all of whom she believes are deceitful and a threat to the honour which alone she prizes (189–92, 235–6, 435–6). Her reaction to the phrase 'fair ladies' (291) and her list of slanders, especially against women (345–7), show more than the alertness, shrewdness and verbal wit for which she is rightly praised. Grateful that she is as yet immune to love (433–41), she seems all too ready to be convinced by Mengo that it is no more than self-centred desire. Not only Fernán Gómez but also the 'over-bold' Frondoso complain repeatedly of her *desdén* (444, 597, 751, 786). But those critics who have seen this lack of sweetness and susceptibility as untypical of Lope's women are completely mistaken.[100] His plays contain many examples (as well as those mentioned above, in *La quinta de Florencia* and *El ejemplo de casadas*), of the *esquiva*, averse to love and marriage. As Melveena McKendrick has shown, this most popular variant of the 'mannish woman' in the *comedia* may well have been a type of Lope's own invention, with the help of the courtly love tradition, classical mythology and real-life examples of contemporary feminists.[101] Such rebelliousness, however, is for Lope a perversity which cries out to be cured, and always is; for while it may be prompted (if not by vanity or pride) by the injustices of men, ultimately it is 'directed against the natural order of things as decreed by God'.[102] Thus Laurencia's asperity seems at odds with the fertility of the fields, and (as Frondoso says) with her own angelic beauty (743–50, 759–64). That her lover's complaint is echoed, in his hearing, by Fernán Gómez, is in several ways ironical, but she has indeed seemed a 'monster', an affront to her Maker's purpose (786–90).

What the Commander cannot know is that a chemical change is occurring, of which he will be the catalyst. Already softening toward Frondoso (772–4), she is moved by his bravery on her behalf to an admiration and concern for his safety which transforms her view of his sex (831–2, 1154–66). Still afraid of the Commander (1194–6), she is no less afraid for her lover (1277–8); she abandons her '*desdeñosos extremos*' and agrees to his wishes (and those of the community) with an amusingly bashful enthusiasm (1303–4, 1309–16, 1405–27).

When the Commander disrupts her wedding, she is both concerned for Frondoso and bold in defence of Esteban (1578, 1637–8). Herself abducted, she reappears in Act II dishevelled and disfigured; but her impassioned (and justly famous) intervention is a model of lucid rhetoric. Denouncing in turn her father, her assailant and the villagers in general, she not only shames them into action but announces the role she herself will enact, as the self-appointed rouser and leader of their womenfolk. In defence of both her old honour and her new love, she becomes, explicitly, that other archetype of the 'mannish woman', the Amazon warrior-queen.[103] With a sense of order apparently lacking in the men (1804–5, 1829–31), she marshals and captains her troops, but is also impelled herself to take the most active part (1899–1903).

At her next appearance, by contrast, she is all love and self-abnegation. Completely committed to the well-being of another – 'I adore my husband, seek his good alone' (2169–72) – she lacks in concern for his safety the least thought of her own. Agonizing over his absence, she is even more anxious when he appears (2161–90). But they remain united before us, as symbols of selfless devotion, to voice our pity, terror and admiration as the community exemplifies the same heroic unselfishness. Both share, too, in the collective celebrations; but it is Laurencia who ends the scene with another outpouring of personal love, both unaffected and total (2288–9). In the last scene she takes little part, except to express to Frondoso both her admiration for the Monarchs and her pious good wishes for their union (2386–9), and to hear him extol the fact that her virtue had not succumbed but triumphed in the face of Fernán Gómez's violence (2410–3). This late-minute revelation that Laurencia had not, as Lope may have meant us to surmise, been raped, is seen by some critics as utterly unrealistic, a sentimental sop to the popular taste of his time.[104]   I have argued elsewhere, on the contrary, that this 'happy ending', as well as poetically 'right', is consistent with all that precedes it, and in particular with the characterisation of Laurencia as a woman of wit, resourcefulness and resolution, in all ways more than a match for the Commander.[105]   I will add here only that if the audience *is* surprised, the actress has not portrayed her as a sufficiently 'iron lady'.

Not surprisingly, she somewhat overshadows her less complex lover, Frondoso.   Yet, he, like her, is a constant opponent of and contrast to the Commander.   His list of flatteries is as shrewd as the list with which she caps it; as Hall points out, 'Lope presents them as a pair of kindred spirits sharing a common concern for honesty and. sincerity'.[106]   Already in love with her, he cannot agree with Mengo, but takes no part in the debate, except to express his frustration at her indifference to his obvious admiration (356–9, 436, 444).   This frustration reappears when she continues to rebuff him, although even she must concede that he stands out from the other young peasants, whom he will later lead and represent (731–4, 1874, 2091–5).   His love, as Lope always makes clear, is directed (unlike Fernán Gómez's lust) towards a Christian marriage,[107] and motivates a defiance which the Commander therefore cannot comprehend (843–5, 1044–9).   Yet in this he remains both coolly shrewd and respectful, aware of limits which unlike the other he is unwilling to overstep.[108]   Not unaware thereafter of his enemy's vindictiveness, his love for Laurencia continues to preclude him from intimidation (1038–43, 1162–6, 1278–84).   When at last it is rewarded by her acceptance, he is delighted, but speaks to Esteban with exemplary correctness, and a naive but honourable disinterest in respect of her dowry (1397–8, 1435–6).

In Act III he is able to understand, and tell the Commander, that the peasants' rebellion was motivated by love (1864), a love which he will later reciprocate by refusing to abandon them in their danger, though his is presumably greater (2189–98).   It is he who at the celebrations which so resemble those at his wedding recites the first *copla* in praise of the royal couple, and he who foresees in their accession the dawn of a new day (2032–42, 2076–7). Confronting them, he is impressed by their power, but makes bold to offer evidence and to proclaim at the close the wisdom of the royal decision.

THE PLAY IN PERFORMANCE

Fuente Ovejuna, since its 'discovery' last century, has become Lope's best-known and most frequently performed play. But though the existence of another play with the same title, by Cristóbal de Monroy (1612–49), would seem to show that its subject continued to be popular, we know nothing of how either was played or received at its first appearance, beyond the fact that a copy of Lope's was one of 31 plays which were bought in far-away Potosí by an actor-manager, one Gabriel del Río, in August 1619.[109] Published that year in Lope's *Dozena parte*, it was never (so far as we know) reprinted or performed before it was edited by Hartzenbusch as late as 1857.[110] It is nevertheless important (even – or indeed especially – if we might choose to direct it differently today) to envisage how Lope expected it to be performed in one of the *corrales* of Madrid, for which he presumably wrote it. These permanent theatres, custom-built (or rather, custom-adapted) in the 1580s, were remarkably similar to some of the rectangular playhouses of the Elizabethans, like the Fortune and the second Blackfriars. Fortunately, we know a great deal about them, and some of similar type, like that in the then important town of Almagro, have survived to our own day.[111] The better acoustics aforded by such theatres probably increased the importance of the aural element in the plays performed there, whereas the increasing use of more illusionistic staging, especially in court performances and theatres, undoubtedly shifted the emphasis toward the visual; but it is an absurd exaggeration, as I have argued elsewhere, to suppose that the *comedias* written for *corrales* were purely aural.[112] The spectators' visual imagination was stimulated not only by the use in their language of imagery, description and 'verbal décor', but by the exploitation of the acting spaces themselves and of scenic devices including furniture, costumes and props, as well as by significant facial and corporal expression. These might be indicated by directions in the text, but much more often were implied or indeed imposed on the actors by the lines they were given to speak. There can be no doubt that so consummate a dramatist as Lope both heard and saw in his mind's ear and eye the kind of performance a play like *Fuente Ovejuna* would be given in such theatres.

'We must imagine a broad end-stage jutting out into a rectangular *corral*, headhigh to the standing *mosqueteros* (groundlings) but flanked and fronted by tiers of seated spectators. Along its rear runs a shallow space covered by a curtain, from which at either side the actors can emerge, and at the centre of which 'discoveries' or simple settings can be displayed. Above this, supported by pillars, runs a gallery (or a pair of them) which can be used for upper-level scenes, musicians or more "discoveries".[113] Even this gallery, however, would not necessarily have been used in *Fuente Ovejuna*, which exploits only the most essential features of such theatres. In a production in the 1960s at Manchester University Theatre, an upper stage was employed for the scene at Ciudad Real, for the assault on the Commander's house, and especially for all three appearances of the Catholic Monarchs, enabling them to be seen, symbolically, at a loftier level than their subjects; but I incline to suppose that Lope imagined the whole of the action as taking place on the main stage.

Most probably no scenery would have been used; the decorated carts full of gifts which Esteban describes, for instance, would not actually have appeared (552–76), although Alonso's remark that 'we've dressed your doorway, Sir, with reeds and rushes' might possibly suggest that the 'discovery-space' was decorated in such a way (583–4).[114] On the other hand, a variety of meaningful insignia would no doubt have been brought on stage. Ferdinand and Isabella, at all their appearances, were probably accompanied by banners bearing the arms of Castile, Leon and Aragon. Such banners are mentioned by Cimbranos (1119–20), and in the scene at Ciudad Real may well have been displayed, above the heads of the defeated Calatravans, on the city's 'battlements' and 'towers' (i.e. the first-floor gallery), together with 'torches', though these (since performances invariably took place in daylight) would possibly have been unlit (1460–2). The Master's satisfaction in that scene that the banner of his Order has not been lost implies that it is visible on stage (1453–5), and indeed it may have appeared in all his other three scenes. When the peasants rebel, moreover, Barrildo proposes that they should raise a banner of their own (1801–2), and this too may have appeared in subsequent scenes (whereas the women, Laurencia tells her 'ensign' Pascuala (1836–43), will have 'no banner but our caps').[115] At their triumph, the Commander's head is brought in on a lance, only to be replaced by an escutcheon which bears the arms of the Catholic Monarchs, and which is set up on the town hall (2069–80) – presumably, that is, over the central 'discovery-space' – where perhaps it remains to the end.

The only furniture required (although the King and Queen could have been enthroned in the 'discovery-space', as they were in the first production of this translation) consists of a few stools (standard equipment, probably pre-set) which are used at the beginning of Act II. At the tense moment of the Commander's entry, some of the villagers are clearly sitting, and respectfully rise to offer him his usual place; but he tells them to resume their seats, with a hypocritical suavity which soon turns, as they demur, to a tone of severe command (940–8).

So spare a style of staging had the enormous virtues of flexibility and 'flow', as well as of requiring the spectators to attend to actors and text, to use their wits and imagination. Whenever the stage was left empty, they would have recognised the end of a scene,[116] and would have imagined, as the next began, a change of place and time, the nature of which would be conveyed by the new characters' lines or costume. It was possible, therefore, as in cinema or television drama, or indeed as in Elizabethan plays (as performed both then and nowadays), to change the setting at will, though in practice the exercise of such licence tended to diminish as the *comedia* matured.[117]

The use of very little scenery or furniture thus had obvious advantages; but it by no means implies a lack of visual impact. The *comedia* makes great use of costume and props, for instance, to indicate character and status, and of changes of either to signal significant changes of time and place or of situation. *Fuente Ovejuna* contains no references to the costumes worn by the Monarchs, and very few (unlike, say, *Peribáñez*) to those of the peasants (203–4, 1034, 1781–3, 1843); but Lope would undoubtedly have expected these opposite poles of society to be visibly distinguished both from each other and from the noblemen, to whose appearance he makes a number of specific allusions. Flores, for instance, describes the battle-array of both the Master and the Commander (469–74, 489–500), and Cimbranos urges Fernán Gómez (1106-8) to exchange for this the green cap and cloak that he first wears, perhaps, when hunting in the last scene of Act I. But above all both Calatravans are conspicuous throughout the play by reason of the emblems they display to denote their noble rank and the proper role of their Order. Cross and sword, seen by the spectators before a word is spoken, should constantly remind such knights – as both soon show they know (33-6, 60-3) – of the solemn obligations which they symbolise, but which the Commander by his every word and deed belies. So indeed, at his bidding, does the Master; but the younger man will learn and by his future conduct fulfil them. These symbols are before our eyes whenever either Calatravan is on stage; our ears ring almost incessantly with reminders of their significance.[118]

The nobleman's sword, however, is not the only weapon or hand-prop which serves as an iconic key to status and role. When he appears as a hunter in the last scene of Act I, Fernán Gómez has abandoned this emblem of nobility for another, a crossbow.[119] When he lays this too aside, to seize Laurencia with his bare hands, the act exposes him as base; when Frondoso recovers it to defend her, the roles of nobleman and peasant, predator and prey, are visibly reversed before us, and the significance of the stage picture will be underlined in Act II (1027–49, 1601–6). Esteban, on the other hand, presumably carries throughout his magistrate's rod, symbolic of justice and the rule of law; significantly, he alludes to its ineffectiveness in the face of tyranny (1341–2), and Fernán Gómez not only usurps but uses it to beat its exemplary bearer. Again, the import of the visual image will be emphasised early in the following act (1691–4). Mengo's humbler role in the community is defined, by contrast, by the sling with which he manages and protects the animals in his charge; in his heroic defence of Jacinta it proves, as he later comments, a quite inadequate weapon (1487–9), and indeed it too is turned against him. Such brutal wrong-doing can only be met, as Frondoso shows, as the other peasants recognise when they seize all available arms, and as the victimised Laurencia comments when she exits sword in hand (1902–3), by the proper use of commensurate force.

Such emblematic visual effect is of course dynamic rather than static, and in no way detracts from the dramatic qualities of the play. Though shorter than most *comedias*, *Fuente Ovejuna* is a complex work, full of parallels and contrasts, cross-references and echoes, with constant variations of pace and mood. Its actors and audience share an almost unlimited diversity of emotions. It has moments of quiet conversation, of sentimental charm, of farcical comedy, of evocative lyricism and exuberant rhetoric. As those who know it well tend to forget, it generates tense expectancy and springs unpredictable surprises. But fundamentally it is a violent drama of passions in conflict, which thrusts continually forward with a relentless energy and intensity.

The action begins, arrestingly, with its protagonist in a state of intense indignation – expressed, no doubt, in restless movement – which his toadies attempt to calm but which is only gradually assuaged when the Master enters, effusively apologetic, and insists on embracing him twice. The speech on which he then embarks, though expository, invites impassioned delivery, and provokes an immediate and active response.

In the dialogue which follows, Laurencia is no less emotionally aroused; even her lyrical description of a day in the country and Pascuala's comic reply are resentful diatribes. The male peasants enter, similarly, in animated discussion, and after the lively battle of wits between Frondoso and Laurencia, their philosophical debate is energetically conducted. The arrival of Flores leads to more expansive but highly coloured narration, but this builds in its turn towards an outburst of collective acclaim at the Commander's triumphant appearance, expressed in song and in Esteban's grandiloquent speech. The festive mood, however, is quickly dispelled when Fernán Gómez ungraciously dismisses the assembled peasants, and attempts instead to lure Laurencia and Pascuala away, only to provoke in them a spirited hostility like that with which the scene began.

The next starts comparatively calmly, with the Monarchs by contrast in agreement; but their concern with pressing affairs of state is intensified by the urgent appeal from Ciudad Real, to which they react with businesslike dispatch. When Laurencia and Frondoso appear, on the other hand, they are entertainingly at odds; but as soon as her waspishness begins to yield to his impassioned wooing, the briefly sentimental mood is shattered by the appearance of the Commander and his crudely physical assault. Frondoso's opportunistic but resolute response produces a confrontation rich in tension, and leaves the Commander – at the act's end, as at its beginning – in an ominously angry mood.

The leisurely conversations with which Act II begins establish a calmer atmosphere, but excitement returns with mention of the Commander and with his unannounced appearance. It mounts as he repeatedly offends and ridicules the peasants' sense of honour, until he furiously orders them to leave. He gives full rein to his uncomprehending resentment, especially against Frondoso, only to turn to a blithe discussion of new adulteries, but is roused again to resolute activity by the news from Ciudad Real.

Equally excited, though out of fear and resentment of him, are Laurencia and Pascuala. But they have barely settled to inveighing with Mengo against his iniquities when they are impelled to flee by the sudden appearance of Jacinta, before the equally dramatic entries of her pursuers and of the Commander himself, to whom Mengo and Jacinta offer both defiance and unavailing pleas for mercy.

Fear spills over into the following scene, but soon gives way to calm and courtesy in the discussion of Frondoso's proposal. Laurencia's emergence from hiding immediately Esteban calls her, and their amusing private conversation, lend humour and charm to the episode, which ends in a moment of ecstatic delight.

The despair of the noblemen defeated at Ciudad Real provides a total contrast, but gaiety and humour return with the wedding festivities. Even amid these, however, the Commander's cruelties cannot be forgotten, and the song intended to celebrate the marriage may in its lyricism distance but cannot exorcise the threat of tyrannical violence. That violence in fact materialises with the startling reappearance of the Commander and his savagery towards Frondoso, Esteban and Laurencia. In this last scene of the act, as in its first, harmony and tranquillity are replaced by disruption and despair.

The debate which opens Act III is characterised by both urgency and indecision; but Laurencia's startling appearance and impassioned harangue provoke in the villagers a readiness for instant action, echoed by that of their womenfolk, which recalls the resolution of the Master and the Commander at the end of previous scenes.

The villain and his henchmen reappear, intent on another atrocity, but are immediately under attack, and the scene becomes very quickly one of almost incessant movement, like that at Ciudad Real which in many ways it parallels. It marks a climax in the action – but a false one, for as its first spectators must have suspected, assuming they knew the proverb, the most dramatic moments are yet to come. The next scene by contrast opens quietly, with the King and Queen responding gravely to Manrique's report of their victory; but excitement returns once more with Flores' lurid account of his master's murder and mutilation, and with Ferdinand's reaction, no less decisive than the one we witnessed in the similar scene in Act I. What follows the Monarchs' exit, however, is Lope's most astonishing conception yet: a 'reprise', though this time in honour of *them* (notwithstanding the ghoulish parading of the common enemy's head) of the wedding celebrations in Act II. Yet this scene too changes gear midway, when the merrymakers suddenly anticipate a royal investigation, and becomes a grimly comic preparation for the ordeal which at its end is announced as imminent.

The brief but important bridging-scene which Lope now neatly inserts, maintaining our interest in the Master without – since his reactions to what has passed are so intense – any diminution of the tension, provides a clear contrast in that it involves only a pair of characters remote from the central action. But the appearance of Laurencia, alone, and her encounter with Frondoso, are an even more surprising introduction to the torture-scene we are expecting; and that this is placed off-stage is not merely, I suggest, a concession to contemporary notions of 'decorum'[120] or to Horace's sound principle that simulated horrors are essentially unconvincing.[121] Distance lends the peasants' suffering an aura of epic or myth; it becomes an unseen but powerful play-within-the play, mediated on stage by a human but archetypal male and female, to which we respond both directly and indirectly by sharing their reactions, at once individual and universal. But Lope has more surprises up his sleeve. He tantalizes the lovers, and us, with the fear that Mengo alone will show fear, only to make his jesting 'confession' the climactic point of his drama, to follow it with a passage of pure farce, and to end this magnificently structured scene with a moment of joyful affection, yet another reaffirmation of the power of love. One might look far to find a better example of tragicomedy, or a better illustration of Montesinos' dictum: 'The baroque is the art of renouncing nothing'.

The final scene, as I have argued elsewhere,[122] is no less masterly in its rapid but balanced and carefully calculated resolution of the plot and recapitulation of its theme. We should note, though, that Lope by no means fails to obey his own shrewd precept in the *New Art* (234–9): 'Don't allow the solution to appear until the very last scene, for once the public knows the ending it turns its face to the exit and its back to the actor who has confronted it for three hours, because it only needs to know how things turn out'.   We cannot know that the Master's contrition will be graciously received, and the Judge's report of the peasants' unanimity ends with a stark but genuine alternative: 'You must either pardon them all, or put the town to death'.   When the 'assassins' are now at last brought face to face with their royal judges, the spectators – mindful, perhaps, of 'modern instances'[123] – may hope but cannot be sure that their crime will go unpunished.   Only in the last twelve lines does Ferdinand deliver, and Frondoso acclaim, a 'judgement of Solomon' which acknowledges that their solidarity, their love, has won them forgiveness.

As well as a drama, however, and in more than one sense, *Fuente Ovejuna* is a musical.   Music, religious or secular, played an important part in the everyday life of both country and city folk, and from medieval times was integral to Spanish drama.   Early dramatists, like Juan del Encina and Gil Vicente (both accomplished composers as well as poets), had included many songs in their plays, and it became the norm in the sixteenth century for dramatic works to be rounded off by a *villancico* or final chorus.   When permanent theatres were established, moreover, they invariably offered not merely a single play but a whole afternoon's entertainment, of which music was a prominent component. Many actors were able singers and dancers, and their companies included musicians, who would normally open and close the programme and remain on hand throughout.   The intervals between the acts of the *comedia* were filled by interludes, which were often musical; in the second, for instance, it was normal for a *baile* or jig to be sung and danced.   But the play 'proper' continued to include any number of songs; most of Lope's have between two and four, and one, *La maya*, has as many as twelve.   In some cases these were 'mere lyrical parentheses or decorative embellishments', but in many they perform an important dramatic function.[124]   In some well-known instances, as in *Peribáñez* or *El caballero de Olmedo*, an existing song was not only Lope's main source of inspiration, but constitutes a crucial part of the action.

Those we find in *Fuente Ovejuna* are not essential to the plot, but serve to emphasise attitudes and crystallize ideas; their ultimate function is to restate, in a different mode, the central theme of the work.   That theme, I have insisted, is the necessity of love, individual and collective, between all human beings.   But if – and only if – he can feel and show such love can man the microcosm perform his proper function in the macrocosm, the very principle of whose continuing existence is concord, expressed for instance in Pythagoras' unheard 'music of the spheres'.   Thus music for Lope is not merely a metaphor but another name for love.   As he makes Barrildo say, paraphrasing Ficino (379–82): '...all the world,/ here and up there, is perfect harmony,/ and harmony is love'.   Thus to be loving is to be 'musical'; to perform music is to express love.   Of *Fuente Ovejuna* – and of Lope's plays in general – we can say with Spitzer: 'Whenever music will be played (or a song sung by the *músicos*) we must infer also the presence of the motif of *love and harmony*'.[125]

Even before actual music is heard, however, and indeed throughout the play, its positive characters are presented as 'musically-minded', are associated in our minds with notions of concord. Laurencia likes to see beef and cabbage in a stew-pot 'cavorting gaily to a frothy tune', likes to 'marry' an aubergine and some bacon (225-32). Mengo, whose most prized possession is his fiddle (286-8), proposes an agreement (a '*concierto*') between the debaters before they consult the women (279-80), and even he does not dispute Barrildo's assertion that all nature is governed by love, defined as '*concierto*' (379-87). Laurencia, long before consenting to her marriage to Frondoso, imagines the rustic music which will accompany it (739-42); Esteban, when Frondoso asks for her hand, takes it for granted that 'they've both agreed' (1392), but insists on confirming the agreement of all concerned. In their rebellion, the villagers 'unite and raise a single cry, since all of us agree' (1806-7). After it, Esteban urges them: 'Agree together what you're going to say' (2089-90); as we hear, and as the Judge reports, they do indeed answer individually but as if in unison, 'with one accord' (2366).

When music is first heard, Flores tells the peasants that love is the best tribute they can offer the victorious Commander (525-8); and in fact, as Esteban's speech clarifies, their song of welcome – cast in a traditional mould, and paralleled in other plays, as shown by Salomon[126] – is just such an offer, as Fernán Gómez has to recognise, though formally and with little sign of reciprocation. The second song – no less traditional in form[127] – is similarly a manifestation of the villagers' love, directed this time toward the peasant lovers Frondoso and Laurencia. The deliberately, comically primitive *estribillo* and *copla* which are performed at their wedding express the collective hope that their life as a married couple may be long and full, that they may die together and so end suitably a union untroubled by envy or jealousy. In this there is perhaps a hint of menace; but the ballad which Juan Rojo calls on all to sing and dance in celebration of the fact that now 'they are as one' both intensifies the threat and clarifies that it is a threat from without. This much more sophisticated pastiche[128] recalls the attempted rape in the last scene of Act I, but even more obviously foreshadows the violence which is to end this last scene of Act II. The song, and the union it is sung to honour, are rudely disrupted by the lustful Commander it alludes to; love and harmony are subverted by the personification of lovelessness and discord.[129]

Such violence can be eradicated only by more violence, as the peasants come to realise and the spectators to accept. Lope has used his first two acts to justify the villagers' rebellion (whereas Rades had used only a hundred words or so); now (though keeping off stage and merely having Flores describe to the Monarchs their less justifiable excesses) he displays that rebellion before us. In doing so he puts in their mouths screams of hatred like those he had found in his source; but we can hear in those screams an excusable transmutation of the offers of love which the song in Act I has implanted in our minds. 'Our lord the Commander we welcome again ... Long live Fernán Gómez' has become, by the Commander's own fault, 'Let traitors and tyrants die ... Death to Fernán Gómez!' But they also raise, as in the Chronicle, a more positive, *loving* cry: 'Long live our lords the King and Queen!'; and in this we also detect, no less transmuted, an echo of their second song: 'See where the happy pair appears; may they live for years and years!'

In the murder scene itself, of course, they raise another cry, which Rades had also reported: '¡Fuente Ovejuna!'; but in this case the echoes are yet to come, for (as he had similarly stated) it became the peasants' unanimous reply to their torturers. Lope proposes therefore to repeat it incessantly (together with the proverbial 'Fuente Ovejuna did it') in three of his five remaining scenes (2092–2124, 2208–87, 2369).

As these cries show, and as Frondoso recognises (1864), the peasants' resort to rebellion was in fact an act of love. By way of celebration, he has them perform another; they lay its fruits, metaphorically, at the feet of the distant Monarchs, whose insignia they display and acclaim. But as they do so, the first and second slogans are once again transmuted; they become the play's fourth and final song, are expressed in the language of love, in music. The *same* music, surely, that we heard in the wedding scene; for the *estribillo* and *coplas* not only paraphrase the cries which accompanied their violence, but echo even more clearly than those cries did the expression of their pious good wishes for the pair of local lovers. 'See where the happy pair appears; may they live for years/ and years … Hear our prayer to Heaven above: may both be spared, as man and wife … and die, exhausted by a life that's full of joy and free of tears' now becomes 'Long life to Isabella fair and Ferdinand of Aragon … she his, he hers, a happy pair; and when at last to Heaven they fare, may Michael lead them by the hand'. At the same time and equally, however, the peasants proclaim their own feat of arms, their defeat of tyranny, as yet another victory for rulers they are happy to serve: 'Long live the Catholic Kings, whose might has given them the victory … May they maintain, whether they fight with giants or dwarves, the upper hand … and all tyrants be dead and damned!' In this sense their song echoes also their first, the one they offered in Act I to the victorious but unworthy Fernán Gómez. They had feted him and the Master, in their innocence, not as cruel self-seeking traitors but as the mild and gentle overlords and stalwart crusaders against the Moors which it was their duty to be (533–8). Now they celebrate instead not only their own recent victory but the past and future victories of the truly benign Catholic Monarchs, who are destined (with the aid of loyal nobles like the regenerate Girón) to conquer the kingdom of Granada.

Fuente Ovejuna, however, can also be described as musical by virtue of the fact that it is written not only wholly in verse but in a rich variety of different metrical forms, which Lope rings the changes on with the inventiveness and assurance of a great composer.

The most distinctive feature of Spanish Golden-Age drama may well be the complexity, in most instances, of its metrical structure. To quote S.G. Morley: 'The extraordinary variety of meters employed in the *comedia* surpassed anything known in any other drama of the world.'[130] Consequently, 'the Golden-Age dramatists have at their disposal a very wide range of metres, any of which at any moment they may choose to employ, to generate the pace, mood or style they have in mind for a particular "beat", very much as a composer may change tempo or key from one musical passage to the next.'[131] Such an analogy, which many critics have drawn, between the *comedia* and music, especially opera,[132] should often be borne in mind, for essentially the drama of Golden-Age Spain is a *dramma lirico*. The progressions from one 'number' or 'movement' to the next may or may not be evident in performance, but 'the successive passages in different metres and stanza-forms are .. the true ... building-blocks of the play; the poetic structure of a *comedia* coincides with, *is* its dramatic structure[133]. When we read a Golden-Age play (especially, of course, as intending performers) we should therefore hope to 'hear' as well as 'see' it, not only to visualise its action but to 'auralise' its poetry, and to try to imagine the effects of its varying verse-forms in the theatre, as they must have been perceived by a seventeenth-century audience.[134]

The criteria by which the dramatists determined their choices of metre are imperfectly understood – and were perhaps not fully known to themselves. Lope himself, the pioneer and unrivalled master of dramatic polymetry, must have thought about them more than anyone, but the only account of his ideas is contained in a mere eight lines of his *New Art*.[135] Of these the first and second are by far the most significant, since they prove that he was aware – more aware than many of his contemporaries, or his critics – of the desirability of suiting poetic form to dramatic content: 'Prudently accommodate your lines to the matters with which you are dealing'. The other six, in which he offers specific examples, have often been read, mistakenly, as if they were meant to represent a fully thought-out system, and have been made to fit (or found not to fit) his own practice. In fact that practice 'evolved both consistently and coherently, without ever becoming a hard-and-fast formula, immune to experimentation'.[136] Because that evolution can be traced, as it was by Morley and Bruerton, we can say for instance that a play like *Fuente Ovejuna* was probably written between 1612 and 1614, or conversely can predict, within broad limits, what metrical forms, and in what proportions, a play by Lope of such a date will contain. For what purposes, what type of scene, what effect he will use one, or change to another, we can be a great deal less certain, notwithstanding the work of other scholars, especially Diego Marín.[137] If we were able to ask the writer himself, he would surely know more of his methods – but perhaps not very much more, for many of his decisions were probably intuitive. For the most part, however, we can make informed guesses about his intentions, conscious or otherwise.

Within a scene, he may use a single verse-form, as in seven of *Fuente Ovejuna*'s sixteen, or make any number of changes, as in the other nine. At its end (i.e. when he empties the stage) he normally emphasises the transition to the next (indicated in his manuscripts by a line across the page) by shifting to another. Failure to do so may indicate, as Marín has observed, a 'desire to underline the thematic link between different scenes',[137] and must produce an unusual sense of continuity. It should not escape our notice, therefore, that in *Fuente Ovejuna* he continues with no change of metre in no less than five out of thirteen cases (at 173, 635, 1277, 2125 and 2290); the first and last of these are especially thought-provoking.

When he does make changes, we should try to distinguish between his habitual or functional and his more affective reasons for doing so. For instance, in the last line of the *New Art* passage he remarked that *redondillas* were suitable for 'matters of love'; and some critics have therefore looked for love-themes in *redondilla* passages.[138] That they have succeeded, more or less, in finding them, is hardly surprising; love, in a broad sense, is Lope's constant theme, in *Fuente Ovejuna* and in general. In fact, though, their suitability for fast-flowing, open-ended dialogue and action made them his favourite form, his work-horse, especially for the beginnings of acts. Between 1609 and 1618, in his certainly authentic and datable plays, he used *redondillas*, on average, about 45 per cent of the time, and for over 75 per cent of his act-openings.[139] We need not therefore be surprised to find that in our play *redondillas* account for 58.3 per cent of the total; what should attract our attention and surmise is that two of its acts do *not* begin in *redondillas*.

Similarly he relied heavily on *romances*, the traditional metre of Spanish epics and balladry. He used them, above all, for narrative-emotive monologue,[140] and they became increasingly the verse-form in which he ended every act. Between 1609 and 1618 his plays have *romances*, on average, as 27 per cent of their lines, and to end 83 per cent of their acts.[141] Thus his use of them in *Fuente Ovejuna* accords with his practice at the time, *except* that his failure to change to *romances* for the final scene is extremely unusual.[142]

Other combinations of octosyllabic lines (and variants thereon) are employed in our play, as they usually were, for the lyrics of songs; but one feature of their use – the 'improvisation' of *coplas* as verses to an *estribillo* – is extremely unusual; we find it in no other play by Lope.[143] The fact that in *Fuente Ovejuna* he introduces it twice, for the celebration both of the wedding and of the rebellion, is a further reason, among many we have noted, for supposing that he intended a parallel between the two scenes.

Such native octosyllabic forms account in fact (after some very early experiments) for over 70 per cent of his lines in every play. But by way of variation he often turns instead, more idiosyncratically and significantly perhaps, to the Italianate forms, with eleven- (or seven-) syllable lines, which Garcilaso and Boscán had first fully 'naturalised' as late as the 1520s. These more leisurely forms had connotations of greater elegance and artifice. Their use by Lope, Diego Marín has argued, is determined by the lofty nature of the sentiments expressed in them, whether by refined or by plebian characters,[145] and thus they should always arouse our interest. We may note, for instance, that in *Peribáñez* (except at the last appearance of the King and Queen, in *octavas reales*) Italianate lines are used only in passages spoken or dominated by its anti-hero, the aristocratic Commander.[146] In *Fuente Ovejuna*, by contrast, apart from 23 lines of blank verse (*sueltos*) for the brief scene at Ciudad Real (intended perhaps to lend it substance and detach it from the scenes at Fuente Ovejuna which surround it), Lope appears to employ Italianate forms to enhance the role and dignity of the peasants. In Act I, 34 *tercetos* – suitable, according to the *New Art*, for solemn matters – are used almost entirely for Esteban's attempt at a grandiloquent speech of welcome; at the beginning of Act III – unusually, as pointed out above – another 60 appear when he and the other leading villagers deliberate on the gravity of their later situation.   Act II opens – also unusually – with a similarly serious discussion, in *octavas reales*, between Esteban and his fellow-magistrate Alonso, on the state of the town's economy; in Act III this form reappears for the climactic scene in which the townsfolk storm the Commander's house and execute their revenge.[147]   The torture scene, on the other hand, begins – arrestingly – with a moment of reflection, a soliloquy cast, as so often in Lope, in the self-advertising, epigrammatic form of a Petrarchan sonnet.   In its quatrains Laurencia meditates, in objective terms, on the effect on an unselfish love of concern for the beloved's well-being, turning only in the tercets, more passionately, to its exemplification in her case,[148] by way of an exordium to its exemplification in Frondoso and in their tortured fellow-villagers. As Wardropper has said, this sonnet 'imposes a tone of immense seriousness on the dramatic moment'; it creates 'a deliberate pause, toward the end of the action, for the purpose of summing up the ideological content of the drama'.[149]

The metrical forms may be tabulated as follows:[150]

ACT I

1–68	redondillas
69–140	romance (a–o)
141–172	redondillas
172–456	redondillas
457–528	romance (e–e)
529–544	romancillo (o–e)
545–578	tercetos
579–590	redondillas
591–594	romancillo (o–e)
595–634	redondillas
635–654	redondillas
655–698	romance (e–o)
699–722	redondillas
723–859	romance (o–o)

ACT II

860–938	octavas reales
939–1102	redondillas
1103–1136	romance (e–a)

1137–1276	redondillas

1277–1448	redondillas

1449–1471	sueltos (4 pareados)

1472–1474	coplilla de estribillo (aaa)
1475–1502	redondillas
1503–1509	copla/estribillo (bccbba/aaa)
1510–1545	redondillas
1546–1569	romance/seguidillas (a–a)
1570–1651	romance (a–e)

ACT III

1652–1711	tercetos
1712–1847	romance (o–e)

1848–1919	octavas reales

1920–1947	redondillas
1948–2027	romance (e–e)

2028–2030	coplilla de estribillo (aaa)
2031–2034	redondillas
2035–2042	copla/estribillo (bccbbaa/aaa)
2043–2046	redondilla
2047–2056	copla/estribillo (bccbbaa/aaa)
2057–2060	redondilla
2061–2068	copla/estribillo (bccbbaa/aaa)
2069–2124	redondillas

2125–2060	redondillas

2161–2174	soneto (abba/abba/cde/cde)
2175–2289	redondillas

2290–2453	redondillas	Changes per act: 12,11,15.

Type	Passages	Lines	Percentage	
Redondillas	15	1432	58.3	
Romance	9	674	27.4	
Seguidillas	2	8	0.3	
Romancillo	2	20	0.8	
Copla/estribillo	6	45	1.8	Castilian lines: 88.5%
Octavas reales	2	152	6.2	
Soneto	1	14	0.6	
Tercetos	2	94	3.8	
Sueltos	1	23	0.9	Italianate lines: 11.5%

THE SPANISH TEXT

Few modern texts of Golden-Age plays are worthy of their authors. Few approximate as closely as possible, that is, to what the dramatists originally wrote, or would ultimately have wished performers or readers to see. In the case of *Fuente Ovejuna*, the last two decades have seen a number of excellent editions, but none has dealt definitively with its textual problems, relatively minor though they are. By building on the work of previous scholars, I have therefore tried to offer here, alongside my translation, as adequate a critical text of the play as can be achieved.

In attempting to reconstruct Lope's intentions, we have essentially a single witness, the text he published in his *Dozena parte* of 1619.[151] But preparing a critical edition is a trickier task than this might suggest. In 1933, C.E. Anibal confirmed that there were two editions of this *Parte*, both printed in Madrid by the widow of Alonso Martín for Alonso Pérez.[152] The one he called A has on its title-page the coat-of-arms of the Cárdenas family; the one he called B, a Sagittarius emblem. It was not until 1982 that Jaime Moll established that B was the later of the two, and was set up from a copy of A.[153] In the process, one line missing from A was supplied (1490), but we cannot know by whom.

Moreover, the surviving copies of edition A (I list on p. 49 those I am aware of) differ slightly among themselves, so that previous editors have designated them A, A_1, A_2, etc. But Moll showed also that their variants were to be explained, for the most part, by press-corrections (for which the author may or may not have been responsible). Corrections were made, he established, to four formes of gatherings Kk and Ll, affecting five pages of *Fuente Ovejuna*; and each of five copies of A which he examined at the Biblioteca Nacional contained, confusingly, both corrected and non-corrected formes.[154]

I have further discovered that corrections were made to the inner forme of the outer sheet of gathering Mm, affecting two more pages of our text.[155] We are indeed faced, therefore, with a number of different copies; but these contain (apart from minor printing imperfections) only three kinds of readings: those which are apparently common to all copies (which we may designate A), those which are found only in corrected formes (Ac), and the original versions of the latter, found in non-corrected formes (Anc).

We may note in passing that one copy of the *princeps* at the British Library, 1072. 1. 9., has emendations in what may be a seventeenth-century hand; these have no authority, but as sensitive attempts to correct the text they deserve an editor's consideration.[156]

A manuscript formerly owned by Lord Holland, and now in the possession of Viscountess Galway at Melbury House, Dorset, is by contrast of little interest; it was clearly transcribed from a copy of the first edition. I have noted some 76 changes made by the copyist, but these are mostly obvious errors or idiosyncratic spellings; nevertheless, it does suggest what I consider a likely reading for one line (302). Even less important is a manuscript at the Biblioteca Palatina, Parma;[157] this too was undoubtedly based on a copy of the *princeps*, but it omits lines 2359–81 and seven others, and has between forty and fifty minor variants, none of which in my view claims our attention.

The first edition of the play to appear in modern times was the one prepared by J.E. Hartzenbusch (H). He evidently used a copy of A, but silently introduced a number of new readings. These were mostly intelligent, but only a dozen (almost all of them corrections of obvious errors) seem acceptable today. Since his was clearly the source of the 'Academy' text, the next serious edition was one published in 1919 by Américo Castro, who by contrast with Hartzenbusch recorded and justified his departures from the *princeps* (C).

For the next half-century, one or other of these three texts was the source of almost every new one (although many made intentional or unintentional changes); but in 1969 – just 350 years after the *princeps* – there appeared the first truly scholarly edition, that prepared by Francisco López Estrada (LE). Further versions of this have appeared, as well as a number of editions of comparable seriousness; in particular, those by Maria Grazia Profeti (P), Juan María Marín (M), Alberto Blecua (Bl) and J. Cañas Murillo (CM).

In view of the above, I have prepared my Spanish text as follows. As base-text I have used a copy of the *princeps* at the British Library, 1072. i. 12, which in respect of the text of *Fuente Ovejuna* has only the corrected versions of those formes which *were* corrected. I have considered, recorded, and in some cases preferred (with reluctance) variants found in other copies of the *princeps*, or in the editions I have mentioned. In a few cases I have suggested and tried to justify readings never printed heretofore (302, 1680, 2279). I have retained the few stage directions found in the *princeps*, but have added none (though a few surprising omissions are mentioned in notes or remedied in the translation). Many are implied by the dialogue,[158] and I assume that the reader will add his own as he directs the play in his mind or indeed on stage; that he will wish to decide for himself, for instance, when lines are spoken 'aside', or heard by others – or both.

Similarly, I have avoided the practice of stating where the action is set; as pointed out in some footnotes, this is either indeterminate or to be inferred from the dialogue; and editorial conjectures, as well as conjuring false visions of illusionistic scenery, can be very misleading.[159] On the other hand, I have clarified the play's dramatic structure by the use of a line across the page (in imitation of Lope himself) at the end of each scene (i.e. when the stage is completely cleared). Similarly, I have clarified its poetic structure by indicating on the right of the page when he has changed to a different metrical form (or has chosen *not* to do so at the start of a new scene).

I have modernized the orthography of the *princeps*, but have respected its apparent inconsistencies,[160] maintained its contractions[161] and avoided obvious changes of pronunciation.[162] I have supplied my own capitals and punctuation, disagreeing in a few cases with all previous editors (404–7, 492–6, 924–5). I have indicated points at which the verse-structure is incomplete,[163] but have not included missing lines in my verse-count; some readers may find it convenient that my numbering thus accords with that of LE and M.

I have listed in a series of end-notes the significant variants found in the other texts I have consulted.

THE ENGLISH TEXT

Translators of Golden-Age plays must face from the outset the difficult and debatable question of form. Some opt for prose; but to my mind, since the *comedia* is an epic and lyric drama, steeped in a diverse poetic tradition, and dependent for much of its impact on the power of verse, to do so is unthinkable, an abdication. As Gwynne Edwards has said in the introduction to his *The Trickster of Seville*: 'A prose version lacks the pulse and the discipline of metre, two of the essential ingredients of Golden-Age and Elizabethan theatre, the framework within which, as in a piece of classical music, emotion is contained and a constant tension between content and form established. Prose dissipates all this.'[164]

To decide on verse, however, raises immediately the further question: what type or types of verse? As pointed out above, *Fuente Ovejuna* is characteristically polymetric. As well as the various songs and *coplas* performed by the peasants, it has five passages of heavily-rhymed hendecasyllables, and one of 'blank verse'. But typically these long, Italianate lines account for less than twelve per cent of the total; for the remainder, Lope uses the much less leisurely native octosyllables. He alternates between *redondillas* (rhyming *abba*) and *romances* (with assonance in every other line). As Nicholas Round has said: 'Taken together, these octosyllabic forms, with their well-defined recurrences of sound, dominate most plays of the time. They furnish the *comedia* in general with a very great deal of its essential character. That character is further defined by the many shifts of pace and density which the polymetric convention makes possible. That is one reason – there are, naturally, others – why the Spanish theatre of this period can seem a faster-moving, more kaleidoscopic, in some senses more superficial, in others more authentically theatrical genre than its English counterpart. This kind of drama – in all senses a "theatre of movement" – was what the Spanish public demanded, and the most immediate function of the metrical structure ... was to give it to them.'[165]

The translator into English, therefore, is at a great disadvantage. Virtually none of the Spanish forms is familiar to himself, his actors or his audience. Rhymes and assonances are far more difficult to find in English; he is likely to be a less competent versifier than the author, especially in the case of a technical master like Lope; and he is or should be far more constrained than an original creator. A few translators of Golden-Age plays – most notably Denis Florence McCarthy, in his nineteenth-century versions of Calderón – have nevertheless attempted a close imitation of the original prosody; but though their virtuosity is often astonishing, such a self-imposed strait-jacket invariably produces excessive paraphrase, unnatural word-order, and forced, false, even unrecognisable rhymes.[166] Others, like Round himself, George Brandt in his *The Great Stage of the World*, or – most successfully, perhaps – Adrian Mitchell in his *The Mayor of Zalamea*,[167] have sought in different ways to replace the original short-line forms by a range of more-or-less similar but freer ones. Such a method preserves the flavour and flexibility of polymetry, but proves to have its own pitfalls. If the new forms are too strict, and too heavily rhymed, they may again impose too rigid a discipline; if too lax, they may leave the audience insufficiently aware that the play is in verse at all. Far less successful, on the other hand, is the use of heavily-rhymed hendecasyllables, as practised on occasion by Roy Campbell.[168] Heroic couplets may well be the only satisfactory form for the translation of rhymed alexandrines, as in Richard Wilbur's versions of Molière,[169] and in theory they should sound like modern equivalents of Dryden or Pope; but in practice they all too often recall to English ears the speeches of Demon Kings and Fairy Queens in pantomime.

My own fundamental preference is for a modern variety of blank verse. I cannot but agree with Nicholas Round, as quoted above, on the differences between Golden-Age plays and the English plays of their time, and the significance among them of a different type of dramatic prosody. But those differences are outweighed by very many similarities; and actors and audiences accustomed to Shakespeare will in my view most readily accept the *comedia* if our translations are couched in the classic metre of English verse drama. Of course Round is also right to warn of the perils of pentameters; as he says, 'their presence tends to carry an unfortunate air of sub-Shakespearean pastiche'.[170] Indeed Roy Campbell's versions, with their pseudo-poetic archaisms, often underline this danger; but it can, I believe, be avoided; we must insist on a flexible line, the word-order of normal speech, and a standard but lively modern lexis. In the present translation, therefore (as also in my version of *El perro del hortelano*), I have chosen to use blank verse – but not entirely. Laurencia's soliloquy, a sonnet in strict Petrarchan form (2161–74), could only be rendered as a sonnet, although I have opted for the frankly less difficult Shakespearean form, which is also more familiar to English ears. Similarly, the peasants' lyrics call, I think, for a measure of rhyme or assonance, and the awkwardness or archaism which this sometimes engenders seems 'in character'. But I have experimented also with another, unrhymed form. In *Fuente Ovejuna* Lope, as we have seen, turns characteristically from *redondillas* to *romance* to end both Act I and Act II, but mostly uses the metre of epic and ballad, more characteristically still, for narrative monologues. Where it serves this second purpose, therefore, I have rendered it not in pentameters but in shorter iambic lines, which I hope will evoke analogous associations in English.[171]

Mostly, however, I have used hendecasyllables to translate a play written mainly in octosyllables. As a result, I have used far fewer lines. The only alternative, evidently, would have been to use far more words, to commit, indeed, one of the cardinal sins of translation: turgidity. Yet all too often, sad to say, the translators of Golden-Age plays make precisely this mistake, and so do less than justice to the dramatic, dynamic qualities of their originals.[172] To give a single example, chosen almost at random: Frondoso's witty catalogue of 25 flattering euphemisms (293–320) is 28 lines long and consists of 108 words. I find I have rendered them in only 15 lines and a similar number of words: 103. Roy Campbell, I discover, used twice as many, 206, and William Colford – though in no more *lines* than Lope – even more: 209. Such prolixity must in itself be mistranslation.

I hope, of course, that my rendering is faithful to the original in some other respects; certainly I have endeavoured to produce a 'literal version'.   But I have aimed no less at a performable script, that actors can speak and audiences enjoy. I may have achieved neither accuracy nor actability; but consciously to have subordinated either to the other would in my view be to have failed outright – by attempting something less than a true translation, to have betrayed both Lope and his potential public today.

Because the English text has far fewer lines, I have left them unnumbered, except to draw attention to many of my footnotes.   Those footnotes, in fact, though keyed to the Spanish text, are addressed to a wide range of readers.   On the one hand I have tried to tackle textual, philological and semantic problems, and relate the text to its literary, socio-political and ideological contexts; on the other I have sought not only to point out what must be lost in translation but to stress what must *not* be lost (whatever is 'modernised') in performance, the essential strengths of the *comedia* as live drama: its directness, its intensity, its 'flow', its kaleidoscopic contrasts of poetry and action, its constant appeal to ear and eye alike.

NOTES TO INTRODUCTION

1. The most recommendable biography is still Américo Castro & Hugo A. Rennert, *Vida de Lope de Vega (1562–1635)*, Salamanca, Anaya, 1968. For a brief account in English of Lope's life, see the edition and translation by James Lloyd, in this series, of his *Peribáñez*.

2. See S.G. Morley and C. Bruerton, 'How many *comedias* did Lope de Vega write?', *Hispania*, 2 (1936), 217–34.

3. See S.G. Morley, 'Lope de Vega's Prolificity and Speed', *Hispanic Review*, 10 (1942), 67–8.

4. Ch.-V. Aubrun, 'Lope de Vega, dramaturge', *Bulletin of Hispanic Studies*, 61 (1984), 271–82 (cf. idem, 'Las mil y ochocientas comedias de Lope de Vega', in *Lope de Vega y los orígenes del teatro español: Actas del Primer Congreso Internacional sobre Lope de Vega*, Madrid, EDI -6, 1981, 27–33) must be almost alone in taking seriously the figures given by Lope and his disciple, and in supposing therefore that many of his plays must have been completed by other writers, or even by actors. Some of the texts which have survived do of course contain later alterations, but there is no evidence that he ever sold an incomplete one. Curiously, the same critic has also said that 'Lope is the author of 850 dramatic works', *La comedia española (1600–1680)*, Madrid, Taurus, 1981.

5. Morley & Bruerton, *Cronología*, 590–601, list 316 certainly authentic plays.

6. Morley & Bruerton, *Cronología*, 330–1. The dates given for all the other plays by Lope I mention are also taken from this study, almost always our most reliable guide.

7. See *Los hechos de Garcilaso de la Vega* (1579–83?), *Los comendadores de Córdoba* (1596), *El cerco de Santa Fe* (1596–8), *El nuevo mundo descubierto por Cristóbal Colón* (probably 1598–1603), *El caballero de Illescas* (about 1602) and *El mejor mozo de España* (1610–1).

8. Rosaldo, 12.

9. See for instance Elliott, 86–9.

10. Aníbal; idem, 'Lope de Vega and the Duque de Osuna', *Modern Language Notes*, 49 (1934), 1–11. Aníbal suggested that Lope may have sent the Duke a copy of *Fuente Ovejuna* when it appeared in print, and that this may explain a gift from him of 500 *escudos* mentioned by Lope in a letter of 6 May 1620 (see Lope de Vega, *Cartas*, edited by Nicolás Marín, Madrid, Clásicos Castalia 1985, 242–3).

11. *Chronica de las tres Ordenes y Cauallerias de Sanctiago, Calatraua y Alcantara*, Toledo, Juan de Ayala, 1572 (three Chronicles, separately foliated). A facsimile, with a study by Derek W. Lomax, was printed at Barcelona, El Albir, 1980.

12. See Moir, 538–9, and Victor Dixon, '*Beatus ... nemo: El villano en su rincón*, la "polianteas" y la literatura de emblemas', *Cuadernos de filología* 3, 1–2 (1981), 279–300; idem, 'Lope's *La villana de Getafe* and the Myth of Phaethon; or, the *coche* as Status-Symbol', in *What's Past is Prologue: A Collection of Essays in Honour of L.J. Woodward*, Edinburgh, Scottish Academic Press, 1984, 33–45 & 157–60.

13. *Crónica de Enrique IV*, translated by A. Paz y Melia, IV (Colección de Escritores Castellanos, 134), Madrid, 1908, 199–203.

14. *Historia General de España ...* Vol. II, Toledo, 1601, Book 24, Chapter 11, 572. This was a free translation of his own *Historiae de rebus Hispaniae libri XXV*, Toledo, 1592–5, in which however the story of Fuente Ovejuna had not appeared. See López Estrada, '*Fuente Ovejuna* en el teatro', 81–3.

15. Kirschner, 45–76, gives a good account of Lope's possible sources. She argues for a 'multiple origin', including oral tradition, and believes that he was acquainted with Palencia's chronicle, which he may have used in *El mejor mozo de España* (1610–1); but the points of similarity she notes between Palencia's account and our play, 71–2, are not convincing. See also Hall, *Fuente Ovejuna*, 11–19, and López Estrada, '*Fuente Ovejuna* en el teatro', who mentions, 80, a study by José Valverde Madrid, 'Fuentes que inspiraron el drama de Lope *Fuente Ovejuna*', *Fuente Obejuna*, No. 107, September 1954, suggesting that Lope may have known a manuscript *Casos notables de Córdoba*.

16. See especially Rafael Ramírez de Arellano, 'Rebelión de Fuente Obejuna contra el Comendador Mayor de Calatrava Fernán Gómez de Guzmán (1476)', *Boletín de la Real Academia de*

la Historia, 39 (1901), 446–512; Anibal; Manuel Cardenal Iracheta, 'Fuente Ovejuna', *Clavileño*, No.

11, September–October 1951, 20–26; Salomon; Raúl Garcia Aguilera & Mariano Hernández Ossorno, *Revuelta y litigios de los villanos de la encomienda de Fuente Obejuna (1476)*, Madrid, Editora Nacional, 1975; Rozas; Angus McKay & Geraldine McKendrick, 'The Crowd in Theater and the Crowd in History: *Fuenteovejuna*', *Renaissance Drama*, New Series 17 (1986), 125-47.

17.   A valuable account of the development of criticism this century, which I cannot trace here (though some of the most important studies are listed in my Bibliography) is contained in Kirschner, 28–41, and idem, 'Evolución de la crítica de *Fuente Ovejuna*, de Lope de Vega, en el siglo XX', *Cuadernos Hispanoamericanos*, Nos. 320–1 (1977), 450–65.

18.   Anibal, 691–2; cf. Hall, *Fuente Ovejuna*, 17–8, and *Chronica*, 80rb.

19.   See 1325-8, 1619-30, 1675-83, 1700-1, 1811-2, 1885-6, 1919, 2038-68, 2434-5.

20.   See 655, 1325, 1468, 1886, 1948, 2066.

21.   See 656–8, 1700, 1949–51, 2039–40, 2344–5, 2357, 2389.

22.   See 177, 236, 240–1, 436, 822, 1021, 1146–7, 1185, 1194, 1251–2, 1275–6, 1316, 1377, 1504, 1541–2, 1577, 1641, 1657, 1702, 1815, 2181–2, 2233, 2255, 2403.

23.   Moir, 542.

24.   In a manuscript *Historia de Córdoba*, quoted by López Estrada, '*Fuente Ovejuna* en el teatro', 79.

25.   Pring–Mill, 7.

26.   'Theories of Revenge in Elizabethan England', *Modern Philology*, 28 (1931), 281–96 (p. 293).

27.   *Marlowe's Tamburlaine*, Nashville, Vanderbilt University Press, 1941, 12. *The Theatre of God's Judgements* was indeed the title of a popular work by Thomas Beard, London, Adam Islip, 1631.

28.   Bruerton, 25–39.

29.   See *Peribáñez*, edited by J.M. Ruano & J.E. Varey, London, Tamesis, 1980, 15–6.

30.   Herrero, 178.

31.   Darst, 146.

32.   See especially the studies by Casalduero, Parker, Ribbans, Spitzer, Wardropper, McCrary and Pring-Mill.

33.   Northrop Frye, *Anatomy of Criticism: Four Essays*, Princeton University Press, 1973, 84.

34.   I cannot here hope to review the innumerable translations, adaptations and performances the play has seen; a good study is provided by Kirschner, 13–27; idem, 'Sobrevivencia de una comedia: historia de la difusión de *Fuente Ovejuna*', *Revista Canadiense de Estudios Hispánicos*, 1 (1976–77), 255–71. See also for instance Jack Weiner, 'Lope de Vega's *Fuente Ovejuna* under Tsars, Commissars, and the Second Spanish Republic (1931–1939), *Annali dell' Istituto Universitario Orientale (Sezione Romanza)*, 24 (1982), 167–223; H.W. Seliger, '*Fuente Ovejuna* en Alemania: de la traducción a la falsificación', *Revista Canadiense de Estudios Hispánicos*, 8 (1984), 381–403.

35.   Anibal,; S.G. Morley, '*Fuente Ovejuna* and its Theme-Parallels', *Hispanic Review*, 4 (1936), 303–11 (p. 310); Bruerton, 39; Albert E. Sloman, The Structure of Calderón's *La vida es sueño*', *Modern Language Review*, 48 (1953), 293–300 (p. 300).

36.   Hall, *Fuente Ovejuna*, 27; see idem, 'Theme and Structure'.

37.   Rozas, 192 (the translation is mine).

38.   'Be it noted that this entity / should have only a single action, observing that the play / should by no means be episodic, / I mean, inflated by other matters / which depart from the primary intention, / and that no component should be able to be removed / without the whole of the context being destroyed' (lines 181-7); Cf.Aristotle, *Poetics* 8: '... the component incidents must be so arranged that if one of them be transposed or removed, the unity of the whole is dislocated and destroyed'.

39.   *Devotions upon Emergent Occasions*, edited by John Sparrow, Cambridge University Press, 1923, 97.

40.   Cf. Everett W. Hesse, 'Los conceptos de amor en *Fuente Ovejuna*', *Revista de Archivos, Bibliotecas y Museos*, 75 (1969–72), 305–23, and Marc Vitse's comments on Dixon, 169.

41.   López Estrada, 'Los villanos', 8–9, has described the lesson in love which the play as a whole affords as 'proceeding, very much in the last instance, from Plato', and has tried to show that Lope was influenced here by the neo-Platonist León Hebreo (Judas Abarbanel). Perhaps he was (see note to 393–9); but as argued by Alan S. Trueblood, 'Plato's *Symposium* and Ficino's commentary in

Lope de Vega's *Dorotea*', *Modern Language Notes*, 73 (1958), 506–15 (p. 506), 'though Lope read him, he was no favorite: Lope apparently found him too abstruse'. In *Fuente Ovejuna*, as in the *Dorotea*, I think Lope went 'to the fountain head, the *Symposium* itself'. He read this in Marsilio Ficino's Latin version, and in conjunction with Ficino's long commentary, which indeed he usually preferred, but 'the two are not always distinct in Lope's mind' (see notes to 379–82, 385–8, 409–20, 421–6).

42.   Antonio Buero Vallejo, 'La tragedia', in *El teatro: Enciclopedia del arte escénico*, edited by G. Díaz-Plaja, Barcelona, Noguer, 1958, 63–87 (p. 84). The translation is mine.

43.   Lope's *New Art of Writing Plays* (1609) is our best guide to his spectators' tastes (and to his reactions); among a host of specific points, note his comments on the need to maintain their interest in the plot (234–9, 300–4), and especially: '... the choleric temper of a seated Spaniard is not assuaged if they do not show him, in the space of two hours, from Genesis to the Last Judgement' (205–8).

44.   Cf. especially A.A. Parker, 'The Spanish Drama of the Golden Age: A Method of Analysis and Interpretation', in *The Great Playwrights*, edited by Eric Bentley, New York, Doubleday, 1970, I, 679–707 (681–2): 'The generic characteristic of the Spanish drama is, of course, the fact that it is essentially a drama of action and not of characterization. It does not set out to portray rounded and complete characters ... We must ... accept the fact that the Spanish drama works on the assumption – which after all has the authority of Aristotle behind it – that the plot and not the characters is the primary thing ... Since the dramatists are out to present, with a strict limitation of time, an action that is full of incident, they generally have no time to elaborate their characters, and must confine their characterization to brief touches. They left it to the audience and the actors to fill in, from these hints and touches, the psychology of the characters'.

45.   Hall, *Fuente Ovejuna*, 40.

46.   Cf. Margit Frenk, 'El personaje singular: un aspecto del teatro del Siglo de Oro', *Nueva Revista de Filología Hispánica*, 26 (1977), 480; she discusses six plays, especially *El médico de su honra*.

47.   Needless to say, I disagree totally with David Castillejo, *Las cuatrocientas comedias de Lope* Madrid, Teatro Clásico Español, 1984, who says of *Fuente Ovejuna* (5–6): 'Its characters lack individual identity. They are only live puppets which perform a particular role: the rapist, the rape-victim, the rape-victim's father, etc. They lack that touch of spontaneity which gives a character life'.

48.   For a c9ounterblast to the notion, now prevalent in Spain, that this was a function imposed from above on the *comedia*, see Charlotte Stern, 'Lope de Vega, Propagandist?', *Bulletin of the Comediantes*, No. 34/1 (Summer 1982), 1–36.

49.   Cf. J.E. Varey, 'Kings and Judges: Lope de Vega's *El mejor alcalde el rey*', *Drama and Society* I (1979), 37–58 (p. 56): 'The play ... looks back to the past, to an idealised and simplified society, in which the King played a more direct role as God's vice-regent on earth. Lope ... saw his ideal society in the past, a golden past to which, if all played their proper part in society, and if God's commandments were truly respected, society might once again return'.

50.   Quoted by J.H. Elliott, 'Self-perception and Decline in Early Seventeenth-Century Spain', *Past and Present*, 74, (1977), 41–61 (p. 50).

51.   Diego Saavedra Fajardo, *Empresas políticas*, Munich 1640 (see especially Empresa 101); Baltasar Gracián, *El Político Don Fernando el Católico*, Zaragoza, 1640.

52.   See Joaquín de Entrambasaguas, 'Fernando "El Católico", personaje de Lope de Vega', *Revista de la Universidad de Buenos Aires*, IV época, 6 (1952), 215–57.

53.   Note that even the Commander's follower Cimbranos refers to Isabella as the Queen of Castile (line 1112).

54.   Elliott, 98, writes for instance that 'their interest in the impartial administration of justice made them set aside every Friday for public audiences in which they personally dispensed justice to all comers. They were the last rulers of Castile to act as personal judges in this way'.

55.   They did so in fact, as Lope must have known (e.g. from the *Chronica*), by ensuring that Ferdinand was given the administration of each Order when its Mastership fell vacant (Calatrava 1487, Alcantara 1494, Santiago 1499); a papal bull of 1523 definitively incorporated all three Orders into the Crown. See Elliott, 88–9.

56.   See Dixon, 164–6.

57.   Hall, *Fuente Ovejuna*, 48.

58. See lines 162–5, 830, 839–48, 987–99, 1217–8, 1241–3, 1254–5, 1615.
59. See lines 1223–50, 1269–74, 1487–96, 1593–1606, 1631–8, 1848–51.
60. See lines 1456, 1582-1602, 1617–8, 1784–7.
61. See the last epithet applied to him (2422), and Hall, *Fuente Ovejuna*, 44–6.
62. Moir, 542.
63. See lines 161, 447, 1148, 1176, 1181–4, 1561, 1568, 1742.
64. See lines 216, 557, 560, 563, 624–5, 768–70, 781–2, 810, 959, 1041–3, 1742, 1758, 1768, 1770.
65. Varey, *passim*; Hall, *Fuente Ovejuna*, 93.
66. See lines 1697, 1711, 1726, 1776, 1808, 1813, 1814, 1877, 1878, 1986, 2030, 2042, 2053, 2056, 2067, 2080, 2394. 'Lope gives Fernán Gómez the traditional characteristics of the tyrant as defined by Aquinas in his *De regimine principum*'; Hall, *Fuente Ovejuna*, 47.   See also idem, 'Theme and Structure', and the studies by Fiore, Carter, Gómez–Mariana and Serrano.
67. When 'quoted' from the *Chronica*, the word suggests the peasants' awareness of his treason (1813–4, 1866, 1883), but elsewhere perhaps their resentment of his creatures' dishonest treatment of them (1727, 1776, 1894, 1912, 1915); see Almasov, 753–4, and Hall, *Fuente Ovejuna*, 46–7, who recalls that according to Lope's *New Art*, lines 333–4, his audiences hated a *traidor* and even the actor who played one.
68. Hall, *Fuente Ovejuna*, 48.
69. See lines 1031–6, 1213, 1241, 1896–7, 1906–7.
70. Hall, *Fuente Ovejuna*, 50.
71. See lines 469, 515–71, 670, 1470–1, 2155–6, 2308–9.
72. Rodrigo Manrique was one of *two* Masters of Santiago, both loyal to Isabella, from the death in 1474 of Juan Pacheco (see lines 81–4) to his own in 1477 (which inspired his son Jorge's famous *Coplas*); he was not therefore living when the Master of Calatrava sought pardon. Lope may have read about him in the Santiago section of the *Chronica*, Chapter 48, fols. 66–8.
73. Exceptions are Laurencia (787), Frondoso (1037, 1863), Pascuala (1595).
74. An anonymous *labrador* speaks 935 and 937–8, and an unidentified *niño* 2214. Short slogans (1812, 1814, 1879–87, 1921) and a shout of *Sí* are attributed to *Todos* or *Todas*.
75. López Estrada, 'Los villanos', 2–16.
76. Cf. Ruano & Varey, Introduction to *Peribáñez*, 37–9.
77. See note to line 217.
78. Cf. *Peribáñez*, lines 730–53.
79. See lines 554–5, 562, 566–8, 570–4, 583–5.
80. On the conventional and fundamental (but transcendable) contrast between town and country, see Ribbans, and Hall, *Fuente Ovejuna*, 78–81.
81. See lines 1007–8, 1189–92, 1325–32, 1619–30.
82. Contrast the *Chronica*, 79va.
83. F. Ruiz Ramón, *Historia del teatro español (desde sus orígenes hasta 1900)*, 3rd edition, Madrid, Cátedra, 1979, 159.
84. The most cogently argued statement of this common view is Kirschner, *passim*. Of course one cannot imagine such sympathy as Lope shows for a popular uprising in any other national theatre of the period.
85. Hall, *Fuente Ovejuna*, 65.
86. See lines 871, 1007, 1377, 1541–2, 1641, 1657, 1700-2.
87. Pring-Mill, 24, finding in the play 63 sententious statements, 42 voiced by the peasants and 12 of these by Esteban, quoted Lope's *New Art* (lines 270–1): 'When the old man speaks, let him make use of a sententious modesty'.
88. Salomon, 803–4; Kirschner, 108–9.
89. Ribbans, 155; Hall, *Fuente Ovejuna*, 58; Profeti's edition, XXXIII.
90. Casalduero, 39; Ribbans, 15⁵ & note.
91. See the end-note to this line.
92. Spitzer, 276.
93. See the footnote to 1503–11.
94. See John Brotherton, *The 'Pastor-Bobo' in the Spanish Theatre before the Time of Lope de Vega*, London, Tamesis, 1975.
95. E.g. *dimuño*, 349 (though *demonio*, 1143); *voto al sol* (1169, 1214); *me emberrincho*

(1214), *soceso*, 1224.

96. See lines 1335–7, 1479–90, 1644–51, 1896–7, 1906–11, 2059–65, 2422–33.

97. Guy Mercadier, '*Fuente Ovejuna*, un mauvais drame?', *Les Langues Neo–Latines*, 58 (1984), 9–30 (p. 22).

98. See lines 193–5, 799–804, 967–70, 1059–1102; but note the possible implications of 1345–50 for the interpretation of 799–801.

99. See lines 936, 961–7, 1031–2, 1656, 1691–2.

100. See for instance the editions of Marín, 135, and Cañas Murillo, 165.

101. McKendrick, 142–73, 281–8.

102. McKendrick, 143.

103. McKendrick, 174–217, 288–98.

104. See Antonio Buero Vallejo, 'Muñiz', in Carlos Muñiz, *El tintero; Un solo de saxofón; Las viejas difíciles*, Madrid, Taurus, 1963, 53–70 (pp. 544–5); Antonio Gala, *Teatro español actual*, Madrid, Cátedra, 1977, 121–2.

105. Dixon, 160–3.

106. Hall, *Fuente Ovejuna*, 55.

107. See lines 189–92, 735–42, 755–7, 767–71, 1297–1300.

108. See lines 825–9, 837–42, 851–42, 1050–1, 1278–84.

109. Salomon, 862, note 37. Monroy's play was edited together with Lope's by López Estrada, who discussed it also in his '*Fuente Ovejuna* en el teatro'.

110. A French translation by J.B. d'Esmenard, with an introduction and notes by A. La Beaumelle, appeared, however, in *Chefs d'oeuvre des théâtres étrangers VIII: Drames de Lope de Vega*, Paris, Ladvocat, 1822; Kirschner, 16 and 153. According to Almasov, 749 (though he gave no reference), *Fuente Ovejuna* was included in a list of 'amoral' plays prohibited in 1644 by a decision of the Council of the Realm.

111. The standard authority is still N.D. Shergold, *A History of the Spanish Stage from Medieval Times until the end of the Seventeenth Century*, Oxford University Press, 1967 (especially Chapters 7 & 8); but see also especially J.J. Allen, *The Reconstruction of a Spanish Golden Age Playhouse: El Corral del Príncipe, 1583–1744*, Gainesville, University Presses of Florida, 1983.

112. Victor Dixon, 'La comedia de corral de Lope como género visual', *Edad de Oro*, 5 (1986), 35–58; I attacked in particular a suggestion that 'the understanding of a work like *Fuente Ovejuna* ... loses nothing if it is listened to with one's eyes shut'.

113. *El perro del hortelano*, 59.

114. This too might of course be 'verbal décor'; cf. Alan C. Dessen, *Elizabethan Stage Conventions and Modern Interpreters*, Cambridge University Press, 1984, Ch. 3 (The logic of 'this' on the open stage).

115. Note that the *Chronica* stated that the women of the town 'had made a banner, and appointed a captain and ensign' (fol. 79vb).

116. 'Scene' is the word I have used throughout this book for the units of action so defined: The obscuring of the dramatic structure caused by old-fashioned editors of *comedias*, who (whereas their seventeenth-century predecessors divided them only into acts) indicated a new *escena* whenever an important character entered or left the stage, has induced myself and other critics to label them *cuadros*; but the contemporary word was *(s)cena* or *salida*. Thus José Pellicer, 'Idea de la comedia en Castilla ...', in *Lágrimas panegíricas a la temprana muerte del Doctor Juan Pérez de Montalbán. Recogidas por Pedro Grande de Tena*, Madrid, 1639, fol. 151r: 'Each act should consist of three *scenas*, which are commonly called *salidas*'.

117. Thus some of Lope's early plays have many scenes; those of Calderón, comparatively few. Yet even Lope in his *New Art* advised that the stage should rarely be emptied, and that necessary leaps of time and place, e.g. in historical plays, should be placed at the act-intervals (194–8, 240–5); and his *El perro del hortelano*, contemporaneous with our play, has only six scenes in its three acts.

118. See lines 117–20, 129–37, 153–6, 465–8, 517–20, 811–2, 825–9, 833–4, 987–94, 1044–5, 1548–9, 1623–30, 1977–9, 2326–33.

119. The hero of *Peribáñez*, as the captain of a company of peasants, orders them to await the departure of a company of *hidalgos*: 'Let lance follow crossbow' (2465).

120. See Duncan Moir, 'The Classical Tradition in Spanish Dramatic Theory and Practice in the Seventeenth Century', in *Classical Drama and its Influence: Essays presented to H.D.F. Kitto*, edited by M.J. Anderson, London, Methuen, 1965, 191–228 (p. 212).

121. Horace, *Ars poetica*, lines 179–88.

122. See Dixon, passim.

123. Salomon, 860–1, refers to the case of the fiefdom of Ariza in Aragon; during the reign of Charles V its vassals, claiming direct dependence on the Crown, rebelled against and killed their overlord don Juan de Palafox. The royal response in this instance was to send an armed force which set fire to and almost destroyed the village of Monreal and punished some of its inhabitants by way of an example.

124. See Gustavo Umpierre, *Songs in the Plays of Lope de Vega: A Study of their Dramatic Function*, London, Tamesis, 1975, 2.

125. Spitzer, 278.

126. See Salomon, 723–38; he refers to this song of welcome, and gives examples from numerous other plays.

127. See Salomon, 699–722.

128. See Salomon, 702–3, and especially López Estrada, 'La canción'.

129. Spitzer, with reference to Fernán Gómez, quotes appositely, 291, *The Merchant of Venice*, Act V, 83–5: 'The man that hath no music in himself,/ Nor is not mov'd with concord of sweet sounds,/ Is fit for treasons, strategems and spoils'. An analogous character is the villain of Buero Vallejo's *El concierto de San Ovidio* (1962), at his most characteristic when he mocks the aspirations of his orchestra of blind men: ('And forget your ... music').

130. S.G. Morley, 'Objective Criteria for Judging Authorship and Chronology in the Comedia', *Hispanic Review*, 5 (1937), 280–5 (p. 283).

131. *El perro del hortelano*, 53.

132. Casalduero, 54; Spitzer, 292; J. Fernández Montesinos, 'La paradoja del *Arte Nuevo*', in *Estudios sobre Lope de Vega*, Salamanca, Anaya, 1969, 1–20 (p.15).

133. Victor Dixon, 'The Uses of Polymetry: An Approach to editing the *comedia* as Verse Drama', in *Editing the Comedia*, edited by Frank P. Casa and Michael D. McGaha (Michigan Romance Studies, Vol. 5), Ann Arbor, 1985, 104–25 (p. 101).

134. Some members at least of that audience, it can be shown, were well aware of metrical changes; ibid., 113–5.

135. 'Suit your lines prudently / to the matters with which you are dealing: / *décimas* are good for complaints; / the sonnet is suitable for those who are left waiting; / narrations demand *romances*, / though they are extremmly elegant in *octavas*; / *tercetos* are for solemn matters, / and *redondillas* for those of love'; lines 305–12.

136. *El perro del hortelano*, 53.

137. Diego Marín, 105 (the translation is mine).

138. E.g. Hall, 75–7; J.W. Sage, *Lope de Vega, 'El caballero de Olmedo'*, Critical Guides to Spanish Texts 6, London, Grant and Cutler, 1974, 76–80.

139. Morley and Bruerton, *Cronología*, 102–7, 201–6. Some contemporaries, like Carlos Boyl (1616) and Cristóbal Suárez de Figueroa (1617), urged that plays should be written entirely in *redondillas*, and some were, e.g. Guillén de Castro's *Los mal casados de Valencia*.

140. Diego Marín, 102.

141. Morley and Bruerton, *Cronología*, 117–25, 201–6.

142. It became such an invariable rule that a play would end in *romances* that dramatists, it has been suggested, could beguile their audience's expectations by using *romances*, as a 'false cadence', earlier in the final act; see Vern G. Villiamsen, 'A Commentary on "The Uses of Polymetry" and the Editing of the Multi-strophic Texts of the Spanish *Comedia*', in *Editing the Comedia*, 126–45 (pp. 136–8).

143. Morley and Bruerton, *Cronología*, 206.

144. Morley and Bruerton, *Cronología*, 184.

145. Diego Marín, 103.

146. The metrical structure thus appears to reinforce the contrast between the world of the peasant and that of the nobleman which is fundamental to the play.

147. One scene is discursive, the other intensely active; neither contains the kind of elegant narration for which Lope suggested in the *New Art* that *octavas* were suitable. It may be more significant that they were the favourite vehicle of the cultivated epic.

148. As pointed out by Diego Marín, 50, 'the combination of general thoughts and personal feeling on the part of a character in a situation of expectancy is the typical form of Lope's

sonnet-soliloquies' (the translation is mine).

149. Wardropper, 163.

150. Morley and Bruerton, *Cronología*, give definitions of the metrical forms used by Lope (38–41), and different metrical data on *Fuente Ovejuna* (330). In *El perro del hortelano*, 54–6, I tried briefly to show how line-lengths may be calculated and metrical forms identified.

151. All the title-pages I have seen bear this date, but the *tassa* on the following leaf, dated 22 December 1618, suggests that it appeared at the end of the previous year. The *aprobación* is dated 15 August 1618.

152. C.E. Aníbal, 'Lope de Vega's *Dozena Parte*', *Modern Language Notes* 47 (1932), 1–7. In both editions, *Fuente Ovejuna* occupies fols. 262v–280v.

153. Jaime Moll, 'Correcciones en prensa y crítica textual: a propósito de *Fuente Ovejuna*', *Boletín de la Real Academia Española* 57 (1982), 159–71.

154. They are the inner and outer formes of the inner sheet of Kk, and the inner and outer formes of the outer sheet of Ll. The pages of *Fuente Ovejuna* affected are fols. 262v, 266r, 266v and 271r.

155. Fols. 273v and 279v. For instance, a copy at the Bibliothèque Nationale, Yg. 282, has the uncorrected forme; the corrected forme is found in two other copies there, 16° Yg. 272 and 8° Yg. 1308, in the British Library's 1072. i. 12, and (according to information kindly supplied by Jaime Moll) in five copies at the Biblioteca Nacional, R. 14105, R. 25183, R. 24983, R. 25182 and R. 25127 (though the last lacks fol. 279). See notes to lines 1517, 2286 and 2296.

156. See notes to lines 491, 638, 650, 860, 981, 1503, 2279.

157. I am extremely grateful to Teresa Krischner for supplying me with a photocopy. For further details, see Profeti's edition, xlv–xlvi.

158. See, for instance, lines 612, 815, 1013, 1631–6, 2338.

159. Cf. Casalduero, 51–4. The author of one of the most perceptive studies of the play states, surprisingly, that Ferdinand and Isabella (the location of whose three scenes is never made clear) 'spend the play moving from Medina del Campo to Toro to Tordesillas'; Carter, 325.

160. e.g. sucesso 647, 722, 1316, socesso 1224; Dexadlo 930, Dexaldos 2254; Lleualde 1245, Lleuadla 1639; accidente 1096, contradicion 1923.

161. i.e. dello, deste, des(s)e, es(s)otro, etc.

162. e.g. ansí, apries(s)a, recebir, destribuye, interrompe, etc.

163. See lines 815–6, 928–9, 2209–10, 2263.

164. Gwynne Edwards, edition and translation of Tirso de Molina, *The Trickster of Sevilla and the Stone Guest*, Warminster, Aris and Phillips, 1986, xxxiv.

165. Nicholas Round, edition and translation of Tirso de Molina, *Damned for Despair*, Warminster, Aris and Phillips, 1986, lxxiv.

166. D.F. McCarthy, *Calderon's Dramas*, London, Henry S. King & Co., 1873. See also R.C. Trench, *An Essay on the Life and Genius of Calderon* (second edition), London, Macmillan and Co., 1880; and Calderón, *La gran comedia, Guárdate de la agua mansa*, edited and translated by David M. Gitlitz, San Antonio (Texas), Trinity University Press, 1984.

167. George W. Brandt, translation of Pedro Calderón, *The Great Stage of World*, Manchester University Press, 1976; Adrian Mitchell, translation of Pedro Calderón, *The Mayor of Zalamea*, Edinburgh, Salamander Press, 1981.

168. See his versions of *Fuente Ovejuna, The Trickster of Seville, Love after Death* and *Life is a Dream*, in *The Classic Theatre*, edited by Eric Bentley, Vol. III, Garden City, N.Y., Doubleday, 1959; and of *The Surgeon of his Honour*, Madison, University of Wisconsin Press, 1960.

169. See for instance his translation of *Tartuffe*, London, Faber 1984.

170. Round, *Damned for Despair*, lxxv.

171. At the end of the monologue, Lope sometimes changes to another metre (e.g. at 141 and 699); but he frequently continues in *romance* to the end of the scene (see 1125–36; 1794–1846; 2008–27). I have imitated him in this, and have similarly extended my use of the corresponding metre to after one narrative (699–712) and before another (1920–47).

172. Gwynne Edwards, for instance, was wrong in my view when in using blank verse for his *The Trickster of Seville* he felt 'a need to lengthen the original line and thus introduce more words', but right to say that 'the result is not a translation but a free adaptation' (xl).

BIBLIOGRAPHY

FUENTE OVEJUNA: PRINCIPAL EDITIONS

A = DOZENA / PARTE DE / LAS COMEDIAS DE / LOPE DE VEGA CARPIO. / *A DON LORENZO DE CARDENAS* / *Conde de la Puebla, quarto nieto de don Alonso de* / *Cardenas, Gran Maestre de Santiago.* / Año [shield with the Cárdenas coat-of-arms] 1619. / CON PRIVILEGIO. / *EN MADRID,* Por la viuda de Alonso Martin. / — / *A costa de Alonso Perez mercader de libros.* Locations of known copies: Biblioteca Nacional R. 14105, R. 25183, R. 25127, R. 24983, R. 25182 (a composite copy; partly B); British Library 1072. 1. 9, 1072. i. 12 (false title-page); Bibliothèque Nationale Yg. 282, 16˚ Yg. 767, 8˚ Yg. 1308; Österreichische National-bibliothek (Vienna) + 38. H. 2. (12); Ambrosiana (Milan) S.N.V.V. 25; Vaticana (Rome) Barberini K. K. K. 19.

B = DOZENA / PARTE... [an identical title-page; but the coat-of-arms is replaced by a block which shows a prancing centaur with drawn bow, encircled by the legend: SALVBRIS SAGITTA A DEO MISSA]. Locations of known copies: Biblioteca Nacional R. 13863, R. 25200; British Library 11726.k. 18; University of Pennsylvania. Copies of the *Dozena parte* at the Estense (Modena) and Casanatense (Roma), T – I – 12, may be either A or B.

H = *Comedias escogidas de Frey Lope Félix de Vega Carpio,* edited by Juan Eugenio Hartzenbusch, Madrid, Biblioteca de Autores Españoles, Vol. XLI, 1857, pp. 633–50.

Obras de Lope de Vega, with prefaces by M. Menéndez Pelayo, Vol. X, Madrid, Real Academia Espanola, 1899, pp. 531–61.

C = Lope de Vega, *Fuente Ovejuna,* edited by Américo Castro, Madrid, Espasa-Calpe (Colección Universal), 1919.

LE1 = Lope de Vega & Cristóbal de Monroy, *Fuente Ovejuna (dos comedias),* edited by Francisco López Estrada, Madrid, Clásicos Castalia, 1969. Revised editions appeared in 1973 (LE 2) and 1979 (LE 3), and the text in Lope de Vega, *Fuente Ovejuna,* edited by María-Teresa López García Berdoy, Madrid, Castalia Didáctica, 1985, is effectively a fourth edition, with minor changes I use 'LE' to indicate readings of all these editions, and 'LE &c.' to indicate readings adopted also by later editors.

P = Lope de Vega, *Fuente Ovejuna,* edited by M.G. Profeti, Madrid, Cupsa, 1978.

M = Lope de Vega, *Fuente Ovejuna,* edited by J.M. Marín, Madrid, Cátedra, 1981.

B1 = Lope de Vega, *Peribáñez & Fuente Ovejuna,* edited by Alberto Blecua, Madrid, Alianza, 1981.

CM = Lope de Vega, *Fuente Ovejuna,* edited by Jesús Cañas Murillo, Barcelona, Plaza y Janés, 1984.

FUENTE OVEJUNA: SOME OTHER TRANSLATIONS

John Garrett Underhill, *Four Plays by Lope de Vega (The Sheep Well),* London, Charles Scribner's Sons, 1936; a mixture of prose and verse.
Roy Campbell, in *The Classic Theatre,* edited by Eric Bentley, Vol. III, Garden City, N.Y., Doubleday, 1959; verse.
Jill Booty, *Lope de Vega: Five Plays* (with a valuable introduction by Robert Pring-Mill), New York, Hill and Wang, 1961; an 'acting version' in prose.
Angel Flores and Muriel Kittel, in *Spanish Drama,* edited and with an introduction by Angel Flores, New York, Bantam Books, 1962; mostly prose.

50] BIBLIOGRAPHY

Lope de Vega, *Fuente Ovejuna*, a bilingual text, with translation and introduction by William E. Colford, Woodbury, N.Y., Barron's, 1969; verse.

Lope de Vega, *Fuente Ovejuna*, texte établi, présenté et traduit par Louis Combet, Paris, Aubier-Flammarion, 1972; prose.

EDITIONS OF OTHER WORKS BY LOPE DE VEGA MENTIONED

Ac = *Obras de Lope de Vega Carpio*, 15 vols., Madrid, Real Academia Española, 1890–1913.

AcN = *Obras de Lope de Vega Carpio* (nueva edición), 13 vols., Madrid, Real Academia Española, 1916–30.

BAE = Biblioteca de Autores Españoles.

Arte nuevo de hacer comedias en este tiempo, in Juan Manuel Rozas, *Significado y doctrina del Arte Nuevo de Lope de Vega*, Madrid, Sociedad General Española de Librería, 1976.

Carlos V en Francia, edited by A.G. Reichenberger, Philadelphia, University of Pennsylvania, 1962.

La desdichada Estefanía, edited by Hugh W. Kennedy, University (Mississippi), Romance Monographs Inc., 1975.

La Dorotea, edited by E.S. Morby, Valencia, Castalia, 1958.

El Duque de Viseo, edited by F. Ruiz Ramón, Madrid, Alianza Editorial, 1966.

La francesilla, edited by Donald McGrady, Charlottesville (Virginia), Biblioteca Siglo de Oro, 1981.

El galán de la Membrilla, edited by Diego Marín & Evelyn Rugg, Madrid, Boletín de la Real Academia Española, 1962.

El mejor alcalde, el rey, edited by J.M. Díez Borque, Madrid, Istmo, 1974.

Peribáñez y el Comendador de Ocaña, edited by J.M. Ruano & J.E. Varey, London, Tamesis,1980.

El perro del hortelano, edited by Victor Dixon, London, Tamesis, 1981.

El primero Benavides, edited by A.G. Reichenberger & A. Espantoso Foley, Philadelphia, University of Pennsylvania Press, 1973.

La prueba de los amigos, edited by L.B. Simpson, Berkeley, University of California, 1934.

El sembrar en buena tierra, edited by W.L. Fichter, New York, Modern Language Association of America, 1944.

Servir a señor discreto, edited by F. Weber de Kurlat, Madrid, Castalia, 1975.

El sufrimiento premiado... atribuida... a Lope de Vega Carpio, con introducción y notas de Victor Dixon, London, Tamesis, 1967.

STUDIES REFERRED TO IN AN ABBREVIATED FORM

Almasov, A., '*Fuente Ovejuna* y el honor villanesco en el teatro de Lope de Vega', *Cuadernos Hispanoamericanos*, 161–2 (1963), 701–55.

Anibal, C.E., 'The Historical Elements of Lope de Vega's *Fuente Ovejuna*', *Publications of the Modern Language Association of America*, 49 (1934), 657–718.

Bruerton, Courtney, '*La quinta de Florencia*, fuente de *Peribáñez*', *Nueva Revista de Filología Hispánica*, 4 (1950), 25–39.

Carter, Robin, '*Fuente Ovejuna* and Tyranny: Some Problems of Linking Drama with Political Theory', *Forum for Modern Language Studies*, 13 (1977), 313–35.

Casalduero, Joaquín, '*Fuente Ovejuna*', in *Estudios sobre el teatro español* (Cuarta edición), Madrid, Gredos, 1981, 24–55.

Darst, David H., 'The Awareness of Higher Authority in *Fuente Ovejuna*', *Oelschläger Festschrift* (Estudios de Hispanófila, 36), Chapel Hill, North Carolina, 1976, 143–9.

Dixon, Victor, '*Su Majestad habla, en fin, como quien tanto ha acertado*: La conclusión ejemplar de *Fuente Ovejuna*', *Criticón*, 42 (1988), 155–68.

Dunn, Peter N., '*Materia la mujer, el hombre forma*: Notes on the Development of a Lopean *topos*', *Homenaje a William L. Fichter*, editado por A. David Kossoff & José Amor y Vázquez, Madrid, Castalia, 1971, 189–99.

Elliott, J.H., *Imperial Spain, 1469-1716*, Harmondsworth, Penguin, 1985.

Fiore, Robert L., *Drama and Ethos: Natural-Law Ethics in Spanish Golden Age Theater* (Studies in Romance Languages, 14), Lexington, University Press of Kentucky, 1975.

Gerli, E. Michael, 'The Hunt of Love: the Literalization of a Metaphor in *Fuente Ovejuna*', *Neophilologus*, 63 (1979), 54-8.

Gómez-Mariana, A., *Derecho de resistencia y tiranicidio: estudio de una temática en las comedias de Lope de Vega* (Biblioteca Hispánica de Filosofía del Derecho, 1), Santiago de Compostela, Porto, 1968.

Hall, J.B., *Lope de Vega: Fuente Ovejuna* (Critical Guides to Spanish Texts, 42), London, Grant & Cutler, 1985.

Hall, J.B., 'Theme and Structure in Lope's *Fuente Ovejuna*', *Forum for Modern Language Studies*, 10 (1974), 57-66.

Herrero, Javier, 'The New Monarchy: a Structural Reinterpretation of *Fuente Ovejuna*', *Revista Hispánica Moderna*, 36 (1970-1), 173-85.

Kirschner, Teresa J., *El protagonista colectivo en 'Fuente Ovejuna'* (Studia Philologica Salmanticensia, Anejos: Estudios, 1), Salamanca, Universidad de Salamanca, 1979.

Larson, Donald R., *The Honor Plays of Lope de Vega*, Cambridge (Mass.), Harvard University Press, 1977.

López-Estrada, Francisco, 'La canción "Al val de Fuente Ovejuna" de la comedia *Fuente Ovejuna* de Lope', in *Homenaje a William L. Fichter*, editado por A. David Kossoff & José Amor y Vázquez, Madrid, Castalia, 1971, 453-68.

López-Estrada, Francisco, '*Fuente Ovejuna* en el teatro de Lope y de Monroy (Consideración crítica de ambas obras)', *Anales de la Universidad Hispalense*, 26 (1965), 1-91.

López-Estrada, Francisco, 'Los villanos filosóficos y políticos (La configuración de *Fuente Ovejuna* a través de los nombres y "apellidos")', *Cuadernos Hispanoamericanos*, 238-40 (1969), 518-42.

Marín, Diego, *Uso y función de la versificación dramática en Lope de Vega* (Estudios de Hispanófila, 2), Valencia, Castalia, 1962.

McCrary, William C., '*Fuente Ovejuna*: its Platonic Vision and Execution', *Studies in Philology*, 58 (1961), 179-92.

McGrady, Donald, 'Lope de Vega's *El mejor alcalde el Rey*, its Italian *novella* Sources and its Influence upon Manzoni's *I promessi sposi*', *Modern Language Review*, 80 (1985), 604-18.

McKendrick, Melveena, *Woman and Society in the Spanish Drama of the Golden Age: A Study of the 'mujer varonil'*, Cambridge University Press, 1974.

Moir, Duncan W., 'Lope de Vega's *Fuente Ovejuna* and the *Emblemas morales* of Sebastián de Covarrubias Horozco (with a few remarks on *El villano en su rincón*)', in *Homenaje a William L. Fichter*, editado por A. David Kossoff & José Amor y Vázquez, Madrid, Castalia, 1971, 537-46.

Moll, Jaime, 'Correcciones en prensa y crítica teatral: a propósito de *Fuente Ovejuna*', *Boletín de la Real Academia Española*, 57 (1982), 159-71.

Morales Blouin, Egla, *El ciervo y la fuente: mito y folklore del agua en la lírica tradicional*, Madrid, J. Porrúa Turanzas, 1981.

Morley, Sylvanus Griswold, and Courtney Bruerton, *Cronología de las comedias de Lope de Vega*, Madrid, Gredos, 1968.

Parker, A.A., 'Reflections on a New Definition of "Baroque" Drama', *Bulletin of Hispanic Studies*, 30 (1953), 142-51.

Pring-Mill, R.D.F., 'Sententiousness in *Fuente Ovejuna*', *Tulane Drama Review*, 7 (1962), 5-37.

Ribbans, G.W., 'The Meaning and Structure of Lope's *Fuente Ovejuna*', *Bulletin of Hispanic Studies*, 30 (1953), 150-70.

Rosaldo, Renato I., Jr., 'Lope as a Poet of History: History and Ritual in *El testimonio vengado*', in *Perspectivas de la comedia*, edited by Alva V. Ebersole (Estudios de Hispanófila: Coleccion Siglo de Oro, 6), University of North Carolina, 1978, 9-32.

Rozas, Juan Manuel, '*Fuente Ovejuna* desde la segunda acción', in *Actas del I Simposio de Literatura Española* (1979), edición dirigida por Alberto Navarro González, Universidad de Salamanca, 1981, 173-92.

Salomon, Noël, *Recherches sur le thème paysan dans la 'comedia' au temps de Lope de Vega* (Bibliothèque des Hautes Études Hispaniques, 31), Bordeaux, Féret et Fils, 1965.

Serrano, Carlos, 'Métaphore et idéologie: sur le tyran de *Fuente Ovejuna* de Lope de Vega', *Les Langues Neo-Latines*, 4 (1971), 31-53.

Spitzer, Leo, 'A Central Theme and its Structural Equivalent in Lope's *Fuente Ovejuna*', *Hispanic Review*, 23 (1955), 274–92.

Varey, J.E., *La inversión de valores en 'Fuente Ovejuna'* (Lectiones, 5), Santander, Universidad Internacional Menéndez Pelayo, 1976.

Wardropper, Bruce W., '*Fuente Ovejuna: el gusto* and *lo justo*', *Studies in Philology*, 53 (1956), 159–71.

Weber de Kurlat, Frida, 'La expresión de la erótica en el teatro de Lope de Vega: el caso de *Fuente Ovejuna*', in *Homenaje a José Manuel Blecua*, Madrid, Gredos, 1983, 673–87.

DICTIONARIES, ETC. REFERRED TO

Autoridades: Diccionario de la lengua castellana... compuesto por la Real Academia Española, 6 vols., Madrid, 1726–39.

Corominas: Juan Corominas, *Diccionario crítico etimológico de la lengua castellana*, 4 vols, Berne, Francke, 1954.

Covarrubias: Sebastián de Covarrubias Orozco, *Tesoro de la lengua castellana o española...* añadido por el Padre B.R. Noydens, Madrid, 1674.

Keniston: Hayward Keniston, *The Syntax of Castilian Prose: The Sixteenth Century*, Chicago University Press, 1937.

Hill: J.M. Hill, *Voces germanescas* (Indiana University Publications, Humanities Series No. 21), Bloomington, Indiana University Press, 1949.

Poesse: Walter Poesse, *The Internal Line-Structure of Thirty Autograph Plays of Lope de Vega* (Indiana University Publications, Humanities Series No. 18), Bloomington, Indiana University Press, 1949.

Propalladia: Bartolomé de Torres Naharro, *Propalladia and Other Works*, edited by J.E. Gillet, 4 vols., Bryn-Mawr – Philadelphia, University of Pennsylvania, 1943-61.

FUENTE OVEJUNA

COMEDIA FAMOSA DE FUENTE OVEJUNA

Hablan en ella las personas siguientes

FERNÁN GÓMEZ
ORTUÑO
FLORES
EL MAESTRE DE CALATRAVA
PASCUALA
LAURENCIA
MENGO
BARRILDO
FRONDOSO
JUAN ROJO
ESTEBAN,
ALONSO   *alcaldes*

REY DON FERNANDO
REINA DOÑA ISABEL
DON MANRIQUE
UN REGIDOR
CIMBRANOS, *soldado*
JACINTA, *labradora*
UN MUCHACHO
ALGUNOS LABRADORES
UN JUEZ
LA MÚSICA

THE FAMOUS PLAY OF FUENTE OVEJUNA

Characters

FERNÁN GOMEZ, the Grand Commander of Calatrava
ORTUÑO,
FLORES, his servants
THE MASTER OF CALATRAVA, Rodrigo Téllez Girón
PASCUALA,
LAURENCIA, peasant-women
MENGO,
BARRILDO,
FRONDOSO, peasants
JUAN ROJO, Laurencia's uncle, alderman
ESTEBAN, Laurencia's father, magistrate
ALONSO, magistrate

KING FERDINAND of Aragon
QUEEN ISABELLA of Castile
MANRIQUE, Master of Santiago
AN ALDERMAN
CIMBRANOS, a soldier
JACINTA, a peasant-woman
BOY
PEASANTS
A JUDGE
MUSICIANS

The list of speakers was compiled without care, and makes no specific mention of
LEONELO (892–929), a PEASANT (935–8) or a SOLDIER (2129–44).
AN ALDERMAN may refer to the one from Ciudad Real who speaks 655–86 and
688–94; there is a second (696–8). The two aldermen of Fuente Ovejuna are not
mentioned; Juan Rojo may be identified as one (see 772, 1313, 1317D). The
other's name is Cuadrado (2113–4).
FERNÁN is the abbreviated form of Fernando (see 52, 190, 450, 2318);
elsewhere (655, 948 &c.), *Fernando* refers to King Ferdinand.

ACTO PRIMERO

Salen el Comendador, Flores y Ortuño, criados.

COMENDADOR.	Sabe el Maestre que estoy en la villa?	[*redondillas*]
FLORES.	Ya lo sabe.	
ORTUÑO.	Está, con la edad, más grave.	
COMENDADOR.	¿Y sabe también que soy Fernán Gómez de Guzmán?	5
FLORES.	Es muchacho, no te asombre.	
COMENDADOR.	Cuando no sepa mi nombre, ¿no le sobra el que me dan de Comendador mayor?	
ORTUÑO.	No falta quien le aconseja que de ser cortés se aleje.	10
COMENDADOR.	Conquistará poco amor. Es llave la cortesía para abrir la voluntad, y para la enemistad la necia descortesía.	15
ORTUÑO.	Si supiese un descortés cómo lo aborrecen todos, y querrían de mil modos poner la boca a sus pies, antes que serlo ninguno se dejaría morir.	20
FLORES.	¡Qué cansado es de sufrir! ¡Qué áspero y qué importuno!	

1–2. Since H, most editors, perhaps influenced by 104–6 & 1123–4, indicate that the *villa* is Almagro, where the Master of the Order resided, whereas Casalduero, 51, proposes Calatrava, quoting 1465; in fact the setting is indeterminate and immaterial.

3. *Gravedad*, in the sense of haughty incivility, is a vice of powerful men often criticised in plays by Lope; see *El ejemplo de casadas*, BAE 249, 48; *El mejor mozo de España*, BAE 41, 618–9; *El Duque de Viseo*, 35–9. The term is also used of course in a positive sense (seriousness); cf. 309, 329, 916.

9. The Grand Commander of the Order was next in rank to the Master, and his chief adviser, esp. in military organization.

ACT ONE

The Commander enters, with Flores and Ortuño, his servants.

COMMANDER.	The master knows I'm in the town?
FLORES.	He knows.
ORTUÑO.	Full of himself, no doubt, now that he's older. 3
COMMANDER.	And knows I'm Fernán Gómez de Guzmán?
FLORES.	He's very young, you needn't be surprised.
COMMANDER.	Even suppose he didn't know my name,
	shouldn't my rank suffice, as Grand Commander? 9
ORTUÑO.	He won't be short of people who'll advise him
	he needn't show respect.
COMMANDER.	He'll not be loved, then.
	Respect's the key that opens all men's hearts; 13
	but foolish disrespect wins only hatred.
ORTUÑO.	Yes, if the man who's no respect for others 17
	could only know how everyone detests him,
	how glad they'd be, in any way they could,
	to make him lick their boots, he'd rather die
	than be so stupid.
FLORES.	Such a man's so tedious,
	so unpleasant, so insufferably odious!

12–4. Cf. 'Dichoso aquel que con prudencia sabe / vencer su condición y ser bienquisto, / que es de la voluntad la mejor llave'; *El Duque de Viseo*, 44. *Voluntad* = goodwill, affection: cf. 527, 554, 577, 1423.

13–36. The exposition is masterly. The Commander, in his misplaced anger, not only identifies himself and reveals his awareness that rank (displayed by the sword he wears and the red cross of Calatrava on his habit) confers rights and (on others!) obligations, but expatiates on the central theme of the play, regard for others, the quality he himself, ironically, will die for lack of.

17–24. The irony is compounded; as the Commander's toadies must know (and maybe intend) they might be talking about him.

25

                    Llaman la descortesía
                    necedad en los iguales,
                    porque es entre desiguales
                    linaje de tiranía.
                    Aquí no te toca nada;
                    que un muchacho aún no ha llegado
                    a saber qué es ser amado.
COMENDADOR.   La obligación de la espada
                    que le ciñó el mismo día
                    que la Cruz de Calatrava
                    le cubrió el pecho, bastaba   35
                    para aprender cortesía.
FLORES.   Si te han puesto mal con él,
                    presto le conocerás.
ORTUÑO.   Vuélvete, si en duda estás.
COMENDADOR.   Quiero ver lo que hay en él.   40

Sale el Maestre de Calatrava, y acompañamiento.

MAESTRE.   Perdonad, por vida mía,
                    Fernán Gómez de Guzmán,
                    que agora nueva me dan
                    que en la villa estáis.
COMENDADOR.   Tenía
                    muy justa queja de vos;   45
                    que el amor y la crianza
                    me daban más confianza,
                    por ser, cual somos los dos,
                    vos, Maestre en Calatrava,
                    yo, vuestro Comendador   50
                    y muy vuestro servidor.
MAESTRE.   Seguro, Fernando, estaba
                    de vuestra buena venida.
                    Quiero volveros a dar
                    los brazos.
COMENDADOR.   Debéisme honrar,   55
                    que he puesto por vos la vida
                    entre diferencias tantas,
                    hasta suplir vuestra edad
                    el Pontífice.

---

28. Flores associates lack of respect for non-equals with *tiranía*, a term which
from 1697 will be applied repeatedly to the Commander and his men. Lope seems

                    Discourtesy towards one's peers is folly;
                    towards others, it's a kind of tyranny.   28
                    Don't take it personally, though; so young,
                    he's not yet learned how much one needs men's love.
COMMANDER.   The sword they girt about him, that same day   32
                    the Cross of Calatrava adorned his breast,
                    should have sufficed to teach him courtesy.
FLORES.   If he's been set against you, you'll be able
                    to know him better soon.
ORTUÑO.   Why, look, he's coming;   39
                    be reassured.
COMMANDER.   I'll see what he can say.

The Master enters, accompanied.

MASTER.   Forgive me, Fernán Gómez de Guzmán!   41
                    I've only just been told of your arrival.
COMMANDER.   I had good reason, sir, to feel aggrieved.
                    My love and my concern, when you were younger,
                    persuaded me to anticipate more deference
                    from you, as Master of our noble Order,
                    toward me, its Grand Commander, and your servant.
MASTER.   I had no notion you were here, Fernando.
                    Embrace me once again.
COMMANDER.   You owe me honour,   55
                    as one who's put his very life at peril
                    through all these troubled times, until the Pope
                    confirmed your youthful claims, in their defence.

---

here to broaden its traditional sense (Aristotle's 'the bad form of monarchy'); as the selfish misuse of power, it may be directed against either inferiors or superiors. Similarly, in *El Duque de Viseo*, 62–4, alleged rebels against the Crown are labelled *tiranos*.

32–6. Our attention is drawn to these visual signs and their symbolism, as it will be repeatedly, e.g. in 60–1.

39. *Vuélvete* here surely means 'turn round', rather than 'go away again'.

41–64. Note that the Master's apologies are effusive and presumably genuine, the Commander's replies sour and grudging.

43. The spelling *agora*, which alternates at this time (and in this text) with *aora* for today's *ahora*, must be retained whenever it appears; it scans as three syllables, *a(h)ora* as two. Cf. esp. 2097–8.

55–9. Cf. *Chronica*, 78vb.

MAESTRE.   Es verdad,
y por las señales santas   60
    que a los dos cruzan el pecho,
    que os lo pago en estimaros
    y, como a mi padre, honraros.
COMENDADOR   De vos estoy satisfecho.
MAESTRE.   ¿Qué hay de guerra por allá?   65
COMENDADOR   Estad atento, y sabréis
    la obligación que tenéis.
MAESTRE.   Decid, que ya lo estoy, ya.
COMENDADOR   Gran Maestre, don Rodrigo   [*romance*]
    Téllez Girón, que a tan alto   70
    lugar os trajo el valor
    de aquel vuestro padre claro,
    que, de ocho años, en vos
    renunció su maestrazgo,
    que después, por más seguro,   75
    juraron y confirmaron
    Reyes y Comendadores,
    dando el Pontífice santo
    Pío segundo sus bulas,
    y después las suyas Paulo,   80
    para que don Juan Pacheco,
    gran Maestre de Santiago,
    fuese vuestro coadjutor;
    ya que es muerto, y que os han dado
    el gobierno sólo a vos,   85
    aunque de tan pocos años,
    advertid que es honra vuestra
    seguir en aqueste caso
    la parte de vuestros deudos;
    porque, muerto Enrique cuarto,   90
    quieren que al Rey don Alonso
    de Portugal, que ha heredado,
    por su mujer, a Castilla,
    obedezcan sus vasallos;
    que aunque pretenden lo mismo   95
    por Isabel, don Fernando,
    gran Príncipe de Aragón,

MASTER.	I know; and by that holy Cross which covers
	your breast and mine, I swear I'm truly grateful,
	and do you honour as I do my father.
COMMANDER.	Well, I'm content.
MASTER.	What news, then, of the war?
COMMANDER.	Listen, and I'll explain the situation,
	and where your duty lies.
MASTER.	Go on. I'm listening.
COMMANDER.	Rodrigo Téllez, proud Girón,

Master of Calatrava
– a lofty title, one you owe
to your illustrious father,
who when you were a boy of eight
renounced it in your favour;
one which was then confirmed on oath
by monarchs and commanders
and ratified by papal bulls
from Pius and Paul, providing
that Juan Pacheco shared your rule,
the Master of Santiago.
Now he is dead, and you alone,
though still so young, are Master,
let me instruct you, where for you
the path of honour lies.
Henry the Fourth being dead, your kin
– whose cause you must espouse –
insist his vassals recognise
the Portuguese Alonso,
whose consort Joan, as Henry's child,
is heiress to Castile.
Of course the Prince of Aragon,
don Ferdinand, proposes
that Isabella should succeed
– his wife and Henry's sister;

69

84

95

69–83. Cf. *Chronica*, 78v a & b.

84–103. Cf. *Chronica*, 78vb – 79ra. Note that the Commander reverses the order of the claims, and underplays that of Ferdinand and Isabella.

95. *pretenden:* strict grammar demands a singular verb-form, but Lope may have felt the royal couple to constitute a plural subject.

95-7. Ferdinand was not in fact *King* of Aragon until the death of his father John in 1479.

no con derecho tan claro
a vuestros deudos, que en fin
no presumen que hay engaño   100
en la sucesión de Juana,
a quien vuestro primo hermano
tiene agora en su poder.
Y así vengo a aconsejaros
que juntéis los caballeros   105
de Calatrava en Almagro,
y a Ciudad Real toméis,
que divide como paso
a Andalucía y Castilla,
para mirarlos a entrambos.   110
Poca gente es menester,
porque tiene por soldados
solamente sus vecinos
y algunos pocos hidalgos,
que defienden a Isabel   115
y llaman rey a Fernando.
Será bien que deis asombro,
Rodrigo, aunque niño, a cuantos
dicen que es grande esa Cruz
para vuestros hombros flacos.   120
Mirad los Condes de Urueña
de quien venís, que mostrando
os están desde la fama
los laureles que ganaron;
los Marqueses de Villena,   125
y otros capitanes, tantos,
que las alas de la fama
apenas pueden llevarlos.

100-1. The *Chronica* ('affirmed') echoes, and Lope underscores, the belief (well-known to Spaniards) that Joan (la Beltraneja) was the illegitimate daughter of Henry's queen and don Beltrán de la Cueva. The Commander is almost made to admit, indeed, that her claim was therefore fraudulent.

104-10. See *Chronica*, 79r.

110. *entrambos* (both) agrees with *reinos* (kingdoms), understood.

but they prefer the claims of Joan,
now in your cousin's power,
and scout those rumours which allege
her parentage is dubious.
I come to urge you, then, to call
the knights of Calatrava
to assemble in Almagro now,
and take Ciudad Real,
which, Janus-like, divides and links
Castile and Andalusia.
We'll not need many men; the town
has very few defenders
– only its own inhabitants
and some few minor nobles
who call don Ferdinand their King
and Isabella Queen.
Though still so young, you would do well,
Rodrigo, to dismay
all those who say that Cross you bear
is heavy for such shoulders.
Remember now Urueña's Counts,   121
the stock from which you sprang;
see where in glory they display
the laurel wreaths they won.
See too Villena's Marquesses,
and other knights, so numerous
the wings of Fame can scarce support
the weight of so much honour.

121. Lope and his contemporaries did use *a* as a sign of the direct object,
esp. with reference to definite persons, but it is often not found, as here, where
it would be normal today (cf. for instance 1004, 1225, 1765); see Keniston 2.4
and P's note.
121–5. See *Chronica*, 78va and 79ra.

	Sacad esa blanca espada,	
	que habéis de hacer, peleando,	130
	tan roja como la Cruz,	
	porque no podré llamaros	
	Maestre de la Cruz roja	
	que tenéis al pecho, en tanto	
	que tenéis la blanca espada;	135
	que una al pecho y otra al lado,	
	entrambas han de ser rojas;	
	y vos, Girón soberano,	
	capa del templo inmortal	
	de vuestros claros pasados.	140

MAESTRE.   Fernán Gómez, estad cierto   [*redondillas*]
que en esta parcialidad,
porque veo que es verdad,
con mis deudos me concierto.

    Y si importa, como paso   145
a Ciudad Real, mi intento,
veréis que, como violento
rayo, sus muros abraso.

    No, porque es muerto mi tío,
piensen de mis pocos años   150
los propios y los extraños
que murió con él mi brío.

    Sacaré la blanca espada,
para que quede su luz
de la color de la Cruz,   155
de roja sangre bañada.

    Vos, adonde residís,
¿tenéis algunos soldados?

COMENDADOR   Pocos, pero mis criados;
que si dellos os servís,   160
pelearán como leones.

    Ya veis que en Fuente Ovejuna
hay gente humilde, y alguna
no enseñada en escuadrones,
sino en campos y labranzas.   165

MAESTRE.   ¿Allí residís?

COMENDADOR   Allí
de mi encomienda escogí
casa entre aquestas mudanzas.

135–6. *la blanca:* B1 (p. 221, n.) also considers the *Parte* reading admissible,

	Unsheathe that blade, which, now so bright,
	shall, when you wield it, show
	as crimson as the Cross; for how
	shall your Commander call you
	the Master of the Cross you wear
	while yet your sword is white?
	Both must be red, one on your breast,
	the other by your side,
	and you, Girón, a worthy scion, 138
	no stripling but a banner
	to top the towering pantheon
	of your immortal race.

MASTER. I see you're right. Believe me, Fernán Gómez,
I shall support my kinsmen in this conflict;
and if, in marching on Ciudad Real,   145
the need arises, you shall see me raze
its ramparts like a blazing thunderbolt.
My youth shouldn't persuade my friends or foes
my valour perished when my uncle died.
I shall unsheathe this blade, and bathe its brightness
in blood as crimson as the Cross I bear.
Can you, from your domain, provide some troops?

COMMANDER. A very few, but faithful followers.
Command them, and they'll fight for you like lions.   161
In my Fuente Ovejuna, there are only
a few poor peasant farmers, better versed
in husbandry than in the arts of war.

MASTER. That's where you live?

COMMANDER.   In troubled times like these,
I chose that fiefdom as my surest stronghold.

---

and proposes its retention; but his text too has *blanca la*.

138–40. Note the puns: *girón* = torn strip of cloth, or standard; *capa* = cloak, or protection. LE recalls that on the title-page of his *Arcadia* (1598), dedicated to the Duke of Osuna, Lope placed the couplet 'Este Girón para el suelo, / sacó de su capa el cielo'.

145–6. My punctuation and translation follow B1: 'Y si importa mi intento ("actuación") como medio para pasar a Ciudad Real'; but very possibly 146 (which H emended 'Ciudad Real al intento') is corrupt, and the sense of 'como paso' is like that in 108. M, CM and LEGB interpret it as 'como pienso', &c.; even if this is admissible, the two lines remain obscure.

161. Note this first association of the Commander and his followers with predatory beasts (cf. 242, 1148, 1184, 1742).

	Vuestra gente se registre;	170
	que no quedará vasallo.	
MAESTRE.	Hoy me veréis a caballo	
	poner la lanza en el ristre. *Vanse, y ...*	

... salen Pascuala y Laurencia.

LAURENCIA.	¡Mas que nunca acá volviera!	[*redondillas*]
PASCUALA.	Pues a la he que pensé	
	que cuando te lo conté,	175
	más pesadumbre te diera.	
LAURENCIA.	¡Plega al cielo que jamás	
	le vea en Fuente Ovejuna!	
PASCUALA.	Yo, Laurencia, he visto alguna	
	tan brava, y pienso que más,	180
	y tenía el corazón	
	brando como una manteca.	
LAURENCIA.	Pues ¿hay encina tan seca	
	como esta mi condición?	
PASCUALA.	¡Anda ya! 'Que nadie diga:	185
	desta agua no beberé'.	
LAURENCIA.	¡Voto al sol que lo diré,	
	aunque el mundo me desdiga!	
	¿A qué efeto fuera bueno	
	querer a Fernando yo?	190
	¿Casárame con él?	
PASCUALA.	No.	
LAURENCIA.	Luego la infamia condeno.	
	¡Cuántas mozas en la villa,	
	del Comendador fiadas,	
	andan ya descalabradas!	195

---

173. The montage seems modern. Forewarned by 162–8, the spectator can assume, when the nobles leave the stage empty and two peasant girls enter, that they are in or near Fuente Ovejuna, and guess (long before 190) that they are giving *their* view of Fernán Gómez.   On ¡Mas que ..! see P's note and *El sufrimiento premiado*, n. to 1827.

Enlist your men, for none will say you nay.
MASTER.   Lance at the ready, then; I ride today.   *They exit.*

Pascuala and Laurencia enter.

LAURENCIA.   Heaven send he'll not come back then!
PASCUALA.   Well, I never!   174
I reckoned when I told you you'd be sorry.
LAURENCIA.   I only pray to God Fuente Ovejuna
won't ever see him again!
PASCUALA.   Oh yes, Laurencia;
I've seen a few as fierce as you, and fiercer,
whose hearts were soft as butter underneath.
LAURENCIA.   Not me! My heart's as hard as any oak.
PASCUALA.   No one should say: 'Not me!' You never know!   185
LAURENCIA.   *I* will, though; let the world say what it may.
What good would it do for me to love his lordship?
D'you think he'd marry me?
PASCUALA.   No.
LAURENCIA.   Well then, it's wicked.
Who knows how many women in the village
have trusted him, and only been dishonoured.

---

174. *A la he* (a la fe) is the first of many *sayagués* (stage rustic) words and
phrases which characterize the peasants' speech. Some are noted in this edition;
for lists, see P, pp. XXIV–V, and López Estrada, 'Los villanos...', 22–3. The
translation does not attempt to render these, but in performance regional accents
and dialectal forms are to be recommended.
186–6. '*Que nadie ... beberé*'; lit. 'Let nobody say: I'll never drink this
water'. A proverb, quoted e.g. by Gerarda, *Dorotea* 229, and listed by Hernán
Núñez & Correas.
187. ¡*Voto al sol* ...!: a euphemistic oath called in Lope's *El valiente
Céspedes*, Ac. 12, 198b, a 'juramento villano'. See LE's note and cf. 1169,
1214.
189. *efeto*: in many words in which today a more Latinate form has
prevailed, and a pair of consonants is used, Lope probably pronounced and
usually wrote only the second. See *El perro del hortelano*, n. to 233, and cf.
1319, 1921, 1928; decienden, 255; satisfación, 440; trecientos, 463, 2370;
prática, 816; desinios, 1456; vitoria, 1459, 2049; vitoriosos, 1462, 2051;
contradición, 1923; solenemente, 2267.

PASCUALA.	Tendré yo por maravilla
	que te escapes de su mano.
LAURENCIA.	Pues en vano es lo que ves,
	porque ha que me sigue un mes,
	y todo, Pascuala, en vano. 200
	Aquel Flores, su alcahuete,
	y Ortuño, aquel socarrón,
	me mostraron un jubón,
	una sarta y un copete;
	dijéronme tantas cosas 205
	de Fernando, su señor,
	que me pusieron temor;
	mas no serán poderosas
	para contrastar mi pecho.
PASCUALA.	¿Dónde te hablaron?
LAURENCIA.	Allá 210
	en el arroyo, y habrá
	seis días.
PASCUALA.	Y yo sospecho
	que te han de engañar, Laurencia.
LAURENCIA.	¿A mí?
PASCUALA.	Que no, sino al cura.
LAURENCIA.	Soy, aunque polla, muy dura 215
	yo para su reverencia.
	Pardiez, más precio poner,
	Pascuala, de madrugada,
	un pedazo de lunada
	al huego para comer, 220

---

204. *copete* has been variously interpreted as a hair-piece, hat or adornment for the head; P quotes Lope's *La serrana de Tormes*, AcN9, 459b: 'No hay villana ni mozuela, / en cualquier pueblo de fama, / que no traiga como dama / su copete y arandela'.

| PASCUALA. | I'll be surprised if you escape his clutches. | |
| LAURENCIA. | He won't get anywhere with me, Pascuala. | |

PASCUALA.   I'll be surprised if you escape his clutches.
LAURENCIA. He won't get anywhere with me, Pascuala.
He's chased me for a month now. Nothing doing!
Flores, that pimp of his, and that Ortuño,
the crafty creature, offered me a bodice,
a necklace and a jewel for my hair,   204
and span me such a yarn about their master
they had me scared, but they won't get their way.
PASCUALA.   Where did they talk to you?
LAURENCIA   Beside the stream,   210
a week ago.
PASCUALA.   Well, I suspect, Laurencia,
they'll win you over.
LAURENCIA.   Me?
PASCUALA.   Why, who d'you think then?   214
LAURENCIA.   Tender I may be, but a sight too tough
to follow the Commander's holy orders.
I swear I'd rather put a piece of ham   217
to cook beside the fire at break of day,

---

210. Streams and fountains are in real life and literary tradition settings for courtship, thanks, as pointed out by Egla Morales Blouin, with reference to our play, 59–60, to 'the common and universal custom whereby women go early in the day to wash clothes or fetch water, thus affording opportunities for suitors'; cf. 723–6.

214. *Que no, sino al cura*; an ironic reply, perhaps related to 'No, sino el alba...', see *Dorotea*, 365.

215. *polla* = chick; 'la gallina nueva, medianamente crecida... Por traslación se llama la muchacha o moza de poca edad y buen parecer'(*Autoridades*).

216. *su reverencia* refers ironically to the Commander, who bore the title Frey don Fernán Gómez de Gúzman; *Chronica*, 81r. Cf. n. to 465–7.

217. *pardiez*: a rustic euphemism for *por Dios*; cf. 837, 954, 961 (*par Dios*). On the formula *más precio... que*, (P, XXIII, n. 27) used by Lope esp. to contrast country with city, see *El sembrar en buena tierra*, n. to 2221–5, with six more examples; P adds another from Lope and one from Luis Vélez's *La luna de la sierra*, BAE 45, p. 191; see also *Los novios de Hornachuelos*, BAE 41, 390, and F. de Rojas Zorrilla, *Del Rey abajo, ninguno*, 494–553.

217–44. In this bucolic but earthy evocation of the peasants' day (largely concerned with food), note the references to pigmeat (219, 232), recalling their freedom from the taint of Judaism; to prayer (236, 240–1); and to notions of harmonious concord (228, 229, 231).

con tanto zalacatón
de una rosca que yo amaso,
y hurtar a mi madre un vaso
del pegado canjilón;
    y más precio al mediodía   225
ver la vaca entre las coles,
haciendo mil caracoles
con espumosa armonía;
    y concertar, si el camino
me ha llegado a causar pena,   230
casar una berenjena
con otro tanto tocino;
    y después un pasatarde,
mientras la cena se aliña,
de una cuerda de mi viña,   235
(que Dios de pedrisco guarde);
    y cenar un salpicón
con su aceite y su pimienta,
y irme a la cama contenta,
y al *inducas tentación*   240
    rezalle mis devociones;
que cuantas raposerías,
con su amor y sus porfías,
tienen estos bellacones;
    porque todo su cuidado,   245
después de darnos disgusto,
es anochecer con gusto
y amanecer con enfado.

PASCUALA.   Tienes, Laurencia, razón;
que en dejando de querer,   250
más ingratos suelen ser
que al villano el gorrión.
    En el invierno, que el frío
tiene los campos helados,
decienden de los tejados,   255
diciéndole 'tío, tío',
    hasta llegar a comer
las migajas de la mesa;

and match it with a bit of twisted bread
I've had to knead myself, and steal from mother
a cup of wine, pitch-flavoured from the jar;
I'd rather see, at noon, some beef and cabbage
cavorting gaily to a frothy tune;
or, when I'm weary from a journey, marry
a bit of bacon and an aubergine;
and later choose some grapes saved from my vineyard   235
– which God protect, I pray, from frost and hail –
to make a snack until my supper's ready;
and dine on mincemeat, soused with oil and pepper,
and so go off contentedly to bed,
to say my prayers, my 'not into temptation';
than heed the foxy talk and amorous ardour
of lying rogues like those, whose whole intention
in stringing us along to do us down
is late-night pleasure but a rude awakening.

PASCUALA.   You're right, Laurencia; men are more ungrateful
when once they cease to love us, than the sparrows.   252
In winter, when the farmer's fields are frozen,
they flutter from his eaves and cry 'Sweet, sweet',
and gobble breadcrumbs even from his table;

---

235. *de una cuerda* refers to the countryman's practice of keeping bunches of grapes hanging from a cord.

238. *pasatarde*: note '... un pasatarde, que hacer / suele la salva al cenar'; *El galán de la Membrilla*, 219–20.

239. *y irme*: *y* was invariably used by Lope for 'and' before initial *h* (*i*); see Poesse, 74–5, and *El perro del hortelano*, n. to 474.

241. *rezalle*: assimilation of the final *r* of an infinitive with the *l* of an enclitic third-person pronoun persisted into the 17th century, especially in verse. See Keniston 9.611, and *El perro del hortelano*, n. to 61, & cf. 1070, 1212, 1388, 1633.

252–64. Whereas in English sparrows twitter 'tweet, tweet', in Spanish they are supposed to cry (*piar*) 'pío, pío'; hence the joke that in winter they call 'tío, tío' (old chap), but in spring 'judío, judío' (jew, a jibe especially insulting to Old Christian peasants; see Salomon, 829). The sparrow is an appropriate metaphor for lecherous men; accordingly to Pliny, as recalled by Covarrubias, 'este pajarillo es lujuriosísimo, y a esta causa vive tan poco que el macho no pasa de año'.

mas luego que el frío cesa,
y el campo ven florecer,   260
no bajan diciendo 'tío',
del beneficio olvidados,
mas saltando en los tejados
dicen 'judío, judío'.
    Pues tales los hombres son: 265
cuando nos han menester,
somos su vida, su ser,
su alma, su corazón;
    pero pasadas las ascuas,
las tías somos judías,   270
y en vez de llamarnos tías,
anda el nombre de las pascuas.

LAURENCIA.	¡No fiarse de ninguno!
PASCUALA.	Lo mismo digo, Laurencia.

Salen Mengo y Barrildo y Frondoso.

FRONDOSO.	En aquesta diferencia 275
	andas, Barrildo, importuno.
BARRILDO.	A lo menos aquí está
	quien nos dirá lo más cierto.
MENGO.	Pues hagamos un concierto
	antes que lleguéis allá, 280
	y es, que si juzgan por mí,
	me dé cada cual la prenda,
	precio de aquesta contienda.
BARRILDO.	Desde aquí digo que sí.
	Mas si pierdes, ¿que darás? 285
MENGO.	Daré mi rabel de boj,
	que vale más que una troj,
	porque yo le estimo en más.
BARRILDO.	Soy contento.
FRONDOSO.	Pues lleguemos.
	Dios os guarde, hermosas damas. 290
LAURENCIA.	¿Damas, Frondoso, nos llamas?
FRONDOSO.	Andar al uso queremos:

but when the cold is past, they see the fields
return to life, and cease to say 'Sweet, sweet'.
They hop along his roof, forget his kindness,
and cry – as if he were a Jew – 'Cheat, cheat'.
Men are the same; when they can't do without us,
they tell us we're their life, their very being,
their heart and soul; but once their passions cool,   269
they change their tune, and we're not 'sweets' but 'cheats'.

LAURENCIA.   You can't trust *one* of them.
PASCUALA.   No, that's what *I* say.

Mengo, Barrildo and Frondoso enter.

FRONDOSO.   This argument is getting out of hand.
    You're too insistent now, Barrildo.
BARRILDO.   Well,
    at least here's someone who can put us right.
MENGO.   Before you tackle them, let's settle *one* thing;
    if they agree with me, then each of you
    owes me a forfeit, as a prize for winning.
BARRILDO.   That's fine by me; but if you lose, what's yours?
MENGO.   I'll give the pair of you my boxwood fiddle.   286
    It's worth a granary full of corn or more,
    because I think so.
BARRILDO.   Fair enough.
FRONDOSO.   Come on, then.
    Greetings, fair ladies!
LAURENCIA.   Us, Frondoso, ladies?
    Why call us that?
FRONDOSO.   Just following the fashion.

---

269. *pasadas las ascuas* = lit. 'when the hot coals (of desire) have cooled'.

272. *el nombre de las pascuas*: Jaime Asensio, 'El nombre de las pascuas en Tirso', *Estudios*, 39 (1983), argues that this insult (Correas: 'putas, bellacas, alcahuetas') was also and originally antisemitic, referring to the scribes and Pharisees (Annas and Caiphas) of the first Easter.

286. *rabel*: 'instrumento músico de cuerdas y arquillo; es pequeño y todo de una pieza, de tres cuerdas y de voces muy subidas. Usan dél los pastores, con que se entretienen, como David hacía con su instrumento' (Covarrubias).

288. *le* was regularly used by Lope as the masculine direct object pronoun referring to *things* (cf. 419–20, 2257).

al bachiller, licenciado;
al ciego, tuerto; al bisojo,
bizco; resentido, al cojo,   295
y buen hombre, al descuidado;
al ignorante, sesudo;
al mal galán, soldadesca;
a la boca grande, fresca,
y al ojo pequeño, agudo;   300
al pleitista, diligente;
al gracioso, entretenido;
al hablador, entendido,
y al insufrible, valiente;
al cobarde, para poco;   305
al atrevido, bizarro;
compañero, al que es un jarro,
y desenfadado, al loco;
gravedad, al descontento;
a la calva, autoridad;   310
donaire, a la necedad,
y al pie grande, buen cimiento;
al buboso, resfriado;
comedido, al arrogante;
al ingenioso, constante,   315
al corcovado, cargado.
    Esto llamaros imito
damas, sin pasar de aquí;
porque fuera hablar así
proceder en infinito.   320

293–320. The list of euphemisms Lope gives Frondoso here is a rhetorical topos of medieval or even Aristotelian origin, applied by Antonio de Guevara in *Menosprecio de corte y alabanza de aldea* (1539) to the language of city flatterers (cf. 321–3), e.g. 'En la corte... al soberbio llaman honrado; al pródigo, magnífico; al cobarde, atentado; al esforzado, atrevido; al encapotado, grave; al recogido, hipócrita; al malicioso, agudo; al deslenguado, elocuente; ... al loco, regocijado; al entremetido, solícito; al chocarrero, donoso' &c.   Se M, Bl and Varey.   A related topos derives from Lucretius 4: 1160–9 on blind lovers.

Your Bachelor is always called a Master;   293
the blind, 'one-eyed'; and those who're cross-eyed, 'squinting';
the lame, 'afflicted'; feckless folk, 'good-natured';
those who know nothing, 'sound'; the boorish, 'bluff'.
Big mouths are called 'full-lipped'; small eyes, 'sharp-sighted';
contentious folk are 'active'; clowns, 'amusing';
chatterers, 'clever'; pushful people, 'bold';
cowards, 'not up to much' and hotheads, 'dashing'.
Your dolt's 'good company'; your madman, 'carefree';   307
sourness, 'solemnity', and baldness, 'presence'.
Folly's called 'wit'; big feet, 'a solid footing';
the pox is 'cold-sores'; haughtiness, 'reserve';   313
fanatics are 'persistent', hunchbacks, 'stooping'.
You see then what I meant when I said 'ladies';
I'll say no more; I could go on for ever.

294–5. *bisojo* and *bizco* are hard to distinguish; for the second, LE suggests 'que guiña los ojos' (winking).

298. *soldadesca*: see Covarrubias (*soldado*): 'Pelea ordinariamente a pie, su exercicio se llama soldadesca'.

302. *gracioso* might seem flattering (witty), and *entremetido* (interfering) is pejorative; hence the emendation by H, &c. But *gracioso* is cited as pejorative (alongside *lascivo* and *mentiroso*) in Mateo Alemán's prologue *Al vulgo* to *Guzmán de Alfarache* I (1599); and cf. Guevara, above: 'al chocarrero, donoso'. In 1971 I therefore proposed, as here, the reading of the Holland ms, which P rejects but LE 2 & 3 consider plausible.

307. *un jarro*: 'al que es necio decimos que es un jarro, presuponemos que es de vino, y si de agua, grosero y basto' (Covarrubias).

313. *al buboso, resfriado*: the nose of Quevedo's miserly *licenciado* Cabra was eaten away by 'unas búas de resfriado' rather than 'de vicio'; genuinely in his case, because catching syphilis costs money.

315. *ingenioso* is explained by Bl as 'maniático'; Combet recalls interpretations of the *ingenioso hidalgo* Don Quixote, and translates: 'maniaque frénétique'.

LAURENCIA. Allá en la ciudad, Frondoso,
llámase por cortesía
de esa suerte; y a fe mía,
que hay otro más riguroso
y peor vocabulario   325
en las lenguas descorteses.
FRONDOSO. Querría que lo dijeses.
LAURENCIA. Es todo a esotro contrario:
al hombre grave, enfadoso;
venturoso, al descompuesto;   330
melancólico, al compuesto,
y al que reprehende, odioso;
importuno, al que aconseja;
al liberal, moscatel;
al justiciero, cruel,   335
y al que es piadoso, madeja;
al que es constante, villano;
al que es cortés, lisonjero;
hipócrita, al limosnero,
y pretendiente, al cristiano;   340
al justo mérito, dicha;
a la verdad, imprudencia;
cobardía, a la paciencia,
y culpa, a lo que es desdicha;
necia, a la mujer honesta;   345
mal hecha, a la hermosa y casta,
y a la honrada ... pero basta,
que esto basta por respuesta.
MENGO. Digo que eres el dimuño.
BARRILDO. ¡Soncas, que lo dice mal!   350
MENGO. Apostaré que la sal
la echó el cura con el puño.
LAURENCIA. ¿Qué contienda os ha traído,
si no es que mal lo entendí?
FRONDOSO. Oye, por tu vida.
LAURENCIA.   Di.   355
FRONDOSO. Préstame, Laurencia, oído.
LAURENCIA. ¿Cómo prestado? Y aun dado.
Desde agora os doy el mío.

LAURENCIA.	Yes, that's the language city people use,	321
	Frondoso, when it suits them to be courteous;	
	but let me tell you, there's a different list	
	you'll hear on other, less respectful lips.	
FRONDOSO.	What do *they* say, then?	
LAURENCIA.	Quite the opposite.	

They always call the man who's serious, 'tedious';
the outspoken, 'rash'; the sober, 'melancholic'.
The man who dares to criticise is 'odious';
the one who offers good advice, a 'meddler';
the man who gives to one and all, a 'softy';
the just man, 'cruel'; the merciful, a 'weakling';
one you can trust, a 'peasant'; one who's generous,
a 'hypocrite'; one who's polite, a 'flatterer';
the honest Christian, 'one who seeks preferment'.
True merit, 'luck', and telling the truth, 'imprudence';
long-suffering, 'fear'; misfortune, 'retribution';
the girl who's modest, 'stupid'; one who's pretty
but chaste, 'ill-favoured'; as for one who's virtuous...
but that'll do, and that's sufficient answer.

MENGO.	You are a devil!	
BARRILDO	By God, that wasn't bad!	
MENGO.	I swear she must have kissed the Blarney stone!	351
LAURENCIA.	Unless I'm much mistaken, you were arguing.	
FRONDOSO.	Listen, Laurencia.	
LAURENCIA.	Well, then?	
FRONDOSO.	Lend an ear.	
LAURENCIA.	Lend one, Frondoso? No, I'll *give* you ear.	

321–6. *cortesia... descorteses*: Laurencia is made to refine the concepts introduced in 10–28. Ironically, in the *corte* (as opposed to the *aldea*), *courtesy* and *discourtesy* have dishonest forms, flattery and slander.

334. On *moscatel*, see C.E. Anibal, in *Hispania*, 17 (1934), 3–18; *El sembrar en buena tierra*, n. to 1508; and P's note.

349–50. *dimuño* is a *sayagués* form of *demonio*, and *soncas*, similarly, a rustic exclamation. Bl interprts Barrildo's line as a question.

351–2. Lit. 'I'll bet the priest (when christening her) threw salt (wit) at her by the fistful'. On *la* as the feminine indirect object pronoun, see Keniston, 7.32 (cf. 1565, 2421).

FRONDOSO.	En tu discreción confío.
LAURENCIA.	¿Qué es lo que habéis apostado? 360
FRONDOSO.	Yo y Barrildo contra Mengo.
LAURENCIA.	¿Qué dice Mengo?
BARRILDO.	Una cosa

que, siendo cierta y forzosa,
la niega.

MENGO.   A negarla vengo,
porque yo sé que es verdad.   365

LAURENCIA.   ¿Qué dice?

BARRILDO.   Que no hay amor.

LAURENCIA.   Generalmente, es rigor.

BARRILDO.   Es rigor y es necedad.
Sin amor, no se pudiera
ni aun el mundo conservar.   370

MENGO.   Yo no sé filosofar;
leer, ¡ojalá supiera!
Pero si los elementos
en discordia eterna viven,
y de los mismos reciben   375
nuestros cuerpos alimentos,
cólera y melancolía,
flema y sangre, claro está.

BARRILDO.   El mundo de acá y de allá,
Mengo, todo es armonía.   380
Armonía es puro amor,
porque el amor es concierto.

MENGO.   Del natural os advierto
que yo no niego el valor.
Amor hay, y el que entre sí   385
gobierna todas las cosas,
correspondencias forzosas
de cuanto se mira aquí;
y yo jamás he negado
que cada cual tiene amor   390
correspondiente a su humor
que le conserva en su estado.

FRONDOSO.	I trust your judgement.
LAURENCIA.	What's your problem, pray?
FRONDOSO.	Barrildo and I are both at odds with Mengo.
LAURENCIA.	What is it Mengo says?
BARRILDO.	He says that something

that's certain, and that has to be, is not.

MENGO.	I say it's not, because I know it's true.	364
LAURENCIA.	What does he *say*?	
BARRILDO.	There's no such thing as love.	
LAURENCIA.	In general? That's too sweeping.	
BARRILDO.	Yes, and stupid.	

The world itself could never last without it.

MENGO.   I can't philosophize – wish I could read!
But if the elements from which our bodies
draw sustenance – phlegm, melancholy, blood,
and choler too – are in perpetual conflict,
it stands to reason.

BARRILDO.   Mengo, all the world,   379
here and up there, is perfect harmony,
and harmony is love, for love is concord.

MENGO.   I don't deny the force of love in nature,
the sort that governs all things that exist,   385
which everything we see must correspond to.
And I've not said there's not a sort of love
within each man, according to his humour,
that helps preserve him in his state of being.

364–5. Mengo means '... I know I'm right'; Lope made him put it clumsily.

379–82.   Lope often expresses such Platonic concepts; e.g. 'La música es divina concordancia / deste mundo inferior y del angélico. / Todo cuanto hay en todo, todo es música', *Los locos de Valencia*, BAE 24, 131b. Eryximachus, in Plato's *Symposium*, compares medicine, the science of creating love and harmony between hostile elements in the body, the opposites hot and cold, wet and dry, with music, which 'produces a harmony out of factors which are first in discord but subsequently in concord, namely treble and base notes', adding (in Ficino's version): 'Harmonia namque concentus est. Concentus vero concordia quaedam'. Lope virtually reproduces this in *Dorotea*, 397.

385–8. Eryximachus also states that love operates not only in men's souls but in 'the bodies of all animals... and plants which grow in the earth, and practically all existing things; in fact Love is a great and wonderful god whose influence extends everywhere, and embraces the world of gods and men alike'.

           Mi mano al golpe que viene
           mi cara defenderá;
           mi pie, huyendo, estorbará   395
           el daño que el cuerpo tiene.
           Cerraránse mis pestañas
           si al ojo le viene mal,
           porque es amor natural.

PASCUALA.   Pues ¿de qué nos desengañas?   400
MENGO.   De que nadie tiene amor
           más que a su misma persona.

PASCUALA.   Tú mientes, Mengo, y perdona;
           porque es materia el rigor
             con que un hombre a una mujer   405
           o un animal quiere y ama
           su semejante.

MENGO.   Eso llama
           amor propio, y no querer.
              ¿Qué es amor?

LAURENCIA.   Es un deseo
           de hermosura.

MENGO.   Esa hermosura   410
           ¿por qué el amor la procura?

LAURENCIA.   Para gozarla.

MENGO.   Eso creo.
           Pues ese gusto que intenta,
           ¿no es para él mismo?

LAURENCIA.   Es así.

MENGO.   Luego, ¿por quererse a sí,   415
           busca el bien que le contenta?

LAURENCIA.   Es verdad.

MENGO.   Pues dese modo,
           no hay amor, sino el que digo,
           que por mi gusto le sigo,
           y quiero dármele en todo.   420

	My hand will fend off blows aimed at my face;	393
	my foot will run, and so protect my body;	
	my lids will close to save my eye from damage;	
	that's natural love.	

PASCUALA.   Then what *do* you deny?

MENGO.   That anyone loves anyone but himself.

PASCUALA.   I'm sorry, Mengo, but you're wrong, because
there's solid proof and substance in the love   404
of man and woman, animal and mate.

MENGO.   You shouldn't call that love, though; that's just *self*-love.
Tell me, what's love?

LAURENCIA   It's a desire for beauty.   409

MENGO.   And why does love want beauty?

LAURENCIA.   Why, to enjoy it.

MENGO.   Yes, I agree; but when it seeks that pleasure,
isn't that for itself?

LAURENCIA.   Well, yes.

MENGO.   And therefore
it wants the thing that gives it satisfaction
because it loves itself?

LAURENCIA.   That's true.

MENGO.   That proves it.
There is no love, except the sort I say,
that I pursue to indulge my private whim
and wholly to give pleasure to myself.

393–9. León Hebreo says of the lover: 'it is very reasonable that he should endeavour to gain that which is most lofty (the beloved), as you will be able to understand by means of a natural example and a moral one. The natural one: when someone is given a blow to the head, he places his arm before his head to save it...' Lope may well be glossing this idea (and giving opportunities for comic business).

404–7. Recent editors all understand these lines as a question, and *materia* as 'merely materialistic or physical'; I suggest the interpretation offered.

409–20. Ficino, in Ch. 9 of his commentary on the *Symposium*, defines love as 'fruendae pulchritudinis desiderium'. Mengo's dialogue with Laurencia is closely similar to the cross-questioning of Agathon by Socrates, and of Socrates by Diotima.

BARRILDO.	Dijo el cura del lugar
	cierto día en el sermón
	que había cierto Platón
	que nos enseñaba a amar;
	que éste amaba el alma sola 425
	y la virtud de lo amado.
PASCUALA.	En materia habéis entrado
	que por ventura acrisola
	los caletres de los sabios
	en sus cademias y escuelas. 430
LAURENCIA.	Muy bien dice, y no te muelas
	en persuadir sus agravios.
	Da gracias, Mengo, a los cielos,
	que te hicieron sin amor.
MENGO.	¿Amas tú?
LAURENCIA.	Mi propio honor. 435
FRONDOSO.	¡Dios te castigue con celos!
BARRILDO.	¿Quién gana?
PASCUALA.	Con la quistión
	podéis ir al sacristán,
	porque él o el cura os darán
	bastante satisfación. 440
	Laurencia no quiere bien;
	yo tengo poca experiencia.
	¿Cómo daremos sentencia?
FRONDOSO.	¿Qué mayor que ese desdén?

421–6. The dual source Barrildo is made to give for his new argument not only lends a touch of verisimilitude to a scene which has eschewed it, but serves 'to underline the basic unity of Christian and Platonic thought' (Spitzer, 276).

BARRILDO.	One day the village priest said in his sermon 421
	some man called Plato taught us how to love,
	and said we should love nothing but the soul
	and virtue of the person whom we loved.
PASCUALA.	This is the sort of thing that academics
	in colleges and schools must boil their brains with.
LAURENCIA.	She's right, you're wrong to tie yourselves in knots
	by copying their contentious arguments.
	Thank heaven, Mengo, you weren't made to love.
MENGO.	Are you in love?
LAURENCIA.	Me? Only with my honour.
FRONDOSO.	God punish you with jealousy. Who wins? 436
PASCUALA.	You'd better take your problem to the sexton;
	he, or the priest, is sure to have an answer.
	Laurencia's not in love, I've no experience;
	how can we judge?
FRONDOSO.	Her scorn's my clearest answer!. 444

The specific reference is probably to a remark by Pausanias in the *Symposium*, which Lope placed at the head of Sonnet 15 in his *La Circe*, in Ficino's version: 'Pravus autem est amator ille vulgaris, qui corpus magis quam animam amat' (see *Dorotea*, p. 167, n. 104); this was surely also the 'aphorism' of Plato referred to by Albano in *El anzuelo de Fenisa*, BAE 247, 264, expressing scepticism about those who 'say that one should love only the soul'. Cf. '... yo sé que basto / a sólo amar el alma con la mía'; *Epístola a Quijada y Riquelme*, BAE 38, 420.

436, 444.   Frondoso's asides establish, economically (as the actor will have shown long before) that he is in love with the self-sufficient Laurencia, and so was hoping (as she must have known) for a more encouraging answer.

437.   *quistión* (cf. 956) is a rustic form of *cuestión*, but also relates the debate to the *cuestión de amor* which was so constant a feature of courtly pastoral.

437–43.   The peasants finally recognise that they have no answer to their theoretical problem (though also, characteristically, that the Church must have one), for lack of practical experience.   That experience, and by implication the answer, will be provided for them (and us) by the actions of the Commander, (whose arrival is immediately announced), and by the reactions they produce.

Sale Flores.

FLORES.	Dios guarde a la buena gente.	445
PASCUALA.	Este es del Comendador	
	criado.	
LAURENCIA.	¡Gentil azor!	
	¿De adónde bueno, pariente?	
FLORES.	¿No me veis a lo soldado?	
LAURENCIA.	¿Viene don Fernando acá?	450
FLORES.	La guerra se acaba ya,	
	puesto que nos ha costado	
	alguna sangre y amigos.	
FRONDOSO.	Contadnos cómo pasó.	
FLORES.	¿Quién lo dirá como yo,	455
	siendo mis ojos testigos?	

Para emprender la jornada   [*romance*]
desta ciudad, que ya tiene
nombre de Ciudad Real,
juntó el gallardo Maestre   460
dos mil lucidos infantes
de sus vasallos valientes,
y trecientos de a caballo,
de seglares y de freiles;
porque la Cruz roja obliga   465
cuantos al pecho la tienen,
aunque sean de orden sacro;
mas contra moros se entiende.

---

447. Laurencia's new allusion to Frondoso's pimping for his master (see 201) introduces the motif of the Hunt of Love (cf. 755–81 &c). Gerli, 447, refers to the symbolism of falcons &c. in Gil Vicente, the *Romancero*, the *Celestina* and St. John of the Cross.

458–9. Ciudad Real, founded by Alfonso X as Villa Real, had been granted its new title by John II half a century before, in 1420. Lope was probably influenced by a phrase in the *Chronica*,   79ra, which 460–4 follow closely.

Flores enters.

FLORES.	God save you all, good people!
PASCUALA.	Here's that Flores,
	his lordship's fellow.
LAURENCIA.	Don't you mean his falcon? 447
	And where have you flown in from?
FLORES.	Can't you see?
	From fighting.
LAURENCIA.	Oh, is don Fernando coming?
FLORES.	The battle's over, though it cost us plenty
	in blood and friends.
FRONDOSO.	Well, tell us how it went.
FLORES.	Who better? Weren't these eyes of mine a witness?
	Preparing for his bold campaign
	against that famous town
	that now they call Ciudad Real, 458
	the gallant Master drew
	from all his fearless followers
	two thousand men-at-arms
	and fifteen score of cavalry,
	both laymen and religious;
	for Calatrava's holy rule 465
	requires that all who wear
	its cross, both friars and cavaliers,
	bear arms... against the Moors. 468

465-7. 'In this Order of Calatrava ... there are Clerical Friars devoted (while they are in the Monastery) principally to the Choir, and to other matters pertaining to divine worship... And they leave the Monastery when His Majesty (as their superior) commands, to serve the advantages of the said Order, that is to be employed also in the Active Life... Also there are in the Order, Knightly Friars devoted principally to the Active Life, which is the employment of arms against the Moors and enemies of our holy Catholic Faith'; F. de Rades y Andrada, *Catalogo de las obligaciones que los Comendadores, Cavalleros, Priores, y otros religiosos de la Orden, y Cavalleria de Calatrava tienen en razon de su avito y Profesion*, Toledo 1571, 11.

468. With some inverisimilitude, Lope has Flores underline the illegitimacy of the campaign against the Catholic Monarchs.

Salió el muchacho bizarro,
con una casaca verde   470
bordada de cifras de oro,
que sólo los brazaletes
por las mangas descubría,
que seis alamares prenden.
Un corpulento bridón,   475
rucio rodado, que al Betis
bebió el agua, y en su orilla
despuntó la grama fértil;
el codón, labrado en cintas
de ante, y el rizo copete   480
cogido en blancas lazadas,
que con las moscas de nieve
que bañan la blanca piel
iguales labores teje.
A su lado Fernán Gómez,   485
vuestro señor, en un fuerte
melado, de negros cabos,
puesto que con blanco bebe;
sobre turca jacerina,
peto y espaldar luciente,   490
con naranjada casaca,
que de oro y perlas guarnece
el morrión, que, coronado
con blancas plumas, parece
que del color naranjado   495
aquellos azares vierte;
ceñida al brazo una liga
roja y blanca, con que mueve
un fresno entero por lanza,
que hasta en Granada le temen.   500

---

479. *codón*, from the Italian *codone*, is the form to be preferred; P gives three other cases in Lope. LE explains *colón* as influenced by *cola*.

482. *moscas de nieve* must refer (*pace* LE) not to darker but to even whiter patches on the horse's white hide; Lope frequently refers to *moscas negras* (see P & Bl).

The handsome youth himself rode out,
his doublet, gleaming green,
embroidered with a gold device
and showing at its sleeves
armlets with six braid fastenings,
astride a mighty steed
– a dappled grey, glad once to drink
the bright Guadalquivir
and crop the verdant grass that grows
about its fertile verge.
A dock of doeskin dressed its tail,
white bows its rippling crest,
matching the snow-white patterning   482
that decked its pallid hide.
Beside him Fernán Gómez rode,
your overlord, his mount
a powerful, honey-coloured beast,
black-hooved, but white of mouth.   487
Over a Turkish coat of mail,
bright armour, breast and back,
with such an orange doublet, topped   493
so aptly by a helm
agleam with snow-white plumes, that these
seemed blossoms to its fruit.
About his arm, a thong, both red
and white, with which he wields
his lance – a whole great tree – whose power
even Granada fears.

---

487. *de negros cabos* probably indicates that all the horse's extremities (tail, hooves, mane and muzzle) were black.

492–6. Every edition I have seen except A, B & LE 3 has a stop or semi-colon after *guarnece*; but I take its subject to be *el morrión*, and *de oro y perlas*, by analogy with 'de oro y azul' and 'de perlas', to mean 'perfectly', and translate accordingly. This interpretation requires also that in 497 we retain *coronado*, despite the improper rhyme (among *romances*) with *naranjado*, and the fact that the line is overlong (unless *morrión* is scanned as two syllables here).

496. *azar(es)* seems to have been Lope's normal spelling of *azahar(es)*.

La ciudad se puso en arma;
dicen que salir no quieren
de la corona real,
y el patrimonio defienden.
Entróla, bien resistida;   505
y el Maestre a los rebeldes
y a los que entonces trataron
su honor injuriosamente
mandó cortar las cabezas,
y a los de la baja plebe,   510
con mordazas en la boca,
azotar públicamente.
Queda en ella tan temido
y tan amado, que creen
que quien en tan pocos años   515
pelea, castiga y vence,
ha de ser en otra edad
rayo del África fértil,
que tantas lunas azules
a su roja Cruz sujete.   520
Al Comendador y a todos
ha hecho tantas mercedes,
que el saco de la ciudad
el de su hacienda parece.
Mas ya la música suena;   525
recebilde alegremente,
que al triunfo las voluntades
son los mejores laureles.

501–4. See *Chronica*, 79ra.

505. *Entróla*: on *entrar* with a direct object, see Keniston, 2.51.

506–24. Lope versifies once more, in 506–9, the account in *Chronica*, 79ra &
b, of the Master's reprisals against the 'rebels', but adds incongruously that he
was loved as well as feared, that in later years he would fight heroically against
the Moors, and that he was generous to all.

The townsfolk rose in arms, proclaimed
their right to self-defence,
their loyalty to the Crown, and will
to stay in its domain.
The Master, though, at last prevailed,   506
and took the town by storm,
had those beheaded who'd presumed
to slander his good name,
and humbler persons gagged and flogged
in public for their pains.
The town is his, and he at once
so feared and yet so loved,
that all foresee that one so young
but so invincible
will prove the scourge, in Africa,
of many a Moorish foe,
and make their proud blue crescents yield
to Calatrava's Cross.
To all – our lord not least – he's shown
such generous largesse,
you'd say he'd plundered not the town
but rather his estate.
But I hear music. Greet your lord
with love and gladness now;
goodwill's the fairest laurel wreath
that crowns the victor's brow.

---

526.   *recebilde*: metathesis between the imperative plural and an enclitic third-person pronoun is frequent in Lope (cf. 965, 1213, 1245, 1249, 1579, 1634, 1851, 2111, 2254) and *recebir* was a common variant of today's *recibir* (cf. 1306, 2190, 2322, 2340).

Sale el Comendador, y Ortuño; músicos; Juan Rojo; y Esteban, Alonso, alcaldes.

MUSICOS *Cantan: Sea bienvenido*   [*romancillo*]
    el Comendadore   530
    de rendir las tierras
    y matar los hombres
    ¡Vivan los Guzmanes!
    ¡Vivan los Girones!
    Si en las paces blando,   535
    dulce en las razones,
    venciendo moricos,
    fuerte como un roble;
    de Ciudad Reale
    viene vencedore,   540
    que a Fuente Ovejuna
    trae sus pendones.
    ¡Viva muchos años,
    viva Fernán Gómez!

COMENDADOR   Villa, yo os agradezco justamente   [*tercetos*] 545
    el amor que me habéis aquí mostrado.
ALONSO.   Aun no muestra una parte del que siente.
    Pero, ¿qué mucho que seáis amado,
    mereciéndolo vos?
ESTEBAN.   Fuente Ovejuna
    y el regimiento que hoy habéis honrado   550
    que recibáis os ruega y importuna
    un pequeño presente, que esos carros
    traen, señor, no sin vergüenza alguna,
    de voluntades y árboles bizarros
    más que de ricos dones. Lo primero,   555
    traen dos cestos de polidos barros.

529–44.   On such songs of welcome by vassals for returning heroes, see Salomon, 724 ff.   He refers esp. to that in Act I of *El Conde Fernán González*, very similar in its metre, *o – e* assonance and use of the archaizing paragogic *e* (*Comendadore, Ciudad Reale, vencedore*).

537.   *venciendo moricos*: Salomon interprets this as a topos of the genre; but Lope is surely making (though the villagers may not be) the ironic point that the Commander has returned from defeating not Moors but loyal Christians.

538.   *fuerte(s)* should probably agree with *el Comendadore*, as P was the first to propose.

The Commander and Ortuño enter, with Musicians, Juan Rojo, and Esteban and Alonso, magistrates.

MUSICIANS *sing:*	*Our lord the Commander*	529
	we welcome again,	
	from conquering lands and	
	from slaughtering men.	
	Guzmán and Girón,	
	God grant them increase;	
	so gentle of speech and	
	so mild when at peace,	
	yet strong as an oak when	
	withstanding the Moor.	537
	From Ciudad Real	
	he returns as of yore	
	to Fuente Ovejuna	
	with banners victorious.	
	Long live Fernán Gómez,	
	ever more glorious!	

COMMANDER.   Good people, I acknowledge as is proper   545
the love you've shown me here.

ALONSO.   Sir, all we've shown
is scarcely a part of what we feel; but then
what wonder that you're loved, when you deserve it?

ESTEBAN.   Fuente Ovejuna, and its village council,
which you've so honoured, beg you and beseech you
to deign to accept, my lord, the humble offering
those carts have brought, with not a little shame,
bedecked with leafy boughs and loving wishes   554
rather than costly presents. First of all,
two baskets full of pots of polished clay.

---

542. The uncorrected reading, a *lectio difficilior*, may be a deliberate archaism (see M), but requires *trae* to be scanned as a monosyllable. This is comparatively rare in Lope; on the other hand, he often wrote *tray*. (Poesse, 22–30).

545–9. Note that the Commander addresses the town as a whole, and that the magistrates reply in its name, stressing its readiness to offer love (cf. 554, 568, 577).

552. The carts and presents are presumably to be imagined offstage; but 584 and 605 ff. will tell us to suppose that the action takes place outside the Commander's doorway; possibly the discovery-space was revealed, decorated as described in 583–4.

                    De gansos viene un ganadillo entero,
                    que sacan por las redes las cabezas
                    para cantar vueso valor guerrero.
                    Diez cebones en sal, valientes piezas,   560
                    sin otras menudencias y cecinas,
                    y más que guantes de ámbar, sus cortezas.
                    Cien pares de capones y gallinas,
                    que han dejado viudos a sus gallos
                    en las aldeas que miráis vecinas.   565
                    Acá no tienen armas ni caballos,
                    no jaeces bordados de oro puro,
                    si no es oro el amor de los vasallos.
                    Y porque digo puro, os aseguro
                    que vienen doce cueros, que aun en cueros   570
                    por enero podéis guardar un muro,
                        si dellos aforráis vuestros guerreros,
                    mejor que de las armas aceradas;
                    que el vino suele dar lindos aceros.
                    De quesos y otras cosas no excusadas   575
                    no quiero daros cuenta: justo pecho
                    de voluntades que tenéis ganadas;
                    y a vos y a vuestra casa, ¡buen provecho!
COMENDADOR   Estoy muy agradecido.   [redondillas]
                    Id, regimiento, en buen hora.   580
ALONSO.   Descansad, señor, agora,
                    y seáis muy bien venido;
                        que esta espadaña que veis
                    y juncia, a vuestros umbrales,
                    fueran perlas orientales,   585
                    y mucho más merecéis,
                        a ser posible a la villa.
COMENDADOR   Así lo creo, señores.
                    Id con Dios.
ESTEBAN.   Ea, cantores,
                    vaya otra vez la letrilla.   590
MUSICOS Cantan: Sea bien venido   [romancillo]
                    el Comendadore
                    de rendir las tierras
                    y matar los hombres...   Vanse.

Next, under nets, a little flock of geese,
craning their necks to sing your warlike valour,
and then ten salted porkers, handsome creatures,
and many another kind of well-cured meats,
in skins as sweet as gloves perfumed with amber.
A hundred brace of capons, and of hens,
whose sacrifice has left their cockerels widowed
in every hamlet here for miles around.
They have no arms to offer here, or horses
caparisoned in cloths of purest gold,
unless you count as gold your vassals' love;   568
and as for purity, I give my word
those dozen wineskins there contain such liquor   570
that though their own were bare, in deep mid-winter,
your troops, once lined with it, could man a wall
better than with steel, for that would steel them better.   573
Of cheese and such obligatory gifts
I'll make no more account, but all are tributes,
true tokens of the love which you've deserved.   577
God give you joy of them, and all your house!

COMMANDER.   I'm very grateful. Councillors, you may go.   579

ALONSO.   Now you may take your ease, my lord; be welcome.
We've dressed your doorway, sir, with reeds and rushes,   584
and wish we could with pearls, for you deserve
far better.

COMMANDER.   Very true. Well, go your ways.   588

ESTEBAN.   Singers, strike up! Let's hear that song again.

MUSICIANS *sing:* *Our lord the Commander*
we welcome again,
from conquering lands and
from slaughtering men...   *The male peasants exit.*

---

570. Note the pun on *cueros* (wineskins) and *en cueros* (naked).

573–4. A similar pun on *armas aceradas* (steel weapons) and *aceros* (valour).

579–80. The Commander, here and in 588–9, 'accepts the homage curtly, rudely'; Wardropper, 164.

584. *espadaña*: '... en las fiestas, por ser verdes y frescas las espadañas, se echan por el suelo y cuelgan por las paredes' (Covarrubias). On their combination in Lope with *juncia* (lit. sedge), see P, and on such festive decoration of houses, of pagan origin, Salomon, 635 ff.

COMENDADOR	Esperad vosotras dos.	[redondillas] 595
LAURENCIA.	¿Qué manda su señoría?	
COMENDADOR	Desdenes el otro día,	
	pues, ¿conmigo? ¡Bien, por Dios!	
LAURENCIA.	¿Habla contigo, Pascuala?	
PASCUALA.	Conmigo no, ¡tirte ahuera!	600
COMENDADOR	Con vos hablo, hermosa fiera,	
	y con esotra zagala.	
	¿Mías no sois?	
PASCUALA.	Sí, señor;	
	mas no para cosas tales.	
COMENDADOR	Entrad, pasad los umbrales;	605
	hombres hay, no hayáis temor.	
LAURENCIA.	Si los alcaldes entraran,	
	que de uno soy hija yo,	
	bien huera entrar; mas si no...	
COMENDADOR	¡Flores!	
FLORES.	Señor...	
COMENDADOR	¡Qué reparan	610
	en no hacer lo que les digo?	
FLORES.	Entrá, pues.	
LAURENCIA.	No nos agarre.	
FLORES.	Entrad, que sois necias.	
PASCUALA.	Harre,	
	que echaréis luego el postigo.	
FLORES.	Entrad, que os quiere enseñar	615
	lo que trae de la guerra.	
COMENDADOR	Si entraren, Ortuño, cierra.	
LAURENCIA.	Flores, dejadnos pasar.	
ORTUÑO.	¡También venís presentadas	
	con lo demás!	
PASCUALA.	¡Bien a fe!	620

---

600.   *tirte ahuera*: a rustic form of *tírate afuera*, lit. = 'get away with you'.

601.   The Commander's metaphor, evoking again the Hunt of Love, recalls ironically those applied to himself and his men (cf. note to 161).

603–4.   On this conflict of attitudes, central to the play, see Salomon, 885, and Serrano, 45–7.

COMMANDER.	You two, remain.
LAURENCIA.	What is your Lordship's pleasure?
COMMANDER.	You were a sight too sour the other day.
	With me, by God!
LAURENCIA.	Does he mean you, Pascuala?
PASCUALA.	What, me? Not likely!
COMMANDER.	No, it's you I mean,

my pretty vixen, and your friend as well.
Don't you belong to me?

PASCUALA.	We do, my Lord,

but not the way you mean.

COMMANDER.	Come on indoors;

you needn't be afraid, there's men there too.

LAURENCIA.	It might be different if the magistrates

were there as well, since one's my father, but...

COMMANDER.	Flores!
FLORES.	My Lord...
COMMANDER.	How dare they hesitate

to do as I command?

FLORES.	Come in!
LAURENCIA.	Don't grab!
FLORES.	Come in, you're stupid.
PASCUALA.	Whoa, you'll shut the postern.
FLORES.	Come in, he wants to show you what he's brought.
COMMANDER.	Ortuño, if they enter, shut the gate. *He exits.*
LAURENCIA.	Flores, just let us pass.
ORTUÑO.	You two belong

with all the other offerings!

PASCUALA.	What a nerve!

600

605

612

---

606. *hayáis*: *haber*, for today's *tener*, was common at this time in such expressions (cf. 1136).

612. *Entrá* may be a rustic form of *Entrad* (cf. 1011, 2072, 2116), though in view of 613 & 615, we should perhaps read *Entrad*, as did H. *Agarre*, addressed to Flores (cf. 447), is an appropriate word, as LE comments, quoting Covarrubias on *agarrar*: 'Asir de alguno con la garra, como hacen las aves de rapiña.'

613. The use of *necias* is ironical, in view of 345. *Harre* is a rustic form of *arre*, often addressed to horses, &c., here expressing scorn.

	Desvíese, no le dé...		
FLORES.	Basta, que son extremadas.		
LAURENCIA.	¿No basta a vueso señor		
	tanta carne presentada?		
ORTUÑO.	La vuestra es la que le agrada.		625
LAURENCIA.	¡Reviente de mal dolor!	*Vanse.*	
FLORES.	¡Muy buen recado llevamos!		
	No se ha de poder sufrir		
	lo que nos ha de decir		
	cuando sin ellas nos vamos.		630
ORTUÑO.	Quien sirve se obliga a esto.		
	Si en algo desea medrar,		
	o con paciencia ha de estar,		
	o ha de despedirse presto.	*Vanse los dos, y...*	

... salgan el Rey don Fernando, la Reina doña Isabel, Manrique y acompañamiento.

ISABEL.	Digo, señor, que conviene	[*redondillas*] 635
	el no haber descuido en esto,	
	por ver [a] Alfonso en tal puesto,	
	y su ejército previene.	
	Y es bien ganar por la mano	
	antes que el daño veamos;	640
	que si no lo remediamos,	
	el ser muy cierto está llano,	
REY.	De Navarra y de Aragón	
	está el socorro seguro,	
	y de Castilla procuro	645
	hacer la reformación	
	de modo que el buen suceso	
	con la prevención se vea.	
ISABEL.	Pues vuestra Majestad crea	
	que el buen fin consiste en eso.	650
MANRIQUE.	Aguardando tu licencia	
	dos regidores están	
	de Ciudad Real: ¿entrarán?	
REY.	No les nieguen mi presencia.	

Just give me room, or I'll give you...
FLORES.   Give up,
they're too pig-headed.
LAURENCIA.   Won't your lord be sated   623
with all the flesh they've brought?
ORTUÑO.   Its yours he fancies.
LAURENCIA.   Let's hope he bursts!   *The girls exit.*
FLORES.   So much for our instructions!
He'll be unbearable when he finds out
we've come without them.
ORTUÑO.   That's the way it goes
if you're a servant; you must either suffer
in silence, and get on, or else get out!   *They exit.*

King Ferdinand, Queen Isabella, Don Manrique and attendants enter.
ISABELLA.   My Lord, we must make ready, now Alfonso   635
is so well placed, and mustering his men.
We should strike first, before he strikes at us;
there's clearly serious danger otherwise.
FERDINAND.   Navarre and Aragon are staunch behind us;
and once I manage to control Castile,
I trust wise planning will ensure our triumph.
ISABELLA.   Be sure, my Lord, such foresight will bear fruit.
MANRIQUE.   My Lord, two aldermen await your pleasure.
They're from Ciudad Real; are they to enter?
FERDINAND.   Why should I not receive them? Bid them welcome.

623–5. *carne*: Laurencia no doubt means to refer to both animal and female flesh; Ortuño's reply perhaps adds an even cruder anatomical allusion. Like 603–4 and 619–20, these lines present starkly the contrast between what the peasants properly offer and what the Commander improperly demands.

635. The gallery above the stage is not required at any point in the play; but it could be used for all the appearances of the Catholic Monarchs. The location of all their three scenes is indeterminate.

637. Like most recent editors, I insert [a] before *Alfonso*; but Lope's autographs suggest that in cases like this (cf. 465–6, 776, 1228 & 1325) he did not write one because it was contained (*embebida*) in the following or preceding *a* (see *El sembrar en buena tierra*, n. to 735; Keniston, 41.32). For cases in which *a* seems clearly not to have been intended, see n. to 121.

Salen dos regidores de Ciudad Real.

REGIDOR I.   Católico Rey Fernando,   [*romance*]   655
a quien ha enviado el cielo
desde Aragón a Castilla
para bien y amparo nuestro;
en nombre de Ciudad Real
a vuestro valor supremo   660
humildes nos presentamos,
el real amparo pidiendo.
A mucha dicha tuvimos
tener título de vuestros,
pero pudo derribarnos   665
deste honor el hado adverso.
El famoso don Rodrigo
Téllez Girón, cuyo esfuerzo
es en valor extremado,
aunque es en edad tan tierno,   670
Maestre de Calatrava,
él, ensanchar pretendiendo
el honor de la encomienda,
nos puso apretado cerco.
Con valor nos prevenimos,   675
a su fuerza resistiendo,
tanto, que arroyos corrían
de la sangre de los muertos.
Tomó posesión en fin;
pero no llegara a hacerlo   680
a no le dar Fernán Gómez
orden, ayuda y consejo.
El queda en la posesión,
y sus vasallos seremos;
suyos, a nuestro pesar,   685
a no remediarlo presto.

679–82. Lope in this scene follows in general (though not closely) *Chronica* 79rb; but the crucial role in the campaign ascribed to Fernán Gómez is a total invention.

681. *a no le dar*: object pronouns, though normally, as today, they followed

Two Aldermen from Ciudad Real enter.

1st ALDERMAN.   Most Catholic King Ferdinand,   655
whom Heaven in its mercy
has sent, from Aragon to Castile,
for our support and succour;
in suppliant humility
we appear before your might
as envoys from Ciudad Real
to seek your royal protection.
We held ourselves most fortunate
and proud to be your subjects;
but now the power of cruel fate
has stripped us of that name.
Rodrigo Téllez, that Girón
whose fortitude and valour
have won him the acclaim of all,
although he's still so young,
ambitious, doubtless, to enhance,
as Master of Calatrava,
the honour of his Order, laid
fierce siege to our fair city.
We opposed his force as best we could,
with resolute resistance,
to such effect, that streams of blood
flowed freely from the fallen.
He took possession, though, at last;   679
yet could not have succeeded
without the initiative, advice
and aid of Fernán Gómez.
And so it stands; Ciudad Real
and we, who would more gladly
be yours, your Majesty, are his,
unless you send and save us.

---

an infinitive, were not uncommonly placed before it at this time, for instance after a negative; see Keniston, 9.6 (cf. 903). Note the similar construction, with imperative forms, in 1148, 1235, 1536, 1543, 2385.

REY.	¿Dónde queda Fernán Gómez?
REGIDOR I.	En Fuente Ovejuna creo,
	por ser su villa, y tener
	en ella casa y asiento.
	Allí, con más libertad
	de la que decir podemos,
	tiene a los súbditos suyos
	de todo contento ajenos.
REY.	¿Tenéis algún capitán?
REGIDOR 2.	Señor, el no haberle es cierto,
	pues no escapó ningún noble
	de preso, herido o de muerto.
ISABEL.	Ese caso no requiere
	ser de espacio remediado,
	que es dar al contrario osado
	el mismo valor que adquiere;
	y puede el de Portugal,
	hallando puerta segura,
	entrar por Extremadura
	y causarnos mucho mal.
REY.	Don Manrique, partid luego,
	llevando dos compañías;
	remediad sus demasías,
	sin darles ningún sosiego.
	El Conde de Cabra ir puede
	con vos, que es Córdoba osado,
	a quien nombre de soldado
	todo el mundo le concede;
	que éste es el medio mejor
	que la ocasión nos ofrece.
MANRIQUE.	El acuerdo me parece
	como de tan gran valor.
	Pondré límite a su exceso
	si el vivir en mí no cesa.
ISABEL.	Partiendo vos a la empresa,
	seguro está el buen suceso.

Marginal line numbers: 690, 695, 700, 705, 710, 715, 720

Marginal stage note: [*redondillas*]

Stage direction: *Vanse todos, y...*

691–4. These lines, an obvious digression in the context, are ignored by the King; but they link the play's two plots, and imply similarities between the Commander's conduct and its effects in both.   For Serrano, 41, they are essentially inconsistent with what we know of the Commander so far, anticipate

FERDINAND.	And where is Fernán Gómez now?
1st ALDERMAN.	In Fuente Ovejuna,
	I should suppose, that's where he's placed
	his residence and stronghold,
	and there, in more licentious ways
	than we can well relate
	deprives its poor inhabitants
	of peace and happiness.
FERDINAND.	And has your cause no leader now?
2nd ALDERMAN.	None, sire, nor could it have,
	for every nobleman we had
	was captured, hurt or slain.
ISABELLA.	This matter must be set to rights
	without the least delay,
	for fear our foes, audacious now,
	may grow still more emboldened;
	the Portuguese Alfonso, once
	his access is assured,
	may march through Extremadura, and
	wreak havoc in our land.
FERDINAND.	Manrique, take two companies
	and lead them out at once.
	Allow the foe no respite till
	this wrong is remedied.
	Diego de Córdoba, the Count
	of Cabra, shall go with you,
	for all the world acknowledges
	his bravery as a soldier,
	and this appears the best resource
	our situation offers.
MANRIQUE.	Such a decision, sire, shows strength
	consistent with your valour.
	I shall indeed curb their excess
	or die in the attempt.
ISABELLA.	Our enterprise is in good hands;
	its triumph is assured. *All exit.*

691

707

709

719

---

what is to come, and so reveal an intention *ab initio* to write a play about 'the Tyrant'.

698.   H commented that this awkward line 'no parece de Lope; lo mismo sucede con varios trozos de la comedia'.

... salen Laurencia y Frondoso.

LAURENCIA.   A medio torcer los paños,   *[romance]*
                quise, atrevido Frondoso,
                para no dar que decir,   725
                desviarme del arroyo;
                decir a tus demasías
                que murmura el pueblo todo
                que me miras y que te miro,
                y todos nos traen sobre ojo.   730
                Y como tú eres zagal
                de los que huellan, brioso,
                y, excediendo a los demás,
                vistes bizarro y costoso,
                en todo el lugar no hay moza   735
                o mozo en el prado o soto,
                que no se afirme diciendo
                que ya para en uno somos;
                y esperan todos el día
                que el sacristán Juan Chamorro   740
                nos eche de la tribuna,
                en dejando los piporros.
                Y mejor sus trojes vean
                de rubio trigo en agosto
                atestadas y colmadas,   745
                y sus tinajas de mosto,
                que tal imaginación
                me ha llegado a dar enojo;
                ni me desvela ni aflige,
                ni en ella el cuidado pongo.   750

FRONDOSO.   Tal me tienen tus desdenes,
                bella Laurencia, que tomo,
                en el peligro de verte,
                la vida, cuando te oigo.
                Si sabes que es mi intención   755
                el desear ser tu esposo,
                mal premio das a mi fe.

LAURENCIA.   Es que yo no sé dar otro.

Laurencia and Frondoso enter.

LAURENCIA. So people wouldn't talk, I've had to leave   723
my washing half wrung out beside the stream
to tell you that you're going too far, Frondoso.
The whole town's whispering now "he fancies her",   728
"she fancies him"; they all keep watching us,
and since you're such a bold upstanding lad,
and dress a sight more smartly than the rest,
there's not a boy or girl now in the village   735
who isn't certain we're as good as married,
and waiting for the day when Juan Chamorro,
the sexton, sends us off, with pipers piping!   742
Good luck to them, say I; I hope at harvest
their granaries may be stuffed with golden grain,
their vats be full of unfermented wine;
but such a notion hasn't crossed my mind.
I'm just not bothered; couldn't give a damn.

FRONDOSO.   Your cruelty's too hurtful, dear Laurencia.
I feel I risk my life each time I see you;
and if you know I want to marry you,
it seems a poor reward.

LAURENCIA.   I can't do better.

723–6.   On the notional setting of this scene near an *arroyo* (in a *locus amoenus* clearly close to Fuente Ovejuna), cf. note to 210, and 782–4.   The washing which Laurencia mentions to Frondoso affords an almost bathetic contrast to the affairs of state which occupy Fernando and Isabella; but his supposed *demasías* toward her (soon to pale beside those of the Commander, which he will check) provide a verbal connection with the *demasías* and *exceso* of the Order of Calatrava, which the loyal noblemen are to limit (709, 719–20, 1322).

728–30.   Note how Laurencia is made to concede repeatedly, here and in 735–43 (and in 1297–1300), that the entire town is united in supposing that she and Frondoso will marry; see Casalduero, 34.

738.   *Para en uno son* was a phrase frequently spoken by bystanders at a marriage and included in wedding-songs (e.g. *Peribáñez*, 27, 145, 165). Stressing the indissoluble unity of the couple, it is used again of Frondoso and Laurencia in 1298 and 1545, and in 2037 of Ferdinand and Isabella.

741.   *tribuna*: 'lugar levantado a modo de corredor en las iglesias, adonde cantan los que ofician misa y vísperas, y las demás horas' (Covarrubias).

742.   *piporro* was lit. a kind of rustic bassoon.

FRONDOSO.   ¿Posible es que no te duelas
              de verme tan cuidadoso,   760
              y que imaginando en ti
              ni bebo, duermo ni como?
              ¿Posible es tanto rigor
              en ese angélico rostro?
              ¡Viven los cielos, que rabio!   765
LAURENCIA.   ¡Pues salúdate, Frondoso!
FRONDOSO.   Ya te pido yo salud,
              y que ambos como palomos
              estemos, juntos los picos,
              con arrullos sonorosos,   770
              después de darnos la iglesia.
LAURENCIA.   Dilo a mi tío Juan Rojo,
              que, aunque no te quiero bien,
              ya tengo algunos asomos.
FRONDOSO.   ¡Ay de mí! El señor es éste.   775
LAURENCIA.   Tirando viene [a] algún corzo.
              ¡Escóndete en esas ramas!
FRONDOSO.   ¡Y con qué celos me escondo!

Sale el Comendador.

COMENDADOR   No es malo venir siguiendo
              un corcillo temeroso,   780
              y topar tan bella gama.
LAURENCIA.   Aquí descansaba un poco
              de haber lavado unos paños;
              y así al arroyo me torno,
              si manda su señoría.   785

---

766. *saludar* = 'curar de mal de rabia por medio del soplo, saliva, y otras ceremonias que usan' (*Autoridades*); on the association of *rabiar* and *saludar* in Lope see P.

767–71. Frondoso's punning reply probably implies the notion that marriage is the best 'cure' for love; see e.g. *El perro del hortelano*, 961–4. Pigeons or doves are, as Covarrubias recalls, 'símbolo de los bien casados'; according to Pliny, X.52 they 'possess the greatest modesty, and adultery is unknown to either

FRONDOSO.   How can you not be moved to see me suffer,
              not eat, not drink, not sleep for thoughts of you.
              Can your angelic face wear such a frown?
              I shall go mad!
LAURENCIA.   You'd better take a cure!   766
FRONDOSO.   It's you I need to cure me, so we both
              can be at peace, like turtle-doves together,
              billing and cooing... once the priest has blessed us.
LAURENCIA.   Well, tell my uncle John. I'm not in love, mind,
              but must admit I do begin to feel...
FRONDOSO.   Oh, heavens, the Commander! Coming here!   775
LAURENCIA.   He must be stalking deer. Hide in those branches!
FRONDOSO.   I'll hide myself, but can I hide my feelings?

The Commander enters.

COMMANDER.   Well, well, I can't complain; I stalk my prey,
              a timid little deer, and in its place
              I come upon a more attractive quarry!
LAURENCIA.   I've just been washing clothes beside the stream,
              and came up here to rest; so now, your Lordship,
              with your permission, I'll go back to work.

---

sex; they do not violate the faith of wedlock, and they keep house in company'.
Note too that Frondoso specifically anticipates the hallowing of marriage by
church ritual (cf. 738, 740–2).

  775–81.   Sentimental banter and the imagery of innocence are interrupted,
almost predictably, by the appearance of the Commander (armed with an
emblematic crossbow).   As in countless other *comedias*, Lope now evokes a
wealth of motifs associated with the Hunt of Love.   Hunting, as well as 'una
imagen de la guerra', was traditionally in many countries an allegory of
courtship; but the allegory often 'degenerated' into the explicit replacement of
the quarry (most frequently a deer; see esp. Marcelle Thiebaux, *The Stag of
Love: the Chase in Medieval Literature*, Ithaca 1974) by a woman (as in the
ballad: 'Iba el Rey a cazar / .../ en vez de encontrar caza, / encontró una linda
romera'); see Edith Randam Rogers, *The Perilous Hunt: Symbols in Hispanic
and European Balladry*, University Press of Kentucky, 1980, and on our play the
study by Gerli.

COMENDADOR: Aquesos desdenes toscos
afrentan, bella Laurencia,
las gracias que el poderoso
cielo te dio, de tal suerte
que vienes a ser un monstro.   790
Mas si otras veces pudiste
huir mi ruego amoroso,
agora no quiere el campo,
amigo secreto y solo;
que tú sola no has de ser   795
tan soberbia, que tu rostro
huyas al señor que tienes,
teniéndome a mí en tan poco.
¿No se rindió Sebastiana,
mujer de Pedro Redondo,   800
con ser casadas entrambas,
y la de Martín del Pozo,
habiendo apenas pasado
dos días del desposorio?

LAURENCIA. Ésas, señor, ya tenían,.   805
de haber andado con otros,
el camino de agradaros,
porque también muchos mozos
merecieron sus favores.
Id con Dios tras vueso corzo;   810
que a no veros con la Cruz
os tuviera por demonio,
pues tanto me perseguís.

COMENDADOR ¡Qué estilo tan enfadoso!
Pongo la ballesta en tierra,   815
....
y a la prática de manos
reduzgo melindres.

LAURENCIA.   ¡Cómo!
¿Eso hacéis? ¿Estáis en vos?

Sale Frondoso, y toma la ballesta.

COMENDADOR ¡No te defiendas!

FRONDOSO.   Si tomo
la ballesta, ¡vive el cielo,   820
que no la ponga en el hombro!

COMMANDER.   Such fierce and coarse rebuffs, my fair Laurencia,
so ill become the graces Heaven's might
has showered upon you, that you seem a monster!
So far you've always managed to avoid
my fond attentions; now this friendly spot
shall be our sole and silent go-between.
Are you alone so proud, you turn your face
and scowl instead of smiling on your lord?   797
Didn't Redondo's wife, young Sebastiana,
though they were married, readily accede?   801
And what about Martín del Pozo's bride,
a bare two days from when they'd been betrothed?

LAURENCIA.   Those women knew, your Lordship, how to please you
because they'd travelled that same road before,
and many others had enjoyed their favours.
So now God speed, pursue your little deer;   810
I might well think, despite that Cross you wear,
you were a devil, you persecute me so.

COMMANDER.   What tedious talk! I'd best put down my bow,   815
and trust my hands to still such silly scruples.

LAURENCIA.   What are you doing? My Lord, are you yourself?

Frondoso enters, and picks up the crossbow.

COMMANDER.   Don't struggle so.

FRONDOSO.   If I pick up that bow,
I swear to God I shan't be shouldering arms!   821

---

790. *monstro*: Lope may never have used the modern spelling *monstruo* (see Poesse, 47).

797-8. A play on words, hard to render, between *tener* and *tener en poco*.

801. It seems improbable (*pace* LE &c.) that *casadas entrambas* can refer forward to *la de Martín del Pozo* as well as backward to *Sebastiana, / mujer de Pedro Redondo*. LE suggests alternatively that we read 800 as *y la de...;* Bl, more plausibly, that two lines (referring to another wife) are missing between 800 & 801. Note how Fernán Gómez boasts of his adulteries; cf. 967-70, &c.

810-2. Three strikingly resonant lines, which bring together dramatically the imagery of the Hunt of Love, the visual symbolism of the Cross of Calatrava, and the archetypal confrontation of hell and heaven (cf. 764, 788-90, 1143-7).

815-8. The Commander's words, after he has laid down his crossbow – a noble weapon – recall (comments Serrano, 33) the proverb: 'juego de manos, juego de villanos', and Laurencia's questions underline how inconsistent is his conduct with what can be expected of a nobleman.

COMENDADOR	Acaba, ríndete.
LAURENCIA.	¡Cielos, ayudadme agora!
COMENDADOR	Solos estamos; no tengas miedo.
FRONDOSO.	Comendador generoso, 825
	dejad la moza, o creed
	que de mi agravio y enojo
	será blanco vuestro pecho,
	aunque la Cruz me da asombro.
COMENDADOR	¡Perro villano!
FRONDOSO.	No hay perro. 830
	¡Huye, Laurencia!
LAURENCIA.	Frondoso, ¡mira lo que haces!
FRONDOSO.	¡Vete! *Vase.*
COMENDADOR	¡Oh,mal haya el hombre loco
	que se desciñe la espada!
	Que, de no espantar medroso 835
	la caza, me la quité.
FRONDOSO.	Pues pardiez, señor, si toco
	la nuez, que os he de apiolar.
COMENDADOR	Ya es ida; infame, alevoso,
	suelta la ballesta luego.
	Suéltala, villano. 840
FRONDOSO.	¿Cómo?
	Que me quitaréis la vida.
	Y advertid que amor es sordo,
	y que no escucha palabras
	el día que está en su trono. 845
COMENDADOR	¿Pues la espalda ha de volver
	un hombre tan valeroso
	a un villano? ¡Tira, infame!
	¡Tira, y guárdate, que rompo
	las leyes de caballero! 850

---

821. The line seems ambiguous; some editors and translators take it that Frondoso is initially anxious not to aim the bow at the Commander, although he soon does so.

825–9. *generoso* was ambiguous at this time, but its primary meaning was 'nobly-born' rather than today's 'generous'; See Covarrubias, and *El perro del*

COMMANDER.	Come on, give in.	
LAURENCIA.	Oh Heaven, defend me now!	
COMMANDER.	Don't be so scared, there's no-one here but us.	
FRONDOSO.	My Lord Commander, leave the girl alone,	825
	or else, believe me, though that Cross dismays me,	
	your breast shall be the target of my anger.	
COMMANDER.	You peasant dog!	
FRONDOSO.	A peasant, but no dog.	
	Laurencia, run!	
LAURENCIA.	Take care, Frondoso!	
FRONDOSO.	Go! *She exits.*	
COMMANDER.	The devil take the man who's such a fool	
	he ventures forth without his sword! To think	
	I was afraid it might alert my prey!	
FRONDOSO.	Well now, by God, if I just touch this trigger,	
	yours are the feet I'll need to truss, my Lord.	838
COMMANDER.	She's got away. You shameless wretch, you traitor,	
	give me that bow at once; at once, you peasant!	
FRONDOSO.	You mean, so you can kill me? Just remember,	
	when love is lord, it's deaf and doesn't listen.	
COMMANDER.	Am I, a nobleman, to turn my back	846
	and flee before a peasant? Shoot, you villain!	
	Shoot and be damned! You'll not make me transgress	
	the code of chivalry.	

---

hortelano, n. to 303–5. Note the tension between Frondoso's jealous outrage and his respect both for the Commander's birth and for the symbolism of his costume (see *Peribáñez*, 2843–9).

833–6.   These lines explain Fernán Gómez's defencelessness, but also emphasise that throughout the scene he has lacked the most obvious symbol of his rank.

838.   *apiolar*: For Corominas (I, 235), this is the first known use of the verb in the sense of *matar*; and in thieves' slang (Hidalgo, in 1609; see Hill, 12) it could mean 'seize' or 'imprison' (see also *Autoridades*).   But probably Frondoso intends its usual sense: fasten the feet of falcons, or of dead game; he is now the huntsman.   (Underhill, half a century ago, translated: 'I'll gyve you like a hawk').   Note that hunting could traditionally prove perilous, even fatal for the hunter, as in the ballads of Don Rodrigo de Lara, el Rey don Pedro and el Rey don Rodrigo.

846–50.   The Commander declares his unwillingness – to the point of death – to contravene, not any moral law, but the aristocratic code, which forbade him for instance to turn his back in flight from an inferior.

FRONDOSO.   Eso no.   Yo me conformo
               con mi estado, y pues me es
               guardar la vida forzoso,
               con la ballesta me voy.
COMENDADOR   ¡Peligro extraño y notorio!   855
               Mas yo tomaré venganza
               del agravio y del estorbo.
               ¡Que no cerrara con él!
               ¡Vive el cielo, que me corro!

851–4.   Frondoso's first words here seem, as Varey comments 24–5, to
contradict the situation, which offers as the act ends an almost emblematic
visualization of the inversion of social values brought about by the Commander's
conduct; yet he can truly claim that, in showing all the respect consistent with his
right of self-defence, he 'knows his place', unlike the nobleman.

FRONDOSO.   Ah no, my Lord.   851
              I know the duty due to rank, but claim
              the right to save my life; so I'll withdraw
              but keep the bow.   [*He exits.*]
COMMANDER.   By God, but that was dangerous!
              But I shall be avenged for this affront
              and this frustration. When I think I failed
              to close with him! By heaven, I swear I'm shamed! [*Exits.*]

The wedding scene, in the Teatro Español production, with kind permission.

ACTO SEGUNDO

Salen Esteban y Regidor 1.

ESTEBAN.   Así tenga salud, como parece   [*octavas reales*] 860
que no se saque más agora el pósito.
El año apunta mal, y el tiempo crece,
y es mejor que el sustento esté en depósito,
aunque lo contradicen más de trece.
REGIDOR 1.   Yo siempre he sido, al fin, deste propósito,   865
en gobernar en paz esta república.
ESTEBAN.   Hagamos dello a Fernán Gómez súplica.
No se puede sufrir que estos astrólogos
en las cosas futuras, y ignorantes,
nos quieran persuadir con largos prólogos   870
los secretos a Dios sólo importantes.
¡Bueno es que, presumiendo de teólogos,
hagan un tiempo el que después y antes!
Y pidiendo el presente lo importante,
al más sabio veréis más ignorante.   875
¿Tienen ellos las nubes en su casa,
y el proceder de las celestes lumbres?
¿Por dónde ven lo que en el cielo pasa,
para darnos con ello pesadumbres?
Ellos en [el] sembrar nos ponen tasa: 880
daca el trigo, cebada y las legumbres,
calabazas, pepinos y mostazas...
¡Ellos son, a la fe, las calabazas!

860D. Since Juan Rojo enters at 931, this must be the other alderman, Cuadrado (see cast-list).

860–7. Note the stress, in this quiet opening, on the town elders' prudence, calm, concern for the general good and respect for the Commander.

860. *Así tenga salud*: most editors make no comment, but the line is ambiguous. Combet translates: 'Ainsi puissiez-vous jouir d'une bonne santé...'; Larson: 'So the town may enjoy health...'; Blecua: 'Que yo conserve la salud, como así parece, si no me equivoco...'

ACT TWO

Esteban and First Alderman (Cuadrado) enter.

ESTEBAN.	I think it's wiser, as I hope to thrive,	860
	not to deplete the granary any further.	
	The year's not shaping well, the weather's worsening;	
	it seems to me we should keep stocks in hand,	
	although there's umpteen people don't agree.	
1st ALDERMAN.	I've always thought that was the prudent way	
	to keep our little commonwealth at peace.	
ESTEBAN.	We'd best petition the Commander, then.	
	What I can't stand is those astrologers,	868
	who claim to know the future, though they don't,	
	and lecture us, in lengthy disquisitions	
	on mysteries that are known to God alone.	
	It's so absurd, they talk like theologians,	
	and when it comes to pressing, present matters,	
	the wisest man amongst them knows the least.	
	Have they got clouds at home, or in their heads,	
	and stars and planets whirling in their courses?	
	How can they say what's shaping up in heaven,	
	so they can plague us with their prophecies?	
	They tell us what we should and shouldn't sow:	
	first wheat, then barley, vegetables, mustard,	
	cucumbers, pumpkins ... they're the pumpkin-heads!	

862. *el tiempo crece*: another ambiguous phrase.   Bl: 'el día se alarga y pronto vendrá la siega'; CM: 'el tiempo se hace largo, pasa despacio'.

868–91. On the frequency in Lope of such attacks on astrologers, see F.G. Halstead, 'The Attitude of Lope de Vega toward Astrology and Astronomy.' *HR*, 7 (1939), 205–19, esp. 206; what Ribbans (155) called 'the sturdy day-to-day empiricism of the countryman' undoubtedly has Lope's approval.

881. *daca*: 'lo mismo que da acá, o dame acá' (*Autoridades*).

Luego cuentan que muere una cabeza,
y después viene a ser en Trasilvania;   885
que el vino será poco, y la cerveza
sobrará por las partes de Alemania;
que se helará en Gascuña la cereza,
y que habrá muchos tigres en Hircania.
Y al cabo, al cabo, se siembre o no se siembre,   890
el año se remata por diciembre.

Salen el licenciado Leonelo y Barrildo.

LEONELO.	A fe que no ganéis la palmatoria,
	porque ya está ocupado el mentidero.
BARRILDO.	¿Como os fue en Salamanca?
LEONELO.	Es larga historia.
BARRILDO.	Un Bártulo seréis.
LEONELO.	Ni aun un barbero. 895

Es, como digo, cosa muy notoria
en esta facultad lo que os refiero.

BARRILDO.	Sin duda que venís buen estudiante.
LEONELO.	Saber he procurado lo importante.
BARRILDO.	Después que vemos tanto libro impreso,
	no hay nadie que de sabio no presuma. 900
LEONELO.	Antes que ignoran más siento por eso,

por no se reducir a breve suma,
porque la confusión, con el exceso,
los intentos resuelve en vana espuma;   905
y aquel que de leer tiene más uso,
de ver letreros sólo está confuso.

---

884. *una cabeza*: not a head of cattle (Colford: 'cow'), but a head of state,
&c.; Bl quotes *Autoridades*: 'Se llama también el Rey, los grandes personajes...'
   885. Transylvania, today part of Rumania, to Lope and his audience was both
remote and turbulent; Istvan Bocskay (1605–6) was succeeded in 1608 by Gabriel
Bathory, its most tyrannical ruler ever, in 1613 by Gabriel Bethlen.
   889. Hyrcania, a region south-east of the Caspian Sea, had been a byword for
its tigers since Antiquity; see Pliny, VIII, 25, and the familiar reference in
Dido's complaint against Aeneas, *Aeneid* IV, 367. For Esteban, all astrologers'
pronouncements prove banal.

They promise some great personage will perish,
and so it proves... in Transylvania;   885
wine, they inform us, won't be plentiful,
but beer will freely flow ... in Germany;
cherries will get the frost in Gascony,
and tigers be abundant in Hyrcania;   889
and in the long run, whether we sow or not,
say what they may, the year ends in December!

The Licentiate Leonelo and Barrildo enter.

LEONELO.   You won't be teacher's pet today, it seems;   892
                there's others here who've got to class before us.
BARRILDO.   How was the University?
LEONELO.   Oh, so-so.   894
BARRILDO.   I expect you know as much as Bartolo.
LEONELO.   Less than a barber, probably; it's just that
                what I was saying's common knowledge there.
BARRILDO.   You've come back quite the scholar, though, I must say.
LEONELO.   I've tried, I trust, to learn what seemed important.
BARRILDO.   You see so many printed books these days
                that everybody thinks they know it all.
LEONELO.   For that same reason, I think they know less,
                now learning's not condensed in summaries;
                so much is printed that it breeds confusion,
                knowledge is mixed with airy-fairy nonsense,
                and those who spend most time in reading find
                so many titles just bemuse the mind.

892–3.   The first pupil to arrive at school was given the teacher's *palmatoria*
(cane), and the privilege of administering punishments.   P quotes three other
metaphorical references in Lope.

893.   *el mentidero*: lit. 'el sitio o lugar donde se junta la gente ociosa a
conversación' (*Autoridades*).

894.   Lit. = 'How did it go with you in Salamanca? – It's a long story'.

894.   Barrildo refers, as Lope characters very frequently do (see P's note) to
the Italian jurist Bartolo de Sassoferrato (1314–1357).   Curiously, as pointed out
by Carter (319, 334), one of his works was a short *Tractatus de Tyrannia*.

No niego yo que de imprimir el arte
mil ingenios sacó de entre la jerga,
y que parece que en sagrada parte   910
sus obras guarda y contra el tiempo alberga;
éste las destribuye y las reparte.
Débese esta invención a Gutemberga,
un famoso tudesco de Maguncia,
en quien la fama su valor renuncia.   915
Mas muchos que opinión tuvieron grave
por imprimir sus obras la perdieron;
tras esto, con el nombre del que sabe,
muchos sus ignorancias imprimieron.
Otros, en quien la baja envidia cabe,   920
sus locos desatinos escribieron,
y con nombre de aquel que aborrecían
impresos por el mundo los envían.

BARRILDO.   No soy desa opinión.

LEONELO.   ¿El ignorante
es justo que se vengue del letrado?   925

BARRILDO.   Leonelo, la impresión es importante.

LEONELO.   Sin ella muchos siglos se han pasado,
y no vemos que en éste se levante
....
un Jerónimo santo, un Agustino.

BARRILDO.   Dejadlo, y asentaos, que estáis mohíno.   930

Salen Juan Rojo y otro labrador.

JUAN.   No hay en cuatro haciendas para un dote,
si es que las vistas han de ser al uso;
que el hombre que es curioso es bien que note
que en esto el barrio y vulgo anda confuso.

---

909. *jerga,* for LE, = jargon, rustic language (and those who use it); for P, = coarse peasant cloth (and those who wear it); for Bl, = rough, unfinished state; all are supported by *Autoridades* (*xerga*).

	I don't deny the art of printing's raised	
	a lot of wits above the common herd,	909
	and does appear to have saved and sanctified	
	their works against the ravages of time,	
	and spread the knowledge of them far and wide.	
	The art of printing was discovered by	
	one Gutenberg, from Mainz, in Germany,	
	to whom report ascribes its first invention;	
	but many men of weighty reputation	
	have found they lost it when their works were printed,	
	and many ignoramuses have published	918
	their follies as the work of learned men,	
	and other, envious men have written rubbish,	
	ascribed it to the man whose name they hated,	
	and spread it round as his, maliciously.	
BARRILDO.	I don't agree.	
LEONELO.	D'you think it's right and proper	924
	that ignorant men should so defame the learned?	
BARRILDO.	But printing is a great advance, Leonelo.	
LEONELO.	We've done without for many centuries now,	
	and I can't see that this one has produced	
	another Saint Jerome, or an Augustine!	
BARRILDO.	Leave it, sit down! You're getting in a temper.	

Juan Rojo and another Peasant enter.

JUAN ROJO.	Weddings, these days, with all the proper presents,	
	can cost you more than four whole family fortunes,	932
	as those who're critical should realise;	
	but people hereabouts don't understand.	

918–23.   Leonelo seems to echo Lope's own constant complaints about those who published inferior plays as his, and about envious detractors.

924–5.   I interpret Leonelo's lines as a question; all modern editions punctuate them as a statement.

932.   *las vistas* may refer to the formal meeting of a betrothed couple, or to the gifts exchanged at this time.

LABRADOR.	¿Qué hay del Comendador? ¡No os alborote!	935
JUAN.	¡Cuál a Laurencia en ese campo puso!	
LABRADOR.	¿Quién fue cual él tan bárbaro y lascivo?	
	Colgado le vea yo de aquel olivo.	

Salen el Comendador, Ortuño y Flores.

COMENDADOR.	Dios guarde la buena gente.	[*redondillas*]
REGIDOR.	¡Oh, señor!	
COMENDADOR.	¡Por vida mía,	940
	que se estén!	
ALCALDE.	Vusiñoría	
	adonde suele se siente,	
	que en pie estaremos muy bien.	
COMENDADOR.	Digo que se han de sentar.	
ESTEBAN.	De los buenos es honrar,	945
	que no es posible que den	
	honra los que no la tienen.	
COMENDADOR.	¡Siéntense! Hablaremos algo.	
ESTEBAN.	¿Vio vusiñoría el galgo?	
COMENDADOR.	Alcalde, espantados vienen	950
	esos criados de ver	
	tan notable ligereza.	
ESTEBAN.	Es una extremada pieza.	
	Pardiez, que puede correr	
	a un lado de un delincuente	955
	o de un cobarde en quistión.	

935–8. The unidentified peasant, as pointed out by Salomon, 854, can be interpreted as a kind of '*vox populi*'.

939–48. Note the tension created by the sudden appearance (did he hear 935–8?) of the Commander, whose very name provokes alarm (935). Those peasants who have seated themselves clearly rise out of proper respect; he, with increasing vehemence, insists that they sit.

941–3. If Alonso has entered, as seems likely (though there is no direction), these lines (and 997–8, 1009–10), with the prefix *Alcalde*, may be spoken by him (cf. note to 1009–10); if he has not, they may be spoken also by the other magistrate, Esteban (cf. note to 1317D).

PEASANT.	What news of the Commander? ... don't take on! 935
JUAN ROJO.	Did you hear how he treated young Laurencia?
PEASANT.	Whoever heard of such a lecherous savage?
	I'd like to see him swinging from that olive!

The Commander, Ortuño and Flores enter.

COMMANDER.	God save you all, good people.
ALDERMAN.	Ah, my Lord!
COMMANDER.	Don't rise, I pray!
MAGISTRATE.	May it please your Lordship sit
	here in your usual place, for we should stand.
COMMANDER.	I say you should be seated.
ESTEBAN.	Such an honour, 945
	your Lordship, is the courtesy of virtue,
	for those who have no honour cannot give it.
COMMANDER.	Be seated! Now, let us converse awhile.
ESTEBAN.	Your Lordship's seen the greyhound? 949
COMMANDER.	Yes, your worship.
	These men of mine were very much astonished;
	they'd never seen one that could run so fast.
ESTEBAN.	It is indeed a most outstanding creature;
	a match, I swear, for any arrant knave
	or errant coward it might be set to chase.

945–7.   Cf. 'Sienpre dan honrra los beunos; / el que la tiene la da'; *El primero Benavides*, 865–6 (the editors quote our passage and two similar proverbs).   Esteban acknowledges the Commander's condescension; but his phraseology (e.g. the double negative) suggests an ironic undercurrent.

949.   *el galgo*, presumably another present sent by the peasants, reintroduces the hunting motif, which is then developed.

COMENDADOR.	Quisiera en esta ocasión
	que le hiciérades pariente
	a una liebre que por pies
	por momentos se me va. 960
ESTEBAN.	Sí haré, par Dios. ¿Dónde está?
COMENDADOR.	Allá; vuestra hija es.
ESTEBAN.	¿Mi hija?
COMENDADOR.	Sí.
ESTEBAN.	Pues ¿es buena
	para alcanzada de vos?
COMENDADOR.	Reñilda, alcalde, por Dios. 965
ESTEBAN.	¿Cómo?
COMENDADOR.	Ha dado en darme pena.
	Mujer hay, y principal,
	de alguno que está en la plaza,
	que dio, a la primera traza,
	traza de verme.
ESTEBAN.	Hizo mal; 970
	y vos, señor, no andáis bien
	en hablar tan libremente.
COMENDADOR.	¡Oh, qué villano elocuente!
	¡Ah, Flores!, haz que le den
	la *Política*, en que lea, 975
	de Aristóteles.
ESTEBAN.	Señor,
	debajo de vuestro honor
	vivir el pueblo desea.
	Mirad que en Fuente Ovejuna
	hay gente muy principal. 980
LEONELO.	¿Vióse desvergüenza igual?
COMENDADOR.	Pues ¿he dicho cosa alguna
	de que os pese, Regidor?
REGIDOR.	Lo que decís es injusto;
	no lo digáis, que no es justo 985
	que nos quitéis el honor.

957–62. The central idea is surely one of *competition* (hare-coursing); but the phraseology may suggest (see Hall, 'Theme and Structure', 66) an unnatural *coupling* of hound and hare, or indeed hare and woman. R.E. Barbera, 'An Instance of Medieval Iconography in *Fuente Ovejuna*', RoN, 10 (1968), 160–2, recalls that the hare was a medieval symbol for the female sex organ.

COMMANDER.	I'd like to have you match the beast directly	957
	to a hare which keeps escaping my pursuit.	
ESTEBAN.	I shall, by God; where is it?	
COMMANDER.	There. Your daughter.	
ESTEBAN.	My daughter?	
COMMANDER.	Yes.	
ESTEBAN.	Is she fair game for you?	
COMMANDER.	Rebuke her for it, pray, your worship.	
ESTEBAN.	What?	

COMMANDER. She seems determined to displease me, though
another, one of note, indeed the wife   968
of someone in the square, at my contriving,
contrived at once to see me.

ESTEBAN. She did wrong;
and you, my Lord, are ill-advised to speak
so brazenly.

COMMANDER. What rustic eloquence!
Flores, arrange to give this man a copy
of Aristotle's *Politics* to read.

ESTEBAN. My Lord, the town is glad to live beneath
your honourable rule; but there are people
of consequence in Fuente Ovejuna.

LEONELO. Whoever saw such utter shamelessness?   981

COMMANDER. Well, Alderman, has something I've just said
upset you, maybe?

ALDERMAN. What you say is wrong.
Don't say such things; it can't be right for you
to take away our honour.

---

960. *hiciérades* = *hicierais*; on the survival of such forms, see *El perro del hortelano*, n. to 2467, and Y. Malkiel, *HR*, 17 (1949), 159–65.

968. *alguno que está en la plaza:* line 1011 will indicate (as the spectators have probably assumed) that this scene is set in the town square, so that the Commander probably means 'someone who is here now'; CM interprets 'someone important enough to reside in the square'.

969–70. The repetition of *traza*, rather than a *'redundancia'* (CM) is surely a pun.

COMENDADOR.	¿Vosotros honor tenéis?
	¡Qué freiles de Calatrava!
REGIDOR.	Alguno acaso se alaba
	de la Cruz que le ponéis,
	que no es de sangre tan limpia.
COMENDADOR.	¿Y ensúciola yo juntando
	la mía a la vuestra?
REGIDOR.	Cuando
	que el mal más tiñe que alimpia.
COMENDADOR.	De cualquier suerte que sea,
	vuestras mujeres se honran.
ALCALDE.	Esas palabras deshonran;
	las obras, no hay quien las crea.
COMENDADOR.	¡Qué cansado villanaje!
	¡Ah! Bien hayan las ciudades,
	que a hombres de calidades
	no hay quien sus gustos ataje.
	Allá se precian casados
	que visiten sus mujeres.
ESTEBAN.	No harán, que con esto quieres
	que vivamos descuidados.
	En las ciudades hay Dios
	y más presto quien castiga.
COMENDADOR.	¡Levantaos de aquí!
ALCALDE.	¡Que diga
	lo que escucháis por los dos!
COMENDADOR.	Salí de la plaza luego!
	No quede ninguno aquí.
ESTEBAN.	Ya nos vamos.
COMENDADOR.	¡Pues no ansí!

990

995

1000

1005

1010

987–94. The Commander mocks the peasants' claim to honour, which belongs only to crusading knights like himself. The Alderman recalls that peasants, as Old Christians, have less suspect bloodlines than many such (see for instance Salomon, pp. 824–5). The Commander bridles at what might seem a personal slur; the Alderman merely replies that evil acts always dishonour. *Alimpia* is a rustic form of *limpia*.

995–8. The Commander's proposition that sex with a nobleman honours any peasant woman is shameful; his behaviour is worse, unbelievable.

COMMANDER.	Do you have honour?	987
	You're holy knights of Calatrava, are you?	
ALDERMAN.	Some proudly wear, perhaps, the Cross you place	
	upon their breasts whose blood's less pure than ours.	
COMMANDER.	D'you mean to say, if I mix mine with yours,	
	yours is defiled?	
ALDERMAN.	Since evil deeds can't cleanse	
	but only stain...	
COMMANDER.	At all events, your women	995
	are honoured in the act.	
MAGISTRATE.	Your words are shameful;	
	your deeds, past all belief.	
COMMANDER.	What tedious yokels!	
	Thank heaven things are different in the cities,	1000
	where men of rank have none to thwart their wishes,	
	and husbands glory when their wives are courted.	
ESTEBAN.	They surely don't; you want us off our guard.	
	God's nearer there, and retribution swifter.	
COMMANDER.	Get out of here!	
MAGISTRATE.	How dare he speak like that	
	to men like us two?	
COMMANDER.	Leave the square at once!	1010
	Go, all of you.	
ESTEBAN.	We're going.	
COMMANDER.	Not like that!	

1000–8. The country v. city contrast again; but vice in the city may be less rife than is supposed, and is more subject to state justice, which should mirror God's.

1009–10. *los dos*: this makes most sense if the speaker is Alonso, protesting to Esteban about the Commander's lack of respect for the office both hold.

1013. *ansi*: Lope clearly preferred this form to *asi* or *assi* (see *El galán de la Membrilla*, n. to 21), but in the *Parte* text it appears only three times out of eleven (here, 1344 & 2320), perhaps reflecting the preference of a copyist or compositor. As 1009–10 anticipate, and 1015–6 & 1019–20 clarify, the peasants begin to exit in small groups, muttering together.

FLORES.	Que te reportes te ruego.	
COMENDADOR.	¡Querrían hacer corrillo	1015
	los villanos en mi ausencia!	
ORTUÑO.	Ten un poco de paciencia.	
COMENDADOR.	De tanta me maravillo.	
	Cada uno de por sí	
	se vayan hasta sus casas.	1020
LEONELO.	¿Cielo, que por esto pasas?	
ESTEBAN.	Ya yo me voy por aquí. *Vanse.*	
COMENDADOR.	¿Qué os parece desta gente?	
ORTUÑO.	No sabes disimular,	
	que no quieres escuchar	1025
	el disgusto que se siente.	
COMENDADOR.	¿Éstos se igualan conmigo?	
FLORES.	Que no es aqueso igualarse.	
COMENDADOR.	Y el villano ¿ha de quedarse	
	con ballesta y sin castigo?	1030
FLORES.	Anoche pensé que estaba	
	a la puerta de Laurencia;	
	y a otro, que su presencia	
	y su capilla imitaba,	
	de oreja a oreja le di	1035
	un beneficio famoso.	
COMENDADOR.	¿Dónde estará aquel Frondoso?	
FLORES.	Dicen que anda por ahí.	
COMENDADOR.	¿Por ahí se atreve a andar	
	hombre que matarme quiso?	1040
FLORES.	Como el ave sin aviso,	
	o como el pez, viene a dar	
	al reclamo o al anzuelo.	
COMENDADOR.	¡Que a un capitán cuya espada	
	tiemblan Córdoba y Granada	1045
	un labrador, un mozuelo	
	ponga una ballesta al pecho!	
	El mundo se acaba, Flores.	
FLORES.	Como eso pueden amores.	
	Y pues que vives, sospecho	1050
	que grande amistad le debes.	

1025. *que no quieren* is a possible reading; Ortuño may be criticizing the peasants' lack of understanding.   But more probably he is trying again to moderate his master's anger.

FLORES.	I beg you, sir, control yourself.
COMMANDER.	Those peasants 1015
	propose to prate and plot behind my back.
ORTUÑO.	Have patience, sir.
COMMANDER.	I wonder I've so much!
	Go home your separate ways, each man of you. 1020
LEONELO.	Oh heaven, can you abide this?
ESTEBAN	*I'm* going this way.
	The peasants exit.
COMMANDER.	What can you think of folk like that?
ORTUÑO.	You can't
	disguise the fact you don't care how they feel.
COMMANDER.	Do they think they're my equals?
FLORES.	Well, it wasn't
	equality they sought...
COMMANDER.	And that Frondoso,
	is he to keep my bow and go unpunished?
FLORES.	I saw a man last night I thought was him,
	wearing a cloak that looked like his, outside
	Laurencia's door, and gave him – as a favour – 1035
	a swingeing slash that scarred him ear to ear.
COMMANDER.	Where can he be?
FLORES.	He's still about, they say.
COMMANDER.	How dare he be, a man who meant to kill me?
FLORES.	We'll snare him soon, like an incautious bird,
	or catch him like a fish with a baited hook. 1041
COMMANDER.	To think a peasant lout could set a bow
	against the breast of one whose knightly sword
	Córdoba and Granada hold in awe!
	I tell you, Flores, the world is out of joint. 1048
FLORES.	It shows the power of love. And I suspect
	that if he spared your life, he must respect you. 1051

1035–6. Cf. '¿Herístela? – A tu servicio. / – ¡Por tu vida! – Un beneficio / de oreja a oreja le di'; *La vitoria por la honra*, AcN 10, 427a.

1041–3. Note this further occurrence, on Flores' lips, of the hunting motif.

1048–9. These two lines encapsulate the conflict and theme of the play. The Commander's *Weltanschauung* is doomed (and he with it), not merely by a young man's passion (as Flores maybe means) but by Love in the broadest sense.

1050–1. *grande amistad le debes* may mean *either* 'he showed love (respect) for you' *or* 'you should show love (gratitude) to him' (because he didn't kill you).

COMENDADOR.   Yo he disimulado, Ortuño,
que si no, de punta a puño,
antes de dos horas breves
pasara todo el lugar;   1055
que hasta que llegue ocasión
al freno de la razón
hago la venganza estar.
¿Qué hay de Pascuala?

FLORES.   Responde
que anda agora por casarse.   1060

COMENDADOR.   Hasta allá quiere fiarse...

FLORES.   En fin, te remite donde
te pagarán de contado.

COMENDADOR.   ¿Qué hay de Olalla?

ORTUÑO.   Una graciosa
respuesta.

COMENDADOR.   Es moza briosa.   1065
¿Cómo?

ORTUÑO.   Que su desposado
anda tras ella estos días
celoso de mis recados,
y de que con tus criados
a visitalla venías;   1070
pero que, si se descuida,
entrarás como primero.

COMENDADOR.   ¡Bueno, a fe de caballero!
Pero el villanejo cuida...

ORTUÑO.   Cuida, y anda por los aires. 1075

COMENDADOR.   ¿Qué hay de Inés?

FLORES.   ¿Cuál?

COMENDADOR.   La de Antón.

FLORES.   Para cualquier ocasión
te ha ofrecido sus donaires.
Habléla por el corral,
por donde has de entrar si quieres.   1080

COMENDADOR.   A las fáciles mujeres
quiero bien y pago mal.
Si éstas supiesen, oh Flores,
estimarse en lo que valen...

1059–63. Presumably this is not the Pascuala who is a major character. The review of 'likely ladies' on which the Commander now embarks is often used in plays by Lope and others to characterise male licentiousness.

COMMANDER.   I have concealed my rage; or else, Ortuño,
I should have decimated this whole town
in two short hours. But I'll restrain my anger
until the time is riper for revenge.
What news of that Pascuala?

ORTUÑO.   Well, she says   1059
she's on the verge of getting married now...

COMMANDER.   And wants to wait to settle my account?   1061

ORTUÑO.   To put off payment, yes; she'll come across.

COMMANDER.   What of Olalla, then?

ORTUÑO.   A bonny answer.

COMMANDER.   She's lively, that one; well?

ORTUÑO.   Says her fiancé
is watching her these days; my messages
and your being there so often with your servants
have made him jealous; when he's off his guard, though,
she'll let you in again.

COMMANDER.   That's good, I swear.
The bumpkin's careful, is he?

ORTUÑO.   He'll get careless.   1075

COMMANDER.   What of Inés?

ORTUÑO.   Which one?

COMMANDER.   Antonio's wife.

ORTUÑO.   Ready and willing, any time you like.
I chatted her up in their stable-yard.
That's your way in.

COMMANDER.   When women are that easy,
I take to them a lot, but give them little.
Ah Flores, girls like that don't know their worth.

1061–3. Note the play on words, significantly of commercial origin.

1072. *como primero* probably = 'as before', rather than 'as the first' (CM).
Note the erotic implication of *entrar* (cf. 1080).

1075. *Andar por los aires* = 'andar levantado de pensamiento, o hacer
diligencia para alguna cosa con grande presteza' (Covarrubias). Like Bl, I take it
as 'but he has his head in the clouds'; it may mean 'and he is watchful'.

FLORES.	No hay disgustos que se igualen	1085
	a contrastar sus favores.	
	Rendirse presto desdice	
	de la esperanza del bien;	
	mas hay mujeres también,	
	por que el Filósofo dice	1090
	que apetecen a los hombres	
	como la forma desea	
	la materia; y que esto sea	
	así, no hay de que te asombres.	
COMENDADOR.	Un hombre de amores loco	1095
	huélgase que a su accidente	
	se le rindan fácilmente,	
	mas después las tiene en poco;	
	y el camino de olvidar	1100
	al hombre más obligado	
	es haber poco costado	
	lo que pudo desear.	

Sale Cimbranos, soldado.

SOLDADO.	¿Está aquí el Comendador?	[*romance*]
ORTUÑO.	¿No le ves en tu presencia?	
SOLDADO.	¡Oh, gallardo Fernán Gómez!	1105
	Trueca la verde montera	
	en el blanco morrión,	
	y el gabán en armas nuevas;	
	que el Maestre de Santiago	
	y el Conde de Cabra cercan	1110
	a don Rodrigo Girón,	
	por la castellana Reina,	
	en Ciudad Real; de suerte	
	que no es mucho que se pierda	
	lo que en Calatrava sabes	1115
	que tanta sangre le cuesta.	
	Ya divisan con las luces,	
	desde las altas almenas,	

1085–6. These two lines are obscure; Flores may mean, by contrast with my version, that in the case of women like those mentioned there are no frustrations to diminish the pleasure of their favours, although....

FLORES.	Rebuffs are never enough to spoil the sport	1085
	of wearing women down, and when they yield	
	too readily, you lose the spice of waiting;	
	but there are some, as Aristotle says,	1089
	who long for us as matter longs for form;	
	there's nothing you should wonder at in that.	
COMMANDER.	Still, when a man's insane with love, he's happy	
	to have his passion quickly satisfied,	1096
	but afterwards he's little time for them.	
	The man who's most committed loses interest	
	when what he wanted wasn't hard to get.	

Cimbranos, a soldier, enters.

SOLDIER.	Is the Commander here?
ORTUÑO.	Why ask?
	He's standing there before you.
SOLDIER.	O gallant Fernán Gómez, now
	put off your cap of green
	and don your white-plumed helmet; change
	your cloak for bright new armour.
	The Master of Santiago and
	the mighty Count of Cabra,
	supporting Isabella's cause,
	surround the young Rodrigo.
	Ciudad Real is like to fall,
	the order of Calatrava
	within an ace of losing what
	you know cost so much blood.
	Already from its battlements
	by torchlight they discern

1089–93.   As usual, 'the Philosopher' is Aristotle (*Physics* I, 9).   As Morby says (*Dorotea* 89), there is scarcely an idea which appears more frequently in Lope.   On the distortion of Aristotle's meaning, in our passage in particular, see Dunn, esp. 196–7.

1096.   On *accidente*, as passion, unhealthy desire, see Weber de Kurlat, 681–2.

	los castillos y leones	
	y barras aragonesas.	1120
	Y aunque el Rey de Portugal	
	honrar a Girón quisiera,	
	no hará poco en que el Maestre	
	a Almagro con vida vuelva.	
	Ponte a caballo, señor,	1125
	que sólo con que te vean,	
	se volverán a Castilla.	
COMENDADOR.	No prosigas; tente, espera.	
	Haz, Ortuño, que en la plaza	
	toquen luego una trompeta.	1130
	¿Qué soldados tengo aquí?	
ORTUÑO.	Pienso que tienes cincuenta.	
COMENDADOR.	Pónganse a caballo todos.	
SOLDADO.	Si no caminas apriesa,	
	Ciudad Real es del Rey.	1135
COMENDADOR.	No hayas miedo que lo sea.	

Salen Mengo y Laurencia y Pascuala, huyendo.

PASCUALA.	No te apartes de nosotras.	[*redondillas*]
MENGO.	Pues ¿aquí tenéis temor?	
LAURENCIA.	Mengo, a la villa es mejor	
	que vamos unas con otras,	1140
	pues que no hay hombre alguno,	
	porque no demos con él.	
MENGO.	¡Que este demonio cruel	
	nos sea tan importuno!	
LAURENCIA.	No nos deja a sol ni a sombra.	1145
MENGO.	¡Oh, rayo del cielo baje	
	que sus locuras ataje!	
LAURENCIA.	Sangrienta fiera le nombra,	
	arsénico y pestilencia	
	del lugar.	
MENGO.	Hanme contado	1150
	que Frondoso, aquí en el prado,	
	para librarte, Laurencia,	
	le puso al pecho una jara.	
LAURENCIA.	Los hombres aborrecía,	
	Mengo; mas desde aquel día	1155
	los miro con otra cara.	
	¡Gran valor tuvo Frondoso!	

the lions and castles of Castile,   1119
and bars of Aragon;
and though the King of Portugal
may favour your Girón
he'll be well served if he returns
to Almagro with his life.
To horse, my Lord, without delay,
for if they only see you,
they'll hurry to Castile again.

COMMANDER. Enough, no more; attend me.
Ortuño, have them instantly
sound trumpets in the square.
How many soldiers have I here?

ORTUÑO. Some fifty, I believe.

COMMANDER. Let every man be mounted then.

SOLDIER. Unless you hasten there,
the King will have Ciudad Real.

COMMANDER. He shall not, never fear. *They exit.*

Mengo enters, with Laurencia and Pascuala, running.

PASCUALA. Don't leave us, Mengo.

MENGO.   Are you frightened here?

LAURENCIA. We find it best to go to town together,   1139
when there's no men about, in case we meet him.

MENGO. Why can't that wicked devil let us be?

LAURENCIA. In sun or shade, we're never safe from him.

MENGO. I pray to Heaven to strike him down and stop him,
the lunatic!

LAURENCIA.   The bloody beast, you mean,
the poisonous pestilence that plagues our town.

MENGO. They tell me young Frondoso set an arrow
against his chest, Laurencia, in the fields here,   1151
and saved you from him.

LAURENCIA.   Yes, I had no time
for men till then, but now I've changed my mind.

1119–20. The first allusion to the combined insignia of Castile and Leon (Isabella) and of Aragon (Ferdinand), an important visual symbol which will already have been brought on (635–722) and will appear throughout (1461–71, 1920–2027, 2071–2124, 2290–2453).

1139–40. These lines, 1151, 1204, and 1245 serve to shift the scene, vaguely, to the countryside outside Fuente Ovejuna.

	Pienso que le ha de costar	
	la vida.	
MENGO.	Que del lugar	
	se vaya, será forzoso.	
LAURENCIA.	Aunque ya le quiero bien,	1160

Pienso que le ha de costar
la vida.

MENGO. Que del lugar
se vaya, será forzoso.

LAURENCIA. Aunque ya le quiero bien, 1160
eso mismo le aconsejo;
mas recibe mi consejo
con ira, rabia y desdén;
y jura el Comendador 1165
que le ha de colgar de un pie.

PASCUALA. ¡Mal garrotillo le dé!

MENGO. Mala pedrada es mejor.
¡Voto al sol, si le tirara
con la que llevo al apero, 1170
que al sonar el crujidero,
al casco se la encajara!
No fue Sábalo, el romano,
tan vicioso por jamás.

LAURENCIA. Heliogábalo dirás, 1175
más que una fiera inhumano.

MENGO. Pero Galván, o quien fue,
que yo no entiendo de historia;
mas su cativa memoria
vencida déste se ve. 1180
¿Hay hombre en naturaleza
como Fernán Gómez?

PASCUALA.   No,
que parece que le dio
de una tigre la aspereza.

Sale Jacinta.

JACINTA. ¡Dadme socorro, por Dios, 1185
si la amistad os obliga!

LAURENCIA. ¿Qué es esto, Jacinta amiga?

PASCUALA. Tuyas lo somos las dos.

JACINTA. Del Comendador criados,
que van a Ciudad Real, 1190
más de infamia natural
que de noble acero armados,

1170. *la que llevo al apero: honda* is understood, rather as a knight often refers to his *espada* as 'la que llevo al lado'. *Apero* lit. = farm tools or animals.

	He was so brave; and yet I think it may	
	cost him his life.	
MENGO.	He'll have to leave the town.	
LAURENCIA.	I tell him so, although I'm fond of him,	
	but that just makes him angry, fierce and scornful,	
	though the Commander swears he'll string him up.	
PASCUALA.	Let's hope he's stricken with the croup!	
MENGO.	No, stoned!	
	If I brought out the sling I mind the sheep with,	1170
	and just let fly, by God, the cords would crack	
	and split his head apart! That Hell-of-a-gabbler	1173
	of Ancient Rome was never half as nasty.	
LAURENCIA.	You must mean Heliogabalus, the tyrant;	
	worse than a beast, he was.	
MENGO.	I'm no historian,	
	but Harry the Gobbler, or whatever you call him,	
	never had such an evil reputation.	
	Did Nature ever spawn a creature like him?	
PASCUALA.	It's given him the temper of a tigress.	

Jacinta enters.

JACINTA.	Help me, for Heaven's sake, if you're my friends!	
LAURENCIA.	Of course we are, Jacinta, what's the matter?	
PASCUALA.	We're both your friends.	
JACINTA.	It's the Commander's men,	1189
	they're making for Ciudad Real, not armed	
	with noble steel, but base depravity,	

1173–80.   Mengo tries to allude to the tyrannical Roman emperor (A.D. 204–222), mentioned elsewhere by Lope (e.g. *La prueba de los amigos*, lines 2832–3), but calls him *Sábalo* (a fish, the shad); corrected, he comes up with *Pero* (a rustic form of *Pedro*) and *Galván*, the name of a Moorish ballad-villain who abducted and cruelly ill-treated Moriana.   P recalls the proverbial phrase 'no me conociera Galván', and cites examples of other rustics' errors; we may add Pelayo's references in *El mejor alcalde, el Rey*, 195–6, to 'el rey Baúl', 'Badil' and 'un gigante que olía' and Marina's in *El Conde Fernán González*, BAE 196, 1156 to 'un tigre arcediano' (= hircano, cf. 889).   The whole passage is a parody of the topos of describing present-day characters as 'outdoing' archetypes of Antiquity.

1189–93.   Note the integration of 'main' and 'secondary' actions (cf. 1214–3).

	me quieren llevar a él.	
LAURENCIA.	Pues, Jacinta, Dios te libre,	
	que cuando contigo es libre.	1195
	conmigo será cruel.	*Vase.*
PASCUALA.	Jacinta, yo no soy hombre	
	que te puedo defender.	*Vase.*
MENGO.	Yo sí lo tengo de ser;	
	porque tengo el ser y el nombre.	1200
	Llégate, Jacinta, a mí.	
JACINTA.	¿Tienes armas?	
MENGO.	Las primeras	
	del mundo.	
JACINTA.	¡Oh, si las tuvieras!	
MENGO.	Piedras hay, Jacinta, aquí.	

Salen Flores y Ortuño.

FLORES.	¿Por los pies pensabas irte?	1205
JACINTA.	Mengo, ¡muerta soy!	
MENGO.	Señores,	
	¿a estos pobres labradores...?	
ORTUÑO.	Pues ¿tú quieres persuadirte	
	a defender la mujer?	
MENGO.	Con los ruegos la defiendo,	1210
	que soy su deudo, y pretendo	
	guardalla, si puede ser.	
FLORES.	Quitalde luego la vida.	
MENGO.	¡Voto al sol, si me emberrincho	
	y el cáñamo me descincho,	1215
	que la llevéis bien vendida!	

Salen el Comendador y Cimbranos.

COMENDADOR.	¿Qué es eso? ¿A cosas tan viles	
	me habéis de hacer apear?	
FLORES.	Gente deste vil lugar,	
	que ya es razón que aniquiles,	1220
	pues en nada te da gusto,	
	a nuestras armas se atreve.	

1205. 'Irse por *pies*. Phrase con que se explica que alguno debió a su ligereza el ponerse en cobro, o escapar...' (*Autoridades*); cf. 959–60.

	and mean to take me to him.	
LAURENCIA.	God must help you,	
	Jacinta, then. I can't; he may be shameless	
	toward you, but he'd be terrible to me.	*Exit.*
PASCUALA.	I'm not a man, Jacinta, I can't save you.	*Exit.*
MENGO.	I am by name and nature, though; I'll be one.	
	Stand here by me.	
JACINTA.	But have you any weapons?	
MENGO.	The first God gave us.	
JACINTA.	Oh, I wish you had!	
MENGO.	Look here, Jacinta, there are stones enough.	1204

Flores and Ortuño enter.

FLORES.	You thought you'd get away?	
JACINTA	I'm frightened, Mengo!	
MENGO.	But sirs, why treat poor peasant folk like us...	
ORTUÑO.	D'you mean you're daring to defend the woman?	
MENGO.	By asking you to, yes. And I'm her kinsman;	
	it's my job to protect her if I can.	
FLORES.	We'll have his life for this!	
MENGO.	By God, if I	1214
	get angry, and let fly this hempen sling,	
	you'll find you pay a heavy price for it!	

The Commander and Cimbranos enter.

COMMANDER.	What trifle's this you're making me dismount for?
FLORES.	Folk from this filthy town, which you'd be right
	to annihilate, they give you so much trouble;
	they think they dare defy our might.

1214–6.   Cf. *La carbonera*, AcN 10, 734a: 'MENGA.   'Por los órganos de Dios, / y por los benditos cregos, / que os mate si me emberrincho'. *Emberrincharse*: 'Enfadarse con demasía, tomarse de cólera y rabia. Es voz baja y vulgar' (*Autoridades*). *Cáñamo*: 'Metaphóricamente se toma por las cosas que se hacen de cáñamo, como la honda' (*Autoridades*). Mengo's heroic stand emblematically recalls the story of David and Goliath, immensely popular in contemporary art and literature (cf. 1171–4, 1202–4); see *El vellocino de oro*, BAE 190, 1106: 'aquél del peto de luciente plata, / ... / es el pastor que derribó el gigante / a los cercos de cáñamo tronante.'

MENGO.	Señor, si piedad os mueve
	de soceso tan injusto,
	castigad estos soldados,
	que con vuestro nombre agora
	roban una labradora
	[a] esposo y padres honrados;
	y dadme licencia a mí
	que se la pueda llevar.
COMENDADOR.	Licencia les quiero dar...
	para vengarse de ti.
	¡Suelta la honda!
MENGO.	Señor!...
COMENDADOR.	Flores, Ortuño, Cimbranos,
	con ella le atad las manos.
MENGO.	¿Así volvéis por su honor?
COMENDADOR.	¿Qué piensan Fuente Ovejuna
	y sus villanos de mí?
MENGO.	Señor, ¿en qué os ofendí,
	ni el pueblo, en cosa ninguna?
FLORES.	¿Ha de morir?
COMENDADOR.	No ensuciéis
	las armas, que habéis de honrar
	en otro mejor lugar.
ORTUÑO.	¿Qué mandas?
COMENDADOR.	Que lo azotéis.
	Llevalde, y en ese roble
	le atad y le desnudad,
	y con las riendas...
MENGO.	¡Piedad!
	¡Piedad, pues sois hombre noble!
COMENDADOR.	... azotalde, hasta que salten
	los hierros de las correas.
MENGO.	¿Cielos, a hazañas tan feas
	queréis que castigos falten?
COMENDADOR.	Tú, villana, ¿por qué huyes?
	¿Es mejor un labrador
	que un hombre de mi valor?
JACINTA.	¡Harto bien me restituyes
	el honor que me han quitado
	en llevarme para ti!
COMENDADOR.	¿En quererte llevar?
JACINTA.	Sí,

1225

1230

1235

1240

1245

1250

Vanse.

1255

MENGO.	My Lord,
	have pity on us when we're so ill treated;
	punish these men who've so misused your name,
	stealing this peasant woman from her husband
	and honoured parents. Give me leave, my Lord,
	to take her home.
COMMANDER.	I'll give them leave instead
	to take revenge. Give me that sling!
MENGO.	My Lord!
COMMANDER.	Flores, Ortuño! Tie his hands, Cimbranos.
MENGO.	Is this how you defend a woman's honour?
COMMANDER.	Who do they think I am, these peasant folk
	of Fuente Ovejuna?
MENGO.	But, my Lord,
	how have the town or I offended you?
FLORES.	Are we to kill him?
COMMANDER.	No, don't stain your swords;
	they'll have more honourable work elsewhere.
ORTUÑO.	What shall we do then?
COMMANDER.	Flog him. See that oak?
	Tie him to that, strip him and use your reins...
MENGO.	Mercy, my Lord, as you're a nobleman!
COMMANDER.	... to leather him until the brasses fly!
MENGO.	Oh heavens, can you leave such crimes unpunished?

1245

1247

The servants and Mengo exit.

COMMANDER.	What about you? Why were you running, woman?
	You'd spurn a man of my rank for a peasant?
JACINTA.	You show your rank, my noble lord, I must say,
	if you restore the honour they've destroyed
	by abducting me yourself!
COMMANDER.	Abducting you?
JACINTA.	Yes, sir; my father is a man of honour,

1224. *soceso*: a rustic form of *suceso* (contrast 647, 722, 1316, 2016, 2443).

	porque tengo un padre honrado,	1260
	que si en alto nacimiento	
	no te iguala, en las costumbres	
	te vence.	
COMENDADOR.	Las pesadumbres	
	y el villano atrevimiento	
	no tiemplan bien un airado.	1265
	¡Tira por ahí!	
JACINTA.	¿Con quién?	
COMENDADOR.	Conmigo.	
JACINTA.	Míralo bien.	
COMENDADOR.	Para tu mal lo he mirado.	
	Ya no mía, del bagaje	
	del ejército has de ser.	1270
JACINTA.	No tiene el mundo poder	
	para hacerme, viva, ultraje.	
COMENDADOR.	Ea, villana, camina.	
JACINTA.	¡Piedad, señor!	
COMENDADOR.	No hay piedad.	
JACINTA.	Apelo de tu crueldad	1275
	a la justicia divina.	*Llévanla y vanse, y ...*

... salen Laurencia y Frondoso.

LAURENCIA.	¿Cómo así a venir te atreves,	*[redondillas]*
	sin temer tu daño?	
FRONDOSO.	Ha sido	
	dar testimonio cumplido	
	de la afición que me debes.	
	Desde aquel recuesto vi	1280
	salir al Comendador,	
	y, fiado en tu valor,	
	todo mi temor perdí.	
	¡Vaya donde no le vean	1285
	volver!	
LAURENCIA.	Tente en maldecir,	
	porque suele más vivir	
	al que la muerte desean.	
FRONDOSO.	Si es eso, ¡viva mil años!	
	y así se hará todo bien,	1290
	pues deseándole bien,	
	estarán ciertos sus daños.	
	Laurencia, deseo saber	

	who may not be as nobly born as you, but acts more nobly.	
COMMANDER.	When a man is angry, such jibes and rustic rudeness don't appease him. Come on!	
JACINTA.	Who with?	
COMMANDER.	With me!	
JACINTA.	Take care, my Lord!	
COMMANDER.	Take care? Yes, I'll take care of you; you shan't be my wench now, but army property.	1269
JACINTA.	While I can breathe, no power on earth can wrong me.	
COMMANDER.	On your way, peasant slut!	
JACINTA.	My Lord, have mercy!	1274
COMMANDER.	You'll find no mercy here.	
JACINTA.	Then I appeal against your cruelty to the throne of God.	

She is carried off; all exit.

Laurencia and Frondoso enter.

LAURENCIA.	How dare you come here, don't you know it's dangerous?	1277
FRONDOSO.	It only goes to show how much I love you. I saw his Lordship leaving, from the hillside, and had such faith in you, I lost all fear. Let's hope we've seen the last of him!	
LAURENCIA.	Don't curse him; the man most people hope will die lives longest.	
FRONDOSO.	If that's the case, I'll hope he'll live forever and so make sure he dies, and put things right. But now, Laurencia, all I want to know	

1265. *tiemplan: templar* is not regularly radical-changing today, but Lope wrote both *templan* and *tiemplan*; see *El perro del hortelano*, n. to 1118–9.

1266. *tirar* is surely *not* used here (*pace* Weber de Kurlat, 683) in an erotic sense.

1269. *bagaje:* 'Vocablo castrense; sinifica todo aquello que es necesario para el servicio del exército, assí de ropas como de vituallas, armas escusadas y máquinas' (Covarrubias); see *El sufrimiento premiado*, n. to 1167.

1277–82. The emptying of the stage implied a probable shift of locale; these lines, 1311–3, 1353–5 and 1429–30 suggest that we are somewhere in Fuente Ovejuna, near Juan Rojo's house but not in the square.

si vive en ti mi cuidado,
y si mi lealtad ha hallado 1295
el puerto de merecer.
  Mira que toda la villa
ya para en uno nos tiene,
y de cómo a ser no viene
la villa se maravilla. 1300
  Los desdeñosos extremos
deja, y responde no o sí.

LAURENCIA. Pues a la villa y a ti
respondo... que lo seremos.

FRONDOSO.   Deja que tus plantas bese 1305
por la merced recebida,
pues el cobrar nueva vida
por ella es bien que confiese.

LAURENCIA.   De cumplimientos acorta,
y, para que mejor cuadre, 1310
habla, Frondoso, a mi padre,
pues es lo que más importa,
  que allí viene con mi tío;
y fía que ha de tener
ser, Frondoso, tu mujer, 1315
buen suceso.

FRONDOSO.   En Dios confío.   *Escóndese.*

Salen Esteban alcalde, y el Regidor.

ALCALDE.   Fue su término de modo
que la plaza alborotó.
En efeto, procedió
muy descomedido en todo. 1320
  No hay a quien admiración
sus demasías no den.
La pobre Jacinta es quien
pierde por su sinrazón.

	is, can you care for me, has my persistence	1294
	not won your love? You must know all the town	
	thinks of us two as one, and nobody	1298
	can understand we're not as good as married.	
	Stop spurning me, and answer yes or no.	
LAURENCIA.	Then you and all the town had better know...	
	my answer's yes.	
FRONDOSO.	I kiss your feet for it;	1305
	it's given me new life, I swear it has.	
LAURENCIA.	Cut out the compliments, and ask my father,	1311
	since that's the proper thing; look, there he is,	
	just coming, with my uncle. See him now.	
	Don't worry, it'll be all right, Frondoso;	
	I'll be your wife.	
FRONDOSO.	I pray to God you will! *(She) hides.*	1316

Esteban (the Magistrate), and the Alderman (Juan Rojo) enter.

MAGISTRATE.	Really, the way he acted was outrageous;	
	everyone in the square was scandalised.	
	We're all astonished by his wild excesses,	1322
	and now he's ruined poor Jacinta too.	

1294. *cuidado* = loving concern, love; 'término abstracto especializado para el amor en la esfera de los sentimientos elevados, no de las bajas pasiones ... significante frecuentísimo en el vocabulario del amor en Lope' (F. Weber de Kurlat, 682). See *El perro del hortelano*, n. to 689.

1297–1304. Note again (cf. note to 729–31) how the marriage is said to be expected – willed, even – by the entire town.

1301. *extremos:* 'demonstraciones o expressiones excesivas' (*Autoridades*).

1305–8. Frondoso's offer to kiss Laurencia's feet for her favour may be a jokey reference to a purely verbal courtly formula; but his conventional phraseology throughout this scene stresses the essential nobility of his *amor purus*.

1316D. It is Laurencia who hides, until called at 1405; Frondoso remains on stage, though not noticed by the newcomers until 1315.

1317D. The alderman with Esteban must be Juan Rojo (see 772, 1313); there is no need to suppose (*pace* P, LE 3) that other characters enter, if we read *Reg.* I before 1387–8 as an error for *Reg.*, and assume that *Alcalde* and *Esteban* are the same speaker. Clearly 1393–6, at least, are spoken by Esteban.

1317. *término:* 'forma o modo de portarse, u hablar en el trato comun' (*Autoridades*). cf. 2420.

REGIDOR.	Ya [a] los Católicos Reyes,	1325
	que este nombre les dan ya,	
	presto España les dará	
	la obediencia a sus leyes.	
	Ya sobre Ciudad Real,	
	contra el Girón que la tiene,	
	Santiago a caballo viene	1330
	por capitán general.	
	Pésame, que era Jacinta	
	doncella de buena pro.	
ALCALDE.	¿Luego a Mengo azotó?	1335
REGIDOR.	No hay negra bayeta o tinta	
	como sus carnes están.	
ALCALDE.	Callad, que me siento arder,	
	viendo su mal proceder	
	y el mal nombre que le dan.	1340
	Yo, ¿para qué traigo aquí	
	este palo sin provecho?	
REGIDOR.	Si sus criados lo han hecho,	
	¿de qué os afligís ansí?	
ALCALDE.	¿Queréis más? Que me contaron	1345
	que a la de Pedro Redondo	
	un día, que en lo más hondo	
	deste valle la encontraron,	
	después de sus insolencias,	
	a sus criados la dio.	1350
REGIDOR.	Aquí hay gente. ¿Quién es?	
FRONDOSO.	Yo,	
	que espero vuestras licencias.	
REGIDOR.	Para mi casa, Frondoso,	
	licencia no es menester;	
	debes a tu padre el ser,	1355
	y a mí otro ser amoroso.	
	Hete criado, y te quiero	
	como a hijo.	
FRONDOSO.	Pues, señor,	
	fiado en aquese amor,	
	de ti una merced espero.	1360
	Ya sabes de quién soy hijo.	
ESTEBAN.	¿Hate agraviado ese loco	
	de Fernán Gómez?	
FRONDOSO.	No poco.	
ESTEBAN.	El corazón me lo dijo.	

ALDERMAN.	The Catholic Monarchs, as they're called already, will soon make Spain respect the rule of law. Santiago as their Captain-General's riding to take Ciudad Real from that Girón. I'm sorry for Jacinta, though; now she was such a decent girl.
MAGISTRATE.	And what of Mengo? You say he had him flogged?
ALDERMAN.	You've not seen flannel as red or black as his poor flesh is now.
MAGISTRATE.	Don't tell me any more, it makes me furious to hear how wickedly the wretch behaves, so that we all revile his very name. Why do I bear this staff, when it's so useless?
ALDERMAN.	Why be so upset? It was his men who did it.
MAGISTRATE.	There's more besides; the other day, I've heard, they came across Pedro Redondo's wife down in the valley, and after he himself had shamed the girl, he gave her to his servants.
ALDERMAN.	There's someone here. Who is it?
FRONDOSO.	It's Frondoso. I hoped I might have leave to speak to you.
ALDERMAN.	You never need my leave, you're always welcome. Your father may have sired you, but you know I'm every bit as fond of you as he is. I've watched you grow and loved you like a son.
FRONDOSO.	I know you have, that's why I dare to hope, sir, you'll grant me what I ask. You know my parents...
ESTEBAN.	What is it? Has that madman Fernán Gómez done you some wrong, my lad?
FRONDOSO.	He has indeed.
ESTEBAN.	I knew it in my bones.

Line markers in right margin: 1342 (at "Why do I bear this staff, when it's so useless?"), 1345 (at "There's more besides; the other day, I've heard,"), 1353 (at "You never need my leave, you're always welcome.")

1325–34. The apparent irrelevance of the alderman's response to the story of Jacinta, to which he returns after 8 lines, serves in fact to underline again the connection between the 'main' and 'secondary' actions, and the necessity of curbing the Commander's *demasías* (1322, cf. n. to 724–8) in both.

1342. *este palo:* the magistrate refers to the *vara* or staff of office he carries throughout, the visual symbol of his authority (and as such the counterpart of the nobleman's weapons). Cf. 1631–6, 1691–4.

1343–4. The alderman perhaps assumes, sarcastically, that Fernán Gómez will misrepresent what happened.

1345–50. This may be a truer version than the Commander's (799–800) of

| FRONDOSO. | Pues, señor, con el seguro | 1365 |

FRONDOSO.   Pues, señor, con el seguro   1365
                        del amor que habéis mostrado,
                        de Laurencia enamorado,
                        el ser su esposo procuro.
                        Perdona si en el pedir
                        mi lengua se ha adelantado,
                        que he sido en decirlo osado,   1370
                        como otro lo ha de decir.
ESTEBAN.   Vienes, Frondoso, a ocasión
                        que me alargarás la vida,
                        por la cosa más temida   1375
                        que siente mi corazón.
                        Agradezco, hijo, al cielo
                        que así vuelvas por mi honor,
                        y agradézcole a tu amor
                        la limpieza de tu celo.   1380
                        Mas, como es justo, es razón
                        dar cuenta a tu padre desto;
                        sólo digo que estoy presto,
                        en sabiendo su intención,
                        que yo dichoso me hallo   1385
                        en que aqueso llegue a ser.
REGIDOR I.   De la moza el parecer
                        tomad, antes de acetallo.
ALCALDE.   No tengáis deso cuidado,
                        que ya el caso está dispuesto;   1390
                        antes de venir a esto,
                        entre ellos se ha concertado.
                        En la dote, si advertís,
                        se puede agora tratar;
                        que por bien os pienso dar   1395
                        algunos maravedís.
FRONDOSO.   Yo dote no he menester;
                        deso no hay que entristeceros.
REGIDOR.   ¡Pues que no la pide en cueros
                        lo podéis agradecer!   1400
ESTEBAN.   Tomaré el parecer della:
                        si os parece, será bien.
FRONDOSO.   Justo es, que no hace bien
                        quien los gustos atropella.
ESTEBAN.   ¡Hija! ¡Laurencia!
LAURENCIA.   ¿Señor?   1405
ESTEBAN.   Mirad si digo bien yo.

FRONDOSO.   Well sir, the love
you've always shown me, emboldens me to say...
I love Laurencia, and I want to marry her.
Forgive my tongue for speaking out so freely;
perhaps I've been too bold, and someone else...   1371
ESTEBAN.   Why no, Frondoso, your request's so timely
I feel it gives me another lease of life,
and sets my heart's most anxious fears to rest.
I offer thanks to Heaven that you, my lad,
should do me so much honour, and to you
for showing such love and virtuous concern.
It would be right and proper, though, for you   1381
to tell your father first; I'll only say
that once we know his mind, I'll be quite willing
and only too delighted to agree.
ALDERMAN 1.   Before you agree, you ought to ask the girl!
MAGISTRATE.   Don't worry, they'll have settled it between them;
they've both agreed before it's come to this.
But now, you know, we could discuss the dowry;   1393
I'll see you get a tidy bit of cash.
FRONDOSO.   You needn't worry, I don't need a dowry.
ALDERMAN.   He'll have her as she stands; you should be glad.
He might have said he'd take her from you naked!
ESTEBAN.   I'd best see what she says, if you don't mind.
FRONDOSO.   Of course, that's only right; it's always wrong   1403
to ride roughshod over other people's wishes.
ESTEBAN.   Where are you, daughter? Hey, Laurencia!
LAURENCIA.   Sir?
ESTEBAN.   There, I was right; you see how quick she answered?

---

what happened in the case of Redondo's wife.

1371. *otro*: Bl supposes that Frondoso refers to his father, but the phrase is very ambiguous.

1403–4.   Pring-Mill, discussing the 63 generalisations he discovered in the play, discussed this one as typical of their use: 'both an indictment of the Comendador and a summary of the "right attitude" held by all those who stand for the maintenance of social order' (7–8).

¡Ved qué presto respondió!
Hija, Laurencia, mi amor,
a preguntarte ha venido...
(apártate aquí) ... si es bien 1410
que a Gila, tu amiga, den
a Frondoso por marido,
que es un honrado zagal,
si le hay en Fuente Ovejuna.

LAURENCIA. ¿Gila se casa?

ESTEBAN.   Y si alguna 1415
le merece y es su igual...

LAURENCIA. Yo digo, señor,que sí.

ESTEBAN. Sí, mas yo digo que es fea,
y que harto mejor se emplea
Frondoso, Laurencia, en ti. 1420

LAURENCIA.   ¿Aún no se te han olvidado
los donaires con la edad?

ESTEBAN. ¿Quiéresle tú?

LAURENCIA.   Voluntad
le he tenido y le he cobrado,
pero por lo que tú sabes... 1425

ESTEBAN. ¿Quieres tú que diga sí?

LAURENCIA. Dilo tú, señor, por mí.

ESTEBAN. ¿Yo? ¿Pues tengo yo las llaves?
Hecho está. Ven, buscaremos
a mi compadre en la plaza. 1430

REGIDOR. Vamos.

ESTEBAN.   Hijo, y en la traza
del dote, ¿qué le diremos?
Que yo bien te puedo dar
cuatro mil maravedís.

FRONDOSO. Señor, ¿eso me decís? 1435
Mi honor queréis agraviar.

ESTEBAN.   Anda, hijo, que eso es
cosa que pasa en un día;
que si no hay dote, a fe mía
que se echa menos después. 1440

Vanse, y queda Frondoso, y Laurencia.

LAURENCIA.   Di, Frondoso, ¿estás contento?

FRONDOSO. ¡Cómo si lo estoy! ¡Es poco,
pues que no me vuelvo loco

	Laurencia, love, they've just been asking me
	(come over here) if it's a good idea
	for your friend Gila to be given in marriage
	to young Frondoso. He's a proper lad,
	and honourable as any in the village.

LAURENCIA.   And Gila's going to...?

ESTEBAN.   Well, if any girl
is good enough to be a match for him...

LAURENCIA.   Then I say yes, sir.

ESTEBAN.   .   Yes? I say she's ugly,
and think he'd do much better marrying you.   1419

LAURENCIA.   Up to your little tricks still, are you then?
At your age, father?

ESTEBAN.   Do you love him, daughter?

LAURENCIA.   I've come to love him, father, more and more,
but you know how it is...

ESTEBAN.   Should I say yes?

LAURENCIA.   Yes, say it for me.

ESTEBAN.   Me? It's up to me?
That's settled, then. Come on, let's go and see
if we can't find my old friend in the square.   1430

ALDERMAN.   Let's go.

ESTEBAN.   Well, son, what shall we say to him
about that dowry? I could well afford
four thousand maravedis.

FRONDOSO.   Sir, how can you?
I'd be offended if you thought I'd take them.

ESTEBAN.   Nonsense, my boy, this love and marriage business
is over in a moment; mark my words,
if you've no dowry now, you'll miss it later.

The older men exit; Frondoso remains, with Laurencia.

LAURENCIA.   Happy, Frondoso?

FRONDOSO.   Happy's not the word!
The wonder is, I've not run mad with pleasure.

1419. On *emplearse* = be romantically involved, marry &c, see *Propalladia*
III, 467.

de gozo, del bien que siento!
Risa vierte el corazón
por los ojos de alegría,
viéndote, Laurencia mía,
en tan dulce posesión. *Vanse.*

Salen el Maestre, el Comendador, Flores y Ortuño.

COMENDADOR.	Huye, señor, que no hay otro remedio.	[*sueltos*]
MAESTRE.	La flaqueza del muro lo ha causado,	1450
	y el poderoso ejército enemigo.	
COMENDADOR.	Sangre les cuesta y infinitas vidas.	
MAESTRE.	Y no se alabarán que en sus despojos	
	pondrán nuestro pendón de Calatrava,	
	que a honrar su empresa y los demás bastaba.	1455
COMENDADOR.	Tus desinios, Girón, quedan perdidos.	
MAESTRE.	¿Qué puedo hacer, si la fortuna ciega	
	a quien hoy levantó, mañana humilla?	
Dentro	¡Vitoria por los Reyes de Castilla!	
MAESTRE.	Ya coronan de luces las almenas,	1460
	y las ventanas de las torres altas	
	entoldan con pendones vitoriosos.	
COMENDADOR.	Bien pudieran de sangre que les cuesta.	
	A fe que es más tragedia que no fiesta.	
MAESTRE.	Yo vuelvo a Calatrava, Fernán Gómez.	1465
COMENDADOR.	Y yo a Fuente Ovejuna, mientras tratas	
	o seguir esta parte de tus deudos,	
	o reducir la tuya al Rey Católico.	
MAESTRE.	Yo te diré por cartas lo que intento.	
COMENDADOR.	El tiempo ha de enseñarte.	
MAESTRE	¡Ah, pocos años,	1470
	sujetos al rigor de sus engaños!	

1449. The lovers, happy in their 'possession' of each other, are replaced on stage by the leaders of the disloyal Order, at the moment (the spectators may guess) of their dispossession and divorce. Lope's debt to the *Chronica*, 79rb, is again evident in this scene, esp. in respect of 1450–1.

My joy to think that you'll be mine hereafter
flows from my heart and fills my eyes with laughter. *Exit.*

The Master, the Commander, Flores and Ortuño enter.

COMMANDER.	Try to escape, there's no alternative.	1449
MASTER.	The wall was weak, the enemy's power too strong.	
COMMANDER.	It's cost them dear in blood and loss of life.	
MASTER.	What's more, they can't include our order's banner among their plunder; that would have sufficed to top all else and crown their enterprise.	
COMMANDER.	And yet, Girón, your plans are brought to nothing.	
MASTER.	What can I do, if Fortune in its blindness one day exalts a man, the next demeans him?	
(Voices off)	Victory for the Monarchs of Castile!	
MASTER.	See how they crown the battlements with torches, and decorate with their victorious banners the windows of the city's topmost towers.	1460
COMMANDER.	The blood it's cost them might bedeck them better. This is no triumph, but a tragedy.	
MASTER.	Commander, I'll return to Calatrava.	
COMMANDER.	And I to Fuente Ovejuna, while you choose if you'll continue in your kinsmen's cause or yield your forces to the Catholic King's.	
MASTER.	I'll let you know what I resolve by letter.	
COMMANDER.	Time will enlighten you.	
MASTER.	Alas, in youth it often seems to blind us to the truth! *They exit.*	

1452. *y* was invariably used by Lope for 'and' before initial (*h*)*i* (see Poesse, 74–5), though some contemporaries, like Covarrubias, approved of the *e* now standard.
1453–62. The banner of Calatrava is evidently visible on stage; an obvious scenic device would be the appearance on the gallery above of the banners of the Catholic Monarchs.

Sale la boda: Músicos, Mengo, Frondoso, Laurencia, Pascuala, Barrildo,
Esteban, y Alcalde.

MÚSICOS.	¡Vivan muchos años	[*coplilla de estribillo*]
	los desposados!	
	¡Vivan muchos años!	
MENGO.	¡A fe que no os ha costado	[*redondillas*] 1475
	mucho trabajo el cantar!	
BARRILDO.	¿Supiéraslo tú trovar	
	mejor que él está trovado?	
FRONDOSO.	Mejor entiende de azotes	
	Mengo que de versos ya.	1480
MENGO.	Alguno en el valle está,	
	para que no te alborotes,	
	a quien el Comendador...	
BARRILDO.	No lo digas, por tu vida,	
	que este bárbaro homicida	1485
	a todos quita el honor.	
MENGO.	¡Que me azotasen a mí	
	cien soldados aquel día!	
	Sola una honda tenía;	
	harto desdichado fui.	
	Pero que le hayan echado	
	una melecina a un hombre	
	que, aunque no diré su nombre,	
	todos saben que es honrado,	
	llena de tinta y de chinas,	1495
	¿cómo se puede sufrir?	
BARRILDO.	Haríalo por reír.	
MENGO.	No hay risas con melecinas,	
	que aunque es cosa saludable...	
	yo me quiero morir luego.	1500
FRONDOSO.	Vaya la copla te ruego,	
	si es la copla razonable.	

1472D.   Presumably both magistrates (Esteban and Alonso) enter here, and also (as most editors note) Juan Rojo, who speaks at 1537 (see note there).   The location must be Fuente Ovejuna (the square?); there is no specific reference.

1472–5.   On the deliberately crude simplicity of this rustic epithalamium, underlined by Mengo, see Salomon, 699.

The wedding party enters: Musicians, Mengo, Frondoso, Laurencia, Pascuala,
Barrildo, Esteban, and the Magistrate (and Juan Rojo).

MUSICIANS.	*(sing:) See where the happy pair appears;*	1472
	may they live for years and years...	
MENGO.	Call that a song? You didn't strain yourselves!	
BARRILDO.	You think you could compose a better one?	
FRONDOSO.	Mengo knows more of bum-beats now than drum-beats.	
MENGO.	I'm not the only one, though, don't you worry.	
	There's one chap in the valley I could name	
	who the Commander caught, and...	
BARRILDO.	No, don't tell us.	
	That murderous swine dishonours all of us.	
MENGO.	When I think how those soldiers leathered me	
	– a hundred of 'em, and me with just a sling –	
	it wasn't too much fun, but then again	1490
	it wasn't like the enema they gave	
	this chap I mean – I won't reveal his name,	
	but everybody here would know him for	
	a man of honour – full of ink and pebbles;	1495
	how can we bear such bloodymindedness?	
BARRILDO.	He must have done it as a joke, I reckon.	
MENGO.	A joke? I'd say, they may be good for you,	
	but enemas are never a laughing matter.	
FRONDOSO.	Let's hear the verse now, if it's any good.	

1490. As shown by Moll, 169–70, B was set up from a copy of A, to which this line had been added by hand; Lope may originally have omitted a line, or have written something quite different; see endnote.

1492. *melecina*: 'un lavatorio de tripas que se recibe por el sieso, y el mismo instrumento con que se echa se llama melecina, que es un saquillo de cuero con un cañuto' (Covarrubias).

1495. *chinas* = pebbles. Bl suggests that the reference may be to *china* (= china-root), 'muy semejante à la raíz del lirio, y notablemente aguda y mordaz. Cocida en agua provoca a sudór' (*Autoridades*).

BARRILDO.	¡*Vivan muchos años juntos*	[*copla*]
	los novios, ruego a los cielos,	
	y por envidias ni celos	
	ni riñan ni anden en puntos!	
	Lleven a entrambos difuntos,	
	de puro vivir cansados.	
	¡*Vivan muchos años...!*	
MENGO.	¡Maldiga el cielo el poeta	[*redondillas*] 1510
	que tal coplón arrojó!	
BARRILDO.	Fue muy presto...	
MENGO.	Pienso yo	
	una cosa desta seta.	

¿No habéis visto un buñolero,
en el aceite abrasando   1515
pedazos de masa echando,
hasta llenarse el caldero?
    ¿Que unos le salen hinchados,
otros tuertos y mal hechos,
ya zurdos y ya derechos,   1520
ya fritos y ya quemados?
    Pues así imagino yo
un poeta componiendo,
la materia previniendo,
que es quien la masa le dio.   1525
    Va arrojando verso aprisa
al caldero del papel,
confiado en que la miel
cubrirá la burla y risa.
    Mas poniéndolo en el pecho,   1530
apenas hay quien los tome;
tanto, que sólo los come
el mismo que los ha hecho.

BARRILDO.	Déjate ya de locuras:	
	deja los novios hablar.	1535
LAURENCIA.	Las manos nos da a besar.	
JUAN.	Hija, ¿mi mano procuras?	
	Pídela a tu padre luego	
	para ti y para Frondoso.	
ESTEBAN.	Rojo, a ella y a su esposo	1540
	que se la dé el cielo ruego,	
	con su larga bendición.	
FRONDOSO.	Los dos a los dos la echad.	

BARRILDO.	*Hear our prayer to heaven above:* 1505
	May both be spared, as man and wife,
	Both jealousy and envious strife,
	With no disputes to spoil their love,
	And die, exhausted by a life
	That's full of joy, and free of tears.
	May they live for years and years...
MENGO.	Who wrote that dreadful doggerel, devil take him? 1510
BARRILDO.	There wasn't too much time.
MENGO.	I'll tell you what

I think of those who turn out stuff like that.
I bet you've seen some fellow frying doughnuts,
tossing great lumps of dough in sizzling oil
until he's filled the pan; so some swell up,
some turn out twisted, crooked and misshapen,
some right, some wrong, some cooked and others burnt;
well, that's how I suppose your poet works.
He gets his subject-matter, that's his dough,
and tosses verses at his pan, his paper,
supposing his absurdities and follies
will pass unnoticed if they're spread with honey.
But when he offers then, he finds no taker
and no one can digest them but their maker.

BARRILDO.	That's enough nonsense; let the lovers speak.
LAURENCIA.	Give us your hands to kiss.
JUAN.	My hand, Laurencia?
	You ought to ask your father, girl, to give
	his hand to you and your Frondoso too.
ESTEBAN.	I pray, old friend, that Heaven itself may offer
	its hand to them, and give its lasting blessing.
FRONDOSO.	Why don't the pair of you bless both of us?

1503–11.   I accept Bl's suggestion that 1503–9 are sung by Barrildo, who composed them and perhaps the banal *coplilla* (cf. 1472–8) and apologises (1512; cf. 2043–4), or by the musicians (which would explain *Men.* in the *Parte* as a misreading of *Musi.*).   If we are right, there is no need to suppose that 1510–1 are spoken by Frondoso; Mengo is the critic.

1546–69.   On every aspect of this lyric, see López Estrada's masterly study, 'La canción ...'.

1547.   *niña en cabello*: a ritual expression of archaic flavour, in law denoting a girl between ten and sixteen, in the traditional lyric symbolising virginity; see Salomon, 693, n.28.

JUAN.	¡Ea, tañed y cantad,	
	pues que para en uno son!	1545
MÚSICOS.	*Al val de Fuente Ovejuna*	[*romance con estribillo*]

la niña en cabello baja;
el caballero la sigue
de la Cruz de Calatrava.
Entre las ramas se esconde,　　　　　　　　　　1550
de vergonzosa y turbada:
fingiendo que no le ha visto,
pone delante las ramas.
"¿Para qué te ascondes,
niña gallarda?　　　　　　　　　　　　　　1555
Que mis linces deseos
paredes pasan."
Acercóse el caballero,
y ella, confusa y turbada,
hacer quiso celosía　　　　　　　　　　　　1560
de las intricadas ramas;
mas como quien tiene amor
los mares y las montañas
atraviesa fácilmente,
la dice tales palabras:　　　　　　　　　　　1565
"¿Para qué te ascondes,
niña gallarda?
Que mis linces deseos
paredes pasan."

Sale el Comendador, Flores, Ortuño y Cimbranos.

COMENDADOR.	Estése la boda queda,	[*romance*] 1570
	y no se alborote nadie.	
JUAN.	No es juego aqueste, señor,	
	y basta que tú lo mandes.	
	¿Quieres lugar? ¿Cómo vienes	
	con tu belicoso alarde?	1575
	¿Venciste? Mas ¿qué pregunto?	
FRONDOSO.	Muerto soy. ¡Cielos, libradme!	
LAURENCIA.	Huye por aquí, Frondoso.	
COMENDADOR.	Eso no; ¡prendelde, atalde!	
JUAN.	Date, muchacho, a prisión.	1580
FRONDOSO.	Pues ¿quieres tú que me maten?	
JUAN.	¿Por qué?	

| JUAN. | Strike up! Sing out, for now they are as one! | 1545 |

MUSICIANS *sing:* *Down Fuente Ovejuna's vale*
the village maiden came,   1547
but Calatrava's noble knight
was following apace.
She hides among the leafy boughs
her shyness and her shame,
pretends she hasn't seen, and draws
the boughs before her face.
'Why hide yourself away, my pretty mate?
My lynx-eyed love stone walls can penetrate.'   1556
The noble Knight draws nearer now;
the maiden, turning pale,
tries to conceal her modesty
amid the tangled shade.
But since a man aflame with love
can easily assail
both ocean depths and mountain heights,
the knight calls to the maid:
'Why hide yourself away, my pretty mate?
My lynx-eyed love stone walls can penetrate.'

The Commander, Flores, Ortuño and Cimbranos enter.

COMMANDER.   What's this, a wedding? That's enough of that.
                         Stay where you are, and don't make any trouble.
JUAN.   This is a serious ceremony, sir,
                         but if you wish we'll stop. Should we give place?
                         Why all this show of military might?
                         Were you victorious? Am I wrong to ask?
FRONDOSO.   Heaven help me now, or I'm as good as dead!
LAURENCIA.   Through here, Frondoso, and you'll get away!
COMMANDER. Oh no, he won't; arrest him, tie him up!
JUAN.   Give yourself up.
FRONDOSO.   You mean, so they can kill me?
JUAN.   Why should they?

1556. *linces deseos*: on this striking expression, see López Estrada, 'La canción...', 466, but add the analogies in Lope noted by P. Note the intensely concentrated association of desire with a predatory beast and the breaking down of a barrier.

1561. *intricadas*: the etymological form (Latin *intricare*; cf. English *intricate*) of modern Spanish *intrincadas*. P notes four other uses in Lope.

COMENDADOR.   No soy hombre yo
que mato sin culpa a nadie,
que si lo fuera, le hubieran
pasado de parte a parte   1585
esos soldados que traigo.
Llevarle mando a la cárcel,
donde la culpa que tiene
sentencie su mismo padre.
PASCUALA.   Señor, mirad que se casa.   1590
COMENDADOR.   ¿Qué me obliga a que se case?
¿No hay otra gente en el pueblo?
PASCUALA.   Si os ofendió, perdonadle,
por ser vos quien sois.
COMENDADOR.   No es cosa,
Pascuala, en que yo soy parte.   1595
Es esto contra el Maestre
Tellez Girón, que Dios guarde.
Es contra toda su Orden,
es su honor, y es importante
para el ejemplo el castigo;   1600
que habrá otro dia quien trate
de alzar pendón contra él,
pues ya sabéis que una tarde
al Comendador mayor
– ¡qué vasallos tan leales! –   1605
puso una ballesta al pecho.
ESTEBAN.   Supuesto que el disculparle
ya puede tocar a un suegro,
no es mucho que en causas tales
se descomponga con vos   1610
un hombre, en efeto, amante;
porque si vos pretendéis
su propia mujer quitarle,
¿qué mucho que la defienda?

1589. *su mismo padre* must surely refer not to Laurencia's father, but to
Frondoso's.   This person was mentioned in 1355, 1381–4, and perhaps in
1429–30, but (strangely) is not obviously present at the wedding; can he perhaps
be identified with the other magistrate, Alonso?

COMMANDER.	Why indeed? I'm not the sort

to kill a man unless it's shown he's guilty;
for if I were, these men of mine would quickly
have run him through. I'm putting him in jail,
where his own father shall decide his guilt.   1589

PASCUALA.   But sir, he's getting married.

COMMANDER.   What's that to me?
Why him? Are there no others in the village?

PASCUALA.   If he's offended you, forgive him, lord,
and show your noble nature.   1594

COMMANDER.   But Pascuala,
I'm not concerned; this is a crime against
Téllez Girón, the Master (God preserve him);
against the Order as a whole, its honour.
The punishment must serve as an example,   1600
for one day other men may seek to raise
the banner of revolt against its Master,
if vassals these days show such true allegiance
that such a man could dare to lay a crossbow
against the person of its Grand Commander.

ESTEBAN.   Since offering a plea in mitigation
is proper to a father-in-law, my Lord,
it isn't strange that one who after all
was so in love, in such a situation,
should fail to keep his head; if you, my Lord,
were seeking to deprive him of his wife,
was it surprising he should try to save her?

1594. *por ser vos quien sois*: a variant on the phrase *soy quien soy*, which appears in countless *comedias* when 'a person of noble birth or character... at the moment of choosing a course of action evokes the ideal to which his personality should aspire, given his inborn nature'; see Leo Spitzer, *NRFH*, I (1947), 113–27 (124); *Propalladia* IV, 177–9; and J.A. Maravall, *Teatro y literatura en la sociedad barroca*, Madrid 1972, 97–104.

1594–1606. The Commander takes refuge in the pretence that he is acting not to avenge himself but to protect his Order from the consequences of a future uprising – ironically, in view of what is to follow.

COMENDADOR.	Majadero sois, alcalde.	1615
ESTEBAN.	Por vuestra virtud, senor.	
COMENDADOR.	Nunca yo quise quitarle	
	su mujer, pues no lo era.	
ESTEBAN.	Sí quisistes; y esto baste,	
	que Reyes hay en Castilla	1620
	que nuevas órdenes hacen	
	con que desórdenes quitan.	
	Y harán mal, cuando descansen	
	de las guerras, en sufrir	
	en sus villas y lugares	1625
	a hombres tan poderosos	
	por traer Cruces tan grandes;	
	póngasela el Rey al pecho,	
	que para pechos reales	
	es esa insignia, y no más.	1630
COMENDADOR.	¡Hola! ¡La vara quitalde!	
ESTEBAN.	Tomad, señor, norabuena.	
COMENDADOR.	Pues con ella quiero dalle,	
	como a caballo brioso.	
ESTEBAN.	Por señor os sufro. Dadme.	1635
PASCUALA.	¿A un viejo de palos das?	
LAURENCIA.	Si le das porque es mi padre,	
	¿qué vengas en él de mí?	
COMENDADOR.	Llevadla, y haced que guarden	
	su persona diez soldados. *Vase èl y los suyos.*	1640
ESTEBAN.	¡Justicia del cielo baje! *Vase.*	
PASCUALA.	Volvióse en luto la boda. *Vase.*	
BARRILDO.	¿No hay aquí un hombre que hable?	
MENGO.	Yo tengo ya mis azotes,	
	que aún se ven los cardenales,	1645
	sin que un hombre vaya a Roma.	
	Prueben otros a enojarle.	

1615. *majadero* = tedious fool; 'majadero llamamos al necio, por ser boto de ingenio, como la mano de mortero, a la que se hace la alusión' (Covarrubias). *Autoridades* and Corominas accept this etymology, which Lope expounds in *El galán de la Membrilla*, 145–60; but his editors there assert that it derives rather from *majada*, a peasant's shelter.

1628–9.   Note the pun on *pecho*, in the senses of 'breast' and 'tribute' (cf. 576).

COMMANDER	Magistrate, you're a fool.	1615
ESTEBAN.	But I appeal	

to your good nature, sir.
COMMANDER.   I never sought
to take his wife, for she was no such thing.
ESTEBAN.   She was, you did, that's all there is to say.
But there are Christian Monarchs in Castile
who'll make new orders and destroy disorders;
and they'll be ill-advised, when they've some respite
from waging war, to allow such men as you
to wield such power in towns and villages,
merely because they wear such mighty crosses.
Only the King should bear one on his breast,   1628
to show that tribute's due to him alone.

COMMANDER.	You, seize his staff.	1631
ESTEBAN.	You take it, sir, and welcome.	
COMMANDER.	Then I shall beat you with it, as I would	

a horse that proved too mettlesome.
ESTEBAN.   Beat on,
I bear your blows because you are my lord.
PASCUALA.   You'd beat a man of his age?
LAURENCIA.   If your reason
for beating him is just that he's my father,
what cause have you to take revenge on me?
COMMANDER.   Take her away, and set ten men to guard her.
He and his men exit.
ESTEBAN.   May Heaven send its justice to destroy him!   *He exits.*
PASCUALA.   No wedding now; it seems more like a wake. *She exits.*
BARRILDO.   Won't any man speak out?
MENGO.   You others may.
I did, and you should see the weals it earned me;   1645
the sort of wheels that get you nowhere fast.

1631–5. The Commander's violent misuse of the magistrate's own insignia (cf. 1341–2) to belabour the critical but exemplarily submissive old peasant is the visual climax of the scene.

1645–6.   The pun on *cardenales* (bruises/cardinals) is a familiar one; see Quevedo, *La vida del buscón*, ed. D. Ynduráin, Madrid 1980, 81. His n. 5 gives 4 other uses.

JUAN.   Hablemos todos.
MENGO.   Señores,
    aquí todo el mundo calle.
    Como ruedas de salmón   1650
    me puso los atabales.

1650–1. *como ruedas de salmón* is a phrase often used (with variants) in such descriptions by Lope's *graciosos*; see *El mejor alcalde, el Rey*, 232; *Los*

Mengo's flogging, in another Spanish production, by kind permission of the Archivo Nacional

JUAN.   We must all talk.

MENGO.   We'd better all be silent.

               He beat my pair of kettle-drums so hard,   1650

               he's left them both as red as fresh-sliced salmon.

---

comendadores de Córdoba, BAE 215, p. 426; *La desdichada Estefanía*, 1412–5. Mengo's coarse jokes may seem out of place; but his resilient 'jesting at scars' lends a touch of comic relief – optimism, almost – to a grimly muted act-ending.

Laurencia's entry (1712), in the Teatro Español production.

ACTO TERCERO

Salen Esteban, Alonso y Barrildo.

ESTEBAN.	¿No han venido a la junta?	[*tercetos*]
BARRILDO.	No han venido.	
ESTEBAN.	Pues más apriesa nuestro daño corre.	
BARRILDO.	Ya está lo más del pueblo prevenido.	
ESTEBAN.	Frondoso con prisiones en la torre,	1655

y mi hija Laurencia en tanto aprieto,
si la piedad de Dios no lo socorre...

Salen Juan Rojo y el Regidor.

JUAN.   ¿De qué dais voces, cuando importa tanto
a nuestro bien, Esteban, el secreto?
ESTEBAN.   Que doy tan pocas es mayor espanto.   1660

Sale Mengo.

MENGO.   También vengo yo a hallarme en esta junta.
ESTEBAN.   Un hombre cuyas canas baña el llanto,
labradores honrados, os pregunta
    qué obsequias debe hacer toda esta gente
a su patria sin honra, ya perdida.   1665
Y si se llaman honras justamente,
    ¿cómo se harán, si no hay entre nosotros
hombre a quien este bárbaro no afrente?
Respondedme: ¿hay alguno de vosotros
    que no esté lastimado en honra y vida?   1670
No os lamentáis los unos de los otros?
Pues si ya la tenéis todos perdida,
    ¿a qué aguardáis? ¿Qué desventura es ésta?
JUAN.   La mayor que en el mundo fue sufrida.
Mas pues ya se publica y manifiesta   1675
    que en paz tienen los Reyes a Castilla,
y su venida a Córdoba se apresta,
vayan dos regidores a la villa,
y, echándose a sus pies, pidan remedio.

ACT THREE

Esteban, Alonso and Barrildo enter.

ESTEBAN.   The council aren't all here yet?
BARRILDO.   No, not yet.
ESTEBAN.   But things are getting worse from hour to hour!
BARRILDO.   Most of the village must have heard by now.
ESTEBAN.   Frondoso's been imprisoned in the tower,
                my girl Laurencia's facing God knows what...
                If heaven in its mercy doesn't help us...

Juan Rojo and the other Alderman enter.

JUAN ROJO.   Why shout so loud, Esteban, when you know
                that secrecy's so vital to our safety?
ESTEBAN.   It's more amazing that I shout so little!

Mengo enters.

MENGO.   I'm here now too; the council can begin.
ESTEBAN.   A man whose whitened hairs are wet with weeping
                stands here before you, honourable peasants,
                to ask what obsequies we all should offer
                to this destroyed, dishonoured town of ours.
                And if such rites are rightly labelled honours,
                who can perform them, when among us all
                there's not one man that monster hasn't shamed?
                I charge you all to answer: is there one
                whose life and honour has escaped unscathed?
                Have all of you not common cause for grievance?
                And if you all have been affronted, tell me:
                what more d'you fear for? What affliction's this?
JUAN ROJO.   The worst the world has ever seen men suffer.
                But now it's well and generally known
                the King and Queen have pacified Castile
                and mean to move their court to Cordoba,
                two aldermen should hurry to the city,
                fall at their feet, and beg them for redress.

BARRILDO.	En tanto que Fernando aquel que humilla	1680
	a tantos enemigos, otro medio	
	será mejor, pues no podrá, ocupado,	
	hacernos bien con tanta guerra en medio.	
REGIDOR.	Si mi voto de vos fuera escuchado,	
	desamparar la villa doy por voto.	1685
JUAN.	¿Cómo es posible en tiempo limitado?	
MENGO.	A la fe, que si entiende el alboroto,	
	que ha de costar la junta alguna vida.	
REGIDOR.	Ya, todo el árbol de paciencia roto,	
	corre la nave de temor perdida.	1690
	La hija quitan con tan gran fiereza	
	a un hombre honrado, de quien es regida	
	la patria en que vivís, y en la cabeza	
	la vara quiebran tan injustamente.	
	¿Qué esclavo se trató con mas bajeza?	1695
JUAN.	¿Qué es lo que quieres tú que el pueblo intente?	
REGIDOR.	Morir, o dar la muerte a los tiranos,	
	pues somos muchos, y ellos poca gente.	
BARRILDO.	¿Contra el señor las armas en las manos?	
ESTEBAN.	El Rey sólo es señor después del cielo,	1700
	y no bárbaros hombres inhumanos.	
	Si Dios ayuda nuestro justo celo,	
	¿qué nos ha de costar?	
MENGO.	Mirad, senores,	
	que vais en estas cosas con recelo.	
	Puesto que por los simples labradores	1705
	estoy aquí, que más injurias pasan,	
	más cuerdo represento sus temores.	
JUAN.	Si nuestras desventuras se compasan,	
	para perder las vidas, ¿qué aguardamos?	
	Las casas y las viñas nos abrasan;	1710
	tiranos son. ¡A la venganza vamos!	

Sale Laurencia, desmelenada.

1680.   No editor, in my view, has satisfactorily explained this line.   Possibly Lope wrote 'Fernando aquieta y umilla' and was misread.

1710.   Note that Lope, preferring to stress Fernán Gómez's sexual excesses, ('taking their daughters and wives by force'), refers only at this point and in 2399 to the other acts of tyranny mentioned in the *Chronica*, 80r.

BARRILDO.	While Ferdinand is so preoccupied
	in putting down so many foes, and righting
	so many wrongs, he'll hardly have the time
	to look to ours; we need some other answer.
ALDERMAN.	If you want my opinion and advice,
	I vote we should evacuate the town.
JUAN ROJO.	How can we, in so short a space of time?
MENGO.	And once he knows the council's up to something,
	I swear it's sure to cost a life or two.
ALDERMAN.	Our little ship of state's so broken-masted,
	it's lost beyond all fear and all forbearance.
	They seize and drag away with savage violence
	the daughter of an honourable man
	who rules the town you live in; on his head
	unjustly break the very staff of justice.
	Was ever any slave so vilely treated?
JUAN ROJO.	So, what do you propose the town should do?
ALDERMAN.	Do? Die itself, or see its tyrants die,
	since we're so many, and they so very few.
BARRILDO.	You mean, take arms against our overlord?
ESTEBAN.	No, under heaven the King alone is lord,
	not men so barbarous they're more like beasts.
	If God above supports our righteous zeal,
	what can we have to fear?
MENGO.	Be careful, sirs,
	and mind you move with caution in such matters.
	I'm here to represent the common peasants;
	they suffer most, but when I say be prudent,
	I'm speaking for their fears and commonsense.
JUAN ROJO.	If all of us are equally afflicted,
	why should we jib at staking life itself?
	They fire our vineyards and destroy our homes.
	Death to the tyrants! Let us have revenge!

1691

1697

1700

1710

Laurencia enters, dishevelled.

1712D.   As noted by Alan C. Dessen, *Elizabethan Stage Conventions and Modern Interpreters*, Cambridge U.P. 1985, 36–7, dishevelled hair was prescribed in numerous English plays of the age of Shakespeare for female characters 'distraught with madness, shame, extreme grief, or the effects of recent violence', including rape.

LAURENCIA.	Dejadme entrar, que bien puedo,	[*romance*]
	en consejo de los hombres;	
	que bien puede una mujer,	
	si no a dar voto, a dar voces.	1715
	¿Conocéisme?	
ESTEBAN.	¡Santo cielo!	
	¿No es mi hija?	
JUAN.	¿No conoces	
	a Laurencia?	
LAURENCIA.	Vengo tal,	
	que mi diferencia os pone	
	en contingencia quién soy.	1720
ESTEBAN.	¡Hija mia!	
LAURENCIA.	No me nombres	
	tu hija.	
ESTEBAN.	¿Por qué, mis ojos?	
	¿Por qué?	
LAURENCIA.	¡Por muchas razones!	

Y sean las principales,
porque dejas que me roben   1725
tiranos sin que me vengues,
traidores sin que me cobres.
Aún no era yo de Frondoso,
para que digas que tome,
como marido, venganza,   1730
que aquí por tu cuenta corre;
que en tanto que de las bodas
no haya llegado la noche,
del padre, y no del marido
la obligación presupone;   1735
que en tanto que no me entregan
una joya, aunque la compre,
no ha de correr por mi cuenta
las guardas ni los ladrones.
Llevóme de vuestros ojos   1740
a su casa Fernán Gómez;
la oveja al lobo dejáis,
como cobardes pastores.
¡Qué dagas no vi en mi pecho!
¡Qué desatinos enormes,   1745

LAURENCIA.	Let me come in, for well I may,	1712
	when men are met in council.	
	A woman has the right to claim	
	a voice, if not a vote.	
	D'you recognise me?	
ESTEBAN.	God in heaven,	
	it's not Laurencia, surely?	
JUAN ROJO.	You mean you don't know who it is?	
LAURENCIA.	I see I'm so much changed	
	you can't be certain who I am.	
ESTEBAN.	Daughter!	
LAURENCIA.	Don't call me that!	
	Your daughter, me?	
ESTEBAN.	Why not, my love.	
	Why not?	
LAURENCIA.	For many reasons!	

But first of all, because you allow
Laurencia to be taken
by tyrants, and don't demand revenge,
by traitors, and don't defend me.
I'd not become Frondoso's wife,
which means you can't pretend
it's up to him to seek revenge;
that's still your obligation.
Until the marriage-night has come,   1732
it's still her father's duty,
and not her husband's, to protect
a woman's name and virtue;
for even though I buy a jewel,
until I take possession
it isn't up to me to see
it's safe from rogues and robbers.
When Fernán Gómez bore me off
before your very eyes,
like cowardly shepherds, you allowed
the wolf to steal your sheep.
What words did he not plague me with,
what daggers at my breast,

1732–9. According to the code of honour, which Laurencia keenly expounds, a woman was the repository of her father's or brother's honour until the consummation of her marriage; thereafter, of her husband's. For *joya* as a symbol of virginity, see Lope's *La francesilla*, 132.

qué palabras, qué amenazas
y qué delitos atroces,
por rendir mi castidad
a sus apetitos torpes!
Mis cabellos, ¿no lo dicen?   1750
¿No se ven aquí los golpes,
de la sangre, y las señales?
¿Vosotros sois hombres nobles?
¿Vosotros, padres y deudos?
¿Vosotros, que no se os rompen   1755
las entrañas de dolor,
de verme en tantos dolores?
Ovejas sois, bien lo dice
de Fuente Ovejuna el nombre.
Dadme unas armas a mí,   1760
pues sois piedras, pues sois bronces,
pues sois jaspes, pues sois tigres...
Tigres no, porque feroces
siguen quien roba sus hijos,
matando los cazadores   1765
antes que entren por el mar
y por sus ondas se arrojen.
Liebres cobardes nacistes;
bárbaros sois, no españoles.
¡Gallinas! ¡Vuestras mujeres   1770
sufrís que otros hombres gocen!
¡Poneos ruecas en la cinta!
¿Para qué os ceñís estoques?
¡Vive Dios, que he de trazar
que solas mujeres cobren   1775

1758–9. Popular etymology appears to have changed Fuente Abejuna (the well
of the bees) to Fuente Ovejuna (see LE, pp. 13–4, n. 14). Some translators have
called our play *The Sheepwell, Font-aux-cabres* or *La Fontaine aux brebis*.

1761–2. *piedras... bronces... jaspes*; lit. = stones... bronzes... jaspers.

1762–7. Neatly, Lope has Laurencia use one Classical topos (cf. 889, 1185) to
refer to the men's insensitivity, and then (as an 'afterthought') a second to
contrast their lack of parental anger with that of the tigress, who (according to
Pliny, VIII, 25) when her cubs are stolen, pursues the hunter at headlong speed
'until he has regained his ship and her ferocity rages vainly on the shore'.   P
cites six other uses of the second in Lope; see also *El sufrimiento premiado*,
1121, 2901 and notes.

what threats, what acts of vile excess,
what gross atrocities,
to force my chastity to yield
to his debased desires?
Does this my hair not tell the tale?
Can you not see these scars,
these signs of savage blows, this blood?
And are you men of honour?
Are you my father and my kin?
Are you so cold, so cruel
your very souls aren't torn apart
to see such suffering?
But no, your town is aptly named,   1758
and you're not men, but sheep!
Let me be armed for battle, then,
if you're so hard of heart,   1761
such stocks and stones, such tigresses...
no, worse than tigresses,
for they, when hunters steal their young
ferociously pursue
and slay them, till they reach the sea
and plunge beneath its waves.
Not tigresses, but timid hares,
not Spaniards, but barbarians,
too chicken-hearted to deny
your women to other men!
Why not wear distaffs at your waists?   1772
Why gird on useless swords?
I swear to God we women alone
shall make those tyrants pay

1768.   *nacistes*: the second person plural of the preterite could at this time end in -*tes*, -*tis* or -*teis*. 'Lope's practice in the autographs reveals a decided preference for the -*tes* ending'; *El sembrar en buena tierra*, 166.

1772-7.   'The image most favoured both in popular and cultured art to represent the inversion of the roles of the sexes is that of the man holding a distaff and the woman a sword', which had its origin in the story of Hercules and Omphale; Helen F. Grant, 'The World Upside-down', *Studies in Spanish Literature of the Golden Age presented to E.M. Wilson*, ed. by R.O. Jones, London, Tamesis, 1973, 115.   Note, though, a parallel between Laurencia and Isabella, who in lines 115-8 of *El mejor mozo de España* had been urged by Spain in a dream: 'O famous Isabella, change your distaff to a sword; you're not one of those women who should spin, you should do battle.'

               la honra destos tiranos,
               la sangre destos traidores!
               ¡Y que os han de tirar piedras,
               hilanderas, maricones,
               amujerados, cobardes!   1780
               ¡Y que mañana os adornen
               nuestras tocas y basquiñas,
               solimanes y colores!
               A Frondoso quiere ya,
               sin sentencia, sin pregones,   1785
               colgar el Comendador
               del almena de una torre.
               De todos hará lo mismo;
               y yo me huelgo, medio hombres,
               porque quede sin mujeres   1790
               esta villa honrada, y torne
               aquel siglo de amazonas,
               eterno espanto del orbe.

ESTEBAN.   Yo, hija, no soy de aquellos
               que permiten que los nombres   1795
               con esos títulos viles.
               Iré solo, si se pone
               todo el mundo contra mí.

JUAN.   Y yo,por más que me asombre
               la grandeza del contrario.   1800

REGIDOR.   Muramos todos.

BARRILDO.   Descoge
               un lienzo al viento en un palo,
               y mueran estos inormes.

JUAN.   ¿Qué orden pensáis tener?

MENGO.   Ir a matarle sin orden.   1805

1783. *solimán* lit. = sublimate of mercury, used as a (pernicious) cosmetic; see *Dorotea* pp. 59, 96, 387; *El loco por fuerza*, AcN 2, 272–3; *El genovés liberal*, AcN 6, 123–4; *El amigo hasta la muerte*, AcN 11, 339b.

1789–93. Elaborating on the sex-change topos, Laurencia concludes with the 'legendary archetype of *varonilidad*'. As shown by McKendrick, pp. 174–84, Lope was fascinated by the Amazons, and brought them on stage in at least three plays, *Las justas de Tebas, Las grandezas de Alejandro* and esp. *Las mujeres sin hombres* (see also his dedication of this play in his *Parte XVI*). The present reference may have been suggested by the actions of the women of Fuente Ovejuna as recounted in the *Chronica*, 79vb (see 1824–46, 1888–1919, 1980–3).

	for our indignities, and bill	
	those traitors for our blood.	
	And you, you effete effeminates,	
	I sentence to be stoned	
	as spinsters, pansies, queens and cowards,	
	and forced henceforth to wear	
	our bonnets and our overskirts,	
	with painted, powdered faces.	1783
	Our valorous Commander means	
	to have Frondoso hanged	
	– uncharged, untried and uncondemned –	
	from yonder battlements.	
	He'll serve all you unmanly men	1789
	the same, and I'll rejoice;	
	for when this honourable town	
	is womanless, that age	
	shall dawn which once amazed the world,	
	the age of Amazons.	
ESTEBAN.	I'm not the sort of man, my girl,	
	to let himself be shamed	
	by calumnies as vile as those;	
	I swear I'll go alone,	
	though all the world opposes me.	
JUAN.	I too, however daunting	
	our adversary's power may seem.	
ALDERMAN.	We all should die together.	
BARRILDO.	Unfurl a banner on the breeze,	1801
	and let those monsters die!	
JUAN.	What order do you mean to keep?	
MENGO.	No order; let the village	

1801–2. The townsfolk, these lines imply, will display their own insignia (see 1453–62, 1837–41, etc.)

1803. *inormes* implies that the tyrant's crimes are not only enormous but 'fuera de norma'; cf. Covarrubias: 'norma... metafóricamente significa la ley, la formula, estilo ajustado y medido. Y porque algunos pecados son grandes y desproporcionados los llamamos enormes'. P cites four adjectival uses in this sense in Lope.

	Juntad el pueblo a una voz; que todos están conformes en que los tiranos mueran.	
ESTEBAN.	Tomad espadas, lanzones, ballestas, chuzos y palos.	1810
MENGO.	¡Los Reyes nuestros señores vivan!	
TODOS.	¡Vivan muchos años!	
MENGO.	¡Mueran tiranos traidores!	
TODOS.	¡Traidores tiranos mueran! *Vanse todos.*	
LAURENCIA.	Caminad, que el cielo os oye.	1815
	¡Ah, mujeres de la villa! ¡Acudid, porque se cobre vuestro honor! ¡Acudid todas!	

Salen Pascuala, Jacinta y otras mujeres.

PASCUALA.	¿Qué es esto? ¿De qué das voces?	
LAURENCIA.	¿No veis como todos van	1820
	a matar a Fernán Gómez, y hombres, mozos y muchachos furiosos al hecho corren?	
	¿Será bien que solos ellos desta hazaña el honor gocen,	1825
	pues no son de las mujeres sus agravios los menores?	
JACINTA.	Di, pues, ¿que es lo que pretendes?	
LAURENCIA.	Que, puestas todas en orden, acometamos un hecho	1830
	que dé espanto a todo el orbe. Jacinta, [a] tu grande agravio que sea cabo responde de una escuadra de mujeres.	
JACINTA.	¡No son los tuyos menores!	1835
LAURENCIA.	Pascuala, alférez serás.	
PASCUALA.	Pues déjame que enarbole	

1806–8.   Note again the stress on the collective will of the town (see 1816–8, 1820, 1829).

1811–4.   Note how these slogans, both affirmative and negative, have been anticipated: *Los Reyes nuestros señores vivan* by 1700; *Mueran tiranos traidores* by 1697, 1711, 1726–7, 1776–7, 1808.

1832–4.   Most editors punctuate: 'Jacinta, tu grande agravio / que sea cabo;

	unite and raise a single cry, since all of us agree the tyrants ought to die.	1806
ESTEBAN.	Take swords, bows, lances, pikes and staves.	
MENGO.	Long live our lords the King and Queen!	1811
ALL.	Long live the King and Queen!	
MENGO.	And let the tyrants and traitors die!	
ALL.	Let traitors and tyrants die! *All the men exit.*	
LAURENCIA.	Go forth, for Heaven hears your cry. Now, women of the town, come join your men, and help restore your honour! All of you!	

Pascuala, Jacinta and other women enter.

PASCUALA.	What is it? Why make such a shout?	
LAURENCIA.	Why, don't you see our men are storming the Commander's house to kill him; don't you see men, lads and boys rush furiously to do so fair a deed? And is it right that they alone should glory in the honour of such revenge? Our grievances are just as great as theirs!	
JACINTA.	What is it you propose we do?	
LAURENCIA.	Unite in ordered ranks, and undertake an enterprise that will amaze the world. Jacinta, it seems right that all the wrongs you've borne should make them the corporal of a platoon.	1832
JACINTA.	Yours are no less than mine!	
LAURENCIA.	Pascuala, you shall be our ensign.	
PASCUALA.	Let me find a staff	1837

---

responde / de una escuadra de mujeres'. I agree with Bl (and H) in understanding 'responde' as 'corresponde', and suggest that *a* is 'embebida' in *Jacinta* (see n. to 637).

1832–47. The 'monstrous regiment of women' – *puestas todas en orden*, by contrast with the men's lack of order (1804–5) – is a detail inspired by the *Chronica*, 79vb, which lends irony, in retrospect, to 162–5.

	en un asta la bandera; verás si merezco el nombre.	
LAURENCIA.	No hay espacio para eso; pues la dicha nos socorre, bien nos basta que llevemos nuestras tocas por pendones.	1840
PASCUALA.	Nombremos un capitán.	
LAURENCIA.	Eso no.	
PASCUALA.	¿Por qué?	
LAURENCIA.	Que adonde asiste mi gran valor, no hay Cides ni Rodamontes. *Vanse.*	1845

Sale Frondoso, atadas las manos; Flores, Ortuño, Cimbranos y el Comendador.

COMENDADOR.	Dese cordel que de las manos sobra [*octavas reales*] quiero que le colguéis, por mayor pena.	
FRONDOSO.	¡Qué nombre, gran señor, tu sangre cobra!	1850
COMENDADOR.	Colgalde luego en la primera almena.	
FRONDOSO.	Nunca fue mi intención poner por obra tu muerte entonces.	
FLORES.	Grande ruido suena. *Ruido suene.*	
COMENDADOR.	¿Ruido?	
FLORES.	Y de manera que interrompen tu justicia, señor.	
ORTUÑO.	¡Las puertas rompen! *Ruido.* ¿La puerta de mi casa, y siendo casa de la Encomienda?	1855
FLORES.	¡El pueblo junto viene!	
JUAN, _dentro._	¡Rompe, derriba, hunde, quema, abrasa!	
ORTUÑO.	Un popular motín mal se detiene.	
COMENDADOR.	¿El pueblo contra mí?	
FLORES.	La furia pasa tan adelante, que las puertas tiene echadas por la tierra.	1860
COMENDADOR.	Desatalde. Templa, Frondoso, ese villano alcalde.	

1845–7.   Laurencia compares herself with the Spanish national hero and one from Ariosto's epic *Orlando furioso* often referred to and put on stage by Lope, e.g. in *Los celos de Rodamonte*; see M. Chevalier, *L'Arioste en Espagne*, Bordeaux 1966.

1854.   *interrompen:* on this form, see *El primero Benavides*, n. to 1998.

	and raise a banner; then you'll see how I deserve that name.
LAURENCIA.	No time for that! Now fortune looks with favour on our cause, we'll have to be content to bear no banners but our caps.
PASCUALA.	We ought to name a captain.
LAURENCIA.	No.
PASCUALA.	Why not?
LAURENCIA.	You'll never see 1845 a Rodamonte or a Cid so valiant as me!

They exit.

Frondoso (with his hands tied), Flores, Ortuño, Cimbranos and the Commander enter.

COMMANDER.	Now that you've tied his hands, there's rope to spare; hang him by that, and make him suffer more.
FRONDOSO.	What honour, Lord, you do your noble blood!
COMMANDER.	String him up now, from yonder battlements! The first to hand!
FRONDOSO.	I vow I never meant to take your life that day.
FLORES.	Wait, what's that noise? *Noise offstage.*
COMMANDER.	A noise, you say?
FLORES.	One loud enough to stay your justice, sir.
ORTUÑO.	They're breaking down the gates! *Noise.* 1850
COMMANDER.	My gates, you mean? The gates of a Commander of Calatrava?
FLORES.	All the town has come!
JUAN ROJO, *off.*	Destroy, demolish, flatten, fire and burn!
ORTUÑO.	When once the people rise against their masters, it's hard to hold them back!
COMMANDER.	They've risen against me?
FLORES.	Their fury's gone so far, they've stormed the gates and brought them to the ground!
COMMANDER.	Untie his hands. Go and appease that peasant magistrate.

1855–1919. Lope follows closely once more the account in the *Chronica*, 79v.

FRONDOSO.	Yo voy, senor, que amor les ha movido. *Vase.*
MENGO, *dentro.*	¡Vivan Fernando y Isabel, y mueran 1865
	los traidores!
FLORES.	Señor, por Dios te pido
	que no te hallen aquí.
COMENDADOR.	Si perseveran,
	este aposento es fuerte y defendido.
	Ellos se volverán.
FLORES.	Cuando se alteran
	los pueblos agraviados, y resuelven, 1870
	nunca sin sangre o sin venganza vuelven.
COMENDADOR.	En esta puerta, así como rastrillo,
	su furor con las armas defendamos.
FRONDOSO, *dentro.*	¡Viva Fuente Ovejuna!
COMENDADOR.	¡Qué caudillo!
	Estoy porque a su furia acometamos. 1875
FLORES.	De la tuya, señor, me maravillo.
ESTEBAN.	Ya el tirano y los cómplices miramos.
	¡Fuente Ovejuna, y los tiranos mueran!

Salen todos.

COMENDADOR.	¡Pueblo, esperad!
TODOS.	¡Agravios nunca esperan!
COMENDADOR.	Decídmelos a mí, que iré pagando 1880
	a fe de caballero, esos errores.
TODOS.	¡Fuente Ovejuna! ¡Viva el Rey Fernando!
	¡Mueran malos cristianos y traidores!
COMENDADOR.	¿No me queréis oír? Yo estoy hablando.
	¡Yo soy vuestro señor!
TODOS.	¡Nuestros señores 1885
	son los Reyes Católicos!
COMENDADOR.	¡Espera!
TODOS.	¡Fuente Ovejuna, y Fernán Gómez muera!

Vanse, y salen las mujeres armadas.

LAURENCIA.	Parad en este puesto de esperanzas,
	soldados atrevidos, no mujeres.

1864.   This striking line, as noted by Spitzer, 284, 'must mean that the rebellion was ultimately an act of love, an attempt to reestablish harmony'. Note the juxtaposition of the following line, shouted offstage.

FRONDOSO.	I'll go, my lord. It's love that's moved them so.	1864
MENGO, *off.*	Long live the King and Queen; let tyrants die!	
FLORES.	My lord, don't let them find you here, for God's sake!	
COMMANDER.	If they persist, they'll find these walls are stout and well defended; that will turn them back.	
FLORES.	But when whole towns, incensed by wrongs, rebel and set their minds to murder and revenge, they're never turned until they're satisfied.	
COMMANDER.	This door's as strong as any iron portcullis; let's arm and make a stand against their fury.	
FRONDOSO, *off.*	Long live Fuente Ovejuna!	1874
COMMANDER	What a hero! I've half a mind to sally forth and brave such blustering.	
FLORES.	It's yours I wonder at.	
ESTEBAN.	Ah, there they are, the tyrant and his toadies! Fuente Ovejuna! Let the tyrants die!	

All the male peasants enter.

COMMANDER.	Good people, wait!
ALL.	Revenge can never wait.
COMMANDER.	Tell me how I've offended; I'll put right what wrongs I've done, I swear it on my honour.
ALL.	Fuente Ovejuna! Long live Ferdinand, and let all traitors and false Christians die!
COMMANDER.	Will you not listen? I demand you hear me; it is your lord who speaks.
ALL.	Our only lords are Ferdinand and Isabella.
COMMANDER.	Wait!
ALL.	Fuente Ovejuna! Death to Fernán Gómez!

The men exit, and the women enter, carrying weapons.

LAURENCIA.	Halt, and wait here in eager expectation, you women – no, you valiant men-at-arms.	1888

1874. Alongside the other slogans, there appears for the first time one recorded by the *Chronica*, 79va, which will encapsulate henceforth the town's collective identity and will (see 1877, 1882, 1887, 1919, 2092 etc.).

1888D. The action shifts, clearly, from inside to outside the Commander's

PASCUALA.	¡Lo que mujeres son en las venganzas!	1890
	En él beban su sangre es bien que esperes.	
JACINTA.	Su cuerpo recojamos en las lanzas.	
PASCUALA.	Todas son de esos mismos pareceres.	
ESTEBAN, *dentro.*	¡Muere, traidor Comendador!	
COMENDADOR	Ya muero.	
	¡Piedad, Señor, que en tu clemencia espero!	1895
BARRILDO, *dentro.* Aquí está Flores.		
MENGO	¡Dale a ese bellaco,	
	que ése fue el que me dio dos mil azotes!	
FRONDOSO, *dentro.* No me vengo, si el alma no le saco.		
LAURENCIA.	No excusamos entrar.	
PASCUALA.	No te alborotes.	
	Bien es guardar la puerta.	
BARRILDO, *dentro.*	No me aplaco.	1900
	¡Con lágrimas agora, marquesotes!	
LAURENCIA.	Pascuala, yo entro dentro, que la espada	
	no ha de estar tan sujeta ni envainada. *Vase.*	
BARRILDO.	Aquí esta Ortuño.	
FRONDOSO.	Córtale la cara.	

Sale Flores huyendo, y Mengo tras él.

FLORES.	¡Mengo, piedad, que no soy yo el culpado!	1905
MENGO.	Cuando ser alcahuete no bastara,	
	bastaba haberme el pícaro azotado.	
PASCUALA.	¡Dánoslo a las mujeres, Mengo! Para,	
	acaba, por tu vida!	
MENGO.	Ya está dado,	
	que no le quiero yo mayor castigo.	1910
PASCUALA.	Vengaré tus azotes.	
MENGO.	Eso digo.	
JACINTA.	¡Ea, muera el traidor!	
FLORES.	¿Entre mujeres?	
JACINTA.	¿No le viene muy ancho?	
PASCUALA.	¿Aqueso lloras?	

---

house.   Men are heard within, but do not appear until 1905.

1890–1.   See the end-notes for these difficult lines and their punctuation.   I take *en él* to repeat *en este puesto*; Pascuala is advising Laurencia to remain outside (cf. 1898–9).   Whether *beban* refers to the men or the women seems ambiguous.

PASCUALA.	What furies women are when they seek vengeance!
	We'd best stay here, so they can drink his blood.
JACINTA.	We'll spike his carcase on our pikes and lances.
PASCUALA.	All of us women want to do the same.
ESTEBAN, *off*.	Die, traitorous Commander! Die!
COMMANDER.	I'm dying!
	Have pity, Lord; I trust your boundless mercy! 1895
BARRILDO, *off*.	Here's Flores too.
MENGO	Don't let that swine escape,
	he was the one who gave me such a flogging!
FRONDOSO, *off*.	I shan't be avenged if I can't have his hide!
LAURENCIA.	We should go in, not wait.
PASCUALA.	Don't get so excited.
	It's best we watch the door.
BARRILDO, *off*.	You won't move me!
	It's too late now for tears, my pretty pansies! 1901
LAURENCIA.	Pascuala, I'm going in; swords shouldn't stay
	so unemployed and useless in their scabbards. *She exits.*
BARRILDO.	Look, here's Ortuño.
FRONDOSO.	Slash the villain's face!

Flores enters fleeing, pursued by Mengo.

FLORES.	Have mercy, Mengo, please, it wasn't *my* fault!
MENGO.	If being his pimp weren't cause enough for blame,
	my flogging would be just as good a reason.
PASCUALA.	Give him to us now, Mengo; you lay off,
	and let us women have him.
MENGO.	Here he is then;
	I wouldn't want to see him better punished.
PASCUALA.	I shall avenge your flogging.
MENGO.	Mind you do!
JACINTA.	Let's do the traitor in!
FLORES.	Be killed by women?
JACINTA.	Isn't it fitting?
PASCUALA.	Why d'you weep at that?

1895.   Killed offstage, the Commander makes a last-minute appeal to God, which rings hollow if we recall 1247–52 and 1274–6.

1901.   On *marquesotes*, see P's full note, including eleven quotations from Lope.

1902–3.   An ironic echo of the Commander's lines in the first scene (129–37).

JACINTA.	¡Muere, concertador de sus placeres!	
PASCUALA.	¡Ea, muera el traidor!	
FLORES.	¡Piedad, señoras!	1915

Sale Ortuño huyendo de Laurencia.

ORTUÑO.	Mira que no soy yo...	
LAURENCIA.	¡Ya sé quién eres!	
	¡Entrad, teñid las armas vencedoras	
	en estos viles!	
PASCUALA.	¡Moriré matando!	
TODAS.	¡Fuente Ovejuna, y viva el Rey Fernando! *Vanse y...*	

... salen el Rey Fernando y la Reina doña Isabel y don Manrique, Maestre.

MANRIQUE.	De modo la prevención	[*redondillas*] 1920
	fue, que el efeto esperado	
	llegamos a ver logrado,	
	con poca contradición.	
	Hubo poca resistencia;	
	y supuesto que la hubiera,	1925
	sin duda ninguna fuera	
	de poca o ninguna esencia.	
	Queda el de Cabra ocupado	
	en conservación del puesto,	
	por si volviere dispuesto	1930
	a él el contrario osado.	
REY.	Discreto el acuerdo fue,	
	y que asista es conveniente,	
	y reformando la gente,	
	el paso tomado esté.	1935
	Que con eso se asegura	
	no podernos hacer mal	
	Alfonso, que en Portugal	
	tomar la fuerza procura.	
	Y el de Cabra es bien que esté	1940
	en ese sitio asistente,	
	y como tan diligente,	

1920D. Ferdinand appears, as if on cue, linking again the two actions. Casalduero suggests, p. 47 (and H indicates) that Isabella, who does not speak in this scene, should not appear. In my view, both monarchs (and their insignia) should appear together, throughout the play.

JACINTA.	You fixed his pleasures for him, we'll fix you!
PASCUALA.	Let's do for him, the traitor!
FLORES.	Mercy, ladies!

Ortuño enters, fleeing from Laurencia.

ORTUÑO.	It wasn't me...
LAURENCIA.	I know you well enough.
	Come in and colour your victorious weapons
	with their foul blood!
PASCUALA.	I'll kill till I can't stand.
ALL WOMEN.	Fuente Ovejuna! Long live Ferdinand! *All exit, and ...*

... King Ferdinand, Queen Isabella and don Manrique, the Master of Santiago, enter.

MANRIQUE.	Our enterprise was well prepared,	1920
	and so the whole campaign	
	.was very smoothly carried out,	
	and we achieved our aim.	
	The enemy afforded us	
	no very great resistance,	
	and even if they had, no doubt	
	it would have posed no problem.	
	The Count of Cabra has remained	
	in charge of the position,	
	in case they're rash enough to risk	
	a counter-operation.	
FERDINAND.	That was a very prudent move;	
	it's wise he should maintain	
	the town and troops in good array	
	and keep that route controlled.	
	It means we can be well assured	
	Alfonso, who's intent	
	on raising strength in Portugal,	
	cannot disturb our peace.	
	It suits us very well the Count	
	should occupy the town	

1920–7. Note that Manrique's description of his victory over the forces of Calatrava offers a comparison and contrast with that of the loyal townsfolk of Fuente Ovejuna.

                         muestras de su valor dé;
                         porque con esto asegura
                         el daño que nos recela,   1945
                         y como fiel centinela
                         el bien del reino procura.

Sale Flores, herido.

FLORES.   Católico Rey Fernando,   [*romance*]
                         a quien el cielo concede
                         la corona de Castilla   1950
                         como a varón excelente:
                         oye la mayor crueldad
                         que se ha visto entre las gentes,
                         desde donde nace el sol
                         hasta donde se escurece.   1955
REY.   Repórtate.
FLORES.   Rey supremo,
                         mis heridas no consienten
                         dilatar el triste caso,
                         por ser mi vida tan breve.
                         De Fuente Ovejuna vengo,   1960
                         donde, con pecho inclemente,
                         los vecinos de la villa
                         a su señor dieron muerte.
                         Muerto Fernán Gómez queda
                         por sus súbditos aleves,   1965
                         que vasallos indignados
                         con leve causa se atreven.
                         Con título de tirano,
                         que le acumula la plebe,
                         a la fuerza desta voz   1970
                         el hecho fiero acometen,
                         y quebrantando su casa,
                         no atendiendo a que se ofrece
                         por la fe de caballero
                         a que pagará a quien debe,   1975
                         no sólo no le escucharon,
                         pero con furia impaciente

1948–51.   Note the parallels between the the beginning of this speech (and the
rest of the scene) and 655–8 &c.

and give such ample evidence
of his heroic zeal
by affording us security
against the threat we fear
– a loyal sentinel who seeks
to serve his country's need.

Flores enters, wounded.

FLORES.   Most Catholic King Ferdinand   1948
whom Heaven in its wisdom
has given so worthily to wear
the crown of fair Castile;
Let me relate the cruellest crime
mankind has ever seen
from where the sun begins its course
to where it sinks to rest.

FERDINAND. Come, calm yourself.

FLORES.   My sovereign lord,
my wounds will not permit
a long account of this sad tale;
I stand too close to death.
I come from Fuente Ovejuna, sire,   1960
by whose inhabitants
their master, the Commander, has
been mercilessly killed.
Sire, Fernán Gómez has been slain
by his seditious subjects;
for serfs who fancy they've been wronged
need little cause to rise.
The peasants call him tyrant, heap
that slander on his name,
and make it their excuse to attempt
so horrible a deed.
They violate his house, ignore
his offer, on his word
of honour as a nobleman,
to settle any scores;
indeed, not only pay no heed,
but vent their reckless rage,

1960–99. Note that Flores' account, though biased, follows closely that in the *Chronica*, 79v a & b.

rompen el cruzado pecho
con mil heridas crueles;
y por las altas ventanas   1980
le hacen que al suelo vuele,
adonde en picas y espadas
le recogen las mujeres.
Llévanle a una casa muerto,
y a porfía, quien más puede   1985
mesa su barba y cabello,
y apriesa su rostro hieren.
En efeto fue la furia
tan grande que en ellos crece,
que las mayores tajadas   1990
las orejas a ser vienen.
Sus armas borran con picas,
y a voces dicen que quieren
tus reales armas fijar,
porque aquéllas las ofenden.   1995
Saqueáronle la casa
cual si de enemigos fuese,
y gozosos entre todos
han repartido sus bienes.
Lo dicho he visto escondido,   2000
porque mi infelice suerte
en tal trance no permite
que mi vida se perdiese;
y asi estuve todo el día
hasta que la noche viene,   2005
y salir pude escondido
para que cuenta te diese.
Haz, señor, pues eres justo,
que la justa pena lleven
de tan riguroso caso   2010
los bárbaros delincuentes.
Mira que su sangre a voces
pide que tu rigor prueben.

REY.   Estar puedes confiado
que sin castigo no queden.   2015
El triste suceso ha sido
tal, que admirado me tiene,

1978. Note how Lope inserts a further reference to the Cross of Calatrava.

and rend the Cross upon his breast
with countless savage blows.
Then from his highest balconies
they fling him to the ground,
where women wait to raise his corpse
on lances, pikes and swords.
They drag his carcase to a house,
and vie persistently
to tug and tear his beard and hair
and mutilate his face.
In fact their fury grows so great,
so vicious is their spite,
they tear his corpse to pieces, till
the largest are his ears.
They rend his coat-of-arms with pikes
and shout that they intend
to raise your coat-of-arms instead,
for his is an offence.
They pillaged all his property
as if it were a foe's,
and gleefully divided out
his goods among themselves.
All this I saw from where I hid,
for my unhappy fate
decreed I should not lose my life
at such a tragic time.
I lay concealed throughout the day,
until the night drew near
and I could safely steal away
to bring you this account.
As you are just, your Majesty,
let your just sentence fall
on those who cruelly carried out
so barbarous a crime.
His blood cries out for them to feel
the rigour of your rule.

FERDINAND.   You can be sure they'll not escape
without due punishment.
An incident so sad and so
astonishing demands

    y que vaya luego un juez
    que lo averigüe conviene,
    y castigue los culpados   2020
    para ejemplo de las gentes.
    Vaya un capitán con él,
    porque seguridad lleve;
    que tan grande atrevimiento
    castigo ejemplar requiere.   2025
    Y curad a ese soldado
    de las heridas que tiene.   *Vanse, y ...*

... salen los labradores y labradoras, con la cabeza de Fernán Gómez en una lanza.

MÚSICOS.   *¡Muchos años vivan*   [*coplilla de estribillo*]
                   Isabel y Fernando,
                   y mueran los tiranos!   2030
BARRILDO.   Diga su copla Frondoso.   [*redondillas*]
FRONDOSO.   Ya va mi copla, a la fe;
                   si le faltare algún pie,
                   enmiéndele el más curioso.
                   ¡Vivan la bella Isabel   [*copla*] 2035
                   y Fernando de Aragón,
                   pues que para en uno son,
                   él con ella, ella con él!
                   A los cielos San Miguel
                   lleve a los dos de las manos.   2040
                   ¡Vivan muchos anos,
                   y mueran los tiranos!

2018–25.   The King's response recalls his very similar reaction to the report from Ciudad Real (707–15).   His promise of an exemplary punishment (after due investigation) contrasts with the hypocrisy of the lawless Commander (e.g. 1582–1606, esp. 1599–1600).

2028D.   The *Chronica* makes no reference to this parading of the villain's head (as in *Macbeth*), or to its symbolic replacement (in 2069–80, anticipated by 1992–5) by the royal coat-of-arms.

2028–30.   The *estribillo* 1) celebrates Ferdinand and Isabella, who have just gone off, and denigrates Fernán Gómez, who is 'present'; 2) recapitulates musically the peasants' slogans (e.g. 1811–4, 1865–6); and 3) recalls the wedding-song, set surely to the same tune.   It too should perhaps begin

that I dispatch a magistrate   2018
to investigate the case,
and punish all the guilty as
examples to mankind.
A captain shall go with him to
protect him in his role,
for such outrageous wrongs require
exemplary redress.
And see this soldier's treated for
the wounds he has sustained.   *All exit,*

---

and the peasants enter, with the head of Fernán Gómez on a lance.

MUSICIANS.   *May Isabella and Ferdinand*   2028
                    ever rule our happy land,
                    and all tyrants be dead and damned!
BARRILDO.   Let's hear Frondoso's verse.
FRONDOSO.   Well, here it is;
                    and if some critic claims it doesn't scan,
                    `I say let him do better if he can!
                    Long life to Isabella fair
                    and Ferdinand of Aragon,
                    who live and love and rule as one,   2037
                    she his, he hers, a happy pair;
                    and when at last to Heaven they fare,   2039
                    may Michael lead them by the hand.
[MUSICIANS].   *May Isabella and Ferdinand...*

(2054 notwithstanding) *Vivan muchos años* (see 2068, and n. to 2041-2). The
fact that it is similarly glossed in *coplas* further associates the royal couple (see
esp. 2037-40, and cf. 1503-6) with Frondoso and Laurencia. Indeed the whole
scene of celebration should be played as a kind of pastiche of the previous one,
underlining the message of the murder; *amor les ha movido* (1864).

2039-40. The Archangel Michael is supposed to weigh souls, and conduct the
righteous after death to God; hence the Offertory of the Roman Mass for the
Dead: 'May Michael the standard-bearer lead them into the holy light'.

LAURENCIA.	Diga Barrildo.	*[redondilla]*
BARRILDO.	Ya va,	
	que a fe que la he pensado.	
PASCUALA.	Si la dices con cuidado,	2045
	buena y rebuena será.	
BARRILDO.	*¡Vivan los Reyes famosos*	*[copla]*
	muchos años, pues que tienen	
	la vitoria, y a ser vienen	
	nuestros dueños venturosos!	2050
	¡Salgan siempre vitoriosos	
	de gigantes y de enanos,	
	y mueran los tiranos!	
MÚSICOS.	*¡Muchos años vivan*	*[copla de estribillo]*
	[Isabel y Fernando.	2055
	y mueran los tiranos!]	
LAURENCIA.	Diga Mengo.	*[redondilla]*
FRONDOSO.	Mengo diga.	
MENGO.	Yo soy poeta donado.	
PASCUALA.	Mejor dirás: lastimado	
	el envés de la barriga.	2060
MENGO.	*Una mañana en domingo*	*[copla]*
	me mandó azotar aquel,	
	de manera que el rabel	
	me daba espantoso respingo;	
	pero agora que los pringo,	2065
	¡vivan los Reyes Cristiánigos,	
	y mueran los tiránigos!	
MÚSICOS.	*¡Vivan muchos años..!*	*[coplilla de estribillo]*
ESTEBAN.	Quita la cabeza allá.	*[redondillas]*
MENGO.	Cara tiene de ahorcado.	2070

2041-2. Frondoso's *copla* seems, by comparison with those that follow, to have a line too many; probably, as Bl suggests, 2041 should follow 2042, and represent a reprise of the *estribillo* (see 2054, 2068).

2054. The *Parte* texts have 'etc.' after this line, indicating that the whole *estribillo* is to be repeated, as probably happens at 2041-2 and 2068.

2058. On Lope's mockery of the *poeta donado* (=lay, i.e. amateur, poet), see *Dorotea*, 265, and P's note.

2059-60. *lastimado / el envés de la barriga* lit. = battered on the backside of the belly.

LAURENCIA.	And now Barrildo's.	
BARRILDO.	Right you are; here goes.	2043
	I've sweated blood on it, I'll tell you straight.	
PASCUALA.	Just say it loud and clear, we'll think it's great.	
BARRILDO.	*Long live the Catholic Kings, whose might*	
	has given them the victory,	
	whose subjects we are glad to be,	
	and whom to serve is our delight.	
	May they maintain, whether they fight	
	with giants or dwarves, the upper hand.	
MUSICIANS.	*May Isabella and Ferdinand...*	2054
LAURENCIA.	It's Mengo's turn.	
FRONDOSO.	Yes, let's hear Mengo's verse.	
MENGO.	I'm not a proper poet, just a layman.	2058
PASCUALA.	You ought to say, a man who's been laid into!	
MENGO.	*That bastard had my backside pasted,*	
	one Sunday morning in the spring,	
	so that it stung like anything	
	as long as the lacerations lasted;	
	but now they're not just beaten but basted,	2064
	long live Isabella and Ferdinandigo,	
	and tyrants all be dead and damnedigo!	2067
MUSICIANS.	*May Isabella and Ferdinand...*	
ESTEBAN.	That head can surely go now.	2069
MENGO.	I should say!	
	It's certainly a skeleton at the feast!	

2063.   *rabel* here (contrast 286) is a comic euphemism (see 1651, 2060, 2424, 2426), no doubt from *rabo* (= tail); 'Festiva y familiarmente se suele llamar al trasero' (*Autoridades*). Cf. '¡Ah, rocín de Bercebú, / cuál me tienes el rabel!'; *Los comendadores de Córdoba*, BAE 215, 43a.

2065.   It was the cruel practice to *pringar* (torture by basting with hot bacon fat) the wound of negroes or jews who had been flogged; by *los* Mengo presumably means either (jokingly) his own wounds (also alluded to in the wedding-scene, 1479–80, 1487–8, 1644–51), or the Commander and his men, on whom he feels he has inflicted in revenge a worse torture (1896–7, 1906–51).

2066–7.   *Cristiánigos ... tiránigos*: 'The formations in *-igo* belong to a pattern familiar in burlesque popular poetry', Spitzer, 286, n. 12; see also LE's note.

Saca un escudo Juan Rojo con las armas.

REGIDOR.	Ya las armas han llegado.	
ESTEBAN.	Mostrá las armas acá.	
JUAN.	¿Adónde se han de poner?	
REGIDOR.	Aquí, en el Ayuntamiento.	
ESTEBAN.	¡Bravo escudo!	
BARRILDO.	¡Qué contento!	2075
FRONDOSO.	Ya comienza a amanecer,	
	con este sol, nuestro día.	
ESTEBAN.	¡Vivan Castilla y León,	
	y las barras de Aragón,	
	y muera la tiranía!	2080
	Advertid, Fuente Ovejuna,	
	a las palabras de un viejo,	
	que el admitir su consejo	
	no ha dañado vez ninguna.	
	Los Reyes han de querer	2085
	averiguar este caso,	
	y más tan cerca del paso	
	y jornada que han de hacer.	
	Concertaos todos a una	
	en lo que habéis de decir.	2090
FRONDOSO.	¿Qué es tu consejo?	
ESTEBAN.	Morir	
	diciendo: '¡Fuente Ovejuna!',	
	y a nadie saquen de aquí.	
FRONDOSO.	Es el camino derecho:	
	¡Fuente Ovejuna lo ha hecho!	2095
ESTEBAN.	¿Queréis responder así?	
TODOS.	¡Sí!	
ESTEBAN.	Ahora pues, yo quiero ser	
	agora el pesquisidor,	
	para ensayarnos mejor	
	en lo que habemos de hacer.	2100
	Sea Mengo el que esté puesto	
	en el tormento.	
MENGO.	¿No hallaste	
	otro más flaco?	
ESTEBAN.	¿Pensaste	

Juan Rojo brings on an escutcheon bearing the royal arms.

ALDERMAN.	Look, here's the royal escutcheon.	2071
ESTEBAN.	Well, let's see.	
JUAN ROJO.	Where shall we put it?	
ALDERMAN.	Why, in pride of place	
	on the Town Hall here.	
ESTEBAN.	What a handsome shield!	
BARRILDO.	A happy sight!	
FRONDOSO.	A shining sun, that shows	

a brighter day's begun to dawn for us!

ESTEBAN.   Salute the lions and castles of Leon
and old Castile, the bars of Aragon!
Long may they live, and see all tyrants die!
But wait, Fuenteovejuna, hear the advice
of this old man; it's never a mistake
to attend to what your elders have to say.
The King and Queen will want to investigate
this incident, especially since it's happened
so near the very route they mean to take.
Agree together what you're going to say.

FRONDOSO.   Well, what do you propose?

ESTEBAN.   That everyone,
on pain of death, should say: 'Fuente Ovejuna',
and none of us should utter another word.

FRONDOSO.   Yes, that's the way. It was Fuente Ovejuna
that did the deed!

ESTEBAN.   Shall that be our reply?

ALL.   Yes!

ESTEBAN.   Right, I'll play the investigating judge,   2097
and we'll rehearse together what to do.
Now, who'll be my first victim? I know: Mengo!

MENGO.   Couldn't you find a weaker one?

ESTEBAN.   D'you mean

2071–80. The arms of Isabella (Castile and Leon) and Ferdinand (Aragon) have been mentioned previously in the text (1117–20, 1460–2, 1992–5). Lope may have meant them to be displayed at 1460–2, and whenever the Catholic Monarchs are on stage.

2097–8. *Ahora ... agora*: see n. to 43.

2101–2. It was taken for granted at this time that interrogation always involved torture. Today we pretend that it doesn't.

	que era de veras?	
MENGO.	Di presto.	
ESTEBAN.	¿Quién mató al Comendador?	2105
MENGO.	¡Fuente Ovejuna lo hizo!	
ESTEBAN.	Perro, ¿si te martirizo?	
MENGO.	Aunque me matéis, señor.	
ESTEBAN.	Confiesa, ladrón.	
MENGO.	¡Confieso!	
ESTEBAN.	Pues, ¿quién fue?	
MENGO.	¡Fuente Ovejuna!	2110
ESTEBAN.	¡Dalde otra vuelta!	
MENGO.	Es ninguna.	
ESTEBAN.	¡Cagajón para el proceso!	

Sale el Regidor.

REGIDOR.	¿Qué hacéis desta suerte aquí?	
FRONDOSO.	¿Qué ha sucedido, Cuadrado?	
REGIDOR.	Pesquisidor ha llegado.	2115
ESTEBAN.	Echá todos por ahí.	
REGIDOR.	Con él viene un capitán.	
ESTEBAN.	¡Venga el diablo! Ya sabéis	
	lo que responder tenéis.	
REGIDOR.	El pueblo prendiendo van,	2120
	sin dejar alma ninguna.	
ESTEBAN.	Que no hay que tener temor.	
	¿Quién mató al Comendador,	
	Mengo?	
MENGO.	¿Quién? ¡Fuente Ovejuna! *Vanse, y* ...	

... salen el Maestre y un soldado.

MAESTRE.	¡Que tal cosa ha sucedido! [*redondillas*]	2125
	Infelice fue su suerte.	
	Estoy por darte la muerte	
	por la nueva que has traído.	
SOLDADO.	Yo, señor, soy mensajero,	

2112. *cagajón* lit. = the dung of horses, asses etc. The expression is
deliberately coarse; '*cagar* ... es una de las palabras que se han de excusar,
aunque sea de cosa tan natural, por la decencia' (Covarrubias).

2113D. This alderman presumably entered at 2028, and spoke 2071 and 2074;
probably, as P suggests, he subsequently left the stage.

	you thought I meant it?
MENGO.	Hurry up.
ESTEBAN.	Who was it
	killed the Commander?
MENGO.	Sir, Fuente Ovejuna!
ESTEBAN.	What if I crucify you, dog?
MENGO.	What if
	you kill me, sir?
ESTEBAN.	Confess, you rogue!
MENGO.	I will!
ESTEBAN.	Who was it killed him, then?
MENGO.	Fuente Ovejuna!
ESTEBAN.	Tighten the screw!
MENGO.	It won't do any good.
ESTEBAN.	The enquiry will be just a load of bullshit!

2112

The Alderman enters.

ALDERMAN.	What are you doing here?

2113

FRONDOSO.	What's up, Cuadrado?
ALDERMAN.	They've sent a judge, and he's arrived.
ESTEBAN.	Let's all
	clear off the other way.
ALDERMAN.	What's more, he's brought
	a captain with him.
ESTEBAN.	So? Suppose he's brought
	the devil himself? You all know what to say.
ALDERMAN.	They're going to arrest us, every living soul.
ESTEBAN.	No need to be afraid. Who was it, Mengo,
	killed the Commander?
MENGO.	Who? Fuente Ovejuna! *All exit, and*

... the Master of Calatrava and a soldier enter.

MASTER.	How terrible a fate, and how outrageous!
	I've half a mind to kill you for such news.
SOLDIER.	I'm nothing but a messenger, my lord;

2129

2129–30. Lope's spectators would have remembered the famous ballad-lines:
'Mensajero eres, amigo, / no mereces culpa, no'; see *El primero Benavides,* n. to
1732–3.

	y enojarte no es mi intento.	2130
MAESTRE.	¡Que a tal tuvo atrevimiento	
	un pueblo enojado y fiero!	
	Iré con quinientos hombres,	
	y la villa he de asolar;	
	en ella no ha de quedar	2135
	ni aun memoria de los nombres.	
SOLDADO.	Señor, tu enojo reporta,	
	porque ellos al Rey se han dado,	
	y no tener enojado	
	al Rey es lo que te importa.	2140
MAESTRE.	¿Cómo al Rey se pueden dar	
	si de la Encomienda son?	
SOLDADO.	Con él sobre esa razón	
	podrás luego pleitear.	
MAESTRE.	Por pleito, ¿cuándo salió	2145
	lo que él le entregó en sus manos?	
	Son señores soberanos,	
	y tal reconozco yo.	
	Por saber que al Rey se han dado,	
	se reportará mi enojo,	
	y ver su presencia escojo	2150
	por lo más bien acertado;	
	que puesto que tenga culpa	
	en casos de gravedad,	
	en todo mi poca edad	2155
	viene a ser quien me disculpa.	
	Con vergüenza voy, mas es	
	honor quien puede obligarme,	
	y importa no descuidarme	
	en tan honrado interés. *Vanse.*	

Sale Laurencia sola.

LAURENCIA.	Amando, recelar daño en lo amado	[*soneto*]
	nueva pena de amor se considera;	
	que quien en lo que ama daño espera,	
	aumenta en el temor nuevo cuidado.	
	El firme pensamiento desvelado,	2165
	si le aflige el temor, fácil se altera,	
	que no es, a firme fe, pena ligera	
	ver llevar el temor el bien robado.	

	I had no thought to rouse you to such anger.
MASTER.	To think a village could be so incensed,
	so savage as to dare to do such things!
	I'll take five hundred men and lay it waste,
	destroy the very memory of their names!
SOLDIER.	My lord, you must restrain your indignation;
	they've given themselves directly to the King,
	and you can ill afford to anger him.
MASTER.	How can they give themselves to him directly,
	when they belong directly to the Order?
SOLDIER.	You'll have to plead that case with him at law.
MASTER.	Since when did anyone regain at law

what he could say was his to give to start with?   2146
Such kings are sovereign, as I must acknowledge.
Yes, now I know they've given themselves to him,
my wisest course will be to calm my rage,
pocket my pride, and humbly wait on him!
for though I've been most grievously at fault,
my youth will be my excuse in everything.
I go in shame, but for my honour's sake,
and must not hesitate when that's at stake.   *They exit.*

Laurencia enters, alone.

LAURENCIA.   When those we love are threatened, we discover
love adds new pain to that in which we burn;
for one who fears some danger to a lover
finds fear provokes a new, more keen concern.
The strongest and most deeply felt devotion,
when fear afflicts it, proves an easy prey,
and knows, though firm and fixed, no mild commotion,
for fear that fear may steal its love away.

2146. *èl* is mysterious. C, followed by Bl, understands: *lo que el pueblo le entregó*; but this is to invent an antecedent. LE understands *lo que el Rey entregó a èl, en las manos de éste*; and Lope may have known and recalled that the Crown in 1460 had given Fuente Ovejuna to the Master's father, but in 1465 to Córdoba. Alternatively, *èl* may repeat *el pleito*, and we might understand: 'what such litigation had placed at the King's disposal'.

Mi esposo adoro; la ocasión que veo
al temor de su daño me condena,   2170
si no le ayuda la felice suerte.
Al bien suyo se inclina mi deseo;
si está presente, está cierta mi pena;
si está en ausencia, está cierta mi muerte.

Sale Frondoso.

FRONDOSO.	¡Mi Laurencia!	[*redondillas*] 2175
LAURENCIA.	¡Esposo amado!	

¿Cómo estar aquí te atreves?

FRONDOSO.   ¿Esas resistencias debes
a mi amoroso cuidado?

LAURENCIA.   Mi bien, procura guardarte,
porque tu daño recelo.   2180

FRONDOSO.   No quiera, Laurencia, el cielo
que tal llegue a disgustarte.

LAURENCIA.   ¿No temes ver el rigor
que por los demás sucede,
y el furor con que procede   2185
aqueste pesquisidor?
Procura guardar la vida.
Huye tu daño, no esperes.

FRONDOSO.   ¿Cómo? ¿Que procure quieres
cosa tan mal recebida?   2190
¿Es bien que los demás deje
en el peligro presente,
y de tu vista me ausente?
No me mandes que me aleje,
porque no es puesto en razón   2195
que, por evitar mi daño,
sea con mi sangre extraño
en tan terrible ocasión.   *Voces dentro.*
Voces parece que he oído,
y son, si yo mal no siento,   2200
de alguno que dan tormento.
Oye con atento oído.

Dice dentro el Juez, y responden.

JUEZ.   Decid la verdad, buen viejo.

>   I adore my husband, seek his good alone;
>   unless kind fortune offers him protection,
>   fear for his safety makes me wish him gone;
>   but can I live without his close affection?
>   His presence is a pain I can't endure;
>   his absence, though, is death, and no less sure.

Frondoso enters.

FRONDOSO.   My darling wife, Laurencia!
LAURENCIA.   Dearest husband!
              How dare you come here?
FRONDOSO.   What, does my devotion
              deserve such coolness? Aren't you glad to see me?
LAURENCIA.   It's dangerous, my love. You must stay hidden.
FRONDOSO.   No, heaven forbid I ever grieve you so.
LAURENCIA.   But aren't you frightened when you see how harshly
              the others have been handled, and how cruelly
              the judge is treating everyone he finds?
              Please, try to get away and save your life.
FRONDOSO.   D'you really want me to behave so badly?
              Could I desert the others in such danger?
              Could I leave you? Don't tell me I should go;
              it can't be right for me to save myself
              and be a stranger to my kith and kin
              at such a dreadful time of trial and torment. *Cries offstage.*
              Was that a cry? I think I heard a scream,
              and if I'm not mistaken, it was someone
              the judge is having tortured. Listen hard.

The Judge speaks and cries are heard offstage.

JUDGE.   Tell me the truth, old man.

2199–2257.   The torture-episode is based on the *Chronica*, 80ra.   Though comically anticipated already (2097–2112), it is kept offstage, as such horrors usually were.   Instead, in counterpoint with the villagers' solidarity, Lope shows us its counterpart, the selfless love and sense of community of Frondoso and Laurencia.

FRONDOSO.	Un viejo, Laurencia mía,
	atormentan.
LAURENCIA.	¡Qué porfía!
ESTEBAN.	Déjenme un poco.
JUEZ.	Ya os dejo.
	Decid, ¿quién mató a Fernando?
ESTEBAN.	Fuente Ovejuna lo hizo.
LAURENCIA.	Tu nombre, padre, eternizo.

....

FRONDOSO.	¡Bravo caso!
JUEZ.	¡Ese muchacho!
	¡Aprieta, perro! Yo sé
	que lo sabes. Di quién fue.
	¿Callas? Aprieta, borracho.
NIÑO.	Fuente Ovejuna, señor.
JUEZ.	¡Por vida del Rey, villanos,
	que os ahorque con mis manos!
	¿Quién mató al Comendador?
FRONDOSO.	¡Que a un niño le den tormento,
	y niegue de aquesta suerte!
LAURENCIA.	¡Bravo pueblo!
FRONDOSO.	¡Bravo y fuerte!
JUEZ.	¡Esa mujer al momento
	en ese potro tened!
	Dale esa mancuerda luego.
LAURENCIA.	Ya está de cólera ciego.
JUEZ.	Que os he de matar, creed,
	en ese potro, villanos.
	¿Quién mató al Comendador?
PASCUALA.	Fuente Ovejuna, señor.
JUEZ.	¡Dale!
FRONDOSO.	Pensamientos vanos.
LAURENCIA.	Pascuala niega, Frondoso.
FRONDOSO.	Niegan niños; ¿qué te espantas?
JUEZ.	Parece que los encantas.
	¡Aprieta!
PASCUALA.	¡Ay, cielo piadoso!
JUEZ.	¡Aprieta, infame! ¿Estás sordo?
PASCUALA.	Fuente Ovejuna lo hizo.
JUEZ.	Traedme aquel más rollizo...
	ese desnudo, ese gordo!
LAURENCIA.	¡Pobre Mengo! Él es sin duda.
FRONDOSO.	Temo que ha de confesar.

2205

2210

2215

2220

2225

2230

2235

FRONDOSO.	It's some old man they're torturing, Laurencia.
LAURENCIA.	They're determined!
ESTEBAN.	Leave me a moment.
JUDGE.	Well, I've left you. Tell me, who was it killed him?
ESTEBAN.	Who? Fuente Ovejuna.
LAURENCIA.	God bless you, father, I'm so proud of you.
FRONDOSO.	How splendid!
JUDGE.	Bring that boy. Pull tight, you dog! I know you know, so tell me who it was. You won't, eh? Tighter!
BOY.	Sir, Fuente Ovejuna.
JUDGE.	In the King's name, I swear I'll hang you all, you peasants! Now, who was the one that killed him?
FRONDOSO.	To think they'd take a child and torture him, and still get no more answer!
LAURENCIA.	What a town! What bravery!
FRONDOSO.	What bravery, what guts!
JUDGE.	Right, grab that girl and get her on the rack. Quick, don't waste time. Now try a turn or two!
LAURENCIA.	He's blind with rage!
JUDGE.	You folk had best believe me, I'll rack you all to death before I'm done. Who was it killed him?
PASCUALA.	Sir, Fuente Ovejuna.
JUDGE.	Again!
FRONDOSO.	He won't get anywhere with her.
LAURENCIA.	Frondoso, that's Pascuala. She's not telling.
FRONDOSO.	Is that so strange, when even children won't?
JUDGE.	You'd think they were enjoying it! Turn tighter!
PASCUALA.	Oh God in heaven, have mercy!
JUDGE.	Tighter, wretch! You must be deaf!
PASCUALA.	It was... Fuente Ovejuna.
JUDGE.	Bring me that fleshy one, who looks half-naked; that fat one, yes.
FRONDOSO.	Poor Mengo, it must be him. He'll tell them, I'm afraid.

MENGO.	¡Ay, ay!	
JUEZ.	Comienza a apretar.	2240
MENGO.	¡Ay!	
JUEZ	¿Es menester ayuda?	
MENGO	¡Ay, ay!	
JUEZ.	¿Quién mató, villano, al señor Comendador?	
MENGO.	¡Ay, yo lo diré, señor!	
JUEZ.	Afloja un poco la mano.	2245
FRONDOSO.	Él confiesa.	
JUEZ.	Al palo aplica la espalda.	
MENGO.	Quedo, que yo lo diré.	
JUEZ.	¿Quién le mató?	
MENGO.	Señor, Fuente Ovejunica.	
JUEZ.	¿Hay tan gran bellaquería?	2250

Del dolor se están burlando.
En quien estaba esperando
niega con mayor porfía.
Dejaldos, que estoy cansado.

FRONDOSO.	¡Oh, Mengo, bien te haga Dios!	2255

Temor que tuve de dos,
el tuyo me le ha quitado.

Salen, con Mengo, Barrildo y el Regidor.

BARRILDO.	¡Vítor, Mengo!	
REGIDOR.	Y con razón.	
BARRILDO.	¡Mengo, ¡vítor!	
FRONDOSO.	Eso digo.	
MENGO.	¡Ay, ay!	
BARRILDO.	Toma, bebe, amigo. Come.	2260
MENGO.	¡Ay, ay! ¿Qué es?	
BARRILDO.	Diacitrón.	

2246-7. *Al palo aplica la espalda* seems ambiguous. In the context, the Judge might be offering respite; Combet translates: 'Laisse-le appuyer le dos contre la poutre'.
2249. *Fuente Ovejunica*: Mengo's diminutive defies translation. As Spitzer notes, 287, it not only shows his linguistic whimsicality and attachment to his town, but stresses the smallness – and yet the 'Roman' cohesion – of that social

ACT THREE [201

MENGO.	Oh! Oh!
JUDGE.	Start tightening.
MENGO.	Oh! Oh!
JUDGE.	D'you need some help?
MENGO.	Oh! Oh!
JUDGE.	Well, peasant,

ACT THREE [201

MENGO.　　　　　　　　　　　Oh! Oh!
JUDGE.　　　　　　　　　　Start tightening.
MENGO.　Oh! Oh!
JUDGE.　D'you need some help?
MENGO.　　　　　　　　　　Oh! Oh!
JUDGE.　　　　　　　　　　Well, peasant,
who was it killed him?
MENGO.　　　　　　　Oh! I'll tell you, sir!
JUDGE.　Ease off.
FRONDOSO.　　　He'll tell!
JUDGE.　　　　　Now, get your back behind it.　　2246
MENGO.　Let up, I'll tell you.
JUDGE.　　　　　Well, who was it killed him?
MENGO.　My Lord, a gang of Fuente Ove-hoodlums!　　2249
JUDGE.　Whoever saw such rogues? They laugh at pain.
The one I had most hope of, proves to be
the most defiant! Let them go, I'm tired.
FRONDOSO.　God bless you, Mengo! I was scared enough
for two, but now I'm not; you've shown the way.

Barrildo and the Alderman enter with Mengo.

BARRILDO.　Mengo, well done!
ALDERMAN.　　　　Well done, indeed!　　2257
BARRILDO.　　　　　　Bravo!
FRONDOSO.　I say so too.
MENGO.　　　　Oh! Oh!
BARRILDO.　　　　　Here, have a drink.
Eat this.
MENGO.　　　Oh! Oh! What is it?
BARRILDO.　　　　　Lemon curd.　　2261

---

cell within the national context. Colford proposes: 'our good old Fuente Ovejuna'; Campbell, 'little old Fuente Ovejuna'; Combet, 'ma soeur Fuente Ovejuna'. See also 2281.
2257D. The Alderman may be Juan Rojo or (more probably) Cuadrado.
2257. 'Victor ... Interjección de alegría, con que se aplaude a algún sujeto, u alguna acción. Dícese mas comunmente Vítor... (*Autoridades*).
2261. *diacitrón* lit. = a conserve made of citrus; P cites three other references in Lope. Note also *El loco por fuerza*, AcN 2, 279a: '¿El no ve que el diacitrón / es caliente para el pecho?'

MENGO.	¡Ay, ay!
FRONDOSO.	Echa de beber.
BARRILDO.	.... Ya va.
FRONDOSO.	Bien lo cuela. Bueno está.
LAURENCIA.	Dale otra vez a comer.
MENGO.	¡Ay, ay!
BARRILDO.	Esta va por mí.
LAURENCIA.	Solenemente lo embebe.
FRONDOSO.	El que bien niega, bien bebe.
BARRILDO.	¿Quieres otra?
MENGO.	¡Ay, ay! Sí, sí.
FRONDOSO.	Bebe, que bien lo mereces.
LAURENCIA.	A vez por vuelta las cuela.
FRONDOSO.	Arrópale, que se hiela.
BARRILDO.	¿Quieres más?
MENGO.	Sí, otras tres veces.
	¡Ay, ay!
FRONDOSO.	Si hay vino pregunta.
BARRILDO.	Sí hay; bebe a tu placer,
	que quien niega ha de beber.
	¿Qué tiene?
MENGO.	Una cierta punta.
	Vamos, que me arromadizo.
FRONDOSO.	Que le acuesten es mejor.
	¿Quién mató al Comendador?
MENGO.	Fuente Ovejunica lo hizo. *Vanse*
FRONDOSO.	Justo es que honores le den.
	Pero decidme, mi amor,
	¿quién mató al Comendador?
LAURENCIA.	Fuente Ovejuna, mi bien.
FRONDOSO.	¿Quién le mató?
LAURENCIA.	Dasme espanto.
	Pues Fuente Ovejuna fue.
FRONDOSO.	Y yo, ¿con qué te maté?
LAURENCIA.	¿Con qué? Con quererte tanto.

Marginal line numbers: 2265, 2270, 2275, 2280, 2285

Vanse, y...

2274.   Frondoso pretends to understand ¡*Ay*¡ as ¿*Hay*? (= is there any...?); hence my attempt at a similar pun.

2278.   *me arromadizo: arromadizarse* = catch a catarrhal head-cold (see 2272); but also Mengo must be drunk by now.

MENGO.	Oh! Oh!
FRONDOSO.	Come on, drink up.
BARRILDO.	Yes, that's the way.
FRONDOSO.	He's putting it away! He'll be all right.
LAURENCIA.	Give him more food.
MENGO.	Oh! Oh!
BARRILDO.	This one's on me.
LAURENCIA.	He's soaking up the wine!
FRONDOSO.	Why shouldn't he?

He kept his mouth shut, now he's got it open.

BARRILDO.	D'you want another one?
MENGO.	Oh! Oh! Yes, yes.
FRONDOSO.	Drink up, you've earned it.
LAURENCIA	Can't he knock it back!
FRONDOSO.	You'd better wrap him up, he must be freezing.
BARRILDO.	D'you want another, friend?
MENGO.	Another three!

2272

Oh! Oh!

FRONDOSO.	Does that mean water?
BARRILDO.	No, you clown,

2274

it's wine he wants. As much as you can down;
no doubt not talking gives a man a thirst!
What's up with it?

MENGO.	It's got a sort of edge.

I'd better go, my head's a little thick.

2278

FRONDOSO.	It'd be best to pack him off to bed.

But tell us, Mengo: Who killed the Commander?

MENGO.	A great big gang of... Fuente Ove-hooligans!

2281

All exit, except Frondoso and Laurencia.

FRONDOSO.	They're right to honour him. But tell me, love,

who was it killed him?

LAURENCIA.	Who? Fuente Ovejuna!
FRONDOSO.	Come on, who really killed him?
LAURENCIA.	You amaze me;

Fuente Ovejuna!

FRONDOSO.	And how did I kill you?
LAURENCIA.	With love, my love. I'm dying of love; you too?

They exit, and ...

... salen el Rey y la Reina, y Manrique.

ISABEL.	No entendí, señor, hallaros	[*redondillas*] 2290
	aquí, y es buena mi suerte.	
REY.	En nueva gloria convierte	
	mi vista el bien de miraros.	
	Iba a Portugal de paso,	
	y llegar aquí fue fuerza.	2295
ISABEL.	Vuestra Majestad le tuerza,	
	siendo conveniente el caso.	
REY.	¿Cómo dejáis a Castilla?	
ISABEL.	En paz queda, quieta y llana.	
REY.	Siendo vos la que la allana,	2300
	no lo tengo a maravilla.	

Sale don Manrique.

MANRIQUE.	Para ver vuestra presencia	
	el Maestre de Calatrava,	
	que aquí de llegar acaba,	
	pide que le deis licencia.	2305
ISABEL.	Verle tenía deseado.	
MANRIQUE.	Mi fe, senora, os empeño,	
	que, aunque es en edad pequeño,	
	es valeroso soldado.	

Sale el Maestre.

MAESTRE.	Rodrigo Téllez Girón,	2310
	que de loaros no acaba,	
	Maestre de Calatrava,	
	os pide, humilde, perdón.	
	Confieso que fui engañado,	
	y que excedí de lo justo	2315
	en cosas de vuestro gusto,	
	como mal aconsejado.	
	El consejo de Fernando,	
	y el interés,me engañó,	

2290D.   Manrique does not in fact enter until 2302 (to exit again at 2309). Frondoso and Laurencia are replaced on stage by Ferdinand and Isabella, and the 'love-duet', which framed the torture-episode, by a 'love-duet' (albeit in courtly terms) between the Catholic Monarchs, which initiates the scene of resolution.

... the King and Queen and (later) Manrique enter.

ISABELLA.   I'd not expected, sir, that you'd be here,   2290
                and count myself most fortunate you are.
FERDINAND.   My eyes regard the joy of seeing you
                as great new glory; I was on my way
                to Portugal, but had to come to greet you.
ISABELLA.   I trust Your Majesty will always make
                such welcome detours, when it proves convenient.
FERDINAND.   How did you leave Castile?
ISABELLA.   At peace, my lord;
                calm and content.
FERDINAND.   Since it was you who strove
                to bring that peace, I cannot be surprised.

Don Manrique enters.

MANRIQUE.   Your Majesties, the Master of Calatrava
                has just arrived, and craves your leave to appear.
ISABELLA.   I had desired to see him; bid him enter.
MANRIQUE.   I pledge my word, my lady, that you'll find him,
                though still so young in years, a valiant soldier.

The Master of Calatrava enters.

MASTER.   Rodrigo Téllez, Master of Calatrava,
                who praises you unceasingly, comes now
                before you both, and humbly begs forgiveness.
                I recognise the errors I've committed,
                the guilty excess that's earned your grave displeasure;
                but I was ill-advised by Fernán Gómez,   2318
                deceived by him and by self-interest,

2296. *le* repeats *paso* in 2294, though there it had a different sense (*de paso* = on the way; *torcer el paso* = change course). Such witty tricks of style are common in Lope.

2310–37.   Note how Lope telescopes events.   As the *Chronica* recorded, 80rb-va, the Master long continued to support Alfonso; only 'passados algunos años, como ya el Maestre auia crecido en edad y entendimiento, conoscio auerlo errado en tomar voz cōtra los Reyes Catholicos', and successfully sought their pardon.   His campaign against the Moors, and his heroic death near Loja, did not take place until 1482.

	injusto fiel; y ansí yo	2320
	perdón humilde os demando.	
	Y si recebir merezco	
	esta merced que suplico,	
	desde aquí me certifico	
	en que a serviros me ofrezco.	2325
	Y que en aquesta jornada	
	de Granada, adonde vais,	
	os prometo que veáis	
	el valor que hay en mi espada;	
	donde, sacándola apenas,	2330
	dándoles fieras congojas,	
	plantaré mis Cruces rojas	
	sobre sus altas almenas.	
	Y más, quinientos soldados	
	en serviros emplearé,	2335
	junto con la firma y fe	
	de en mi vida disgustaros.	
REY.	Alzad, Maestre, del suelo,	
	que siempre que hayáis venido	
	seréis muy bien recebido.	2340
MAESTRE.	Sois de afligidos consuelo.	
ISABEL.	Vos, con valor peregrino,	
	sabéis bien decir y hacer.	
MAESTRE.	Vos sois una bella Ester,	
	y vos, un Xerxes divino.	2345

Sale Manrique.

MANRIQUE.	Señor, el pesquisidor	
	que a Fuente Ovejuna ha ido,	
	con el despacho ha venido	
	a verse ante tu valor.	
REY.	Sed juez destos agresores.	2350
MAESTRE.	Si a vos, señor, no mirara,	
	sin duda les enseñara	
	a matar Comendadores.	
REY.	Eso ya no os toca a vos.	

2319–20. *el interés ... injusto fiel*: Bl explains 'el interés no es un justo fiel de la balanza del comportamiento'; less convincingly, LEGB understands: 'el interés le hizo cometer injusticia pensando que era fiel a sus designios'.

2332. A final reference to the insignia of Calatrava (contrast 1453–62).

	another evil arbiter; and therefore	2320
	kneel now in penitence and crave your pardon,	
	and promise, if I merit such indulgence,	
	henceforth to offer my devoted service.	

another evil arbiter; and therefore   2320
kneel now in penitence and crave your pardon,
and promise, if I merit such indulgence,
henceforth to offer my devoted service.
The conquest of Granada you propose
shall see, I swear, the valour of my sword,
which, scarcely drawn, shall fright the afflicted Moor,
and set my crimson Crosses on his towers: 2332
In fine, I bring five hundred men to serve you,
and pledge and promise never more to offend.

FERDINAND.   Rise, Master, from your knees; be sure such service,
come when you may, will always make you welcome.

MASTER.   Such graciousness is comfort to the contrite.

ISABELLA.   We recognise your own especial merit,
as skilled in speech as daring in your deeds.

MASTER.   You, madam, are as fair and wise as Esther;   2344
you, sire, more righteous than her consort Xerxes.

Manrique enters.

MANRIQUE.   The judge whom you dispatched to investigate
in Fuente Ovejuna, has returned
to offer his report.

FERDINAND.   I call on you
to judge how we should deal with such assassins.   2350

MASTER.   Except that I defer to you in this,
I'd teach them, sire, in no uncertain manner,
to murder the Commander of an Order.

FERDINAND.   That is no longer a concern of yours.

2334–7.   *soldados ... disgustaros*: such false rhymes are rare in Lope; cf.
866–7.   Note that the Master previously proposed to take five hundred men to
destroy Fuente Ovejuna (2133–4).
2344–5.   The Master compares Ferdinand and Isabella to Xerxes (King of
Persia 486–465 B.C.) and Esther, who according to the Book of Esther was his
wife between the seventh and twelfth years of his reign.   In lines 2076–8 of
Carlos V en Francia (1604), Charles V is called a 'claro Xerxes'; and in 1610
Lope wrote his play *La bella Ester* (although the King's name appears there as
Asuero).
2350.   This line is probably addressed to Isabella (see also 2390); but the
Master interposes and has to be silenced.

ISABEL.   Yo confieso que he de ver   2355
                 el cargo en vuestro poder,
                 si me lo concede Dios.

Sale el Juez.

JUEZ.   A Fuente Ovejuna fui
                 de la suerte que has mandado,
                 y con especial cuidado   2360
                 y diligencia asistí.
                 Haciendo averiguación
                 del cometido delito,
                 una hoja no se ha escrito
                 que sea en comprobación;   2365
                 porque, conformes a una,
                 con un valeroso pecho,
                 en pidiendo quién lo ha hecho,
                 responden: 'Fuente Ovejuna'.
                 Trecientos he atormentado,   2370
                 con no pequeño rigor,
                 y te prometo, señor,
                 que más que esto no he sacado.
                 Hasta niños de diez años
                 al potro arrimé, y no ha sido   2375
                 posible haberlo inquirido
                 ni por halagos ni engaños.
                 Y pues tan mal se acomoda
                 el poderlo averiguar,
                 o los has de perdonar,   2380
                 o matar la villa toda.
                 Todos vienen ante ti
                 para mas certificarte;
                 dellos podrás informarte.
REY.   Que entren, pues vienen, les di.   2385

Salen los dos alcaldes, Frondoso, las mujeres, y los villanos que quisieren.

LAURENCIA.   ¿Aquéstos los Reyes son?
FRONDOSO.   Y en Castilla poderosos.
LAURENCIA.   Por mi fe, que son hermosos:
                    ¡bendígalos San Antón!
ISABEL.   ¿Los agresores son éstos?   2390

| ISABELLA. | For my part I confess I mean, God willing, | 2355 |
| | to see that office under your control. | |

The Judge enters.

JUDGE.   I went, as you commanded, to the town,
                and exercised all diligence and care
                to investigate the crime that was committed,
                but could not pen one page of evidence;
                for everyone, with fearless fortitude,   2367
                when I demanded who had done the deed,
                replied with one accord: 'Fuente Ovejuna'.
                Three hundred souls I tortured, showed no mercy,
                and swear I could extract no more than this.
                I went as far as stretching boys of ten
                upon the rack, and still could learn no more,
                whatever tricks or blandishments I tried.
                No more can be determined; you must either
                pardon them all, or put the town to death.
                They all have come to offer further proof,
                and you may question them.

FERDINAND.   Then bid them enter.

The two magistrates, Frondoso and the women enter, with any number of peasants.

LAURENCIA.   Are those the King and Queen?

FRONDOSO.   Those are the rulers
                of all Castile.

LAURENCIA.   I swear to heaven they're handsome;
                Saint Anthony preserve them!   2389

ISABELLA.   And are these
                the assassins, then?

2355–7. Isabella is addressing not, as is sometimes supposed, the Master, but Ferdinand, who with Papal authority assumed command of the Order of Calatrava after the death of the next Master; see Introduction, note 55.

2367. Note that the Judge himself is made to admire the villagers' fortitude. His whole speech is based on the *Chronica*, 80ra.

2389. The young bride, like a bystander at a wedding, invokes the blessing of St. Anthony of Padua – the patron saint, in popular devotion, of lovers and of marriage – on the couple at the head of the social hierarchy.

ALCALDE [ESTEBAN.] Fuente Ovejuna, señora,
    que humildes llegan agora
    para serviros dispuestos.
     La sobrada tiranía
    y el insufrible rigor   2395
    del muerto Comendador,
    que mil insultos hacía,
     fue el autor de tanto daño.
    Las haciendas nos robaba
    y las doncellas forzaba,   2400
    siendo de piedad extraño.
FRONDOSO. Tanto, que aquesta zagala
    que el cielo me ha concedido,
    en que tan dichoso he sido
    que nadie en dicha me iguala,   2405
     cuando conmigo casó,
    aquella noche primera,
    mejor que si suya fuera,
    a su casa la llevó;
     y a no saberse guardar   2410
    ella, que en virtud florece,
    ya manifiesto parece
    lo que pudiera pasar.
MENGO.   ¿No es ya tiempo que hable yo?
    Si me dais licencia, entiendo   2415
    que os admiraréis, sabiendo
    del modo que me trató.
     Porque quise defender
    una moza de su gente,
    que, con término insolente,   2420
    fuerza la querían hacer,
     aquel perverso Nerón
    de manera me ha tratado
    que el reverso me ha dejado
    como rueda de salmón.   2425
     Tocaron mis atabales
    tres hombres con tal porfía,
    que aun pienso que todavía
    me duran los cardenales.
     Gasté en este mal prolijo,   2430
    porque el cuero se me curta,
    polvos de arrayán y murta,
    más que vale mi cortijo.

ESTEBAN.   These, madam, are the peasants
of Fuente Ovejuna, who have come
to offer you their humble service here.
The late Commander's tyrannous excesses,
his cruelties, his countless provocations,
which passed all human bearing, were the cause
of so much strife; he plundered our possessions
and raped our girls, with utter ruthlessness.

FRONDOSO.   This girl, for one, whom Heaven gave to me,
and so made me the happiest man on earth,
the very night we married, the Commander
stole from my side as if she were his own,
and what would have ensued is plain to see,
had her unsullied virtue not prevailed.

MENGO.   Isn't it time I spoke? If you'll allow me,
I know you'll be astonished when you hear
the way he treated me. Because I tried
to save a girl from certain of his soldiers
who meant with shameless savagery to rape her,
that vicious Nero had me so belaboured,
he left my rear as red as fresh-sliced salmon.
Three men beat my backside with such a will,
I'm sure the scars must still be plain to see.
I've spent more cash to cure my battered hide,
on myrtle powders, than my farm would fetch.   2432

2432. *arrayán* 'es planta que siempre está verde... y en medicina sirve esta
planta con su raíz, hoja y fruto para grandes remedios'; *murta*: 'el arrayán
pequeño llamamos murta' (Covarrubias).   See Pedacio Dioscórides Anazarbeo,
Acerca de la Materia Medicinal... Traduzido de la lengua Griega... por el
Doctor Andrés de Laguna, Antwerp 1555, Libro primero, cap. 128, pp. 99–100:
'*Del Arrayhan, y del Myrtidano...* Las hojas secas, y pulverizadas, tienen gran
fuerça de restriñir, apretar, y repercutir: y ansi meritamente se aplican sobre las
partes aporreadas'.

ESTEBAN.   Señor, tuyos ser queremos
                   Rey nuestro eres natural,   2435
                   y con título del tal
                   ya tus armas puesto habemos.
                   Esperamos tu clemencia,
                   y que veas, esperamos,
                   que en este caso te damos   2440
                   por abono la inocencia.
REY.   Pues no puede averiguarse
                   el suceso por escrito,
                   aunque fue grave el delito,
                   por fuerza ha de perdonarse.   2445
                   Y la villa es bien se quede
                   en mí, pues de mí se vale,
                   hasta ver si acaso sale
                   Comendador que la herede.
FRONDOSO.   Su Majestad habla, en fin,   2450
                   como quien tanto ha acertado.
                   Y aquí, discreto senado,
                   Fuente Ovejuna da fin.

Ferdinand and Isabella, in the first production of this translation at the Atrium,
Trinity College, Dublin, March 1989

ESTEBAN.	Your Majesty, we want to be your vassals.	2434
	You are our natural lord, as we've proclaimed,	
	displaying your escutcheon in our town.	
	We seek your clemency, and trust you'll find	
	our innocence a plea in our defence.	
FERDINAND.	This was a serious crime; but since it cannot	2442
	be verified by written evidence,	
	I cannot choose but pardon it. Moreover,	
	now that the town's appealed direct to me,	
	I shall myself assume its jurisdiction,	
	until a new Commander can be found	
	to whom perhaps authority may pass.	
FRONDOSO.	His Majesty's as wise in this as in	
	so many other ways. And thus, my friends,	
	the tale of Fuente Ovejuna ends.	

2452–3. *Comedias* regularly ended with such a brief address to the *senado* (see *Dorotea*, 451), incorporating the title of the play.

TEXT VARIANTS

8	sobra Ac, B, H, C, LE &c.; sabra Anc.
18	lo A, C, LE &c.; le B, H.
33	le A, B, LE 1 & 2, M, B1, CM; se H, C, P, LE 3.
41D	*Sale* A, B, C, LE, B1, CM; *Salen* P, M.
95	pretenden A, B, B1; pretende H, C, LE, P, M, CM.
110	mirarlos A, B, LE &c.; tomarlos H; mirarlas a entrambas C.
112	tiene A, B, LE &c.; tienen H, C.
135	la blanca A, B, C; blanca la H, LE &c.
169–70	A, B, H, C, P, CM attribute these lines too to the Comendador; LE, M, **]** unnecessarily, give 169 to the Maestre, 170 to the Comendador.
173D	*Pascuala* H, C, LE &c.; *Pascual* A, B.
200	Pascuala H, C, LE &c.; Pasqual A, B.
260	ven A, H, C, LE &c.; ver B.
285	darás A, H, C, LE &c.; diràs B.
302	al gracioso, entretenido (see footnote); al gracioso, entremetido A, B, LE 2 & 3, gracioso, al entremetido H, LE 1, P, B1, CM.
317	Esto llamaros imito A, B, LE &c.; Esto al llamaros imito H, C.
330	venturoso, al descompuesto A, B, C, LE &c.; al que es veraz, descompuesto H.
334	al liberal, moscatel H, C, LE &c.; liberal al moscatel A, B.
404	materia A, B, LE &c.; mentira H, C.
413	A repeats *Men.* before this line, an error corrected by B, C, LE &c.
431–4	A, B, H, P, M, CM attribute these lines as shown. In LE 1 & 2 LAURENCIA is omit⟨ before 431; thus 431–4 are attributed to Pascuala. In LE 3, B1, LAURENCIA appe⟨ before 433; thus 431–2 are attributed to Pascuala, 433–4 to Laurencia.
469	entiende A, B, H, C, LE &c.; two copies of A (R 14.105 and 8° Yg 1308) have enti⟨ no doubt because of type-slippage.
472	brazaletes Ac, B, H, C, LE &c.; braçateles Anc.
479	codón Ac, H, C, P, LE 3, B1, CM; colón Anc, B, LE 1 & 2, M.
480	rizo Ac, H, C, LE &c.; rico Anc, B.
491	casaca P, LE 3, B1, CM; las saca A, B, C, LE 1 & 2, M; orla saca H. I proposed reading *casaca* in 1971, and in 1972 D.W. Cruickshank explained *las saca* as a misread of *cassaca* from a ms. We had both been anticipated by the ms. emendations in 1702 9.
493	coronado Anc, B, LE, P, M, CM; corona Ac, H, B1.
538	fuerte P, M, LE 3; fuertes A, B, H, C, LE 1 & 2, B1, CM.
542	trae sus Ac, H, LE 3, B1; trae los sus Anc, B, C, LE 1 & 2, P, M, CM.
570	cueros... cueros H, C, LE &c.; queros... queros Anc; cueros... que ros Ac (i.e. 'corrected' reading has further typographical errors); cueros... queros B.
608	uno Ac, B, C, LE &c.; una Anc, H.
623	No B, H, C, LE &c.; Na A.
630	ellas A, H, C, LE &c.; ella B.
634	o ha de despedirse presto B, H, LE &c.; o ha despedirse de presto A, C.
637	ver Alfonso A, B, B1, CM; ver a Alfonso H, C, LE, P, M.
638	y su A, B, C, LE &c.; que su H (anticipated by the ms. emendations in 1072. 1. 9).
650	eso H, LE &c.; esto A, B (a clear error, which destroys the rhyme, corrected by the **]** emendations in 1072. 1. 9).
672	él, ensanchar A, B, C, LE &c.; el ensanche H.
673	el honor A, B, C, LE &c.; y el honor H.
684	sus A, B, C, LE &c.; tus H.
723D	*Laurencia* H, C, LE &c.; *Laura* A, B.
727	decir A, B, C, LE &c.; diciendo H.
750	cuidado A, H, C, LE &c.; descuido B.
758	Es que yo B, H, C, LE &c., es que que yo A.

76   viene algún A, H, CM; viene a algún B, C, LE, P, B1, M.

15   At least one line (with o – o assonance) is missing.

46   espalda H, C, LE &c.; espada A, B.

60   como A, B, H, C, LE &c. The ms. emendations in 1072. 1. 9 propose: q̃ me.

69   futuras, y ignorantes A, B, LE &c.; futuras ignorantes H, C.

73   el que después A, B, C, LE &c.; el de después H.

80   en el sembrar H, C LE &c.; en sembrar A, B; the line is a syllable short, unless emended.

90   Y al cabo al cabo se siembre A, B, C, LE &c.; Y al cabo que se siembre H. The line has an extra syllable; P favours H's emendation, perhaps with ya for ˘que.

08   de imprimir C, LE &c.; del imprimir A, B, H. The line is a syllable too. long, unless emended.

13   Gutemberga A, H, C, P, LE3, M, B1, CM; Cutemberga B, LE 1 & 2. (In some copies of A, the G is indistinct and appears to read C).

24   des(s)a A, CM; de es(s)a B, H, C, LE &c.; P, M, B1.

29   A line (rhyming -ado) is missing from the octava, before this one. Agustino A, H, C, LE &c.; Augustino B.

30   dejadlo A, C, LE, P, CM; dejaldo B, H, M, B1.

31D   Sale A, B, P; Salen C, LE, M, B1, CM.

31   en A, B, H, C, LE &c.; B1 emends entre, on the grounds of scansion and sense.

38   le A, H, C, LE &c.; la B.

55   a un lado A, B, LE &c.; al lado H, C.

58   que le hiciérades pariente A, B, C, LE &c.; que le echarais diligente H.

81   LEONELO A, B, H, C, LE &c. The ms. emendations in 1072. 1. 9 attribute this line Regidor.

94   que el mal A, B, C, LE &c.; es mal H.

97   deshonran H, C, LE, P, M, CM; les honran A, B, B1.

98   obras A, B, H, LE &c.; otras C. LE 3 punctuates: ¡Esas palabras deshonran / las obras! ¡No hay quien las crea...!

021   Cielo A, H, C, P, LE 3, M, B1, CM; Cielos B, LE 1 & 2.

024   No sabes A, B, C, LE &c.; No saben H.

025   que no quieres C, LE, M; que no quieren A, B, P, B1, CM; y no quieres H.

050–1 H, C, and others, though no recent editor, attribute these lines to Ortuño, presumably because 1052 is addressed to him (it may be a reply to 1024-6).

090   por que (porque) el Filósofo dice A, B, H, C, B1, CM; y el Filósofo lo dice LE, P, M. If por que = por quienes, there is no need for emendation.

096   accidente A, H, C, P, B1, CM; acidente B, LE, M.

136   The stage is evidently cleared here, though A & B have no direction.

138   aquí tenéis temor A, H, LE &c.; aquí tenéis aquí temor B; a qué tenéis temor C.

177   Pero Galván A, B, C, LE &c.; Pelicálvaro H.

205D Ortuño. C, LE &c.; Ortun. A, B.

316D Escóndese A, B, C, P, B1, CM; Escónde[n]se LE, M.

317D Salen Esteban Alcalde, y el Regidor A, B, C, M, CM; Salen Esteban, alcalde y el Regidor [Juan Rojo] LE 1 & 2; Salen Esteban, Alcalde, y el Regidor y Juan Rojo P; Salen Esteban [Alonso, el otro] alcalde y el Regidor [y Juan Rojo] LE 3.

401   Tomaré A, B, C, LE, P, M, CM; Tomar H, B1.

409   preguntarte B, H, C, LE &c.; pregunrarte A.

471   The stage is evidently cleared here, though A & B have no direction.

472D Esteban, y Alcalde A, P, LE 3, B1, CM; Esteban y Alcalde [Juan Rojo] C; Esteban, Alcalde B, LE 1 & 2, M.

490   harto desdichado fui B, LE &c.; the line is not found in A, H, C. The ms. emendations in 1072. 1. 9 propose: y aun me le desceñi.

503   BARRILDO B1; MENGO A, B, H, C, LE, P, M, CM. B1's emendation was anticipated in 1072. 1. 9.

505   envidias A, B, LE, P, M, CM; envidia H, C, B1. The s is faint in A, and may in some copies be missing.

510   MENGO A, B, B1; FRONDOSO H, C, LE, P, M, CM.

1514   buñolero A, H, C, LE &c.; buñuelero B.
1517   llenarse Ac, B, H, C, LE &c.; llegarse Anc.   P gives llegarse as the reading of B, probably in error.
1547   en cabello B, LE, P, M; en cabellos A, H, C, B1, CM.
1544–5 These lines, 1556–7, 1566–7 and 1568–9 are printed in the *Parte* as single lines.
1570D   *Sale* A, B, C, LE, CM; *Salen* P, M, B1.
1607   disculparle A, H, C, LE &c.; disculparse B.
1639   Llevadla A, LE &c.; Llevadle B; Llevalda H, C..
1657   lo A, B, LE &c.; los H, C.
1664   esta A, B, H, LE, B1, CM; esa H, P.
1680   Fernando aquel que humilla A, B, C, P, M, CM; Fernando al suelo humilla H; [aquel Rey] Fernando humilla LE; Fernando, aquel que humilla, / ha tantos… B1.
1687   entiende A, B, H, P, M, B1; entiendo C, LE, CM.
1694   quiebran A, H, C, LE &c.; quiebra B.
1737   la A, H, C, LE &c.; le B: compre H, LE &c.; compren A, B, C.
1751–2 ¿No se ven aquí los golpes / de la sangre, y las señales? A, B, C, LE &c.; ¿Las señales de los golpes / no se ven aquí, y la sangre? H.
1773   ceñís A, H, C, LE &c.; ecñís B.
1832   Jacinta, tu grande agravio / que sea cabo responde A, B; Jacinta, a tu grande agravio / que seas cabo corresponde H; for later editions, see footnote.
1837   enarbole A, B, H, C, P, LE 3, M, B1; enarbolo LE 1 & 2, CM. Some copies of A appear to read *enarbolo*; others clearly have *enarbole*, which the assonance requires.
1845   *adonde* is missing, presumably because of type-slippage, in at least one copy of A (1072.i.12).
1848D   Cimbranos H, C, LE &c.; Cimbrano A, B.
1854   interrompen A, B, H, LE &c.; interrumpen C.
1873   defendamos A, H, C, LE &c.; defendemos B.
1890–1 Lo que mugeres son en las venganças, / en el beuan su sangre, es bien que esperes A, B; ¿Los que mujeres son en las venganzas, / En él beban su sangre, es bien que esperes? H; C; ¡Lo que … venganzas! / ¡En él … sangre! ¡Es bien que esperes! LE, CM; ¡Lo que … venganzas! / ¡En él … sangre! ¿Es bien que esperes? P, M; Lo que … venganzas. / En él … que esperes. B1.
1968–70 Con título de tirano / que le acumula la plebe / a la fuerza A, B, H, LE &c.; En títul de tirano / le acumula todo el plebe / y a la fuerza C; other editors (Entrambasaguas &c.) further emend En to El.
2044   a fe que A, B, H, C, LE &c.; a la fe que B1, on the grounds that otherwise the line is syllable short.
2096–7 …así / – ¡Sí! – Ahora pues, yo quiero ser C, P; …así? – ¡Sí! / – Ahora pues, yo quiero ser A, B, LE, M, B1, CM; …así? / – Sí, sí! – Pues yo quiero ser H.   For reasons of scansion, Sí must belong to 2097.
2125D   *salen* A, C, P, M, CB; *sale* B, LE, B1.
2146   lo que él le entregó A, B, C, LE &c.; lo que se entregó H.
2150   se reportará LE &c.; me reportará A, B, H, C.
2176   Cómo estar A, B, LE &c.; cómo a estar H, C. LE and P suggest that *a* may be embebida, but this seems uncertain.
2188   Huye tu daño, no esperes A, B, LE, B1; Huye, tu daño no esperes H, C, P, CM.
2209   The last line of the *redondilla* (rhyming with *Fernando*) is missing.
2248   le mató A, B, LE, M, B1, CM; lo mató H, C, P.
2263   The first five syllables of this line are missing. P suggests that Mengo repeats his ¡Ay!
2279   Que lea, que este es mejor A, B, LE, CM; Es aloque: este es mejor H; Que beba, que éste es mejor C; Que vea, que éste es mejor P, M (suggested by LE); Que le acuestes mejor B1. B1 in my view has come closest to correcting this line; my further attempt based on a ms. emendation in 1702. 1.9, supposes that *acuesten* was written *aqueste*.
2286   Dasme espa(n)to Ac, B, H, C, LE &c.; Dasme espã Anc.
2296   le tuerza Ac, B, H, C, LE &c.; no tuerza Anc.
2320   injusto fiel A, B, C, LE &c.; injusto fué H.
2331   dándoles A, H, C, LE &c.; dándole B.

CHRONICA DE LAS tres Ordenes y Cauallerias de San-
ĉiago, Calatraua y Alcantara: en la qual ſe trata de ſu origen y ſucceſſo, y
notables hechos en armas de los Maeſtres y Caualleros de ellas: y de muchos Señores de Titulo y otros Nobles que deſcienden de los
Maeſtres: y de muchos otros Linages de Eſpaña. Com
pueſta por el Licenciado Frey Franciſco de
Rades y Andrada Capellan de ſu
Mageſtad, de la Orden de
Calatraua.

¶ Dirigida a la. C.R.M. del Rey don Philippe nueſtro ſeñor,
Adminiſtrador perpetuo deſtas Ordenes.

¶ Impreſſa con licencia en Toledo, en caſa de
Iuan de Ayala. Año. 1572.
¶ Con Priuillegio Real por diez años.

Chronica de las tres Ordenes y Cauallerias de Sanctiago, Calatraua y Alcantara... Compuesta por el Licenciado Frey Francisco de Rades y Andrada... Impressa con licencia en Toledo, en casa de Iuan de Ayala. Año. 1572.

Chronicle of the three Orders of Chivalry of Santiago, Calatrava and Alcántara... Written by the Licentiate Brother Francisco de Rades y Andrada... Printed with permission in Toledo, at the printing-house of Juan de Ayala. 1572.

[Fol. 78va] ... Del Maestre don Rodrigo Tellez Giron. Capitulo. 38.

EL XXIX Maestre de Calatraua fue dõ Rodrigo Tellez Girõ, hijo de dõ Pedro Girõ Maestre de la
mesma Orden, y hermano de don Alfonso y don Iuan Tellez Giron Condes que fueron de Vrueña.
Sucedio a su padre en el Maestradgo, por la renunciacion que en el auia hecho con autoridad
Apostolica: y para mayor seguridad de su derecho, los Comendadores, Caualleros y Religiosos que se
hallaron en Villarruuia [Fol. 78vb] al tiẽpo que su padre murio, y otros muchos que alli acudieron,
eligieron de nueuo por su Maestre al dicho dõ Rodrigo Tellez Girõ, y despues otra vez lo ratificaron
ellos y los demas en el Conuento de Calatraua. Fue esto en el año de mill y quatrociẽtos y sesenta y
seys, por el mes de Mayo, reynando en Castilla y Leon dõ Enrrique el quarto. Era el Maestre a
tiẽpo de su election niño de ocho años: y por esto la Orden suplico al Papa Pio segundo, supliesse de
nueuo la falta de edad, y confirmasse la election o postulacion que auian hecho. El Papa viendo que
hombre de tan poca edad no podia tener el Maestradgo en titulo, dioselo en Encomienda: y despue
Paulo segundo le dio por Coadjutor a don Iuan Pacheco su tio Marques de Villena. Este don Iua
Pacheco fue despues Maestre de Sanctiago...

El octauo año de su election (siendo de edad de diez y seys años, y auiendo ya muerto don Iua
Pacheco su tio (que como dicho es gouernaua el Maestradgo) començo a gouernarle por su persona
El mesmo año murio el Rey dõ [Fol. 79ra] Enrrique: por cuya muerte se continuaron y aumẽtaro
los vãdos y parcialidades entre los Grandes del Reyno: por q̃ la mayor parte de ellos obedescieron
por su Reyna y señora a doña Ysabel, hermana del Rey don Enrrique, y por ella a dõ Fernãdo s
marido Rey de Sicilia y Principe de Aragon: y otros deziã pertenescer el Reyno a doña Iuana,
affirmauan ser hija del Rey don Enrrique, la qual estaua en poder de don Diego Lopez Pached
Marques de Villena, primo del Maestre. Auiase desposado esta señora cõ don Alonso su tio Rey d
Portogal: y cõ este titulo seguian su partido para hazerle Rey de Castilla todos los Girones, Pachecos
y otros Grandes del Reyno. El Maestre (como mãcebo q̃ era de diez y seys años) siguio este partid
de doña Iuana y del Rey de Portogal su esposo, por induzimiẽto del Marques de Villena su primo,
del Cõde de Vrueña su hermano: y cõ esta voz hizo guerra en las tierras del Rey en la Mancha
Andaluzia.

En este tiempo el Maestre junto en Almagro trezientos de cauallo entre Freyles de su Orden
segiares, con otros dos mill peones, y fue cõtra Ciudad Real, con intento de tomarla para su Orde
Dezia pertenescerle por virtud de la donacion q̃ el Rey don Sancho el Brauo auia hecho de aqu
pueblo (q̃ entõces se dezia Villa Real) a esta Ordẽ de Calatraua. Los de Ciudad Real se pusierõ e
defensa, por no salir de la Corona Real: y sobre esto vuo guerra entre el Maestre y ellos, en la qu
de ambas partes murierõ muchos hõbres. Finalmente el Maestre tomo la ciudad por fuerça c
armas... [Fol. 79rb] Tuuo el Maestre la ciudad muchos dias, y hizo cortar la cabeça a much
hombres de ella, por q̃ auian dicho algunas palabras injuriosas cõtra el: y a otros de la gente plebey
hizo açotar cõ mordazas en las lenguas. Los de la ciudad se quexarõ alos Reyes Catholicos del
agrauios y afrentas q̃ los de la Orden de Calatraua les hazian, y dixerõ como en aquella ciudad au
pocos vezinos, y ninguno de ellos era rico ni poderoso para hazer cabeça del cõtra el Maestre: sino
todos erã gẽte comũ y pobre, por estar la ciudad cercada de pueblos de Calatraua, y no ten
terminos ni aldeas. Los Reyes Catholicos viẽdo q̃ si el Maestre de Calatraua quedaua cõ Ciud
Real, podia mas facilmẽte acudir cõ su gẽte a juntarse cõ la del Rey de Portogal, q̃ ya auia entra
en Estremadura, embiarõ cõtra el a dõ Diego Fernãdez de Cordoua Cõde de Cabra, y a don Rodri
Mãrrique Maestre de Sãctiago, cõ mucha gẽte de guerra. Llegarõ estos dos Capitanes a Ciudad Re
dõde el Maestre dõ Rodrigo Tellez estaua, y pelearõ la gẽte delos vnos cõ la delos otros a la entra
y por las calles, que no es pueblo de fortaleza ni castillo, sino solamente cercado de una ruyn cerc
Todos pelearõ valerosamẽte, y de ambas partes murierõ muchos hõbres: mas como los dichos d
Capitanes auiã lleuado mucha gente, y los de la ciudad erã cõ ellos, vẽcierõ, y echarõ fuera
Maestre cõ los suyos. Estuuierõ alli los dos Capitanes mucho tiẽpo haziẽdo guerra en las tierras de
Ordẽ, a fin q̃ el Maestre por defenderlas dexasse de acudir al Rey de Portogal.

Of the Master don Rodrigo Téllez Girón. Chapter 38.

CHRONICLE [219

e twenty-ninth Master of Calatrava was don Rodrigo Téllez Girón, son to don Pedro Girón, the ster of the same Order, and brother to don Alfonso and don Juan Téllez Girón, who were Counts Urueña. He succeeded his father in the Mastership, by virtue of the latter's renunciation in his our with apostolic authority: and further to assure his right, the Commanders, Knights and ligious who were present in Villarubia at the time of his father's death, and many others who aired thither, re-elected the said don Rodrigo Téllez Girón as their Master, and thereafter they d the remainder ratified it once more at the Monastery of Calatrava. This was in the month of y of 1466, in the reign of Henry IV of Castile and Leon. The Master at the time of his election s a boy of eight: and for this reason the Order appealed to Pope Pius II to make good his lack of ars, and confirm the election or petition that they had made. The Pope, seeing that so young a n was not qualified to hold the Mastership, gave it to him by way of commission; and thereafter ul II gave him as Coadjutor his uncle don Juan Pacheco, Marquis of Villena. This don Juan checo was later Master of Santiago...

the eighth year after his election (he being now sixteen, and his uncle don Juan Pacheco, who as s been said had exercised the Mastership, having died) he began to exercise it in person. The me year saw the death of King Henry, by reason of which the factions and dissensions among the randees of the realm continued and increased: for the greater part of them gave allegiance, as to eir Queen and ruler, to doña Isabella, the sister of King Henry, and because of her to her husband n Ferdinand, King of Sicily and Prince of Aragon, while others said that the realm belonged by ght to doña Juana, whom they affirmed to be a daughter of King Henry, and who was in the power the Master's cousin don Diego López Pacheco, Marquis of Villena. This lady had been betrothed her uncle don Alonso, King of Portugal: and by reason of this claim all the Girones, Pachecos and her Grandees of the realm supported his faction, in order to make him King of Castile. The aster also (being as he was a youth of sixteen) supported the faction of doña Juana and of her sband the King of Portugal, at the persuasion of his cousin the Marquis of Villena, and of his other the Count of Urueña: and in pursuit of this claim he waged war in the royal lands, in La ancha and Andalusia.

t this time the Master assembled in Almagro three hundred horsemen from among the knights of his rder, both religious and lay, with a further two thousand foot-soldiers, and moved against Ciudad eal, with the intention of taking it for his Order. He claimed that it was his by reason of the gift at King Sancho the Brave had made of that town (which was then called Villa Real) to the Order f Calatrava. The inhabitants of Ciudad Real took up arms in self-defence, in order not to pass out f Crown control: and battle was joined on the matter between the Master and themselves, in which any men on both sides died. Eventually the Master took the city by force of arms... The Master eld the city for many days, and had many of its men beheaded because they had said some offensive ords against him, and had others of the common folk gagged and flogged. The inhabitants of the ity complained to the Catholic Monarchs of the wrongs and affronts afflicted upon them by those of he Order of Calatrava, explaining that in that city there were few inhabitants, none of whom was ich or powerful enough to be its leader against the Master: on the contrary, all were common and oor folk, because the city was surrounded by townships that belonged to Calatrava, and it had no ands or villages. The Catholic Monarchs, seeing that if the Master of Calatrava remained in ossession of Ciudad Real, he could the more easily repair with his troops to unite with the King of ortugal, who had already entered Extremadura, sent against him don Diego Fernández de Córdoba, Count of Cabra, and don Rodrigo Manrique, the Master of Santiago, with many men-at-arms. These wo captains arrived at Ciudad Real, where the Master don Rodrigo Téllez was, and the troops of the ormer fought with those of the latter at the gate and in the streets, for it is not a fortified town or astle but is encircled only by a weak wall. All fought bravely, and many men died on both sides: ut since the two captains previously mentioned had brought many troops, and the inhabitants of the ity supported them, they were victorious, and drove out the Master and his followers. The two captains remained in that place a long time, waging war in the lands of the Order, so that the Master, needing to defend them, should not support the King of Portugal.

[Fol. 79va]
El hecho de Fuenteouejuna.

Estando las cosas desta Orden en el estado ya dicho, dõ Fernã Gomez de Guzman Comendador mayor de Calatraua, q̃ residia en Fuenteouejuna villa de su Encomiẽda, hizo tantos y tan grandes agrauios alos vezinos de aquel pueblo, que no pudiendo ya suffrirlos ni dissimularlos, determinaron todos de vn consentimiẽto y voluntad alçarse contra el y matarle. Con esta determinaciõ y furor de pueblo ayrado, con voz de Fuenteouejuna, se juntaron vna noche del mes de Abril, del ano de mill y quatrocientos y setenta y seys, los Alcaldes, Regidores, Iusticia y Regimiẽto, cõ los otros vezinos, y cõ mano armada, entrarõ por fuerça en las casas de la Encomienda mayor, donde el dichõ Comendador estaua. Todos apellidauan Fuenteouejuna, Fuenteouejuna, y dezian, Viuan los Reyes don Fernando y doña Ysabel, y muerã los traydores y malos Christianos. El Comendador mayor y los suyos quãdo vieron esto, y oyeron el apellido que lleuauan, pusieronse en vna pieça la mas fuerte dela casa, con sus armas, y alli se defendieron por horas, sin que les pudiessen entrar. En este tiempo el Comendador mayor a grandes vozes pidio muchas vezes a los del pueblo, le dixessen que razon o causa tenian para hazer aquel escãdaloso mouimiento, para que el diesse su descargo, desagrauiasse a los que dezian estar agrauiados del. Nunca quisieron admitir sus razones, antes cõ grande impetu, apellidãdo Fuẽteouejuna, combatieron la pieça y entra- [Fol. 79vb] dos en ell matarõ catorze hombres que con el Comendador estauan, por que procurauan defender a su señor Desta manera con vn furor maldito y rauioso, llegaron al Comendador, y pusieron las manos en el: le dierõ tantas heridas, que le hizieron caer en tierra sin sentido. Antes que diesse el anima a Dios tomaron su cuerpo con grande y regozijado alarido, diziẽdo, Viuan los Reyes y mueran los traydores y le echaron por vna vẽtana a la calle: y otros que alli estauan cõ lanças y espadas, pusieron la puntas arriba, para recoger en ellas al cuerpo, q̃ avn tenia anima. Despues de caydo en tierra, l arrancaron las barbas y cabellos con grande crueldad: y otros con los pomos de las espadas l quebraron los dientes, A todo esto añadieron palabras feas y deshonestas, y grandes injurias cõtra e Comendador mayor, y contra su padre y madre. Estando en esto, antes que acabasse de espira acudieron las mugeres de la villa, con Panderos y Sonages, a regozijar la muerte de su señor: y auia hecho para esto vna Vandera, y nombrado Capitana y Alferez. Tambien los mochachos a imitacio de sus madres hizieron su Capitania, y puestos en la orden q̃ su edad permitia, fueron a solenizar dicha muerte, tanta era la enemistad que todos tenian contra el Comendador mayor. Estãdo junt hombres, mugeres y niños lleuaron el cuerpo con grande regozijo a la plaça: y alli todos hõbres mugeres le hizieron pedaços, arrastrandole, y haziendo en el grandes crueldades y escarnios: y r quisieron darle a sus criados, para enterrarle. Demas desto dieron sacomano a su casa, y le ro- [Fo 80ra] baron toda su haziẽda. Fue de la Corte vn Iuez Pesquisidor a Fuenteouejuna, con comision los Reyes Catholicos, para aueriguar la verdad de este hecho, y castigar a los culpados: y avn q̃ dio tormento a muchos de los que se auiã hallado en la muerte del Comendador mayor, nun ninguno quiso confessar quales fueron los capitanes o primeros mouedores de aquel delicto, dixeron los nombres de los que en el se auian hallado. Preguntauales el Iuez, Quien mato Comendador mayor? Respõdian ellos, Fuenteouejuna. Preguntauales, Quien es Fuenteouejun. Respondian, Todos los vezinos desta villa. Finalmente todas sus respuestas fueron a este tono, por estauan conjurados, que avn que los matassen a tormentos no auian de respõder otra cosa. Y lo q̃ mas es de admirar, que el Iuez hizo dar tormento a muchas mugeres y mancebos de poca edad, tuuieron la misma constancia y animo que los varones muy fuertes. Cõ esto se boluio el Pesquisid a dar parte a los Reyes Catholicos, para ver q̃ mandauan hazer: y sus Altezas siendo informados, las tyranias del Comendador mayor, por las quales auia merescido la muerte, mandarõ se quedasse negocio sin mas aueriguaciõ. Auia hecho aquel Cauallero mal tratamiento a sus vassallos, tenien en la villa muchos soldados para sustentar en ella la voz del Rey de Portogal, que pretendia ser R de Castilla: y consentia que aquella descomedida gente hiziesse grandes agrauios y afrentas a los Fuenteouejuna, sobre comerseles sus haziendas. Vltra desto, el mesmo Comẽdador mayor auia hec grandes agrauios y deshõ [Fol. 80rb] rras a los de la villa, tomandoles por fuerça sus hijas y mugeres, y robãdoles haziendas, para sustentar aquellos soldados que tenia, con titulo y color que el Maestre dõ Rodri Tellez Giron su señor lo mandaua, por q̃ entoces seguia aquel partido del Rey de Portogal...

The action of Fuente Ovejuna.

The affairs of this Order being in the state already described, don Fernán Gómez de Guzmán, the Grand Commander of Calatrava, who resided in Fuente Ovejuna, a town that formed part of his concession, inflicted so many and such great wrongs upon its inhabitants, that being no longer able to endure or excuse them, they all decided with one consent and will to rise up against him and kill him. With this determination and the fury of an angered township, raising the cry 'Fuente Ovejuna', the Magistrates, Aldermen, Justices and Councillors, together with its other inhabitants, assembled one night in the month of April 1476, took up arms and entered by force the property of the concession, in which the said Commander was residing. All kept clamouring 'Fuente Ovejuna, Fuente Ovejuna', and crying 'Long live the King and Queen. Ferdinand and Isabella, and let traitors and false Christians die'. The Grand Commander and his followers, observing this and the cries they were raising took up position with their weapons in the stoutest chamber of the house, and there defended themselves for two hours, without the townsfolk being able to enter. The Grand Commander during this time demanded loudly and repeatedly of the townsfolk that they should tell him what reason or cause they had to make that outrageous uprising, so that he might offer his defence and satisfy those who claimed that they had been wronged by him. But they at no time were willing to accept his appeals, and instead in a mighty rush, crying 'Fuente Ovejuna', assaulted the chamber and once they had entered it killed fourteen men who were with the Commander, because they were trying to defend their lord. In this way, with accursed and rabid fury, they reached the Commander and laid hands on him; and they inflicted on him so many wounds, that they made him fall senseless to the ground. Before he surrendered his soul to God, they seized his body with a great delighted shriek, crying 'Long live the King and Queen and let traitors die': and they flung him through a window into the street, and others who were there with lances and swords, raised their points upward, to receive upon them his body, which was still alive. After he had fallen to the ground, they tore his beard and hair with great cruelty, and others broke his teeth with the pommels of their swords. To all this they added foul and indecent words, and great insults against the Grand Commander and against his father and mother. At this point, before he finally expired, the women of the town approached, with tambourines and rattles, to rejoice in the death of their lord: and for this purpose they had made a banner and appointed a captain and ensign. The young too, in imitation of their mothers, elected officers, and forming up in such order as their age allowed, went to celebrate that death, so great was the enmity all harboured against the Grand Commander. When men, women and children were gathered, they bore the body with great rejoicing to the square: and there all, both men and women, hacked it to pieces, dragging it about, and inflicting great cruelties and indignities upon it: and they refused to give it to his servants for burial. In addition to this they sacked his house and stole from it all his property. An investigating Judge went from the court to Fuente Ovejuna, with a commission from the Catholic Monarchs, to discover the truth about this deed and punish the guilty; and although he tortured many of those who had been present at the death of the Grand Commander, at no time was any one of them willing to confess who were the captains or instigators of that crime, or to give the names of those who had been present at it. The Judge kept asking them: 'Who killed the Grand Commander?' They kept answering: 'Fuente Ovejuna'. He kept asking them: 'Who is Fuente Ovejuna?' They kept answering: 'All the inhabitants of this town'. To the last all their answers were in this same vein, because they had conspired together, that even though he should torture them to death they were not to give any other answer. And what is most to be wondered at is that the Judge had many women and lads of tender age put to the torture, and they showed the same constancy and spirit as the strongest men. With this the Investigator returned to report to the Catholic Monarchs, to see what they commanded to be done: and their Highnesses, being informed of the tyrannies of the Grand Commander, for which he had deserved death, commanded that the matter should be left without further investigation. That knight had ill-treated his vassals, maintaining many soldiers in the town in order to support in it the cause of the King of Portugal, who was claiming to be King of Castile: and he allowed those insolent troops to commit great wrongs and offences against the people of Fuente Ovejuna, as well as consuming their property. Besides this, the Grand Commander himself had inflicted great wrongs and dishonour on the inhabitants of the town, taking their daughters and wives by force, and robbing them of their property to maintain those soldiers he kept, on the pretext that it was at the command of his lord the Master don Rodrigo Téllez Girón, who at that time was supporting the faction of the King of Portugal...

Los de Fuenteouejuna despues de auer muerto al Comendador mayor, quitaron las varas y cargos de justicia a los que estauan puestos por esta Orden, cuya era la jurisdicion: y dieronlas a quien quisierõ. Luego acudieron a la ciudad de Cordoua, y se encomendaron a ella, diziẽdo querian ser subjetos a su jurisdicion, como auian sido antes que la villa viniesse a poder de don Pedro Giron...

Boluiendo a las cosas del Maestre don Rodrigo Tellez Giron, es de saber, que en su tiempo avnque el anduuo en el partido del Rey don Alonso de Portogal muchos años, no por esso [Fol. 80va] se ha de entender que todos los Caualleros de su Orden siguieron este partido...
Assi fue que passados algunos años, como ya el Maestre auia crescido en edad y entendimiento conoscio auerlo errado en tomar voz cõtra los Reyes Catholicos, y puso intercessores para que boluiendo a su seruicio le perdonassen lo passado. Los Reyes viendo que auia errado por ser de tierna edad, y por seguir el parescer del Marques de Villena su primo y del Conde de Vrueña su hermano, perdonaronle con liberalidad, y avn holgaron de que el se combidasse a seruirles, por ser tan poderoso. Con esto boluio a su seruicio: y de alli adelãte siempre les fue muy leal vassallo, y les hizo todo seruicio en lo que le mandaron, assi en la paz como en la guerra, y assi fue muy priuado suyo...

Muerte del Maestre sobre Loxa.

Año de mill y quatrociẽtos y ochẽta y dos, el Maestre partio de Almagro con trezientos de cauallo y grãde numero de peones, para seruir a los Reyes Catholicos en la guerra que hazian cõtra Moros. Fue cõ ellos a su villa de Porcuna, que es en Anda [Fol. 80vb] luzia: alli se le juntaron otros ciente de cauallo y ochocientos peones, de los pueblos q̃ esta Orden tiene en Andaluzia...

The people of Fuente Ovejuna, after having killed the Grand Commander, took away their rods and offices from those appointed by this Order, to whom jurisdiction belonged, and gave them to whoever they wished. Then they had recourse and entrusted themselves to the city of Cordoba, saying that they wanted to be subject to its jurisdiction, as they had been before the town came into the power of don Pedro Girón...

To return to the affairs of the Master don Rodrigo Téllez Girón, it should be known that at this time, although he belonged for many years to the faction of King Alonso of Portugal, it must not on that account be understood that all the knights of his Order supported that faction... So it was that after some years had passed, and since the Master had now increased in years and understanding, he recognised that he had erred in espousing a cause opposed to the Catholic Monarchs, and sought through intermediaries that if he returned to their service they would forgive him for what had passed. The Monarchs, seeing that he had erred because he had been of tender years, and because he had followed the advice of his cousin the Marquis of Villena and of his brother the Count of Urueña, generously forgave him, and indeed were pleased that he should offer to serve them, since he was so powerful. With this he returned to their service: and thereafter he was always their very loyal vassal, and did them every service in what they commanded him, both in peace and in war, and thus was very much their trusted minister...

The death of the Master in the attack on Loja

In 1482 the Master set out from Almagro with three hundred horsemen and a large number of foot-soldiers, to serve the Catholic Monarchs in the war they were waging against the Moors. He went with them to his town of Porcuna, which is in Andalusia: there he was joined by another hundred horsemen and eight hundred foot-soldiers, from the townships this Order possesses in Andalusia...

Printed in the USA/Agawam, MA
January 20, 2011

556213.041